These gor...
are in need of a wife!

By Request

Her Greek
Tycoon

EXPECTANT BRIDE
by
Lynne Graham

HUSBAND ON TRUST
by
Jacqueline Baird

CONSTANTINE'S REVENGE
by
Kate Walker

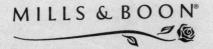

MILLS & BOON®

*All the characters in this book have no existence outside the imagination
of the author, and have no relation whatsoever to anyone bearing the
same name or names. They are not even distantly inspired by any
individual known or unknown to the author, and all the incidents are
pure invention.*

*All Rights Reserved including the right of reproduction in whole or in part
in any form. This edition is published by arrangement with Harlequin
Enterprises II B.V. The text of this publication or any part thereof may not
be reproduced or transmitted in any form or by any means, electronic or
mechanical, including photocopying, recording, storage in an
information retrieval system, or otherwise, without the written
permission of the publisher.*

*This book is sold subject to the condition that it shall not, by way of trade
or otherwise, be lent, resold, hired out or otherwise circulated without the
prior consent of the publisher in any form of binding or cover other than
that in which it is published and without a similar condition including this
condition being imposed on the subsequent purchaser.*

*MILLS & BOON and MILLS & BOON with the Rose Device
are registered trademarks of the publisher.*
Harlequin Mills & Boon Limited,
Eton House, 18-24 Paradise Road, Richmond, Surrey, TW9 1SR

HER GREEK TYCOON © by Harlequin Enterprises II B.V., 2003

Expectant Bride, Husband on Trust and *Constantine's Revenge*
were first published in Great Britain by Harlequin Mills & Boon Limited
in separate, single volumes.

Expectant Bride © Lynne Graham 1999
Husband on Trust © Jacqueline Baird 2000
Constantine's Revenge © Kate Walker 1999

ISBN 0 263 83590 1

05-0503

*Printed and bound in Spain
by Litografia Rosés S.A., Barcelona*

Lynne Graham was born in Northern Ireland and has been a keen Mills & Boon® reader since her teens. She is very happily married with an understanding husband, who has learned to cook since she started to write! Her five children keep her on her toes. She has a very large dog, which knocks everything over, a very small terrier which barks a lot, and two cats. When time allows, Lynne is a keen gardener.

Modern Romance™ brings you Lynne Graham's passion-filled trilogy *Brides of L'Amour*, which starts in July with:

THE FRENCHMAN'S LOVE-CHILD

EXPECTANT BRIDE

by

Lynne Graham

CHAPTER ONE

'WHAT on earth are you wearing on your head?' Meg Bucknall demanded as she pressed the button for the service lift.

Ellie raised a self-conscious hand to the floral scarf which covered her hair. 'It'll keep the dust off.'

'Since when have you been so fussy?'

Ellie heaved a sigh and decided to be honest with the older woman. 'There's this guy who often works late on my floor...and, *well*, he's—'

'Making a nuisance of himself, is he?' Meg's round face tightened with disapproval but she wasn't surprised by the news. Even in an overall Ellie would attract keen male attention. Fashioned on petite but shapely lines, the young woman had hair so naturally fair it gleamed like silver, and clear green eyes enhanced by unexpectedly dark brows and lashes. 'I bet he thinks he's onto a sure thing with a humble cleaner. Old or young?'

'Young.' Ellie stood back to let Meg enter the lift first. 'He's really getting on my nerves. I've been thinking about mentioning him to the supervisor.'

Meg grimaced. 'No, whatever you do, don't make it official, Ellie. If this lech works late, he must be quite important. Let's face it, you're more expendable than some business whizzkid!'

'Don't I know it.' Ellie sighed. 'It's still a man's world.'

'He must be pretty persistent if he's getting *you* down...' Meg frowned, thinking of how feisty Ellie could be, although nobody would ever think it to look at her. 'Look, you do my floor tonight and I'll do yours. That'll give you a break. Then

5

maybe one of the other cleaners will consider doing a permanent switch with you.'

'But I haven't got security clearance to clean the top floor,' Ellie reminded the older woman reluctantly.

'Oh, never mind that!' Meg dismissed impatiently. 'Why should anyone need special permission just to polish floors and empty bins? But if the security guard does a round while you're up there, take yourself off out of sight if you can. Some of those blokes *would* report us. And don't go through those big double doors at the front. That's Mr Alexiakis's office suite and I'm not allowed in there…OK?'

As the older woman pushed her trolley out onto the floor that was usually Ellie's responsibility, Ellie gave her a grateful smile. 'I really appreciate this, Meg.'

Ellie had never been on the top floor of the Alexiakis International building before. When she emerged from the service lift, she realised that the layout was different from the floors below. Rounding a corner, she saw a large, luxurious reception area to her right. Beyond it, all the lights had been turned off, but she could dimly see an impressive set of double doors in the gloom.

But when she looked to her left, another set of plainer double doors also greeted her at the far end of the corridor. She raised her eyebrows, but assumed the unlit passage closer to Reception housed the office suite that was off-limits. Deciding to start at the opposite end and work her way back along the corridor, Ellie relaxed. She was delighted by the prospect of any evening shift uninterrupted by Ricky Bolton and his suggestive remarks.

Her canvas-shod feet making little sound, Ellie opened one of the heavy double doors and had crossed the room to reach for the overflowing wastepaper basket before she registered that the interconnecting office beyond was still occupied. The door stood slightly ajar, spilling out the unmistakable sound of male voices.

Usually she would have announced her presence, but, having taken Meg's advice on board, she decided it would be wiser just to beat a quick, quiet retreat. The very last thing she wanted to do was get the older woman into trouble. Just as she was about to step back out again she heard male footsteps coming down the corridor, and practically had a heart attack on the spot.

Without even thinking about what she was doing, she shot behind the door to conceal herself, her heart hammering like a piston. The steps got closer and closer, and then stopped *right* on the other side of the open door. At that point Ellie just stopped breathing altogether.

In the rushing silence she could now hear every word of the dialogue carrying through from the office next door.

'…so as long as I continue to *appear* to be interested in acquiring Danson Components, Palco Technic will remain a sitting duck,' a dark-accented male drawl was murmuring with satisfaction. 'I'll make my move the minute the market opens on Wednesday.'

Ellie heard whoever else was on the other side of the door catch their breath audibly. She felt like a total idiot. What the heck had she been thinking of? The maintenance trolley parked outside supplied visible proof of her presence somewhere nearby.

However, the man in the doorway advanced no deeper into the room. To her surprise and relief, she heard him start back down the corridor much more quietly than he had walked up it. Ellie slowly sucked in much-needed air. She was creeping out from concealment on literal tiptoe when the door of the interconnecting office suddenly shot wide to frame an intimidating male, who seemed at that moment to be as tall as a skyscraper. She froze, green eyes huge in her flushed and discomfited face.

Eyes as black as pitch raked over her in a challenging appraisal as aggressive as a loaded gun.

'What the hell are you doing in here?' he shot at her in angry disbelief.

'I was just leaving—'

'You were hiding behind the door *listening*!' he contradicted in pure outrage.

'No, I wasn't listening.' Ellie was genuinely shocked by the level of his annoyance, and then, as she recognised him, her own tension rocketed right off the scale.

No, they hadn't met before, but there was a dirty great enormous portrait of the guy in the ground-floor foyer. That portrait was the target of much teasing and admiring female comment. Why? Dionysios Alexiakis was drop-dead gorgeous. Dionysios Alexiakis, popularly known as Dio, the ruthless, asset-stripping Greek billionaire who ran Alexiakis International. Oh, dear heaven, she registered sickly, she'd picked the wrong set of double doors to intrude behind. Now both her job *and* Meg's had to be on the line!

A grey-haired older man appeared from behind Dio Alexiakis. Frowning at her in dismay, he dug out a mobile phone. 'She's not the regular cleaner, Dio. I'll get onto security straight away.'

'There's no need for that,' Ellie protested through teeth that were starting to chatter. 'I'm just covering for the usual cleaner tonight…that's all. I'm sorry. I didn't mean to interrupt you…I was just about to step back outside—'

'But you had no business being here in the first place,' the older man condemned.

Dio Alexiakis studied her broodingly, eyes so dark they glittered like reflective mirrors and unnerved her. 'She was hiding behind the door, Millar.'

'Look, it may have *looked* like I was hiding behind the door,' Ellie argued in growing desperation. 'But why would I be hiding? Does that make sense? I'm just a cleaner. I can see I made a mistake coming in here, and I'm really sorry. I'll get out right now—'

Without warning, a large brown hand stretched out to close round her narrow wrist and halt her backward drift towards the door. 'You're not going anywhere. What's your name?'

'Ellie...I mean, Eleanor Morgan...what are you *doing*?' she gasped.

But it was too late. Dio Alexiakis had already tugged loose the scarf she had tied round her head. Her silvery pale hair fell round her shoulders in tumbled disarray. He towered over her, easily six foot three. Feeling menaced by his sheer size, Ellie gazed up at him, green eyes locking into fathomless black.

Her tummy clenched as if she had dropped from a height, the oddest sensation of dizziness making her head swim and her knees tremble. His frowning appraisal had become an outright smouldering stare of sexual assessment.

'You don't look like any cleaner I've ever met,' he finally breathed in a roughened, accented undertone.

'You meet a lot?' Ellie heard herself ask foolishly, but then she had been thrown way off balance by what she had seen in his eyes. That age-old oversexed male to female reaction she despised.

'Ellie...there *is* an Eleanor Morgan on the maintenance roster,' the older man he had referred to as Millar cut in flatly. 'But she's supposed to be working on level eight, and Security haven't cleared her for this floor. I'll have her supervisor sent up to identify her.'

As the other man relayed that information, the Greek tycoon's hard, dark features tautened. '*No.* Get off that phone now. The fewer people who know about this intrusion the better.' Releasing her wrist, he stepped back to swing out a swivel chair. 'Take a seat, Ellie.'

'But I—'

'*Sit!*' he emphasised, as if he was dealing with a puppy in dire need of basic training.

Her teeth locking together at that style of address, Ellie

dropped down, her slim back rigid but her heartbeat still racing. So she had walked in where she shouldn't have. She had apologised. In fact she had all but grovelled, she reflected resentfully. So why the continuing fuss?

'Perhaps you'd care to explain what you're doing on this floor? Why you came into this particular office and why you chose to stay and eavesdrop behind a door?' Dio Alexiakis spelt out with harsh exactitude.

The silence simmered. Momentarily, Ellie wondered if bursting into tears would get her off the hook. She met those hard black eyes and her heart skipped a startled beat. With Dio Alexiakis already behaving as if she had committed a criminal offence, honesty now seemed the wisest and safest course.

'I've been having a bit of a problem with this bloke who works late on level eight,' Ellie admitted with fierce reluctance.

'What sort of problem?' Millar prompted.

Dio Alexiakis let his intense dark gaze roam with bold intimacy over Ellie's small tense figure, lingering at length on the tilted thrust of her breasts defined by the overall and the slender perfection of her legs. As mortified colour ran up beneath her fair skin his wide, sensual mouth quirked. 'Look at her, Millar. Then tell me you still need an answer to that question,' he advised drily.

Still reeling resentfully from that shameless clothes-stripping appraisal, Ellie breathed jerkily. 'I mentioned the situation to the woman who normally works up here and asked if I could switch floors with her for a night. After a *lot* of persuasion, she agreed, and she did warn me not to clean the office behind the double doors…but unfortunately there are two sets of double doors—'

'So there are,' Dio Alexiakis conceded, his agreement smooth.

'I made a simple mistake, and I was about to slip out again

when I heard somebody coming,' Ellie confided tautly. 'I was scared it was a security guard. He might've asked what I was doing up here, and that could have got Meg into trouble. I dived behind the door so that I wouldn't be seen. It was a stupid thing to do—'

'Security haven't been up here since six,' the older man interposed, unimpressed. 'And when Mr Alexiakis arrived just ten minutes ago this entire floor was empty.'

'Well, I don't know who it was. He stood in the doorway for about twenty seconds and then went away again…' Wondering why her reasonable explanation was being challenged, Ellie found her voice trailing away.

Expelling his breath in a slow, measured hiss, Dio Alexiakis lounged back against the edge of a nearby desk and glanced at the anxious older man. 'Go on home, Millar. I can deal with this.'

'I should stay and sort this out for you—'

'You have a dinner date to keep,' Dio reminded him drily. 'I've made you late enough as it is.'

Millar looked as if he was about to protest, and then, meeting his employer's expectant scrutiny, he nodded. Just before he took his leave, he paused to remark gruffly, 'My thoughts will be with you tomorrow, Dio.'

Dio Alexiakis tensed, his eyes veiling. 'Thank you.'

He closed the door in the older man's wake and swung back to survey Ellie.

'I'm afraid I can't trust your word on this, Ellie,' he drawled in a tone of daunting finality. 'You listened to a very confidential dialogue—'

'I wasn't listening…I wasn't interested!' Ellie told him frantically, intimidated much against her own will.

'I've got two questions for you,' Dio Alexiakis advanced softly. 'Do you want to keep your job?'

Ellie stiffened even more, despising him for using such bullying tactics. 'Of course I do—'

'And do you want the other lady who allowed you to come up here and work in her place to keep her job?'

Ellie sagged as if he had punched her, and turned very pale. 'Please don't involve Meg in this,' she argued strickenly. 'This was *my* mistake, not hers!'

'No, she chose to break the rules,' Dio Alexiakis contradicted with lethal cool. 'She's as much involved in this as you are. And if you *are* some kind of spy, in the pay of one of my competitors, you must've made it well worth her while to agree to tonight's switch.'

'A *spy*? What on earth…?' Ellie whispered unevenly, her whole attention focused on that strong, dark face.

'Right at this moment, I find your reference to another unseen and unidentifiable individual's presence rather too convenient,' Dio Alexiakis admitted bluntly. 'If there is an information leak, you have already supplied yourself with the excuse of a third party to take the heat.'

'I d-don't know what you're talking about.' He had her so much on edge that for the first time in her life Ellie couldn't think straight.

'For your sake, I hope you don't,' Dio Alexiakis conceded, with every appearance of grim sincerity. 'But you must understand that to just let you walk back out of here is too big a risk for me to take. If you shared what you heard with the wrong person it could seriously damage my plans.'

'But I wouldn't dream of repeating what I heard!'

'So you *do* remember what you overheard. And yet only a minute ago you swore that you weren't even interested enough to *listen*!'

At that silken reminder, a frank look of dismay leapt into Ellie's eyes. She stared back at him with a sinking heart. She did have perfect recall of what he had said, but had intended to play dumb and keep that news to herself. However, he had tied her in verbal knots and tripped her up. He had a mind like a steel trap, she conceded furiously. Keen, suspicious, quick and deadly in its accuracy.

Dio Alexiakis glanced at the slim gold watch on his wrist and then back at her. 'Allow me to show you the bigger picture here, Ellie. As long as this deal goes down on Wednesday, you and your foolish friend will still be gainfully employed in this building. But until Wednesday comes, you're not moving out of my sight!'

'I b-beg your pardon?'

'Naturally, I'll pay you well for the inconvenience—'

'Inconvenience?' Ellie interrupted in a hopelessly squeaky voice.

'I assume you have a passport?'

'A *passport*? Why are you asking me that?' she gasped.

'I have to fly to Greece tonight. Keeping you under surveillance to ensure that you make no phone calls will require you to fly to Greece with me,' he delivered with perceptible impatience.

'Are you absolutely mad?' Ellie mumbled shakily.

'Do you live alone or with your family?' he questioned.

Transfixed by her own bewilderment, Ellie muttered, 'Alone, *but*—'

'A winged ebony brow rose at that news, black eyes briefly welding to her beautiful face. 'You surprise me. Where do you keep your passport at home?'

'In my bedside cabinet, but *why*—?'

Dio Alexiakis punched out a number on his mobile phone. 'I don't see any alternative to a trip to Greece,' he informed her in a sardonic aside. 'I could lock you up without a phone, but I think you'd be even less happy with that option. And I can hardly ask my household staff here in London to keep you imprisoned while I'm out of the country! You *have* to accompany me of your own free will.'

Free will? What free will? Ellie's lower lip finally dropped away from her upper as she appreciated that he was deadly serious. In the simmering silence she listened to him talk at some length on the phone in what she assumed to be Greek, his tone brusque, commanding. She heard her own name mentioned and tensed up even more.

'But I...I *swear* I won't tell anyone a word of what I heard!' she protested feverishly as he came off the phone again.

'Not good enough. By the way, I've just instructed one of my staff to open your staff locker in the maintenance department and extract your keys.'

'You've *what?*' Ellie flew upright, angry colour lighting her cheeks.

'Your address is in your personnel file. Demitrios will pick up your passport and bring it to the airport.'

Eyes wide with incredulity, Ellie snapped, 'I don't think so...I'm going home right now!'

'Are you? It really is do or die time, Ellie,' Dio Alexiakis advanced with a measuring look of challenge. 'You *can* walk out through that door. I can't stop you. But I can sack both you and your friend, and believe me, if you walk out, I *will!*'

Halfway to the door, Ellie stilled with a jerk.

'I think it would be much more sensible for you to accept the inevitable and come along quietly. That is, assuming you're the innocent party you say you are,' he completed softly, studying her with brilliant black questioning eyes.

'This is crazy! Why would I risk my job by telling anyone what I overheard?' Ellie demanded starkly.

'That information could sell for a great deal of money. I think that would supply sufficient motivation.' Dio Alexiakis strode to the threshold of the inner office he had emerged from earlier. 'Are you coming?'

'Coming where?' Ellie muttered.

'I have a helicopter waiting on the roof. It'll take us to the airport.'

'Oh...' He might as well have admitted to having a dinosaur waiting on the roof. She could not have been more taken aback. 'A helicopter?' she repeated weakly.

Seeming finally to appreciate that she was paralysed by sheer disbelief at what he was calmly demanding of her, Dio Alexiakis strode back across the room, closed a powerful hand over hers and urged her in the direction he wanted her to go. Pausing only to lift a heavy dark overcoat off a chair-arm, he hurried her across a palatial office with huge corner windows and pressed her through a door on the far side of the room.

'This can't be happening to me,' Ellie whispered dazedly as she stumbled up a flight of steps.

'That wish cuts both ways,' he drawled curtly from behind her. 'I have no desire for company on this particular trip.'

As he reached a long arm past her to open the steel door at the top, a blast of cold spring air blew her hair back from her face and plastered her thin overall to her slight body. She shivered violently. Having already donned his overcoat, Dio Alexiakis side-stepped her to stride towards the silver helicopter and the pilot stationed by its nose.

'Hurry up!' he shot at her over a broad shoulder.

'I haven't even got my coat!' Ellie heard herself shriek at him, losing her temper with a suddenness that shook her.

He stopped dead and wheeled round. With an air of grim exasperation and quite unnecessary male drama, he began to shrug back out of his coat.

'Don't waste your time!' Ellie snapped, temper leaping even higher at that display of grudging gallantry. 'I wouldn't wear your stupid coat if I had pneumonia!'

'So freeze in silence!' Dio Alexiakis launched back at her at full throttle, black eyes flashing like forked lightning.

Ellie squared her slight shoulders. Only the frank fascination of the watching pilot persuaded her to put a lid on her anger. Quite untouched by a slashing response that would have intimidated ninety per cent of the population, and keeping her wind-stung face stiff as concrete, Ellie stalked past Dio Alexiakis and climbed gracefully into the rear seat of the helicopter.

'I'll buy you some clothes at the airport,' the abrasive Greek slung at her as he swung in beside the pilot. He turned his head towards her, putting his hard, classic profile into stark view, adding thinly, 'We'll have plenty of time to kill. Waiting for your passport to arrive will probably cost the jet its take-off slot!'

'You are so gracious,' Ellie framed in an unmistakable tone of sarcasm, and his brows drew together in disconcertion a split second before the deafening whine of the rotor blades shattered the tense silence and she turned away again.

This is not happening to me. This *cannot* be happening to me, Ellie told herself all over again as the helicopter first rose in the air and then went into a stomach-churning dip and turn to head out across London. Having employed the equivalent of blackmail, Dio Alexiakis was now set on practically kidnapping her! What choice had he given her? *No* choice! How could she possibly run the risk of getting Meg fired? The older woman didn't have the luxury of a second salary to fall back on, and her husband was disabled.

But was she herself *really* any more independent? Ellie asked herself tautly. If it had simply been a question of survival, she could have managed without her earnings as a cleaner. After all, she had a day-job as well, and a healthy savings account. In fact, Ellie lived like a church mouse, squirrelling away every penny she could, willing to make just about any sacrifice if it meant she could attain her ultimate goal.

And that goal was buying the bookshop where she had worked since she was sixteen. However, if the steady flow of savings into her bank account ceased just when she was on the brink of asking for a large business loan, her bank manager would be most unimpressed, and her ambition to own the shop she loved would suffer a serious, indeed potentially fatal setback. Right now, with her elderly boss becoming increasingly eager to sell and retire, time was of the essence.

Dio Alexiakis was paranoid, absolutely paranoid, she decided helplessly. A *spy*? Did he read a lot of thrillers? So a cleaner had accidentally entered his precious inner sanctum and overheard him discussing confidential business plans. A cleaner who didn't have permission to work on the top floor, a little voice reminded her. A cleaner who shouldn't have been there, shouldn't even have entered that office, caught sneaking out from behind a door looking guilty as hell...

OK, Ellie conceded grudgingly, so she must have looked a bit suspicious in those circumstances. But that still didn't justify his outrageous insistence that he couldn't trust her out of his sight for the next thirty-six hours. And to demand that she travel abroad with him into the bargain was, in her opinion, proof of sheer insanity!

That wasn't his *only* problem either. The way Dio Alexiakis had looked at her a couple of times had infuriated her. Even in the midst of what he had clearly seen as a very serious situation, Dio had still been eying her up like a piece of female merchandise on offer. Compressing her generous mouth into a most ungenerous line, Ellie ruminated on that fact.

Ricky Bolton had been hard enough to tolerate, refusing to take no for an answer and convinced that he only had to persist to wear her down. That she had experienced that strange sense of disorientation when Dio Alexiakis had looked down at her didn't surprise Ellie in the slightest. This arrogant Greek had merely incited a stronger sense of revulsion than even his subordinate did. But then he was one of those *very* earthy guys, she decided grimly, the sort who couldn't look at any reasonably attractive woman without wondering what she might be like in bed!

* * *

Quite impervious to Ellie's growing antipathy, which she expressed in frigid silence, Dio Alexiakis marched her through the airport to a busy shopping area. Striding straight into an exclusive boutique, he headed for a rack of lightweight black skirt suits. Dumping the smallest size available into Ellie's startled arms, he snatched a hat, purse and long black gloves down from the display shelf above and added them.

The remainder of the tastefully concocted display fell flat on the stand. Flushing to the roots of her hair beneath the aghast scrutiny of the saleswoman surging forward, Ellie whispered in a mortified undertone, 'What on earth do you think you're doing?'

'Shopping,' Dio Alexiakis delivered succinctly, quite indifferent to the staff eyes now trained on their every move. Like a steamroller, he headed for another rack, to pull a blue cotton shift dress from a hanger and stuff it with equal unconcern into her dismayed grasp. A long black coat was thrust at her in the same careless fashion. Then he paused by a severely undersized candy-pink shorts outfit on a dummy. With an imperious inclination of his dark head, he hailed the frozen-faced older woman already moving their way. 'We'll have this as well.'

'I'm afraid that item is sold out, sir,' he was told acidly.

'Take it off the dummy, then,' Dio instructed the woman, whose badge proclaimed her managerial status.

'Mr Alexiakis!' Ellie hissed, cringing with embarrassment.

On the clear brink of making a deflating retort, the older woman's mouth fell open when she heard that name and took a better look at the tall black-haired male towering over Ellie. 'M-Mr Alexiakis?' she stammered in incredulously.

'Yes, the owner of this chain of shops,' Dio confirmed, surveying the unfortunate woman with menacing disapproval. 'Tell me, do your staff usually stand around chatting when there are customers requiring attention? And since when has a display been more important than making a sale?'

'You're quite right, sir. Please allow me to assist you,' the manageress muttered unevenly, her discomfiture unconcealed.

'This lady needs lingerie. Pick some out for us.' His attention falling on the shoe racks, he dragged Ellie across to them. 'What size are you?'

'I don't think I've ever been more embarrassed in my life.' Ellie was trembling with rage and chagrin. 'Is this the way you normally behave in public?'

'What's the matter with you?' he demanded with ringing impatience. 'We don't have time to waste. Choose some shoes.'

In the background the manageress was struggling to strip the shorts outfit from the mannequin with hands that were visibly trembling.

In a sudden move of desperation, Ellie stretched up and heaped all the garments into his arms instead. 'Why don't you just go over to the checkout and wait for me there?'

'I'll stay here to expedite matters—'

'You are *not* standing around while I choose undergarments!' Ellie hissed up at him, like a viper ready to strike, infuriated green eyes flaming bright as jewels. 'I don't need so much stuff either.'

Black eyes scorched down into hers. 'I'm paying you to do as you're told—'

'If I have to put up with you, it'll need to be plenty!'

His brilliant gaze literally shimmered, a dark flush of colour accentuating the savage slant of his sculpted cheekbones. Incredulity emanated from him in waves. *Nobody* speaks to me like that—'

'Oh, stop throwing your weight around,' Ellie told him witheringly.

'I—'

'You've behaved atrociously from the moment we walked in here,' Ellie condemned fiercely. 'Go over to the checkout and keep quiet, and try not to terrify the life out of anybody else!'

Turning her back on him, unperturbed by the rasp of Greek invective Dio Alexiakis was audibly struggling to restrain, Ellie chose a pair of high-heeled black sandals and tried them on. They fitted. She passed them to him without a backward glance before joining the ashen-pale manageress at the lingerie section and hurriedly selecting a nightdress and some sets of bras and briefs. Argument, she sensed with a shudder, might well lead to further public mortification. She would leave the clothes behind when she was finally free of the dreadful man. And already the mere thought of another thirty-six hours in Dio Alexiakis's domineering and boorish radius daunted her.

He handed the blue dress and the shoes back to her. 'Put them on,' he commanded with studied insolence.

Cheeks adorned with flags of outraged scarlet, Ellie stalked into a cubicle. He had no manners. He was incredibly confrontational, unnervingly uninhibited and outspoken. As for the way he reacted when he got a taste of his own medicine back—well, he went up in flames like a rocket! When she emerged again, the entire staff were engaged in wrapping the rest of the purchases. Never had Ellie been more grateful to leave a shop.

'I suppose you want to go in there,' Dio condemned with unconcealed exasperation as he surveyed a busy outlet which sold cosmetics and toiletries.

'No…no, I'll manage fine!' Ellie swore in haste. 'Prehistoric man cleaned his teeth with a twig. Maybe I'll pick one up somewhere on the way.'

Dio dealt her an arrested glance. And then he really shocked her. He flung back his imperious dark head and laughed with spontaneous amusement. Ellie simply gaped, heart-rate speeding up, pulses jumping. His even white teeth flashed against bronzed skin, dark, deep-set eyes gleaming with appreciation. Humour drove all brooding darkness from his lean, powerful face, leaving her bemusedly conscious of just how stunning he was in the looks department.

'I'm not into shopping,' he confided huskily, as if she might not already be aware of that reality. 'Other people usually do it for me.'

Her complexion uncomfortably warm, Ellie dragged her attention from him and studied the floor, but that Mediterranean dark and devastating face was still imprinted in her mind's eye. He really *was* spectacular. That stark acknowledgement, that very thought, seriously unsettled Ellie. Dio Alexiakis wasn't making the tiniest effort to impress or please her. Yet somehow he still made her effortlessly aware of his high-voltage male sexuality. She didn't like that sensation, didn't like the unease and tension he provoked inside her.

She might be only twenty-one, but it was over a year since Ellie had gone out on a date. Men, she had decided, were a waste of precious time and effort, and she hadn't once regretted that decision. She didn't consider herself a man-hater, but she did get a secret kick out of jokes that suggested the male sex was useless and increasingly surplus to female requirements. After all, by and large, that *had* been Ellie's experience from childhood.

As Dio urged Ellie at speed through the crowded terminal, he rested a lean hand lightly on her taut spine to keep her moving. She stiffened defensively. 'Excuse me,' she heard herself say stiltedly, stepping back, suddenly determined to escape him, even if it could only be for a little while.

'Where do you think you're going?' he demanded.

'The ladies' cloakroom,' Ellie framed with frigid emphasis. 'Are you planning to come with me?'

His aggressive jawline squared. 'I'll give you two minutes.'

Pointedly dumping the carrier bags she was loaded down with at his feet, she began to walk away.

'Ellie…' He extended a comb to her with a sardonic look. 'Maybe you should do something with your hair while you're in there.'

Gritting her teeth at the realisation that she hadn't taken the time to check her appearance in the shop, and strongly resisting an unusually feminine urge to start smoothing her hair down, Ellie vanished into the cloakroom.

It was the work of a moment to tame her bright hair back into a straight heavy fall just below her shoulders. She frowned at her reflection, noticing the animated pink in her cheeks, the surprising sparkle in her eyes. The dress had a cool simplicity she liked, but it wasn't her style.

Her full pink mouth tightening, Ellie studied the expensive silver comb he had given her and recalled the ease with which he had accurately assessed her dress size. But then that had not been a surprise to her. At twenty-nine years of age, Dio Alexiakis was an unrepentant, totally unreconstructed womaniser. Naturally he was, Ellie reflected cynically. Men with money and power lived in a buyers' market of all too willing women. Dio was a real babe magnet, and he *knew* it. He had undoubtedly never had to worry too much about honing the rough edges from his less than presentable manners.

But, even so, she was to get a free trip to Greece. Private jet, five-star luxury all the way. The drawback? Dio Alexiakis breathing down her neck. An adventure, she told herself staunchly. Even with *him* around it ought to be more fun than polishing endless floors.

Heavens, she realised abruptly, she'd have to ring Mr Barry. Tomorrow morning her boss would be expecting her to open up as usual. He never turned in until noon, and when he found the shop still locked up he'd go straight upstairs to her bedsit and hammer on the door, thinking she had fallen ill. Regardless of Dio's embargo, she *had* to phone Mr Barry, and as she could hardly tell the older man the truth, she would have to lie to excuse her absence.

Carefully concealing herself behind a pair of large, gossiping women, Ellie slipped out of the cloakroom and lunged breathlessly at the public phone only a few yards away. Dio Alexiakis was now standing in the centre of the busy concourse, talking on his mobile phone, his attention conveniently distracted.

Ellie dialled the operator. Since she had no cash on her at all, she would have to request a reverse-charge call. But just as the operator answered, Dio turned his dark, arrogant head. She crashed the receiver back on the hook, but she wasn't quick enough. Dio saw her before she could put some space between herself and the phone.

Ellie froze like a criminal as glittering black eyes locked to her in instantaneous judgement, his lean, strong face darkening as he strode towards her. And Ellie, who knew all too well what it felt like to be irritated or bored by a member of the male sex, discovered for the first time in her life what it felt like to be *scared*...

CHAPTER TWO

EYES as dangerous as black ice scanned Ellie's pale face. 'The instant I allowed you out of my sight, you rushed to the phone to pass on the information you overheard. You have betrayed my trust!' Dio Alexiakis condemned with scantily suppressed savagery.

Even trembling, and with her stomach knotted light with apprehension, Ellie was fascinated by the volatile charge of that explosive Mediterranean temperament and that innate sense of drama. Both were so utterly foreign to her.

'Mr. Alexiakis—' she began, keen to disabuse him of his eagerness to assume the worst.

'You have made your choice. So be it.' Dio surveyed her with cold, lethal menace. 'I will destroy you for this.'

Ellie's tummy performed an unpleasant somersault. 'You've got it wrong,' she protested feverishly. 'I only got as far as dialling the operator!'

With a look of thunderous derision, Dio swung on his heel and strode away, outrage etched in every line of his lean, tight, powerful body.

For an instant, disconcertion froze Ellie to the spot. Oh, yeah, just drag me out to the airport on your stupid helicopter and then dump me with no money and a very nasty threat! Only unfreezing as fear for her co-worker Meg's future job security assailed her, Ellie raced after Dio Alexiakis, hating him like poison.

'Get out of my way,' he growled when she got in front of him.

'That call I was trying to make wasn't what you thought it was either!' Ellie argued hotly.

He simply side-stepped her.

'You are so *stubborn*!' Ellie flung wrathfully in his wake. 'All I did was try to make a reverse-charge call to my boss at the bookshop…all right?'

Stilling, Dio swung back with stormy reluctance. 'What bookshop?' he ground out.

Ellie stared at him with a frown, sensing something missing, and then she exclaimed, 'What the heck have you done with the bags? For goodness' sake, you just walked off and left them lying on the floor, didn't you?'

Ellie went into automatic reverse, spinning round to retrace his steps. Her attention settled on the abandoned carrier bags with relief. Hurrying back, she grabbed them up.

'What bookshop?' Dio repeated stonily when she'd made it back to his side, laden like a packhorse.

'I work in one during the day. I also live above the shop…' Ellie paused to get her breath back. 'I *have* to contact Mr Barry to warn him that I'll be taking time off. He'll call the police if I suddenly vanish—'

'Rubbish! He'll assume that you've taken off with some boyfriend. Staff of your age are often unreliable,' Dio Alexiakis asserted, unimpressed.

Affronted by the response, Ellie breathed in very deep to control her temper, but it didn't work.

'You know, I've had it up to here with you!' she told him bluntly, tipping back her silvery fair head to survey him with angry resentment. 'I do not have a boyfriend and I am *not* unreliable. Don't underestimate me and don't talk down to me, Mr Alexiakis. I always turn in for work. I've been in the same job for five years, and for the past two I've virtually been running the business—'

'So what are you doing slogging as a cleaner five nights a week?' he incised drily.

'I need the money…OK?' she flared. 'Is that really any of your business?'

'Your insolence outrages me.' Shimmering dark, deep-set eyes raked over her, the lean, bronzed features hard as steel.

'So I don't like you…what do you expect? I haven't done anything wrong. I made a silly mistake, but it's being treated like a major crime!' Ellie recounted in an accusing undertone. 'You're blackmailing me into doing what I don't want to do…and I don't appreciate your conviction that because I'm poor I'm more likely to be dishonest!'

'Are you quite finished?'

Feeling as if she had run smash-bang into a brick wall and bruised herself all over, Ellie reddened and compressed her lips.

'Today of all days,' he breathed with harsh emphasis, 'I am not in the mood for this nonsense. Come on. We have wasted enough time.'

'You believe me, then…?' Ellie prompted a minute or two later as she struggled to keep up with his long, powerful stride.

'All I believe is that I caught you *before* you contrived to disobey my explicit warning not to telephone anyone,' Dio contradicted with succinct bite. 'You're little *and* sneaky. Why does that not surprise me?'

'I am not sneaky!'

'You could have explained that you had another employer. I'm not an unreasonable man,' Dio stated grimly. 'But you chose to sneak instead of being open and honest.'

If he said 'sneak' again, she swore she would slap him. Her cheeks flamed, but the threat of thirty lashes at dawn wouldn't have dragged an apology from her. Asking him permission to do anything would have choked her. And, whether he liked it or not, that call to Mr Barry still had to be made. Unfortunately the prospect of telling little white lies to Mr Barry in Dio Alexiakis's presence made her squirm.

Ellie didn't make a habit of lying. If anything, she tended to be too honest, too blunt. She knew her own failing well, but some of her failings were also her strengths. She was fiercely independent and had never been a team player. She loved having the freedom to make her own decisions. As a result, both her jobs suited her perfectly. She preferred to work alone and without interference.

Almost an hour later, when Dio's brooding silence was fraying her nerves, her passport and her keys were handed over at a prearranged meeting point by an older man in a dark suit, whom Dio called Demitrios. Both men totally ignored her, and talked for what felt like a very long time in Greek.

'I hope you didn't leave my place in a mess,' Ellie finally remarked, rather loudly.

When she spoke, Demitrios frowned in complete surprise, much as if a suitcase had suddenly opened its mouth and tried to chat.

'And I hope you locked up properly again.' At that point a strangled groan erupted from Ellie. 'For goodness' sake, how the heck did you get past the alarm system in the first place? And did you *reset* the—?'

'My security staff are not stupid,' Dio interposed crushingly, openly aggravated by her interruptions. 'The premises will have been left in order.'

Ellie tilted her chin. 'It must be comforting to know that you have staff who can trespass as efficiently as burglars.'

Dio dealt her a thunderous glance from brilliant black eyes.

'It's rude to ignore people,' she told him stubbornly, and spun away.

But then you're just a cleaner, she reminded herself in exasperation. The lowest of the low in any staff hierarchy. Even worse, she was stuck with a guy used to being waited on hand and foot by servants. Behaving as if she was the invisible woman didn't tax Dio in the slightest. He expected her to maintain a respectful silence unless first invited to speak. But she had never been that good at keeping her tongue between her teeth, she acknowledged ruefully.

Feeling cold now that she was no longer being kept warm by carting heavy bags around, not to mention the need to walk at about five times her natural speed, Ellie took out the black coat, ripped off the sale label and put it on. The hem hit the floor. If she pulled up the collar she would look like a small moving blanket.

'Here…' Dio Alexiakis extended his mobile phone to her.

Ellie blinked in complete disconcertion.

'Your story checks out. Demitrios confirms it. You may call the owner of the bookshop.'

Ellie punched out the number. As soon as he heard her voice, Mr Barry asked anxiously if something had happened at the shop. Reassuring him, but resentfully conscious of Dio listening to every word, she explained that she would be off work for a couple of days, and apologised for the lack of warning she was giving him. She said a close friend was ill.

Ending the call with relief, she returned the phone to Dio Alexiakis.

He shot her a grim, measuring look. 'You're a very convincing liar.'

Several hours later, Ellie was appreciatively conceding that the interior of the Alexiakis private jet was something else.

Her eyes roved with keen curiosity in every direction. Opulent cream leather seating, plush carpet and elegant dcor. The cabin was far more like a luxurious reception room than mere passenger space. And did Dio Alexiakis realise how lucky he was? Did he heck!

Ellie surveyed her reluctant host. While they had waited endlessly at the airport for a fresh take-off slot for the jet he had paced the VIP lounge, exuding frustration and wrathful impatience in enervating waves. Now they were finally airborne, but from what she could see he was in no better a mood.

Even so, she still found herself studying him. The dense blue-black hair so perfectly styled to his well-shaped head. The spectacular eyes enhanced by luxuriant ebony lashes. Eyes the colour of midnight that could glint like diamond stars. The hard planes and hollows of his fabulous bone structure. Strong cheekbones added character. His arrogant nose gave warning. And that wide, perfect mouth? Passion and sensuality. She pondered on the mystery of how a particular set of features could add up to such a devastating whole.

And by the time she surprised herself at that stage, she'd got distinctly hot and bothered, and acknowledged a truth she would sooner have denied. She fancied the socks off Dio Alexiakis! Who had she been trying to kid when she'd told herself he revolted her? But it had been such a very long time since Ellie had been physically attracted to a man that she was sincerely stunned by the revelation. Just hormones playing a trick on her to remind her that she could be as foolish and fallible as any other woman, she told herself. Urgently.

But even in a filthy mood, Dio Alexiakis *was* incredibly sexy. If she had noticed, he *had* to be! Possessed of that rare fluidity of a male totally in touch with his own body, he moved like a big cat prowling on velvet paws. And he was beautifully built. Broad shoulders, taut, flat stomach, slim hips, long, lean powerful thighs, she assessed, taking individual note of each attribute. *Fantasy man*…well, until he opened his mouth, she conceded, or left her carting the bags, or looked through her with supreme disdain while never once enquiring if she was hungry or thirsty. Not a feeling guy. Tough, selfish, single-minded and utterly ruthless in attaining his own ends…

Caught staring, Ellie clashed in shock with Dio's narrowed intent gaze. Eyes that could turn to the glowing gold of topaz in sunlight, she registered, suddenly running alarmingly short of breath. But it was a kind of alarm new to Ellie's experience. Edge-of-the-seat excitement, she labelled in disbelief, finding it impossible to break free of that smouldering golden appraisal. Feverish tension held her fast, the thunder of her accelerated heartbeat pounding in her ears like surf as her mouth ran dry. An arrow of twisting heat coiled up through her and warm colour stained her face.

'It's three in the morning Greek time. You should lie down for a while and try and get some sleep,' Dio murmured thickly.

The very sound of that deep, dark drawl was like honey drenching her every straining sense, sending a delicious little shiver through her taut frame.

Ellie blinked like a sleepwalker waking up. 'Lie down?' she mumbled.

A dark line of blood now accentuated the hard arc of his cheekbones. He reached out and pressed a service button. His astonishing eyes were semi-veiled by his lush lashes. The raw tension churning up the atmosphere turned her stomach over. Complete bewilderment assailed her, followed by a sudden stark flood of intense embarrassment.

As Ellie rose jerkily upright, looking everywhere but at Dio Alexiakis, the female flight attendant appeared. Ellie was shown into a sleeping compartment. She sank down on the edge of the surprisingly large bed, powerfully disconcerted by the lingering ache in her swollen breasts and the still urgent tautness of her nipples. Never before had a man simply looked at Ellie and made her feel a hunger so powerful it hurt. But Dio Alexiakis had.

Ellie was shattered by that discovery, and ashamed of a physical reaction she had been quite unable to control. Had *he* realised what was happening to her? Had *he* recognised the effect he was having on her? She shut her eyes tight. She was appalled by the suspicion that Dio had not only recognised her helpless sexual response to him but banished her from his sight because of it.

A couple of hours later, a quiet but insistent voice roused Ellie from her uneasy doze. 'Miss Morgan…?'

Ellie came up slowly on one elbow. The flight attendant was hovering with a tray and a look of uncertainty. Ellie reached up with a grateful smile to accept the food finally being offered to her. 'Thanks…yes?'

'We…well, the cabin staff wondered if perhaps *you* would like to wake Mr Alexiakis,' she confided tautly. 'We'll be landing in fifty minutes, and naturally we're all anxious not to intrude any more than we have to—'

'Intrude?' Ellie queried, all at sea and wondering why on earth such a strange request should be made of her. Was Dio a grizzly bear when he was woken up? Had she qualified for the short straw? Did she look like cannon fodder?

The other woman sighed. 'Someone has to wake Mr Alexiakis up now so that he can dress for the funeral.'

'The funeral…' Ellie echoed, her voice just fading out altogether.

'I'm afraid this flight is very late, Miss Morgan. The delay back in London and the further delay in landing means that you'll have to travel to the funeral direct. I hope you won't think I'm being too personal, but we all think it's wonderful that Mr Alexiakis has brought someone with him for support,' she shared, and slipped out again.

Fully awakened now by sheer horror, Ellie stared into space. Oh, dear heaven, Dio Alexiakis was flying out to Greece to attend a funeral! That was why he had bought her all that black clothing! And the cabin staff had decided that she had to be somebody important in Dio's life because she was accompanying him. She remembered him saying that he hadn't wanted company on this particular trip, and groaned out loud at the memory while wondering whose funeral it was. Obviously somebody close. A relative? A dear friend?

After hurriedly choking down the breakfast on the tray, Ellie got up and rushed into the compact bathroom. She would have loved to take advantage of the shower but there wasn't time. She took out the black suit and put it on.

Her appearance in that suit astonished her. The light jacket fitted like a glove, nipping in at her tiny waist, hugging her slim shoulders, the deep vee-neck moulding her full breasts. The narrow skirt outlined the all-female curve of her hips and then tightened to outline her slender thighs. She looked sensational, she registered in amazement. Then, reddening at a vanity that seemed inappropriate, she turned from the mirror, irritated with herself for being so superficial.

Returning to the cabin, she saw Dio's impossibly long and powerful length sprawled at a most uncomfortable angle across one of the fancy leather seats. Her now tenderised and conscience-stricken heart smote her.

Shorn of his formal jacket and tie, his silk shirt open at his strong brown throat and his jawline darkly shadowed by stubble, he looked so much younger and less intimidating. He also looked absolutely exhausted, and if it hadn't been for her presence he would naturally have enjoyed the comfort of his own bed.

Ellie tensed even more. To think the cabin staff had clearly been nervous of intruding on his grief! She herself had done nothing *but* intrude! Recalling every angry combative word she had slung at the airport, Ellie cringed with guilt and shame. So the poor guy had been in a rough mood. In the circumstances, that was hardly a surprise, and his preoccupation had been equally understandable.

With a gentle hand on his shoulder, she shook him awake. His incredibly long lashes lifted off his flushed cheekbones, and with a soft sigh, he lifted his tousled head to check his watch. With a stifled expletive, he then plunged forcefully upright and headed for the sleeping compartment.

'Mr Alexiakis…?'

He stilled, but he didn't turn round.

'I didn't know you were attending a funeral,' Ellie said awkwardly. 'I wish somebody had mentioned it.'

He swung back, frowning at her in genuine surprise. 'Don't you read newspapers?'

'I don't get time to read them.'

'It's my father's funeral,' he responded curtly, and strode away.

Ellie slowly breathed in deep, but it didn't make her *feel* any better. His father! What could be worse? Of course he hadn't wanted to be lumbered with a total stranger over the next couple of days. So why on earth had he insisted that she had to accompany him?

Those extremely confidential business plans he was so fired up about, this pretending to be interested in one company while really being interested in another, she recalled in exasperation. She wished she understood how that information could be as hugely important as *he* seemed to think it was. A spy, she thought afresh, shaking her head in wonderment. Cops and robbers. Thriller territory. Way beyond anything she could even imagine.

But then Dio Alexiakis lived in a gilded world of immense wealth and privilege. He wheeled and dealed in incredibly high-powered circles. Even the night before his own father's funeral he had still been talking business. Had it been a very sudden death? Whatever, on reflection, Ellie was surprised that he hadn't already been in Greece. Even before she had entered the equation and complicated matters, hadn't he been cutting things a bit fine?

It was after seven in the morning and a bright and beautiful day when Dio Alexiakis and Ellie finally walked into Athens airport.

Wearing the suit combined with the long dramatic gloves, the extravagant-brimmed hat and the designer sunglasses which Dio had given her, Ellie felt as if she was taking part in a fancy dress parade. They were waved on by grave-faced officials. But as they passed through the barriers a wave of shouting men with cameras surged forward, held at bay only by a squad of equally determined security guards.

Ellie just froze in the glare of flashing cameras. Dio closed a powerful arm round her and carried her on through the crush as if it wasn't there, impervious to the questions being thrown in several different languages.

'Who's the woman?' she heard a man roar loudly in English.

Ellie was unnerved by the aggressive behaviour of the paparazzi. Dio was coming home to his father's funeral. What had happened to privacy? The giving of a little respectful space? For goodness' sake, was Dio hounded like this everywhere he went? Ellie hadn't the slightest idea.

But during breaks in evening shifts she had frequently heard her co-workers discussing Dio's private life in the most lurid of terms. He lived in the fast lane. He featured in glossy magazines and made endless gossip column headlines. Having enjoyed affairs with a string of gorgeous, high-profile women, he was a real sex god to the cleaning staff. But Ellie had always felt rather superior during those sessions. She hadn't had the slightest interest in the exploits of a male she neither knew nor ever expected to meet. So she hadn't listened any further.

They changed terminals and ended up in a small, plainly furnished waiting room. Ellie was still trembling. 'Is it always like that for you?'

Dio shrugged a broad shoulder. Dark, deep-set awesomely beautiful eyes briefly touched her. 'Yes...but I'm afraid I overlooked the more extreme interest your presence would excite.'

'I hope to heaven I'm not going to be recognisable in any of those photos,' Ellie confided tautly.

Dio said nothing.

'What are we waiting for now?'

'A flight out to the island where the burial will take place.'

Another flight. She suppressed a groan. The journey seemed endless. 'The island?' she queried.

'Chindos. You really do know nothing about me,' Dio remarked with a slight frown. 'I'm not used to that.'

'But I bet it's good for you…puts a dent in your belief that you are the sun around which the entire world must turn,' Ellie muttered, and then froze in dismay. She grimaced. 'I'm sorry, I'm sorry. I was just thinking out loud!'

'That disastrous lack of tact must get you into trouble.' Dio surveyed her with a shadowy suspicion of a smile momentarily softening the hard line of his expressive mouth.

Ellie swallowed hard, grateful he hadn't exploded. 'It's been known.'

'Why are you always in search of a fight?' Dio scanned her with penetrating eyes that tightened her very skin over her bones and made her shift uneasily on her seat. 'You look so wonderfully feminine and delicate—'

Ellie winced. 'Not delicate…*please*!'

'Cute?'

'Worse,' she censured without hesitation. 'Men refuse to take me seriously. It's a big drawback being small and blonde—'

'But you're not blonde. Your hair is the colour of platinum. It's extremely eye-catching,' Dio informed her with definitive derision and the distinct air of a male unimpressed by her protest. 'If you genuinely don't want to invite that type of male attitude, you shouldn't dye it that shade.'

Ellie dealt him the weary glance of a woman who had

heard it all before. 'My hair's natural. My grandmother was Dutch, and very fair.'

'Natural? I don't believe you. Take your hat off,' he urged, startling her.

After a moment's hesitation, Ellie did so, and flung back her head as if she was challenging him. Her bright hair shone like heavy silver silk against the darkness of her jacket. 'You see, *not* fake.'

His black eyes flared gold and lingered on that shimmering fall. The silence set in then, thick as a sheet of solid steel. She watched him covertly from beneath her lashes. So very tall, so exotically dark, so still and silent. Sheathed in a sensationally well-cut black double-breasted suit, he looked truly amazing. Stop it, *stop it*. What's the matter with you? a shaken voice screamed inside her bemused head.

Perspiration beading her short upper lip, Ellie quivered, agonised by the awful reality that her own brain seemed to be romping out of control. In directions it had never gone in before. Even in the depths of infatuation at nineteen, with the latest and last of the users and abusers she'd seemed to attract, she hadn't felt overwhelmed and taken over, her very thoughts no longer her own. And there hadn't been this ghastly, utterly desperate sexual craving which flooded her every time she looked at Dio Alexiakis. She just could not *cope* with feeling like that around a man. It was so weak, so irrational, so humiliating...

'What's it like being a cleaner?' Dio enquired with quite staggering abruptness.

'Look, you don't have to make conversation with me.'

'It was a sincere question.'

'OK...it's very boring, repetitive and poorly paid,' Ellie told him with a touch of defiance. 'So if you're expecting me to say I'm some weirdo who gets a real high out of dusting and polishing—well, sorry to disappoint you!'

'So why are you doing it?'

'The hours suit me and I've got nobody on my back. I don't like being ordered around.'

'I noticed. You should deal with that problem and then consider the possibility of more challenging employment. But perhaps you have no training for any other sphere.'

'I've got plans of my own. I'm an ambitious woman in my own small way. I won't be polishing your floors for much longer,' Ellie told him with open mockery.

Dio studied her with hard black eyes. 'In the situation you're in, it's not a good idea to drop hints of that variety. I never joke about business, Ellie.'

'Neither do I. Business comes first and last in my life—'

'Really?'

'And you're running up quite a bill already,' Ellie informed him gently. 'You do realise that I expect you to pay me for every hour of the last twelve?'

'Naturally.'

'Double time too,' Ellie specified, tilting up her chin and ready to fight her corner. 'I take a dim view of being starved, deprived of breaks and kept up until three in the morning.'

Grudging amusement stirred in his brilliant eyes. 'You're your own worst enemy,' he murmured silkily. 'I'd have paid one hell of a lot more if you had just kept quiet.'

'I'm not greedy, and by the way, when I said I wouldn't be working in the maintenance department for much longer, I wasn't thinking about that stupid conversation I overheard,' Ellie told him impatiently. 'I'd forgotten about that.'

'How *could* you have forgotten about it?' Dio growled in disbelief.

'Even if I did understand the importance of what you said in that office—which I don't—I'm an honest person and I wouldn't take advantage.'

'Those who stress how honest they are, are almost always lying in their teeth,' Dio countered crushingly.

Feeling oddly hurt that his barriers had gone up again, Ellie felt her beautiful face stiffen and flush. 'Obviously you're going to believe what you want to believe. Suit yourself!'

'You can't blame me for taking every possible precaution.'

That confident assertion filled Ellie with furious resentment. Who did he think he was kidding? Without hesitation, he had used his infinitely superior power like the weapon it was! The fact that she was endeavouring to make the best of a bad situation didn't alter that brutal reality. 'Don't you *dare* try to justify yourself!' she warned him. 'Tell it like it is. If you weren't who you are and I wasn't who I am, I wouldn't *be* here! If Meg and I didn't need our jobs, I would have told you exactly where to go—'

'I can imagine,' Dio slotted in silkily.

'And, you know, dragging me along on a trip like this…well, it's not exactly a dream treat, is it? No offence or disrespect intended, but I'm not heavily into funerals,' Ellie confided.

A disconcerting flare of amusement lit Dio's steady scrutiny. 'My father would have adored your irreverence!'

Her full mouth softened. 'Was he one of the good guys?'

All his tension returned, his amusement fading as quickly as it had come. In silence, he slowly nodded, bronzed features setting hard. He swung away and she wished she had kept her stupid, clumsy mouth closed. Just for a little while he had emerged from his brooding reserve and contrived to forget what lay ahead of him.

A knock sounded on the door. It was time to move on again. Under the growing heat of the sun they walked out across the tarmac to board a small plane. A dream treat? Ellie cringed at the recollection. How could she have been that tactless? Now he was wishing she would vanish again! So why should it bother her that he felt like that? After all, how did she expect him to feel?

The plane flew out over the gleaming waters of the Aegean. In a silence filled only with monotonous engine noise,

Ellie's eyes grew heavier and heavier. She sank down lower in her seat and slid into a deep, dreamless sleep.

Feeling incredibly languid, Ellie took her time about waking up again. But she frowned in sleepy disorientation when she finally focused on her surroundings. She was lying on the capacious back seat of an enormous limousine with tinted windows.

With a thick, expensive metal clunk, the passenger door opened. A black-haired young man backed by bright golden sunlight gaze down at her with patronising amusement. 'So you're Dio's latest woman... I've got to hand it to my cousin. He's got taste. No wonder he kept you out of the church. Some of his late mother's relatives are pretty narrow-minded. I'm Lukas Varios.'

Tensing with annoyance under the earthy glide of the eyes trailing over the slender length of her exposed legs, Ellie pulled herself hurriedly upright and tugged down the skirt which had ridden up while she slept. 'I am *not* Dio's woman!' she snapped.

'Nice to have a piece of good news today.' With a cocky grin on his handsome face, Lukas Varios slid in beside her and closed the door. 'So, if you don't belong to Dio, what are you doing waiting outside the cemetery for him?'

Ellie compressed her ripe pink mouth into a rigid line. 'I just work for him...OK?'

'Oh, it's *very* much OK with me...' Impervious to her frozen expression, Lukas stretched out a confident hand to finger the silvery fall of hair lying against her flushed cheekbone and murmured, 'You are a real babe—'

The passenger door opened again, this time framing Dio. He took one look at the apparently intimate scene he had interrupted and smouldering fury blazed in his spectacular eyes. He reached in a powerful hand, closed it over the younger man's shoulder and hauled him out of the limo to shoot a raw flood of guttural Greek down at him.

Lukas Varios backed off, struggling to reassert his cool by smoothing down his jacket, but his shaken face was red as fire. As Ellie sat there, immobilised by sheer shock at Dio's extraordinary behaviour, Lukas sent her a fiercely accusing glance. 'She said she wasn't yours...do you think I'd have come on to her if she'd told me the truth?'

Lean, strong face cold and hard as bronze, Dio swung into the limo and slammed the door without another word. Black contemptuous eyes flamed over Ellie. 'I didn't bring you here to behave like a tramp!' he told her with splintering derision.

CHAPTER THREE

ELLIE's quick temper, already taxed to its limits by Lukas's offensive familiarity, simply erupted.

Reacting on instinct alone, her hand flew up and she slapped Dio Alexiakis so hard across one cheekbone her fingers stung like mad. 'No man calls me a tramp!' she bit out in furious condemnation.

As the livid marks of that slap sprang up across one slashing cheekbone, Dio stared back at her with truly stunned black eyes.

Even though Ellie instantly knew that she had gone too far, she was far too angry to acknowledge her mistake. 'And your conceited mega-ego of a cousin deserves the same!' she launched in defiant addition. 'Who does that little squirt think he is? Calling me a *babe*, and smirking and pawing my hair like I'm some kind of toy to be played with! And how dare you behave in such a way as to give him the impression that I would stoop to be something as utterly disgusting as *your* woman?'

'Disgusting…?' Dio gritted, not quite levelly, eyes now as scorching a gold as the heart of a bonfire.

'Yes, disgusting!' Ellie repeated with a feeling shudder. 'Women do not belong like objects to men—'

'I could persuade you to belong to me,' Dio declared in a wrathful growl.

Ellie breathed in so deep on that staggering claim she was vaguely surprised that she didn't explode. She studied him with scornful green eyes. 'What with? A Stone Age hammer? Because let me tell you, knocking me out and dragging me by force back to the family cave would be the only way!'

41

Without the slightest warning, Dio reached for her with powerful hands that brooked no refusal. He brought his mouth crashing down hard on hers. Shock paralysed Ellie. But a far deeper level of shock awaited her. When that wide, sensual mouth possessed hers with hungry force, it was as if the world came to a sudden screeching halt and sent her flying off into the sun.

The surge of heat Dio ignited could have burned up an entire planet. Ellie's head swam, all rational thought suspended beneath that shattering shower of instant sensation. As he hauled her into a crushing and deeply satisfying embrace, her blood pounded madly through her pliant body.

He tasted like water after a long summer drought. He created a thirst she had never known she had. She was so hooked on that electrifying excitement that she clung like a vine to a tree, moaning low in her throat as his tongue invaded the moist sensitivity of her mouth in an erotic invasion that drove her wild.

Dio dragged her back from him, his breathing fractured, his eyes blazing over her with a primitive satisfaction he couldn't hide. 'I wouldn't need to use force with you, Ellie. You'd come back to the family cave like a little lamb,' he contended thickly.

As the haze of intoxicating passion evaporated, Ellie gazed up into his darkly handsome features, aghast. Simultaneously, Dio stiffened, veiled his eyes and set her back from him. A boiling wave of hot embarrassment enveloped Ellie. She couldn't believe that what had happened had happened. She couldn't believe that she could possibly have felt what he had made her feel when she hadn't wanted to feel anything. And the silence lay there, thick and treacherous as a swamp that neither of them wanted to risk trying to cross.

'I…I…' Ellie began unevenly, suddenly eager to give both of them an acceptable excuse. 'I shouldn't have slapped you. I made you angry—'

'Greek men don't like having their masculinity challenged.' Dio loosed a sardonic laugh and dealt her a bleak glance. 'But I kissed you because I wanted to. As you said to me, tell it like it is.'

Taken aback by that blunt acknowledgement that the attraction playing havoc with her own self-discipline was not solely her problem, Ellie gazed at him in frank perplexity. Then she swiftly turned her head away.

'Naturally we won't be repeating the experiment,' Dio completed with flat finality.

Ellie's delicate profile tautened. Although he was only stating the obvious, only saying what she would have said herself, angry mortification still engulfed her. Conscious that she was being warned off, she felt humiliated. *He* had kissed *her*! Yet he still evidently saw a need to depress any foolish ideas she might be developing. Who the heck did he think he was?

Mr Totally Irresistible? *Yes*, she answered for herself. And that blazing confidence wasn't vanity, she acknowledged with driven reluctance. He had it all. The looks, the money, the power. How often did Dio Alexiakis meet with rejection? How much more often must he meet with blatant encouragement?

But still Ellie felt the need to defend herself. 'I lashed out because you were extremely ru—'

'I don't wish to discuss this any further,' Dio interposed harshly. 'I'm not myself today. My reactions are on a very short fuse.'

But in the space of a heartbeat he had blown Ellie's belief that she wasn't a very sexual person right out of the water. She could only cringe when she recalled the almost irresistible temptation to snatch him greedily back into her arms. She had never dreamt that *any* man could rouse her to that level of excitement, hunger and craving. That Dio Alexiakis had that power shook her to her very depths.

The limousine drove up the steep road at a stately crawl,

other vehicles now falling in behind to follow in their wake. Above them, perched on the spectacular height of a cliff, the large domed roof of a pale building came into view. The higher they climbed, the bigger that building seemed to become. It couldn't be called a villa, Ellie decided wide-eyed, it could only be called a *palace*.

'Is this your home?' she prompted tautly.

As the limo glided to a halt in front of the massive entrance, Dio gave a bleak nod of confirmation.

'If you're going to be socialising with friends and family now, just find me a room somewhere and lock the door. I don't want to intrude—'

'You're staying with me,' Dio countered steadily.

'But what am I supposed to say if anyone speaks to me?' Ellie's dismay was unhidden. 'I don't even know what your father was called!'

'His name was Spiros. He was seventy-one and I was his only child,' Dio framed, his accent thickening to roughen his vowel sounds, his jawline squaring. 'He was one of those good guys you mentioned. He may have passed away peacefully in his sleep, but his death was both sudden *and* unexpected.'

'You had no chance to say goodbye. That's very hard to bear.' As she had listened Ellie had paled, briefly plunged into her own memories of the loss of a loved and loving parent.

Dio sent her a flashing glance of pure disdain. 'Spare me the platitudes,' he derided harshly. 'My father and I had been estranged for some time before his death.'

'It wasn't a platitude. Whose fault was it that you were…estranged?' she dared to ask.

'*Mine…*' She watched his lean brown hands slowly clench into powerful fists and then carefully unclench again the instant he realised she had noticed that betraying gesture.

'You couldn't have known—'

'This is none of your business!' Dio ground out thunderously.

They climbed out of the car. Ellie stole a troubled glance up at Dio's rigid profile and suppressed a rueful sigh, recognising the stoic, all-male but unnatural control he was determined to maintain. Maybe it was easier for women to let go emotionally, talk it out, forgive themselves. It was certainly wiser, she reckoned. Right now Dio Alexiakis was like a big simmering volcano, struggling to swallow back a surging lava flow. Hanging back, she let him stride ahead of her,.

A large cluster of staff were waiting in the huge, opulent entrance hall. Dio spoke a few words. Ellie hovered awkwardly in the centre of the marble floor, her attention roaming over statues in alcoves and magnificent paintings and then centring on the gorgeous brunette who had unexpectedly appeared in a doorway.

Not having noticed the other woman, Dio swung back an imperious head. 'Ellie!' he gritted impatiently.

Her colour rising as every watching eye swivelled to examine her with keen interest, Ellie quickened her step. Just as Dio clamped a large imprisoning hand over hers, the sophisticated brunette strolled forward. She looked to be in her late twenties. She had short, glossy black hair, exotic dark eyes and creamy skin. Her designer dress and her jewellery were simply breathtaking.

'Helena…' Dio drawled, his long fingers suddenly closing so tightly over Ellie's smaller hand that she almost yelped with discomfort.

Helena planted a cool kiss on his cheek and then addressed him in Greek. She ignored Ellie. But Ellie was grateful to be ignored because she was embarrassed by Dio's stubborn determination to keep her by his side. Still conversing with Helena, whom Ellie now assumed to be a close relative, Dio walked them both into a vast reception room.

Other people began to arrive. Helena took up position like

a seasoned hostess. Dio's grip on Ellie's fingers had mercifully loosened, and she tried to pull away, hoping to retire to a dark corner. But not only did Dio retain his hold on her, he also swept her forward and introduced her, although nobody got the chance to engage her in any actual conversation. Many curious eyes lingered on her, but Dio kept both of them on the move. He exchanged a word here, a sentence there, his bleak, brooding tension forestalling any more intimate dialogue.

'*Cristos*...I *hate* this!' he bit out rawly under his breath at one stage.

Some minutes later, an exuberant older man grasped him in a bear hug, forcing him to release Ellie. Ellie backed away and then walked out onto the balcony that appeared to stretch the entire length of the house. She breathed in deep in the hot still air. The view out over the bay was really incredible. An endless blue sky arched over the lush, forested pine slopes sprinkled with wild flowers and the majestic rock formations that jutted out into the sparkling turquoise sea far below. It was so beautiful it almost hurt.

She stood there for a long time before she turned away again, becoming conscious of how very tired she still was. A couple of catnaps hadn't made up for the stress of a long trip and the loss of a decent night's sleep.

As she glanced back into the crowded room, she immediately noticed Dio. He was so tall he couldn't be missed. He had a dark frown on his starkly handsome features as he glanced restively around himself, only paying part attention to what was being said to him. Then his keen gaze lit like a falling star on Ellie, where she stood outside in the sun, her silver hair gleaming like precious metal. The marked strain on his lean, strong face instantly eased.

Across the distance that separated them, Ellie collided with glittering black eyes. Her heart gave a sudden violent lurch and her mouth ran dry. She watched Dio plough through the crush surrounding him. She could focus on nothing but him, and was as blind as he was to the buzz of speculation his abrupt departure had created.

'Where the hell have you been?' he breathed in a driven undertone.

But a couple of feet from her Dio ground to an equally sudden halt, an almost bemused frown pleating his winged ebony brows. Emanating megawatt tension in abundance again, he studied Ellie with ferociously intent black eyes that questioned even before he demanded, 'Why do I *want* to be with you right now?'

As tense now as he, Ellie jerked a slight shoulder in an awkward movement. 'Keeping tabs on me to ensure I don't get near a phone has b-become a real bad habit?' she stammered in a strained and breathless rush.

At that moment, Helena Teriakos strolled unhurriedly out to join them. Beneath her coolly enquiring scrutiny, Ellie found herself reddening with fierce discomfiture, although she could not have explained why.

'Miss Morgan looks quite exhausted, Dio,' the other woman commented. 'I believe she might appreciate the opportunity to retire to her room.'

'Yes…yes, I would,' Ellie agreed tautly.

The beautiful brunette awarded her a faint but dismissive smile of approval. His strong jawline clenching, Dio summoned a maid with an imperious snap of his fingers, his habit of command so ingrained in that gesture it caught Ellie's attention and made her look away.

'I'll see you later,' he informed Ellie flatly, and strode back indoors.

Why do I feel like I'm abandoning him? Ellie asked herself in genuine bewilderment as she followed the maid. Where had this ridiculous sense of connection come from? She barely knew Dio Alexiakis. She didn't even like the guy, did she? What on earth was the matter with her?

Jet lag, exhaustion, she told herself, but she knew it was more. Helpless sympathy had flared when Dio had admitted that he'd been at odds with his father before his death. She understood that he didn't feel entitled to play the grieving role of a loving son for the benefit of an audience. Yet it was patently obvious to her that he *had* been a loving son. But right now, Dio was so tormented by his conscience he couldn't see the wood for the trees.

The maid led her into a lift off the huge entrance hall. They travelled down and then traversed a corridor which took them straight back out into the open air again. Mystified, but intrigued, Ellie followed the girl down a short sloping path to a low building sited right on the edge of an endless dreamy stretch of golden sand.

The interior was wonderfully cool. It was some sort of self-contained guest suite, Ellie assumed, admiring the spacious lounge and adjoining dining area. The tall windows had elegant shutters to keep out the sun; inviting sofas adorned the marble floor. There was no kitchen, just a concealed fridge the size of a walk-in larder, packed with snacks and soft drinks. Two *en suite* bedrooms completed the accommodation. Her assorted carrier bags already sat in a rather pathetic huddle on one of the beds.

With alacrity, Ellie took the opportunity to strip off every stitch she wore and head straight for the shower. Smothering yawns, she washed, but she was conscious of the weirdest sense of dislocation. Dio drifted back into her mind, and his lean, dark, devastating image wedged there, refusing to be driven out again. She frowned in confusion.

Suddenly she remembered the way Dio had stridden towards her, and she shivered then, reluctant to examine her own response. 'Why do I *want* to be with you right now?' he had demanded, his incredulity unconcealed. Why, she should have asked herself, had she stood there waiting for him, strung out on such a high of anticipation she could hardly breathe?

That was not how Ellie acted around the opposite sex. In fact, Dio Alexiakis should already have sunk like a stone under the weight of her prejudices. Ellie thoroughly distrusted good-looking men, and was all too well aware that rich men saw women as mere trophies with which to embellish their all-important image. Her own father had been just such a man.

Only now, all of a sudden, Ellie was being forced to accept that even her most cherished convictions didn't necessarily influence how she actually behaved. Dio had spellbinding physical magnetism, but that didn't excuse her for acting like a silly little schoolgirl. In real life, Cinderella would have watched her prince waltz over the horizon and out of reach with a real princess, Ellie reflected cynically. No, she didn't see Dio Alexiakis as an essentially superior being, but in terms of cold, hard cash and status, he was as far removed from someone like her as a royal prince.

She was attracted to him, that was all, she told herself uneasily. Unfortunately that didn't explain why only self-conscious embarrassment in Helena Teriakos's presence had driven her into walking away from Dio. For after the way Dio had looked at her, exhausted or not, she had the horrendous urge to stick to him like superglue.

Donning the sheer, strappy midnight-blue nightdress because it was cool, blanking out her unproductive thoughts, Ellie padded out to the lounge again. The maid reappeared with a tray. Ellie tucked into the delicious buffet-style offerings with appetite and then curled up on a sofa, too sleepy to keep her eyes open any longer.

The arrival of yet another meal was what finally awakened Ellie, but she wasn't hungry enough to eat anything more. The sun was beginning to go down and she couldn't believe that she had slept away the entire afternoon. She would never manage to sleep again later, and what a terrible waste it had been not to at least walk along that beautiful beach outside!

She rummaged through the eclectic mix of CDs stored in the state-of-the-art entertainment centre. Smiling to herself, she put on flamenco music, remembering the endless dance and drama classes which her mother had insisted she attend. Dancing was still her favourite method of working out. She performed a few exploratory movements, letting the rhythm flow until all her muscles had loosened up. Then, picking up on the faster tempo, she gave herself up to the passionate music.

Her breasts heaving with the rapidity of her breathing, the sheer strain clinging to her damp skin, Ellie came to a fluid halt as the CD moved to an end. She let her head slowly fall back, her slender spine arching into a perfect curve.

'That was *incredible*…' Dio Alexiakis murmured with ragged emphasis.

Ellie whirled breathlessly round on her toes, the faraway look in her eyes banished by dismay and disconcertion.

Shorn of his jacket and tie, both of which trailed carelessly from one clenched hand, Dio stood in the shadows near the entrance door. He was still as a bronze statue. Then he suddenly moved an expressive hand and spread long brown fingers, the extent of his appreciation of the performance he had witnessed unconcealed.

Brilliant, dark deep-set eyes sought hers. 'Quite extraordinary,' he told her with husky intensity. 'So much fire, so much pathos, every single movement, every tiny gesture telling a story.'

As slow-burning colour swept up from her extended throat Ellie trembled, outraged that he had not immediately announced his presence. 'You should've told me you were here…you had no *right* to watch me!'

'I didn't want to interrupt you…' A shimmer of gold as

bright as a flame glimmered in Dio's semi-screened gaze as it lingered on her ripe pink mouth.

Her lips parted, an alien ache stirring low in her belly as the silence stretched.

'That's not an excuse…' she protested unevenly, her slight frame tautening in instinctive reaction to the growing tension in the atmosphere.

Dio Alexiakis threw his darkly handsome head back and surveyed her. '*Cristos*…is there a man alive who would have interrupted you?' he demanded with roughened urgency.

Ellie was so still and so tense she could feel every beat of her heart—even, she was dimly convinced, the very pulse of her blood through her veins. She collided with Dio's shimmering gaze and she felt intoxicated. Dizzy, disorientated, no longer able to get her brain to send a message to her tongue. Indeed, it was suddenly such a challenge to keep a grip on a single coherent thought that she simply stared at him in bewilderment. Her body was already responding far in advance of her brain, her breasts swelling heavily, tautened peaks pitching into almost painful prominence.

A feverish flush on his sculpted cheekbones, Dio let his stunning eyes roam hungrily over her beautiful face, and then at an incredibly slow pace over her slim figure. The fabric of the nightdress clung like a second skin to her surprisingly lush shape, moulding her straining nipples, the shapely curve of her hips and the slender line of thigh. The high-voltage charge of his powerful sexuality entrapped her, filling her with excitement and leaving her utterly without defence.

'Watching you dance was the most erotic experience I have ever had outside the bedroom door,' Dio confessed with driven urgency. 'I have never known such an overpowering need to possess a woman. And right now I'm just revelling like a crazy teenager in the pleasure of feeling something *this* intense!'

Ellie quivered, shocked rigid by that bold speech and sufficiently jarred to begin reasoning again. A crazy teenager? *Him?* What sort of a line was that? Involuntarily, she glanced down at herself and froze. Belatedly appreciating how very little she was wearing, she was quite unable to comprehend how the need to cover herself up had not been her first thought when she'd seen him!

In a stumbling surge, shorn of her usual grace, her face hot as hellfire, Ellie snatched up a throw from the nearest sofa and hauled it round herself like a screening blanket. No blooming wonder he was coming on to her! Men were not very discriminating when a woman put on a provocative display. In fact it was her belief that most men lived on the constant edge of succumbing to illicit temptation.

Dio released a soft, ruefully amused laugh. His strong features were no longer hard with tension as he scanned Ellie standing there, green eyes huge, gripping the colourful throw tightly around herself. 'Half-child, half-woman. What a confusing combination you are!'

'Stop talking like that,' Ellie urged him uncomfortably, evading his scrutiny. 'You don't know what you're saying. I'll just pretend I didn't hear what you said. I know you can't help being like that, so I'm not taking offence—'

'Perhaps this is not the moment to tell you that you have supplied the only glimmer of light in an exceedingly dark day,' Dio breathed grittily, switching mood at volatile speed as he swung with restive fluidity away from her.

'Because I'm a stranger...don't you realise that?' Ellie prompted in a voice that shook with sudden strain. She was touched against her own volition by that roughened sincerity, but eager to tell him why she believed he was acting like somebody temporarily bereft of all sanity. 'I have no expectations of you, no knowledge of your life. I don't ask anything of you. I make no judgements.'

'On the contrary, you never stop making arbitrary judgements,' Dio contradicted grimly.

'I'm going for a walk on the beach.' Shaken by the warring emotional storm beginning to make its presence felt inside her, Ellie wrenched open the door and hurriedly walked outside.

Moonlight shimmered on the sea as the surf whispered onto the shore. It was a clear night, and the air was warm and still. She trudged barefoot through the soft silky sand, fighting the turmoil he had unleashed—because she understood all too well what Dio Alexiakis was going through.

And the way Dio looked at her might scare the hell out of her on one level, but on another it electrified her. Even without him in front of her she still felt drunk. It was as if some giant, crazy infatuation had mushroomed inside her and stolen all common sense. In the space of twenty-four hours Dio had turned her inside out, dissolving her defensive shell, luring out the soft, vulnerable feelings she usually kept under lock and key.

Now that she was being honest with herself, she knew that she couldn't trust herself around him. She *wanted* Dio Alexiakis. She wanted him as she had never wanted any other man, and that alone was terrifying. But, far more dangerously, she ached to talk to him, listen to him, *be* with him…

Every alarm bell she possessed was clanging as loud as Big Ben. Dio couldn't deal with his own emotions right now so he had focused on her instead. That was the cruel reality of his supposed desire, she told herself urgently. Standard male avoidance technique. Target the nearest reasonably attractive woman and try to blot out every painful feeling with the comforting familiarity of the physical. And right now Dio Alexiakis would dance on broken glass sooner than admit his desperate need to talk about his late father.

Reaching an impulsive decision, Ellie suddenly turned in her tracks and set off back in the direction she had come. Dio was staring out to sea, both hands dug in the pockets of his well-cut trousers, his pale shirt glimmering in the shadows of the overhanging roof that shaded the entrance to the beach house.

'I bet nothing really bad has ever happened to you before,' Ellie breathed.

He swung round. 'What the hell are you talking about?'

'Did you have a happy childhood?'

'Yes!' he gritted.

'A close relationship with your father before you became estranged?'

'Of course,' Dio confirmed in a shuttered tone that would not have encouraged the wise or wary to continue.

'So why can't you just concentrate on the good times you had?' Ellie asked bluntly.

'How could *you* understand how I feel now?' he demanded with splintering aggression.

'I understand. I just don't think you appreciate how very lucky you are to have enjoyed so many years of love and support,' Ellie admitted ruefully.

Dio turned to stare at her, speechless with disbelief, his whole stance shouting his blistering anger at such a contention.

'I mean…I had a father who wouldn't even let my mother put his name on my birth certificate, a father who once walked past me in the street and pretended not to know me,' Ellie confided tightly. 'And a mother who still worshipped the ground he walked on.'

Dragged with a vengeance from his own brooding self-absorption, Dio frowned at her with frank incredulity.

'I had a major fight with my mother the day before she died,' Ellie volunteered, her throat convulsing with the sickness of tears. 'I was sixteen. I loved her so much and I was worried sick about her. I was trying to snap her out of her depression, persuade her that there was a life worth living *without* my worthless creep of a father…'

Dio had moved without her noticing. He closed two arms

round her and pulled her slight, shaking body close. Dimly it occurred to her that nothing was working quite the way she had imagined it working. Then the warm, intimate scent of him drenched her senses and she breathed in deep, loving the heat and stability of his big, powerful frame.

Without the slightest hesitation, Dio was the one asking questions now. And Ellie told him about her mother. The only child of a prosperous widower, beautiful and sweet-natured Leigh Morgan had been cocooned from life's tougher realities by a parent who had idolised her. At twenty-two she had fallen in love and got engaged to Ellie's father, Tony. Then her own father had gone bankrupt and the happy days had come to an end.

'Tony didn't want Mum without her father's money,' Ellie confided. 'He broke off the engagement and not long afterwards he married the daughter of a wealthy manufacturer.'

'So he ditched your mother when she was pregnant—?'

'No, it wasn't that simple. A few weeks after he got married he went to Mum and told her that he'd made a dreadful mistake, that he still loved her. I was conceived the same day. She thought he would leave his wife.'

'Ah…' Dio murmured with expressive softness. 'But he had no such intention.'

'Mum was as green as grass and still mad about him,' Ellie conceded heavily, and then she sighed. 'I don't want to talk about them any more.'

'No problem,' Dio told her huskily, letting his big hands slide down her taut spine to curve over her hips and mould her against his lean, hard body.

'Now it's your turn…' Ellie muttered unevenly as she quivered, thought about pulling away, decided to *do* it, and then discovered that she didn't have that much will-power.

'My turn…?' Dio echoed thickly.

'Your turn,' she repeated unsteadily, a twist of heat snaking through her lower belly and tightening every tiny muscle she possessed.

'My father told me it was time I got married. I said, No, I'm not ready yet…and *he* said, ''I don't want to see you or speak to you until you *are* ready,''' Dio recited with raw-edged emphasis, half under his breath.

Ellie tipped back her head to frown up at him. 'That's your joky way of telling me to mind my own business…right?'

'Wrong.'

'You mean your father just expected you to get married when *he* said so?' Ellie couldn't hide her astonishment.

'My own parents didn't just meet and date, Ellie. They knew each other from childhood, grew up knowing what was expected of them, and when the time seemed right,' Dio specified in a taut undertone, 'their fathers got together and set the wedding date.'

'For goodness' sake, that's medieval!'

'To you, perhaps. But my parents were very happy together.' Dio smoothed her tousled hair back from her damp brow with incredibly gentle fingers, making her shiver and automatically curve closer, her legs increasingly wobbly supports. 'Marriage can still be very much a family affair in Greece.'

'I don't want to criticise your father…' Ellie began hesitantly, turning the side of her face into his palm, like a sensuous cat begging to be stroked, and snatching in a fracturing breath as she struggled to concentrate. 'But I think he should've appreciated that times have changed. You're a grown man and he treated you like—'

'He knew what was best for me,' Dio slotted in with velvet-soft finality. 'I may speak public school English, Ellie, but I *am* Greek, and marriage *is* a very serious step. The English rely on love and have a very high divorce rate—'

'Yes, *but*—'

'It's more important to pick a life partner with intelligence,' Dio stated, and then he lifted her high in his strong arms, as if he was tired of that particular subject, and sealed his sensual mouth with hungry mastery to hers.

Ellie's head spun, her heart jumping violently. He needed to talk. This wasn't what she had planned; this *wasn't* what was supposed to happen. In another minute, she swore feverishly, she would pull back, stop this before it got out of hand. But somehow her arms had got round his neck and her fingers were already sliding into the thick luxuriance of his black hair. A cloud of such debilitating weakness enveloped her that by the time she promised herself another thirty seconds she could no longer recall why that strange idea of a time-frame should come into her head.

'This was inevitable,' Dio growled, sweeping her right off her feet when she stumbled on her no longer reliable lower limbs and carrying her back into the beach house.

CHAPTER FOUR

A THOUGHT almost made it to the surface of Ellie's blank mind. And then she locked into Dio's black glittering eyes. Her heart lurched; her pulses raced. Dizzy and mindless euphoria took a hold again.

She raised an uncertain hand to cover one hard flushed cheekbone with a shy possessiveness entirely new to her. Her spread fingers rejoiced in the rougher texture of his skin, her dilated pupils searching out every tiny detail of him that close.

The lush black spiky lashes, so ridiculously long, the dramatic set of his eyes below those dark defined brows; the sheer masculine beauty of his hard bone structure; the lean, arrogant perfection of his nose. She caressed his aggressive jawline with wondering tenderness, her whole being intensely absorbed in that appraisal. Nothing had ever felt so right or so natural.

'You really are gorgeous,' she told him helplessly.

Dio brought her down on something firm and deliciously comfortable and leant over her. He stared down into her dazed eyes, his own flaming gold, and groaned, 'I thought you were the most perfect thing I ever saw in my life when I took that scarf off. Your hair, your skin, your eyes. You stunned me—'

'Guess you're s-stunning me,' Ellie stammered, wit returning to take in the fact that she was lying on a bed in a dimly lit room, sudden dismay blossoming at the edge of her euphoria.

'You're really very sweet underneath the tough front...' Dio lowered his proud dark head.

Ellie could have drowned in those topaz eyes, could literally feel weakness escaping like a honeyed dam breaking its walls inside her, sentencing her to mesmerised stillness.

He took her lips again, prying them apart with the wicked dart of his tongue. Her heart banged and her tummy quivered and she couldn't get breath back into her lungs. Her submission was absolute, instinctive. She could not have resisted the erotic allure of that kiss had her life depended on it. It was like being reborn, every sensation so sharp, so fresh, so intense she was hooked in helpless, urgent longing for the next.

'So *sweet*,' Dio growled low in his throat as Ellie moaned and gasped under his expert mouth with shivering responsiveness.

Peeling off his shirt, he raised her to him. Ellie stiffened. The whole of her vision was filled with that broad bronzed chest and the thick, dark curling hair marking his pectoral muscles before snaking down into a fine silky furrow over his taut flat stomach. He lifted her hands and put them on him, as if it was the most natural thing in the world that she should touch him.

'Dio…' she said jerkily, shock waves running through her as the hard, hair-roughened warmth of him met her splayed fingers.

Heavens, there was so much of him, and suddenly she felt wildly out of her depth, recognising that he was encouraging and expecting an experienced partner.

'Touch me,' he invited raggedly.

She studied her own hands as if she was hoping they would lift from him without any conscious message from her brain. But he felt so fascinatingly, wonderfully good. 'This is…this is a little bit fast for me,' she mumbled with serious understatement, because she still couldn't grasp how they had got as far as undressing on a bed.

He covered her small hands with his. 'You want me to leave, I will.'

A cold stab of fear made Ellie's stomach flip. She lifted her head up to encounter sizzling dark eyes set in a lean, taut-boned face that made her ache with longing. Leave or stay. Nothing in between. And if he leaves now, maybe he'll never ask again; maybe he'll think I'm just a tease, she reflected in anguish, finally appreciating that he saw no reason why they shouldn't enjoy each other immediately.

'But I…' she began, not even knowing what she was going to say, terrified of sounding like some old-fashioned virgin and turning him off completely.

'Make your mind up.' Dio's dark drawl was urgent with stress and tension, pure, masculine need stamped on his lean dark features. 'I'm not made of steel and I am *burning* for you…'

Ellie's taut hands quivered under his. She just couldn't take her eyes off him. His intensity melted her deep down inside. 'I want you too…*so* much.'

Dio settled her gently back onto the mattress. 'I won't do anything you don't want me to do, *pethi mou*.'

'Of course not, *but*—'

'Open your mouth for me,' he urged raggedly.

And she did, taking instant fire from that passionate onslaught. She didn't notice him skimming her nightdress straps down her arms. Then he coiled back from her to remove the tangle of fabric from round her hips and she focused in shock on her own bare breasts, rising wantonly full, crested by taut pink nipples.

'You're exquisite,' Dio groaned.

Coming back to her, he let his thumb stroke a swollen bud, his palm cupping the underside of her firm breast, and then he closed his mouth there instead. He sent such a jolt of startling sensation through Ellie she cried out loud, her head falling back on the pillows, all thought suspended. Her hands gripped his smooth brown shoulders as over and over again he caressed her sensitive flesh with his tongue and his teeth and his lips. Now she was the one burning, maddened by every sure, knowing stroke, driven to a height of frantic yearning need that consumed her like a greedy fire.

Without warning Dio rolled back from her and slid off the bed backwards, burnished golden eyes welded to her pale pink body. It was like being visually consumed. She was hot and out of breath, in a state of mindless hunger beyond anything she had ever imagined possible. Her eyes followed him. She simply couldn't bear him that far away from her.

'Dio…?' she muttered uncertainly.

'You respond to me like you were made for me,' Dio told her with primal satisfaction.

She watched him unzip his well-cut pants. Her eyes widened, a shred of awareness returning. His black boxer shorts were skimmed off his lean hips a split second later. Receiving her first view of a fully aroused adult male shook Ellie. And although Dio was even more beautiful than she had naively imagined, he was considerably more intimidating. Belatedly conscious of her own nakedness, Ellie sat up and wrenched at the sheet so that she could squirm beneath its cover, her heart pounding against her breastbone as if she had run a three-minute mile.

The knowledge of her own inexperience provoked a current of panic. Dio strolled back to the bed without inhibition. In fact she doubted that Dio had ever had the slightest urge to hide himself in the bedroom. 'You're shy,' he murmured almost tenderly, but he threw back the sheet to join her, with scant allowance for that reality.

'Yes… Dio—'

'I want to look at you,' he confessed, curving her into the hard, abrasive heat of his powerfully masculine body with a long possessive arm. 'You're shaking…'

'You're making me nervous.'

He meshed lean fingers into her thick hair and brought her mouth up to his, tasting her with deep, sensual appreciation until her head swam and the nerves were squeezed out of her by more physical reactions.

He lifted his imperious dark head then. Brilliant golden eyes gazed down into hers. 'This isn't a one-night stand. This is something exceptional and special. I don't sleep around,' he asserted with husky sincerity.

Ellie raised an unsteady hand and brushed the tousled black hair off his brow, her heart banging somewhere in the region of her throat. She couldn't believe the power he had over her. She couldn't believe that a man finally had her hanging on his every word, hoping and praying that he was worthy of her trust. It was a terrifying feeling, but when he held her eyes and touched her there wasn't a fibre of her being capable of resisting him.

Dio ran an exploring hand over her trembling length. She jerked and gasped, her whole body already so sensitised he could reawaken her with the slightest touch. When he teased the soft silver-gilt triangle at the juncture of her thighs she moaned, and thrust her burning face into his hard shoulder. With devastating expertise, he traced the hot, swollen centre of her and located the most sensitive place of all. And from that point on Ellie was lost, without hope of reclaim, stormed by endless exquisite sensations that just as quickly became a kind of sustained torture.

'You are so tight,' Dio muttered in a sensual groan of appreciation.

The ache of need he aroused was unbearable. Ellie writhed out of control, tormented gasps wrenched from her as she clutched at any part of him she could reach. 'Dio, *please…*' she moaned in desperate appeal.

He slid over her, rearranging her with urgent hands. She clashed with blazing eyes and exulted in her femininity, sensing his control was as ragged as her own was non-existent.

Fierce hunger seethed in her shamelessly at that instant. She would have walked through fire to lie under him. And then he plunged into her, and the sharp, wrenching pain of that passionate invasion startled her into crying out in surprise.

Dio stilled. Stunned black eyes looked down into hers. '*Cristos*…you can't be!' he exclaimed.

'Not any more…'

Something primitive flared then in his tense gaze. 'You like shocking me, don't you?'

Ellie was blushing like mad now, maddeningly conscious of the tiny smooth shifts with which he was easing his hungry passage all the way inside her. 'Can't talk now,' she mumbled, wholly intent on this new and fascinating experience.

A ragged laugh was torn from Dio. He kissed the crown of her head and began to demonstrate how much more exciting it could get. Raw, out-of-control need possessed her as thoroughly as he did. She couldn't breathe for the insane race of her heart. The world could have ended, and nothing but the pounding surge of his body into hers would have mattered. The intensity of the pleasure drove her wild, and finally off the edge into a hot, wrenching paroxysm of shattering release.

'You should have told me I'd be the first, *pethi mou*,' Dio rasped, out of breath.

'Didn't seem important,' Ellie muttered evasively, revelling in the way he was holding her close to his hot, damp magnificent length, tears of reaction in her softened eyes which she was glad he couldn't see.

Was it possible to fall in love in the space of twenty-four hours? she wondered dreamily, struggling to recognise the person she now felt inside herself, but too happy and fulfilled to feel threatened by that change. *Special?* How special was special? She already knew how special he was to her. She wanted to wrap him up in a big blanket of affection and hug him to death, and Ellie had never felt that soppy in her life before.

'It was important to me,' Dio confided softly. 'Are you hungry?'

'Not really.'

'I can't remember when I last ate,' Dio muttered reflectively.

'Not very sensible,' she told him.

Releasing her, Dio rolled over and reached for the internal phone by the bed to order some food. Then, reaching for her hand, he pulled her out of bed with him. Her arms wrapped round herself as if she was freezing cold, Ellie hovered in the bathroom, watching him switch on the power shower. All of a sudden she felt so horrendously shy. She was being thrown into the deep end of sexual intimacy.

Dio tugged her into the shower with him, either not noticing or deliberately ignoring her discomfiture. 'You really are tiny,' he sighed.

She could feel him staring down at her. 'I'm five foot one inch,' she muttered—adding the inch.

'You looked so funny in that coat at the airport...like a little girl dressing up.'

Ellie couldn't think of anything witty to respond with.

'Why have you gone so quiet?' Dio demanded with sudden force.

'I'm not wearing any clothes and I'm not used to holding conversations in a shower.'

A reluctant laugh of appreciation was dredged from Dio. He lifted her up into his arms like a doll, and hooked her arms round his shoulders. Holding her level with him, he stared into her eyes, his own dark and deep and curiously unguarded. 'Are you on the contraceptive pill?'

Ellie frowned and reddened, wondering why he was asking such a question when she knew that he himself had protected her. 'No...'

'I didn't think you would be. The condom broke,' Dio admitted with unflinching exactitude.

'No…' The warm colour drained from Ellie's complexion as the implications of that admission sank in. Cold fear snaked through her.

'If anything happens—which I think unlikely—we'll deal with it together.' Dio's breath fanned her parted lips and he slowly, gently kissed her again with incredible expertise.

Snatched in the nick of time from the pessimistic image of having her life ruined by an unplanned pregnancy, as her mother had, Ellie clung to his clearly more optimistic outlook and hurriedly pushed the matter out of her mind. Reality for her had evaporated well over an hour ago, and she was in no hurry for it to intrude again.

'I have plans for you,' Dio shared teasingly between drugging kisses that made Ellie tremble. 'You're going to enjoy being with me.'

They picnicked on the bed. They ate deep-fried courgette, followed by lobster and a Greek salad. Ellie had never eaten lobster in her life, and just about died when she saw it on her plate. She kept on sipping her wine until Dio got around to *his*, and then copied what he did with it. Her own ignorance embarrassed her, reminded her of what vastly different worlds they inhabited, and that was not something she could bear to be reminded of.

'Thank you for what you said on the beach earlier,' Dio murmured levelly. 'It helped me to put the situation into perspective. If either I or my father had once suspected that he had so little time left we would have been instantly reconciled. The biggest irony is that I was already working in that direction.'

'How?' she prompted.

'That conversation you overheard,' Dio reminded her wryly. 'That company I plan to buy out in a few hours' time.

My father lost it a long time ago. The reacquisition was to have been a subtle olive branch.'

'Oh, Dio,' Ellie sighed in sympathy. 'So that's why it was so important to you.'

'I'll toast his memory instead. He was a strong, vital man who lived life to the full. He would not want me to remember him with sadness.'

'Explain to me the significance of what I overheard in that office,' Ellie invited, to drive away the vulnerable darkness in his eyes and distract him.

'Let's say we have company A and company B,' Dio responded. 'You buy company A stock, and start a rumour that you're interested in acquiring it. The stock price rises. You resell that stock at a major profit. Then, without warning, you pounce on company B, where the stock price has not risen, and you stage a company buy-out at a good price.'

Ellie shook her head. 'Pretty devious.'

Dio was anything but insulted by that assessment. 'I have that reputation in business. If word of my true intentions were to escape, the stock price of company B would rocket and I wouldn't buy.'

Innately tidy, Ellie couldn't relax until she had removed all the dishes from round the bed. When she returned to the bedroom, Dio had fallen asleep. Her heart, which felt as soft as melted caramel, lurched all over again at the sight of him. He looked exhausted, but rather more at peace than he had looked at the outset of the day when she had woken him up on board the jet. Just for once in her life she was going to go with the flow, she told herself. As a rule she was very, very cautious, preferring to see everything etched in clear black and white before she risked herself. But it was too late for that *now*…

Ellie didn't open her eyes until eight the following morning. Dio was still sound asleep. He even looked gorgeous asleep, she decided, rather glad he wasn't awake, because she was sure she herself looked a mess. But Dio was a long, lithe version of sheer masculine perfection. Even his bronzed skin glowed against the pale bedding.

She crept out of bed, feeling considerably less brave than she had the night before. The intimate ache of her body rather embarrassed her. In the clear light of a beautiful Greek morning Ellie was painfully aware that she had taken a plunge from which there was no turning back. Her emotions were involved up to the hilt, and the level of her absorption in Dio felt frankly scary.

When she put on the candy-pink shorts outfit, she was amused to discover that it wasn't one bit undersized on her. But then she didn't have four-foot-long legs like the store mannequin. She poured herself a glass of iced water from the fridge and pinched an orange and an apple from the bowl on the dining table. In need of fresh air and some temporary physical distance from the male in the bedroom, she went for a walk along the beach.

There was definitely something reassuring about a guy who mentioned having plans for you right from the word go, Ellie told herself urgently, stamping down hard on her anxious misgivings. Dio seemed so honest and open. All right, so she wasn't happy that she had fallen into his bed so quickly, but she was glad that he had been her first lover. At least Dio couldn't get the idea that she made a habit of that sort of thing.

Furthermore, it was a sort of inverted snobbery to imagine that she couldn't possibly have a relationship with Dio just because she was a part-time cleaner in his wretched monolith of a building, wasn't it? It didn't seem to bother him, did it? And she managed the bookshop for Mr Barry. She had a responsible position even if she didn't earn very much. She decided that as soon as she got home she would approach the bank about a loan to buy the bookshop. Only fear of refusal had made her hang back so long.

When she checked her watch, she was surprised to realise that she had been out for a couple of hours. She walked back towards the beach house. From a distance, she saw Dio poised on the verandah, apparently waiting for her. Her mouth ran dry. The closer she got, the more she drank him in. He looked sensational. The unstructured beige jacket he wore over a black tee shirt simply shrieked cool designer elegance. Tailored black chinos hugged his long, powerful thighs. She wished he wasn't wearing sunglasses which masked his eyes.

'I got a call on my mobile,' Dio drawled when she was still several feet away.

And, that quickly, Ellie realised that something was badly wrong. His tone was ice-cold, and so empty of emotion it ran a real chill down her spine.

She came to a halt, green eyes betraying her anxious uncertainty. 'What's wrong?' she asked tautly.

'The minute the market opened, the price of stock in Palco Technic started heading for outer space,' Dio informed her with lethal quietness.

Ellie stared back at him in bewilderment, too shaken by the change in him to immediately understand what he was telling her.

'You said you didn't manage to make that phone call from the airport. But evidently you *did*,' Dio continued with the same lack of emotion. 'You passed on that confidential information you overheard and naturally it's been used. I hope the tip-off paid handsome dividends.'

Ellie unfroze and started forward. 'The *only* call I made from the airport was made on your phone! For goodness' sake, Dio…' she protested feelingly. 'If something's gone wrong, it's got nothing to do with me. I haven't passed on any information…I wouldn't even know where to pass it *to*!'

'One too many coincidences, Ellie. Like where were you when I woke up this morning?'

She blinked in disconcertion. 'I—'

'Tell me, were you afraid of how I might react when the bad news broke and the balloon went up?' Dio enquired flatly. 'You knew that I'd find out what you'd done before you got off this island, but you were too greedy to stop and think about that, weren't you?'

The sun was beating down on Ellie. Perspiration was dampening her skin. But inside herself the coldness of shock was spreading like a glacier. Now that she had finally grasped what she was being accused of—selling the content of that wretched conversation in some covert phone call—if anything, she felt even more bemused.

'Dio, you've got this all wrong,' Ellie protested. 'If that information has got out somehow, I'm sorry, but I don't like being accused of something I didn't do. I did warn you that there was someone else listening at that doorway—'

Savage derision curled Dio's expressive mouth. 'Don't insult my intelligence—'

'What intelligence?' Ellie demanded thinly, an unstable combination of anger and piercing fear beginning to rise out of her shock. 'If you had any, it *should* be telling you that it's highly unlikely to be me responsible for any information leak!'

'You blew my deal. And then you crawled into bed with me and practically prostituted yourself in the hope of placating me,' Dio spelt out with menacing softness.

That savage judgement hung there in the hot, still air. Ellie shivered, white as death, her beautiful face a frozen oval.

Dio whipped off his sunglasses and surveyed her with eyes that glittered black as night over her. 'No…looking at you now, I *do* believe it was a little more personal than that,' he drawled with silken insolence, his accent licking around every vowel sound in the stillness.

'You bastard,' Ellie whispered, reacting to that calculated cruelty with instinctive recoil.

'So I went slumming for one night,' Dio derided. 'It was an experience, but not one I ever intend to repeat.'

Ellie threw back her bright head, eyes burning like emerald daggers. 'No, *I* was the one slumming, Dio. All you've got is a bottomless bank account. You have as much class as an illiterate goat-herd!'

Dio jerked and froze to the spot. Ellie stalked up onto the verandah, brushing past him to gain entry to the beach house. All that was guiding her was a somewhat formless desire to get some shoes on and escape. She sped into the bedroom, where her clothing was.

As she crossed the threshold, a powerful hand suddenly closed round her forearm. 'Say that again,' Dio invited in a raw undertone of pure menace.

'You have as much class as an illiterate goat-herd,' Ellie framed woodenly, staring blindly into space. 'And, in making that comparison, I have no doubt that I am insulting the goat-herd. He might well be poor and decent, and if he's poor and mean, well, at least he's got some excuse—'

'Whereas I?' Dio slotted in, a whole octave louder in volume.

Ellie's heart was hammering like a storm warning. She could feel his rage like a hurricane, churning up the atmosphere, but she couldn't suppress her overwhelming need to hit back. 'You are rich and privileged and pig-ignorant. Now get your hands off me!'

A split second later, her feet left the marble floor and a strangled screech escaped her. Dio brought her down on the bed in a startlingly fast landing that left her breathless and pinned her there. He was ashen pale beneath his bronzed skin, dark, deep-set eyes now a blaze of flashing gold intimidation. 'If you were a man, I'd kill you for such insults!'

'You're f-frightening me…' Ellie mumbled truthfully.

An expression of extreme distaste flashed across Dio's darkly handsome features. He straightened up and backed off instantaneously. 'The helicopter's waiting up at the villa for you,' he delivered between clenched teeth, with openly challenged restraint. 'Pack and get out! Don't set foot in the Alexiakis International building again.

Pale as the pristine white sheet spread beneath her, Ellie swung her legs off the side of the bed and sat there. 'I thought I could love you, and now I hate you,' she muttered sickly.

With a contemptuous gesture of one lean brown hand, Dio sent a handful of banknotes fluttering down onto the soft deep carpet at her feet.

Ellie stared speechless at all those fifty pound notes.

'As you said, business comes first and last in your life. If it's any consolation, you gave me a great night.'

Ellie's innate survival skills rose above the devastating sense of betrayal that momentarily threatened to overwhelm her. 'Is this my plane fare home from Athens?'

'*Cristos*...what's that supposed to mean?' Dio raked at her.

'That little people like me have to think of practical stuff like that. I don't know how much a flight home would cost,' she extended doggedly, refusing to look at him, refusing to let herself *feel* anything at all.

'You collect your ticket at the terminal.'

'Then all I need is transport home once I get back to London.' Ellie picked up one note, resolving to send him the change, and then she stiffened. 'What about Meg?'

'The other cleaner? What do you think?'

'That if you sack Meg too, you will live to regret it.' Slowly, very slowly, Ellie raised her head, eyes as cold as his own now as she made the worst threat she could imagine. 'I'll go to the newspapers, Dio. Since they seem so interested in you, I'll give them chapter and verse on this whole sleazy little episode and then compensate Meg with the proceeds...'

Dio studied her with a quality of incredulous disgust that was unmistakable. Inwardly, Ellie cringed from that look and, terrified of betraying any further weakness, she got up on cotton wool legs. Turning her back to him, she tipped her old canvas shoes out of the relevant carrier bag and slid her feet into them. With a nerveless grip on the bag that contained the rest of what she had been wearing that first evening, she walked past him, her head as high as she could hold it.

It seemed to take for ever to reach the lift in the villa, for ever to walk the length of that opulent endless hall, shoulders and spine aching with the rigidity of unnatural control. The helicopter was parked on the heli-pad a hundred yards from the entrance. She climbed in and closed her eyes tight, shallowly breathing in and out, struggling to maintain control and, most of all, not to actually *think* about what she had foolishly brought on herself.

But the first stab of self-loathing still escaped and pierced deep long before she reached Athens. Ellie wasn't used to making mistakes. In fact, Ellie was very cautious, particularly with men. So when the events of the previous thirty-six hours flashed before her, she could not begin to credit her own foolish wanton behaviour. Before long she decided that she had got exactly what she deserved. She had invited all that pain and humiliation.

When had she contrived to forget that she was with the same modest guy who had announced earlier in the day that he could 'persuade' her to belong to him? She shivered beneath the sting of that memory. It was even more of a hard lesson to acknowledge that she had actually felt *close* to a male capable of misjudging her to such an extent. He hadn't even listened to her attempt to defend herself.

What did she want with somebody that stupid and prejudiced anyway? The trouble was, nothing had ever hurt Ellie so much in five long years...

CHAPTER FIVE

ELLIE rearranged the book display in the window for the second time that day.

'Cup of tea, Ellie?' Horace Barry suggested.

It was a lashing wet day and there wasn't a customer in the shop. Ellie focused on her elderly employer, the kindly concern visible in his lined features, and forced a strained smile. 'Lovely…thanks.'

Grateful that the older man would never dream of asking prying questions, Ellie stood behind the counter sipping her tea and watching the rain stream down the window and the door. She had been back home for two days, but what had happened on the island of Chindos haunted her more with every passing hour. How could she have been such an idiot?

Sex was a dangerous fire to play with; she had always known that. She had always believed that physical intimacy belonged in stable relationships. It was humiliating to accept that she had recklessly gone to bed with a man she had known for little more than a day. She had had a choice and, relying on feelings rather than intelligence, she had made the wrong choice. She should have kept Dio Alexiakis at arm's length. And if that little accident with contraception which Dio had mentioned with such supreme cool had consequences, she would have nobody to blame but herself, she reflected fearfully.

Mr Barry went home early. Just before closing time, a delivery man arrived with a large bouquet. 'Miss Eleanor Morgan?'

'I don't think I'm the Eleanor Morgan you're looking for,'

Ellie told him drily, never having received flowers in her life, and certainly not an enormous bunch of costly white roses.

'This is the address.'

Her heart beating very fast as she thought of the only person she knew who could afford such a gesture, Ellie signed for the bouquet and tore the accompanying card out of the envelope. Three words. 'From the goat-herd.'

Ellie turned white, and then furious pink. She tore the card into pieces as small as confetti and tossed them in the bin below the counter.

Evidently the roses were Dio's idea of an apology. Her soft full mouth compressed. Had he somehow established that she wasn't the source of the information leak? Someone else must have rammed that reality down his arrogant throat, Ellie decided bleakly. Certainly Dio himself hadn't cherished the slightest doubt of her guilt. No, Dio had had no trouble whatsoever believing that the sneaky little cleaner had lied to him, deceived him and finally betrayed his precious plans. She hoped he's lost a mint of money on the deal going wrong. He deserved to.

The phone rang. She answered it.

'I'd like to speak to Ellie…'

Ellie froze at the startling familiarity of Dio's rich, dark drawl.

Silence filled with static buzzed on the line.

'What do you want?' she enquired curtly.

'I'll be back in London by nine this evening. I want to see you.'

'Nothing doing,' Ellie said after a truly staggered pause in which to absorb that smooth announcement of intent.

'Ellie…' Dio breathed, and the way he said her name made her clench the phone so tight that her fingers ached.

'Is Meg still employed?' she demanded brittly.

'Yes.'

'Fine…' Ellie released her pent-up breath in a jerky exhalation of relief. 'I presume that means that I can have my job back too?'

'We'll discuss that later—'

'Dio, we are never going to meet again in this lifetime,' Ellie asserted, her temper steadily climbing. 'All I've got to say to you I can say now. You *owe* me my job back!'

'I can find you alternative employment—'

'Look, what's it to you if I'm working on level eight?' Ellie raked down the line at him with furious resentment. 'You think I'm going to gossip about you with the women I work with? You've just got to be joking! Electric shock treatment wouldn't drag a confession from me!'

'We'll talk about it this evening.'

'I'm not seeing you again. I don't *want* to see you again! You're trying to bully me and I'm not having it. If you don't let me go back to work, I'll go to an employment tribunal with a complaint of unfair dismissal. I know my rights, Dio.'

'Ellie, you just said that electric shock treatment wouldn't drag a confession from you,' Dio reminded her in a maddeningly lazy drawl. 'It wouldn't work to be that sensitive with a tribunal.'

'Surely you don't believe I'd tell the whole truth? A convincingly *sneaky* little liar like me?' Ellie hissed in a sizzling undertone. 'Naturally, I'd lie!'

The silence full of static returned.

'If you want to return to work next week, I won't stand in your way.' Dio ground out that concession with audible exasperation.

'I'm going in tonight. Just forget we ever collided, Dio. *I* certainly have,' Ellie told him, and slammed down the phone.

Did he think she was prepared to see him just to hear some explanation about who had really blabbed about his confidential plans? Did he really think she was interested? Did he fondly imagine an apology was likely to change anything? Were all rich men that arrogant? Fizzing with turbulent emotion, Ellie locked up the shop and mounted the stairs to her bedsit behind the storeroom on the first floor.

The very last thing she needed was to *see* Dio Alexiakis again. Who would wish to be faced with the reminder of their lowest moment? Throwing together a sandwich with trembling hands, Ellie took two bites of it and then dumped it. Twenty minutes later, she set out for work at the Alexiakis International building. Why couldn't he just leave her alone? Couldn't he appreciate that he was just embarrassing and annoying her?

When Ellie walked into the building, the big portrait of Dio in the ground-floor foyer really offended her. On canvas, Dio just emanated cool, sophisticated charm. Fresh flowers always adorned the side table below the painting. It looked remarkably like a shrine to her embittered and unimpressed gaze.

The supervisor, a thin, sour woman, frowned when Ellie signed in. 'You took off on Monday night without a word to anyone,' she censured. 'You didn't even phone in sick. I had to put in a report to Personnel.'

'Yes. I expect you did. I'm sorry.' Ellie added another pound of flesh to Dio's mounting tally of sins and fumed all the way up to level eight.

Midway through her shift, she went down to the basement restroom for her usual cup of coffee. Meg dropped into the vacant seat beside her. 'Where on earth did you go on Monday evening?' she demanded. 'I was so worried when you didn't come down for your break. I was scared there'd been a row, because that bloke you told me about—'

'What bloke?'

'You know, the one that was annoying you.' Meg frowned at her. 'Big blond bloke called Bolton. He walked right up to me the minute I began work on your floor and demanded to know where you were.'

Ellie paled. 'Sorry.'

'I *had* to tell him, love. Did he come upstairs looking for you?'

Ellie stilled. 'I don't know…I didn't see him,' she muttered, suddenly wondering if it was Ricky Bolton who had overheard Dio's wretched profiteering plans.

The conversation of two other women nearby attracted her attention.

'I bet she's just a secretary or something…'

'Not the way she was done up, with the hat and all,' the other argued vehemently. 'Anyway, why would he take a secretary to his dad's funeral?'

Ellie cleared her dry throat. 'Who are they talking about?'

'The mystery blonde Mr Alexiakis arrived in Athens with. A secretary!' Meg chuckled. 'Not in *those* clothes!'

'Some secretaries are very highly qualified and earn top salaries,' Ellie hastened to point out.

One of the other women leant across the gap separating them and said, 'That blonde piece was a dead ringer for you, Ellie.' She gave an outrageous wink. 'And you did go AWOL that night. Anything you'd like to confess?'

'Me…*me*?' Ellie repeated, sharply disconcerted and striving for more convincing vigour.

'Ellie would be too busy lecturing our Dio about sexism in the workplace to get off with him!' someone else mocked.

'I'm rather behind tonight. I'd better get back to work,' Ellie told Meg breathlessly as the dialogue roamed away from her again, leaving her limp.

She caught the bus home at the end of her shift, feeling both tired and stressed out. As she walked down the street where she lived, she could not help but notice the long silver limousine parked outside the shop. Fierce tension tautened her slim figure and her heart raced so fast it was a challenge to breathe. As she approached, Dio Alexiakis got out of the car, the movement fluid and controlled, without any suggestion of haste.

As usual, he looked spectacular. Charcoal-grey suit, crisp shadow stripe shirt, elegant silk tie in muted shades. Ellie's heart went from racing to sinking. Dio looked every inch what he was, she acknowledged dully. A very rich and powerful businessman, highly sophisticated and exquisitely well groomed. How she had *ever* for one second imagined that she could have a relationship with someone like him?

Ellie removed her keys from her bag with an unsteady hand. 'You're not playing fair, Dio. I told you I didn't want this,' she reminded him.

'I hurt you and I'm sorry,' Dio murmured steadily.

Unprepared for a blunt assertion of that ego-battering truth, Ellie twisted her head away. Her strained eyes stung with tears as she fumbled blindly to get the key into the lock and get the shop door safely shut behind her again.

Dio plucked the key from her nerveless grip, opened the door and stood back.

Ellie stepped inside and adjusted the alarm so that it wouldn't go off. 'I just don't want to speak to you...OK?' she said stiltedly.

'No. It's not OK. I want to talk to you.'

Ellie swallowed hard. All he probably wanted to do was explain and go away again. With as much dignity as she could muster, she simply shrugged as if she didn't really care either way. Dio followed her up the steep narrow staircase behind the counter. She unlocked the door of her bedsit and switched on the lamp by her bed.

It was a spacious room and she was proud of it. She had painted the walls a sunny yellow, put up posters, and covered the armchair with a colourful throw. Tossing her keys on the gate-leg table by the window, she turned back to him with pronounced reluctance.

Dio studied her with an intensity she could feel right through to her bones. She flushed and folded her arms, suddenly horribly conscious of her serviceable rain jacket, faded jeans and sweater. In the act of tilting her chin, she connected with glittering black eyes. She quivered, treacherous heat pooling between her thighs, a strength of craving that appalled her instantly awakened.

'Come home with me' Dio demanded thickly.

'No!' Ellie gasped, reeling in bemusement from that invitation.

Dark colour scored his hard cheekbones. His dense lashes swept down low over his stunning gaze and he breathed in deep, his tension as strong as her own. 'You're right. We have to talk this out first,' he conceded with gritty reluctance.

First? Ellie spun away on legs that trembled, shattered that he could reduce her to such a level with just one smouldering glance.

'I went off on a tangent with you on the island,' Dio admitted without hesitation. 'When my chief accountant called me with the bad news, I cut him short. I didn't want to discuss it any further. I'm afraid I just assumed that you had made that phone call from the airport. I was outraged.'

'Yes,' Ellie conceded stiffly.

'But this morning I learnt that you had been telling the truth all along. There *was* someone else there that night. His arrival and his departure were recorded by the security camera in the corridor,' Dio revealed ruefully. 'If I had been in a more focused frame of mind at the time, I would've recalled the presence of that camera and I would have been able to check out your story immediately.'

Ellie nodded in silence without looking back at him, her delicate profile taut.

'I have a hot temper. But I don't usually rush into making instant judgements on the basis of circumstantial evidence,' Dio continued.

'Well, it didn't look good for me, did it?' Ellie responded with determined lightness, keen to bring his visit to a speedy conclusion. 'You didn't know me, so how could you know that I wouldn't do something like that?'

'You're being very generous, but that's not an excuse I need to hide behind. We had spent enough time together. I *should* have known,' Dio contradicted levelly. 'I very much regret the way I treated you on Chindos. I was…brutal.'

Ellie didn't argue that point. She stared at her own feet, eager to focus on anything that helped her to resist the temptation to look at him again. He was making resistance difficult. He hadn't leapt on the excuse she had offered him, as most men would have done. He wasn't trying to lessen his own offence. He wasn't trying to deny that he had cruelly humiliated her.

The silence stretched and stretched. She knew he was waiting for her to say something, but she had nothing to say.

Dio exhaled in a soft hiss. 'The employee who tipped off one of my competitors was an accounts manager called—'

'Ricky Bolton?' Ellie interrupted before she could think better of it.

His dark eyes narrowed. 'How did you know who it was? I thought you didn't see the man.'

'I didn't, but during my break this evening Meg told me that he'd asked where I was that night, and he is an accounts manager—'

'Why would Bolton have been asking where you were?'

Ellie grimaced. 'He was the guy who was always trying to chat me up on level eight.'

At that admission, Dio's jawline took on an aggressive slant. 'I was even denied the pleasure of sacking him. He resigned from his job the next day. He exchanged the information he had picked up for a more senior position in the other company—not that he'll be there for long.'

'Why not?'

A grim smile curved Dio's wide, sensual mouth. 'He has

no company loyalty. How can he be trusted? The first excuse they get, he'll be fired.'

'Oh…' Her shadowed gaze clung to that lean strong face, her mouth running dry, her breath feathering in her throat. 'You don't seem as angry as I thought you'd still be.'

'I put my plans for a buy-out on hold. And before word got out I made a healthy profit selling the stock I held in company A…' His brilliant dark eyes held hers as he utilised the same terminology he had employed to explain his tactics as they had lain in bed together at the beach house.

Ellie flushed, but she still couldn't break that enervating visual link.

'As for company B, my competitors mistakenly assumed that if *I* was interested, company B must have some wonderful new technology under wraps. They bought a massive amount of their stock,' Dio continued with a sardonic edge to his deep-pitched drawl. 'Having now discovered otherwise, when they unload that stock, they are likely to make a loss.'

'So in the end you'll probably pick up that company for a song…'

Silence fell and lingered. Dio studied her with dark, deep, intent eyes. Ellie tensed like a mouse sensing a cat. She was unbearably aware of his potent masculinity. Indeed, beneath that slumbrous appraisal her breasts stirred and ached, their sensitive peaks straining to wanton tautness. Hot pink embellished her cheekbones.

In one fluid movement, Dio closed the distance between them. 'I won't hurt you like that again, Ellie.'

The colour in her face receded. 'I think you should leave now, Dio.'

His winged ebony brows pleated, his surprise unconcealed. 'Why?'

And with that one word, which revealed just how easily Dio had expected to win her forgiveness, Ellie was armoured against him. All weakness put back under safe lock and key. 'Surely that's obvious?' she murmured drily. 'What happened on the island isn't ever going to happen again. We've got nothing more to say to each other.'

'I won't let you go,' Dio declared in a silken tone of steel.

Her green eyes flared bright with resentment. 'Who the heck do you think you are to say that to me?'

'Your lover,' Dio responded softly.

Ellie paled at that retaliation.

'I told you I wasn't into one-night stands,' he reminded her steadily. 'You're still angry with me, Ellie. I understand that, but it's hardly an insurmountable problem.'

'Whether I'm angry or not is irrelevant,' Ellie protested tautly. 'On the island…*us*…well, it was more like a fantasy, a dream.'

Dio dealt her a sizzling smile. 'Thanks.'

Ellie stiffened, annoyed that he wasn't taking her seriously. 'But now we're back in the real world, Dio.'

'Even on Chindos, I was not aware that we had left it—'

'Well, I *certainly* had,' Ellie countered vehemently. 'It was my natural environment. Idyllic moonlit beach, handsome foreigner saying all the right things…and pow, suddenly we're in bed!'

Dio frowned. 'What are you trying to say?'

'We let ourselves forget who we both are,' Ellie stated curtly.

'And what are we but two people who desire each other?' Dio demanded forcefully.

'I'm an ordinary working girl and you're a super-rich Greek tycoon! Stop trying to duck the issue,' Ellie told him in exasperation. 'I could have been the cleaner on the top floor all my life and you'd never have noticed that I was even alive!'

'I would have noticed you—'

'No, you *wouldn't* have!' Ellie was determined to drive

her point home. 'Because someone like you doesn't really ever look at someone like me—'

'But now that I have looked, I'm not backing off,' Dio interrupted with stubborn assurance. 'As for you being an ordinary working girl, that's a problem I would be happy to deal with.'

'A problem?' Ellie gave him a bemused look. 'What are you talking about?'

'I want to keep the fantasy going. Fantasy I understand,' Dio confessed as he calmly linked his arms round her small but taut figure. 'I think you're adorable, *yineka mou*.'

'A-adorable...' Ellie echoed weakly, feeling like a woman trying to stem a damburst with a piece of paper.

'There's no need for you to work,' Dio murmured with a husky intimacy that sent a flick of fire dancing over her entire skin surface. 'I'll buy you an apartment—'

'An a-apartment?' Ellie stammered in total bewilderment.

Dio ran a long brown forefinger in a silken caress along her sensitive jawbone and tipped up her chin to gaze hungrily down into her widening eyes. 'I'm Greek. I want to take care of you in every way. You look stunned. Why? I told you on Chindos that I had plans for you.'

In serious shock, Ellie parted her lips, but no sound came out the first time. Her vocal cords had seized up. The second time, a thready version of her usual brisk voice emerged. 'Let me get this straight...*you* are asking *me* to be your mistress?'

'I am asking you to be my woman,' Dio countered with megawatt cool.

'Your little toy...' Ellie squeezed out, since her lungs felt as if they were on the brink of collapse. Oh, what a bitter irony that he should make such a suggestion! She didn't know whether to laugh or scream.

Dio studied her with a reproachful light in his dark gaze. 'That is not how it would be between us.'

'Would you ask a woman from your own background to be your mistress?' Ellie could not resist demanding.

Dio flung back his arrogant dark head, black eyes glittering with stars. 'You are the only woman I have ever asked.'

'Sorry, I'm not available,' Ellie told him without a single shade of regret.

Dio slid lean brown fingers into the fall of her silvery hair, holding her imprisoned. Scorching eyes roamed over her flushed and angry face. 'You're hooked. You just won't admit it yet. You want me as much as I want you—'

'Right now, I could give you freezer burn!' Ellie warned him.

'Let's see…shall we?'

'Dio, no—'

But Dio crushed her soft mouth under his. And then he sent his tongue delving with carnal expertise into the tender interior of her mouth. Plunging and withdrawing, he set fire to her every skin cell in a charged and erotic reminder of how he had once invaded her quivering and eager body. Her thighs trembled. Helpless in the grip of that excitement, she pushed into the lean, hard heat and muscularity of his powerful frame. Recognising the bold thrust of his erection against her, she melted into hot liquid honey inside herself.

With a shuddering groan, Dio cupped two big hands round her face and stared down at her with raw sexual hunger. 'Why shouldn't I offer you financial support? It would be as much for my own convenience as yours. I want you to travel with me. I want you to *be* there for me…'

The fevered heat in Ellie's bloodstream drained away, axed by his physical withdrawal of passion but even more by his candour. 'What you want is a sex slave on tap…'

'I'd be bored rigid with a sex slave,' Dio retorted with unblemished cool.

A ragged and involuntary laugh escaped Ellie. But, raising her hands, she firmly detached herself from him and stepped back. 'You are *so* smooth, Dio. And this ridiculous conversation is totally pointless. You're wasting your time.'

His dark, deep-set eyes rested on her, his strong bone structure clenching. 'You belong with me—'

'No, I definitely don't.' Ellie tossed back her head as she challenged that contention. 'Nor do I have the slightest desire to be kept by anyone. The hours I work, I haven't even got room for a man in my life. I should be furious with you for asking me to be your mistress. But you *did* remind me that you are Greek. I suppose I have to make allowances for cultural differences…'

A dark rise of blood now marked Dio's spectacular cheekbones. 'I think you want me to chase you—'

'That's your ego talking. What I *want* is to forget we ever met,' Ellie contradicted with fierce conviction, her fingernails biting into her palms. 'But you're so used to being top of every woman's wish list that when I say no you can't accept that I *mean* no!'

Black eyes burned into hers in ferocious challenge. 'If I walk away now, it's over.'

At that warning, and in spite of all she had said, Ellie's breath snarled up in her throat. She felt hollow in the taut, waiting silence which followed.

Without another word, Dio strode to the door. And then he was gone.

Ellie waited for a few minutes, and then went downstairs to lock up after him. When she came back up, the room felt empty and cold. It was as if Dio had taken all the light and energy with him. She dismissed that fanciful impression and strove without success to appreciate the irony of the proposition he had laid before her. After all, no persuasion known to mankind would have persuaded Ellie to even *consider* such a lifestyle…

Her mother had been her father's mistress for sixteen years, a covert relationship full of lies and endless pretences.

From the day she was old enough to finally understand why her mother had no friends in the small coastal town where they had lived, Ellie had been bitterly ashamed of her parentage. Leigh Morgan had decided that she could not live without the married father of her child, and in so doing, she had wrecked her own life.

Ellie suppressed her memories of her less than idyllic childhood and grimaced. No, she would never be guilty of repeating her mother's mistakes. In a couple of weeks Dio probably wouldn't even remember her name. Unfortunately, she suspected that she was going to be remembering him for a very long time...

Slicing through her defences, Dio had sent her flying high into the realms of romantic fantasy. He had taken her to paradise in bed. But within hours he had mercifully brought her back down to earth with a jarring crash. He had hurt her more than she had known she could be hurt. She had learnt that she was far more naive than she would ever have been prepared to admit.

Not a bad lesson to learn, Ellie told herself, striving to feel more upbeat. The excitement was over now. She had resisted Dio Alexiakis. She had done the right thing. But why hadn't she appreciated how dreadful doing the right thing might make her feel?

CHAPTER SIX

MIDWAY through the following week, Ellie told Mr Barry that she had finally made an appointment at the bank.

'Why?'

Ellie smiled, thinking that her elderly employer was becoming very absent-minded. 'So that I can apply for a loan to buy this business,' she reminded him gently.

Horace Barry looked dismayed. 'Leave that for a while yet, Ellie,' he urged.

Bewildered by that reaction, Ellie murmured reluctantly, 'I suppose I *could* cancel the appointment—'

'Yes…yes, much the best thing for now,' he cut in to agree with a pronounced air of relief.

With a muttered reference to some books that required sorting, the older man then took himself off without offering any further explanation. Ellie frowned. Wasn't he quite as eager to retire as he had always said he was? What else could it be? Keen to save on estate agency fees, Horace Barry had given her to understand that if she was able to offer a fair price by the end of the year, the shop was hers. Ellie told herself not to make mountains out of molehills. It wouldn't hurt her to wait, but she was disappointed. Just then, the challenge of taking on her own business would have been very welcome.

Another two weeks passed by on leaden feet for Ellie. Mr Barry was a quiet man, but he had become exceptionally quiet. Almost evasive with her. Troubled and distracted by that suspicion, Ellie had to glance at the calendar in her room one evening before she belatedly noticed the absence of a certain telling pen-mark. All of a sudden Ellie saw that she had something far more immediate to worry about.

Stress and sleepless nights had probably disrupted her monthly cycle, she told herself in dismay. She was only about a week late. But the more she worried about the possibility of being pregnant, the more likely a development it seemed. She might well have conceived. She was young and healthy and, according to her calculations, the timing of that contraceptive failure could not have been worse.

As Ellie entered the Alexiakis International building for work that same evening, she saw Dio for the first time in almost three weeks. Tall, blue-black hair gleaming under the lights, his bold, bronzed profile commanding, he was striding towards the executive lift, three other men in his wake. Shock made Ellie's stomach flip right over. She came to an involuntary halt on legs that felt distinctly wobbly. Her head swam and she gulped in oxygen, feeling perspiration break out on her skin.

'How are you, Ellie?' a deep, dark drawl enquired with leaden casualness.

Blinking furiously, Ellie focused on a pair of polished hand-stitched leather shoes and slowly lifted her head. Her wide, incredulous gaze centred on Dio and stayed there, locked onto him like a guided missile, her heart pounding like crazy. Black fathomless eyes stared down into hers.

'You look like a ghost facing an exorcist,' Dio murmured in flat continuation, looking her over with unashamed and even more inappropriate thoroughness.

Noticing his three former companions holding the lift for his benefit while watching the encounter with the equivalent of dropped jaws, Ellie forced her brain to spring back into gear. 'Go away, for goodness' sake!' she urged, her colour high. 'You're not supposed to know me!'

'Damned if I do and damned if I don't,' Dio rhymed with sardonic amusement. 'Why are women so irrational?'

'Why are men so unbelievably thick?' Ellie breathed, side-stepping him to hurry on past with a downbent head. Before she had completed that escape, however, she noticed a couple of the other cleaners nearby. Their attention was welded to her with speculative heat. Ellie's heart sank.

When she went down for her break later, she was intensely uncomfortable. If one of her co-workers had challenged her openly about her encounter with Dio, she would have known that nothing suspicious had been detected. But the sudden silence which greeted her appearance, the covert glances and the buzz that broke out when she left again told her other-wise. And what other reaction could she have expected? she asked herself sickly.

Dio hadn't just given her a fleeting nod or a passing word. In the act of stepping into the lift, Dio had come all the way back across the foyer to acknowledge her and embark on a conversation. What on earth had possessed him? Didn't he appreciate how much he had exposed her to adverse com-ment?

Meg Bucknall followed her into the service lift. 'I thought I'd better wait and have a word with you in private,' she admitted frankly.

Ellie tried not to stiffen and nodded.

'Ellie, the girls were adding two and two and making four before you even started your shift,' Meg shared ruefully. 'Everyone knows you switched with me that night and then just vanished for most of that week.'

'I didn't think anyone would be that interested.'

'In the normal way of it, they wouldn't have been. But a few of them had already joked about how much you looked like that blonde with Mr Alexiakis in Greece. None of them were suspicious…but him going out of his way to speak to you tonight was strange enough to confirm the wildest ru-mours.'

Ellie had too much respect for the older woman to embark

on frantic denials. On her first night back to work she had known that Meg was disconcerted by her failure to offer an explanation of her disappearance. 'I'll ride out the gossip,' she muttered tautly.

The older woman sighed. 'A couple of weeks ago, Mr Alexiakis walked past me and said, "Goodnight, Mrs Bucknall," for the *first* time ever. I couldn't help but know that something had changed somewhere. I would have sworn he didn't even *know* my name, never mind take note of me being around!'

Ellie coloured as she recalled accusing Dio of not even noticing his more humble employees.

'I've no time for gossip.' Meg's eyes were troubled. 'It's *you* I'm worrying about—'

'I'm fine…sadder but wiser,' Ellie confided tightly as the lift reached her floor.

Meg grimaced. 'I wish I could give that young man a piece of my mind—'

'I'm not a child, Meg.'

'No,' Meg conceded grudgingly as Ellie stepped out. 'But you needn't try to kid me that you're in *his* league either!'

It was no comfort to be reminded of that salient fact. Ellie was already far too well aware of it. One reckless night which could well change the whole course of her life, she reflected with a feeling shiver. Her mother had been a single parent. Ellie knew better than most just how difficult it was to raise a child alone. She was probably being foolishly pessimistic, she told herself. Even so, she decided to buy a kit and do a pregnancy test for herself the following day. It would be a lot quicker than waiting to get an appointment with her doctor.

She was emerging from one of the offices on level eight when the lift next to the reception area pinged. She turned her head, expecting to see the security guard on his round, and froze when she saw Dio Alexiakis striding down the corridor towards her.

This time she noticed every tiny detail of his appearance. He was wearing a superb silver-grey suit, cut to enhance every powerful line of his magnificent physique. Her heartbeat thudded preternaturally slow in her eardrums. His lean, dark features had a slightly keener edge then she recalled; his sensational cheekbones were more defined, the hollows below a little deeper. But even the faint shadows now etched beneath his stunning eyes added an exotic tinge of drama to his spectacular good-looks, she reflected in a sudden surge of bitter anger. She hated the way he made her feel. Breathless and excited, and then foolish and unbearably sad...

Ellie spun away and plugged in the floor-polisher, determined just to get on with her job. The polisher fired into noisy motion but almost as suddenly lost power.

Ellie whirled round. Having switched off the electric current, Dio straightened, surveying her disconcerted face with brilliant black eyes of challenge. 'Stop running away,' he derided.

Unprepared for that angle of attack, Ellie said tautly, 'I don't know what you're talking about—'

'Yes, you do. You're trying to hide behind the fact that you work for me. But it's too late for that,' Dio told her with sardonic cool.

'I just want you to leave me alone.'

Dio gazed steadily back at her. 'Every time you look at me, you tell me the exact opposite.' He reached down for her hand before she could guess his intention. 'Your pulse is racing. You're trembling—'

'With annoyance!' Ellie tugged her wrist free and spun away again. 'I know what I want out of life and, believe me, you're not part of the package!'

'What features in the package?'

'You really want to know?'

'I really want to know,' Dio confirmed levelly.

'All right. I'm hoping to buy the bookshop. That's why I run two jobs. I've been saving up for a long time and I'll be applying for a loan soon,' she admitted flatly.

'I'll offer you a loan now, on a straight business basis,' Dio informed her lazily.

Ellie groaned out loud in frustration, marched into the next office down the corridor and snatched up the wastepaper bin. 'You just don't get it, do you?' she condemned when she emerged again. 'I don't want any favours. I don't *need* any help.'

'But you're making your employment here a barrier between us.'

'Dio…you wouldn't recognise a solid brick wall as a barrier!' Ellie snapped.

'I shouldn't have asked you to be my mistress,' he murmured sibilantly.

Ellie was tempted into looking at him again, the hard knot of anger inside her loosening ever so slightly. 'No—'

'It was too soon,' Dio completed.

'You are a *really* slow learner!' Ellie delivered with waspish bite.

Vibrant amusement shimmered in his stunning dark eyes. 'I've missed having you around, *pethi mou*.'

That smile warmed her like summer sunshine. She dragged her eyes from him, as if that sudden heat burned her. 'So you're bored with sycophancy and in need of novelty. Have you ever thought of a dating agency?'

'You finish work soon. Let me take you out to eat somewhere.'

Ellie studied him where he lounged up against the door like a sleek, dark predator at rest. He aroused the most terrifyingly powerful hunger in her. She thought of all the nights she had tossed and turned, unable to get him out of her mind and hating herself for being so weak she couldn't control her own thoughts. But there it was, this aching, hurting craving that went way beyond physical desire…

'Ellie…' Dio prompted gently.

'I finish work and go to *bed*, Dio,' she stressed curtly, bending down to plug in the polisher again.

'So we skip the food.'

Anger lancing through her in response to that provocative suggestion, Ellie came upright again very fast. But that sudden movement engulfed her in a wave of dizziness. Her view of Dio and the well-lit corridor lurched, and then blurred out of focus. With a muffled gasp of fright she went down and down into the beckoning darkness, her legs crumpling beneath her.

When Ellie began to recover consciousness, she felt nauseous and dazed. Her lashes lifted slowly. Dio was so close she could see the tiny golden lights in his eyes and every inky individual spike of his lush lashes. They were in a lift and he was carrying her, she finally registered, twin discoveries which confused her even more. 'Dio…'

'What?' he demanded with unconcealed aggression, powerful arms tightening round her to keep her firmly wedged against his hard, muscular chest.

'What happened?' she mumbled heavily.

'You fainted.'

A frown indented her damp brow as she fought to regain her wits. 'I don't faint…'

'I've had it with this cleaning lark,' Dio ground out, his jawline squaring. 'It's obvious that you're not fit for it.'

'Dio…put me down!'

'If I put you down, you'll fall over again! You look terrible, but then that's not very surprising, is it?' Dio continued in the same accusing tone. 'You work six days a week in that bookshop, and more than half the time you're left to cope on your own there.'

'How do you *know* that?' Ellie gasped, taken aback by his knowledge.

'I made it my business to know.' Black eyes gleamed down into hers. 'Your other employer has got it made. He wanders in around lunchtime and heads home again mid-afternoon. How can you expect to work all day and then put in five nights here in a physically demanding job?'

'I'm young, and healthy as a horse,' Ellie protested as the lift doors sprang open, belatedly prompting her to demand to know where on earth he was taking her.

'I'm taking you home.' With long, forceful strides, Dio headed out across the ground-floor foyer towards the line of exit doors.

With difficulty, Ellie dragged her attention from him and took in the presence of the security guards at the main reception area. One of them was rushing to get a door open. The other two were gazing rigidly into space with the fixed expressions of men who had had a really good look at them coming out of the lift but were determined not to betray any reaction that might cause offence.

Belatedly appreciating the spectacle Dio was making of them both, Ellie groaned out loud. 'How am I ever going to work here again after this?'

'Goodnight, Mr Alexiakis,' the guard swinging open the door said stiltedly.

'*Ne*…yes, it *is* a good night,' Dio drawled with a truly staggering lack of self-consciousness.

Ellie just closed her eyes tight, feeling the cool air of outdoors chill her burning cheeks. 'If I didn't still feel so awful, I'd strangle you for this, Dio!'

Unrepentant, Dio stowed her in the back seat of the waiting limousine and swung in beside her. 'We have to wait,' he advanced. 'Demitrios is clearing your locker out.'

Ellie noted the finality of that statement, but she was past caring. With the slamming of a door, the car moved off a few minutes later. Only when mind over matter appeared to be winning and her stomach had settled back to normality did she risk opening her eyes again. Dio was lounging back in one corner, surveying her with slumbrous dark eyes filled with satisfaction.

'Don't look at me like that!' she told him thinly.

'What way am I looking at you?' he murmured huskily.

The same way she had once seen a man study his new car. With the proud possessiveness of ownership. 'Nothing's changed,' she warned him feverishly.

'Sometimes,' Dio responded with indolent cool, 'you are incredibly naive.'

'On the island. *Not* any more,' Ellie qualified with deliberate acidity. 'And if naive is what you like, well…with your money I'm sure you'll find plenty of takers.'

A slow-burning smile curved his wide, sensual mouth. 'Where would I find a woman with the courage to be as scathing as you?'

'If I were you, I'd be getting worried about what you find attractive in a woman!'

Dio loosed an appreciative laugh. 'You challenge me. I enjoy the fact that you're not impressed by who I am and what I possess. You have no idea how rare a quality that is in my world.'

Ellie tore her attention from the devastating magnetism of his lean dark features, her mouth running dry at the effort even that small amount of self-denial took. She remembered the deference of his relatives at the villa, the invisible boundary line which had enabled him to mix without once being challenged by a more personal approach. His icy reserve had held them all at a polite and formal distance. Only *not* her. Her pride had demanded that she be treated like an equal.

Yet, had she been awestruck and silent around Dio Alexiakis, she would not now be facing potential disaster, Ellie conceded heavily. If she *was* pregnant, how on earth was she going to cope? Ellie's careful plans for her future had not catered for the possibility of a child. Indeed, those plans had revolved round the necessity of working very long hours well into the foreseeable future. Servicing a large business loan would swallow up a good deal of the income the shop brought in; increasing profit margins would take both time and further investment. Ellie breathed in shakily and struggled to suppress her growing apprehension. Until she had confirmation one way or the other tomorrow, it was foolish to get herself into a state.

'All of a sudden you're a thousand miles away,' Dio drawled.

Ellie blinked and looked back at him, only then realising that the limo had drawn to a halt.

'Of course, you're exhausted,' he conceded grimly.

'No, I think I might be pregnant.' Ellie blurted out that admission without the slightest forethought.

Dio froze in shock. Indeed 'shock', she noted, was not an excessive word to describe his reaction. Stunned black eyes clashed with hers. His strong bone structure clenched hard and he turned pale beneath his bronzed skin.

'Maybe…maybe I should've worked up to saying it…somehow,' Ellie mumbled, although she couldn't imagine any way in which such a bombshell could be delivered gently. She hadn't meant to tell him, hadn't even toyed with the idea of telling him, but the level of her stress had betrayed her.

In the enervated state she was in, she had left the car and allowed herself to be pressed across an imposing entrance hall and straight into another lift before she actually registered that she was not where she had expected to be.

Ellie frowned in bemusement. 'You *said* you were taking me home…'

'I thought we'd be more comfortable at my apartment,' Dio imparted.

'You called *me* sneaky. I don't know where you get the nerve,' Ellie remarked brittly.

All of a sudden every silence simply screamed. She didn't want to think about what she had impulsively blurted out in the limo. She definitely *didn't* want to talk about it. What had she expected from Dio? In this scenario a trouble shared would not mean a trouble halved.

Dio lived in the penthouse apartment. A Greek manservant ushered them in to the high-tech interior. Seeming acres of space ran in every direction. The furniture was stark and elegant, an effective backdrop for what appeared to be an extensive and fabulous art collection. She focused on one canvas. It looked like a Picasso she had once seen in a book. She realised that it might well be the real thing. Swallowing hard, she looked away again, suddenly utterly intimidated by her surroundings.

'I want to get changed,' she said stiltedly.

Dio showed her into a luxurious guest room. Ellie peeled off her overall and her canvas shoes. She freshened up in the bathroom, noting in disgust that her hands were trembling. She tipped her clothing out of the bag which Demitrios had removed from her locker. After wriggling into her stretchy short black skirt and fine short-sleeved sweater, she hauled on her knee boots. She left the overall lying in a heap. No way would she ever be walking back into work at Alexiakis International again. There were plenty of other evening jobs available…only few of them would be suitable for a pregnant woman.

On her reluctant passage back to rejoining Dio, Ellie noticed a large gilded photo on prominent display on a cabinet in the hall. The photo was of three people. Dio with a tall, older man, so like himself that he simply had to be his late father, and Helena Teriakos, all of them wearing evening dress. The Greek woman had signed it across one corner.

Realising that she was only putting off the inevitable confrontation, Ellie breathed in deep, smoothed down her skirt and walked back into the airy drawing room. She started speaking before Dio even got to turn round to face her.

'I didn't mean to tell you. It was stupid. I'm going to do a pregnancy test tomorrow,' she shared tautly.

Dio swung round. 'You've made an appointment with your doctor?'

'No—'

'I'll make one—'

Ellie stiffened. 'That's not necessary.'

'I think it is,' he contradicted steadily. 'A medical examination would give a more reliable result.'

Ellie folded her arms in a defensive motion. 'But I—'

'I'm as much involved in this as you are,' Dio spelt out stubbornly.

No, she thought strickenly, he *wasn't*. She could feel the distance in him already. He was saying the right things, going through the motions of being decent and supportive, but naturally he was praying hard for a negative result and probably wishing he had never set eyes on her. 'It's very stuffy in here,' she said tautly. 'Can I go out on the balcony? I could do with some fresh air.'

'It's very cold tonight.'

'So shut the doors after me!' Ellie advised sharply.

Dio swept up a remote control. The wall of glass glided back. Ellie headed out with alacrity and was totally unappreciative of his magnificent view of the Thames. She gripped the rail girding the parapet until her knuckles showed white. All she could see in front of her still were Dio's cloaked dark eyes. Those beautiful midnight-dark eyes that haunted her dreams. She heard him behind her.

'Oh, go inside, for heaven's sake!' she urged without turning her head. 'I know you're freezing.'

'I'm not—'

'Look, I boiled alive when you switched off the air-conditioning at the beach house in the middle of the night! We don't even match temperature-wise,' Ellie completed accusingly, swallowing back the thickness in her throat.

'Ellie…' Dio released his breath in an audible hiss and closed his arms round her, easing her slight body back into the lean, hard strength of his.

Every fibre of her longed to luxuriate in that physical contact, but she gritted her teeth and held herself rigid, refusing to give way to her own weakness. She loved him; she really, *really* loved him. It was a waste of time hoping that those feelings were about to magically go away and leave her free of pain and vulnerability. He wasn't in love with her. At most all Dio had wanted was a casual affair, and now he probably didn't even want that. Unlike Cinderella, she had blown it. She hadn't gone home alone at midnight.

'You feel like ice.' Dio ran long gentle fingers down over her bare arms. 'Come inside.'

'I just want to go home,' she enunciated with great care.

'Not tonight. You shouldn't be on your own.'

'Don't be wet. I've been on my own for a long time.' She hesitated. 'I really shocked you again, didn't I?'

'What do you mean?'

'What I said to you on the beach that night. You just *don't* expect bad things to happen to you.'

'That is not at all how I would describe this situation.' Losing patience, Dio closed a determined arm round her and urged her back indoors. 'You need something to eat.'

Pulling free of him, Ellie sank down on a sofa. 'I'm not hungry.'

Dio sent the wall of glass gliding shut again in the teeth of the wind. He tossed the remote aside and studied her with black fathomless eyes. 'What happens happens, *yineka mou*,' he murmured wryly.

'You still didn't think it was going to happen to you.' Ellie felt like a dog with a bone she had to keep on digging up, even though she knew she ought to leave it buried.

His expressive mouth quirked. 'I have to admit that I am so accustomed to more experienced women who protect themselves from pregnancy that I didn't quite compute the true level of risk we faced.'

'Why do you keep on saying *we*? It leaves me cold,' Ellie told him thinly. 'After all, we don't have a relationship.'

'You are *very* angry with me.'

Colliding with far too perceptive dark eyes, Ellie flushed and squirmed. There was a kind of rage inside her desperate to break out, but he had recognised it before she had.

'Come here…' Dio urged with the sort of rueful exasperation an adult employs with a difficult child.

Ellie could feel a giant well of tears gathering behind her eyes. Instantly she scrambled upright. 'It's late, and if I'm staying, I might as well go to bed…it's not like you're going to make a move on me *now*, is it?'

'Not without a whip and a chair,' Dio agreed with dulcet cool.

Ellie moved a couple of steps away and then paused, discovering that she was oddly reluctant to leave him. 'I thought you'd be punching walls and swearing by now,' she confided without turning round.

'Public school followed by so many years in business teaches a reasonable amount of self-control,' Dio advanced with gentle irony.

'Well, the Mr Smooth and Cool act really annoys me. You haven't given me one genuine emotional reaction since I told you!' she condemned grittily.

But even as Ellie voiced that accusation she saw how foolish it was. How could he give her a genuine reaction? Did she really want him to show her the volatile flipside of that cool, controlled façade which he had donned like armour? *Yes*, she acknowledged. She needed a good excuse to hate him. Everything would be so much more bearable if she *hated* him.

Closing his hand over her knotted fingers, Dio spun her back to him. Ellie dropped her head, struggling desperately to control her emotions. Dio turned her face up to his and met defiant green eyes that shimmered with unshed tears.

A roughened groan escaped him. 'You're panicking. Why? You are not alone with this. Trust me.'

'How do I *trust* a guy who asked me to be his mistress?' Ellie demanded with raw, incredulous force.

'What has that got to do with this?' Dio asked with a frown.

'Everything!' Ellie condemned unevenly. 'You were thinking of what suited *you*…you certainly weren't thinking about my wellbeing! Do you honestly think I'm stupid, Dio? How could I possibly trust you? If I'm pregnant, your solution will be a discreet termination…exactly what my loving father planned for *me*!'

His hard, bronzed features froze. As a ragged sob broke from Ellie's throat, her vision of him mercifully blurred and she twisted away. With a stifled expletive in his own language, Dio closed his arms round her. She made a frantic effort to pull free, but he was so much stronger she might as well have been trying to break through solid steel bars.

Ellie finally subsided against him, weak as water after that outburst which had come from the very depths of her. Crushed against his chest, she listened to the solid, reassuring thump of his heart and drank in the achingly familiar scent of him. She shut her eyes tight and wished the world could stop for ever at that moment.

'I can promise you that I will not suggest *that* as a remedy,' Dio breathed, his Greek accent very thick.

The tight knot of fear inside her began to uncoil. 'I just don't want that pressure put on me…it's not fair,' she muttered shakily.

'At least your mother withstood that pressure—'

A humourless laugh was dredged from Ellie. 'Only because she was terrified of what the procedure might involve.' She snatched in a jagged breath. 'She didn't even *see* that my father just didn't want me to be born. He told her that he couldn't bear the thought of her having to live as an unmarried mother and she believed him.'

'You never did tell me the rest of that story.'

'There was no happy ending.'

'So?' Dio challenged, his deep-pitched drawl reverberating through his chest, making her quiver in reaction.

Ellie lifted her head and looked up at him. It was a long way up, but those stunning black eyes of his could have gripped and held her at a hundred yards. She fought to concentrate. 'Mum was his mistress for sixteen years…'

Taken aback by that bald admission, Dio expelled his breath in a fracturing hiss.

'So you really weren't on a winning streak with that offer you made,' Ellie pointed out, a pained attempt at a teasing smile curving her soft full mouth. 'But at least you're not someone else's husband, like he was…'

Dio had gone very still. His incredible lashes lowered to screen his gaze.

'And even though it wasn't what I wanted to hear, I guess you were honest,' Ellie conceded jerkily. 'Which *he* never was.'

Tension snaked through Dio's big powerful frame. His arms tightened round her. Ellie felt whole again for the first time since she had left Chindos, but all the more conscious that the emotional hold which Dio had on her was stupendously strong.

Dio smoothed the tumbled silvery hair from her damp brow, his eyes liquid dark with emotion. 'You were right,' he murmured with a roughened edge to his dark, deep voice.

'When I asked you to be my mistress, I didn't consider you. I wanted you back in my bed. That was the bottom line.'

Ellie trembled, defenseless against her own hunger to be as close to him as his own skin. 'Well, I don't want to be your mistress,' she whispered shakily. 'But I *do* want to be with you tonight…'

Dio wasn't quite quick enough to hide his surprise.

Shocked by her own daring, Ellie reddened, not even sure where that frank confession had come from.

'I really *don't* deserve you,' Dio grated quietly as he bent and lifted her easily off her feet and up into his arms.

Ellie buried her hot face in his shoulder and gloried in his physical strength. At that instant being with Dio was all she wanted in the whole wide world. He settled her down on a divan in a low-lit elegant bedroom. He ran the zips down on her boots and eased them off. He sprang upright again with that fluid grace she adored and began to undress.

Watching him discard his clothes, Ellie was weak with longing. She shimmied out of her tights and clumsily tugged off her sweater.

'Stop it,' Dio scolded with shimmering golden eyes full of mingled reproach and anticipation. 'I want to do that.'

Her mouth ran dry as he came back to her, his bold arousal flagrant proof of his powerful masculinity. He was like a bronze sculpture, but far too erotic to ever be put on public view. Nor could any metal ever have portrayed his sheer vibrance. Stinging sexual awareness shot through Ellie like an electric current.

Dio unclipped her bra. Her full breasts were adorned by pouting pink nipples. His slumbrous eyes burning her temptingly exposed flesh, Dio suddenly groaned, '*Cristos*…I shouldn't be doing this!'

Ellie frowned in bewilderment. His tension pronounced, Dio raised his scorching gaze to her moist parted lips and then to her confused eyes. Just as suddenly he appeared to reach a decision, and he closed his hands over hers to haul her all the way into his arms. He possessed her mouth with a raw, hungry heat that provoked a startled gasp from her, and then he eased her over him to deftly dispose of the rest of her clothing.

'I want you *every* way there is,' he intoned, lowering her to the pillows and running sure hands over the straining sensitivity of her breasts. 'But gently, *pethi mou*.'

Excitement already running like fire through her as he teased her prominent nipples, Ellie could only manage a shaken moan, and then she reached up, plunging her fingers into his thick black silky hair to draw his gorgeous mouth back to hers again. She let her fingers slide down over his taut flat stomach, reveling in the sudden tightening of his muscles as she traced the fine furrow of hair to its magnificent source.

With a ragged laugh at her new boldness, Dio flung himself flat on the bed and watched her explore him with golden eyes full of indulgence. Then he drew her up to him with lazy eroticism and began to show her what he liked. And, shy and uncertain as she was, she was driven by the most intense need to give him pleasure.

'Enough,' Dio groaned all too soon, lifting her up to him with powerful arms and kissing her breathless. He studied her with deeply appreciative eyes. 'I love teaching you…but you're too fast a learner.'

'Am I?' Ellie shivered, shockingly aroused by the excitement of touching him, loving him. She sank down on his lean, hard all-male length to lose herself in another carnal kiss with the ease of a programmed doll.

He rolled her over and began to systematically drive her wild. Her heart hammered like crazy. Nothing existed for her but Dio and the tormenting need which now controlled her. He found the swollen, aching sensitivity at the very heart of her and she couldn't stay still. Her breath sobbed in her throat then as she twisted and jerked beneath a tidal wave of exquisite sensation.

'*Please…*' she gasped helplessly.

Eyes burning pure gold, Dio slid between her parted thighs and entered her with an earthy growl of satisfaction. The feel of him stretching her gave her the most intense tormenting pleasure. He moved fast and deep, and a low, keening sound was wrenched from her. His every thrust burned her with liquid fire. All control was decimated, her overwhelming hunger driven higher and higher. She clung to him in wild abandonment, out of her senses with pleasure long before he pushed her to a shattering climax.

Ellie came back to herself with tears in her eyes and a dazed sense of wonder. She relived the instant when Dio had shuddered over her, reaching down his own zenith with dominant power, and she stroked loving fingers through his tousled damp hair and pressed her reddened mouth reverently against his shoulder. 'You make me feel so special…' she whispered unsteadily.

Really special, for the first time in her entire life, she realised ruefully—just as the phone by the bed buzzed and Dio's long, lithe length suddenly tensed above hers.

'Don't answer it,' she muttered urgently, not wanting anything to intrude.

'I'm expecting a call.' Dio eased free of her to roll over and reach for the phone.

Lying on her stomach, Ellie watched him recline back against the padded headboard. His brilliant black eyes were screened from her but she could feel his sudden distance like a cold chill in the air. He was talking in Greek, his darkly handsome features grave and taut.

Ellie frowned, anxiously wondering what the call was about.

A couple of minutes later, Dio cast the phone aside. 'I need a shower, and then I might work for a while,' he announced, his stunning eyes veiled, his jawline clenched. 'Try to get some sleep, Ellie.'

When he sprang off the bed without another word, Ellie paled. 'What's wrong?'

'Nothing that need concern you.'

'Maybe you'd just like me to vanish in a puff of smoke now!' Ellie exclaimed rawly.

Dio drove exasperated fingers through his hair and swore long, low and viciously in his own language. Black eyes glittering, he drew in a deep, shuddering breath, visibly attempting to control a temper that was now, it seemed, on a hair trigger. 'Ellie, just lie down and go to sleep—'

'I'm going home.' Her face a furious pink, but her eyes mirroring her pain and confusion, Ellie swung her legs over the edge of the bed.

Dio loosed a savage groan. 'I *want* you to stay!'

Ellie flung back her head in challenge. 'It doesn't feel like it.'

'I'm not about to beg, *yineka mou*,' Dio incised in stark warning.

It was the endearment that soothed her. At least she assumed that the thing he'd called her was a term of affection. She listened to the shower running in the bathroom, but all happy contentment had now been wrested from her. Maybe he had got some bad news during that phone call. But if that was true, why hadn't he just said so? Her insecurity level began to climb. Inevitably she started questioning the renewed intimacy she had personally invited, and her misgivings mushroomed.

In a desperate need to convince herself that they *did* have a relationship, she had just thrown herself at Dio. All right, she loved him, and was currently suffering from the most humiliating need for reassurance, but that was certainly not an excuse. Tonight, prompted by the fear that she was pregnant, she had tried to attach strings that didn't exist, hadn't she? If Dio was feeling in need of some space now, how could she possibly blame him? She should have resisted her own weakness and slept elsewhere. Why, oh, why did she *always* get it wrong with Dio? she asked herself in positive anguish.

Getting out of bed, Ellie hurriedly gathered up her clothes. She crept down the corridor to the room in which she had changed earlier and climbed into the bed there. If Dio really wanted her with him, he would come and get her. If he didn't—well, then she had done the right thing, hadn't she?

Ellie lay awake for a long time, but Dio didn't put in an appearance to persuade her back into his arms.

Dio's manservant brought her breakfast in bed the following morning. Then Dio called her on the internal phone to tell her that he had made a provisional appointment for her with a consultant gynaecologist willing to see her at noon.

'Nathan Parkes is a personal friend. If you feel uncomfortable with that fact, I'll make other arrangements,' Dio asserted with scrupulous care and tact.

'I don't care who I see,' Ellie responded flatly, worn down by her sleepless night and thoughts that overflowed with regret and self-loathing.

She was impervious to Dio's every impossibly smooth conversational sally on the drive across London. A pretence of polite cool was beyond her. She might love him, but just then she hated him for succumbing to her moment of weakness the night before. Succumbing with enthusiasm and *then* making her feel ten times worse. She wished she had never met him. She wished it so hard that she said it out loud just as she climbed out of his fabulous sleek black Ferrari.

'I don't wish that,' Dio delivered grittily as he strode up onto the pavement beside her, six foot three inches of aggressive masculinity. 'And neither do you.'

'What do you know about how I feel?' she demanded shakily. 'And why have you got out of your car?'

'Naturally I'm coming in with you—'

'Like heck you are! This is one thing I do on my own!'

Twenty minutes later, Ellie's suspense came to an end.

'You're pregnant,' Nathan Parkes informed her levelly.

'Definitely... That is, without any room for doubt?' Ellie prompted jerkily.

'Definitely. No room for doubt.'

Ellie dropped her head and studied her tightly linked hands. Why had she even bothered to question his diagnosis?

'At this stage, feeling a little sick is normal,' the lanky blond man continued. 'But I'm not entirely happy with your weight. You're quite thin.'

'I've been skipping meals recently,' Ellie admitted grudgingly.

'Nausea does tend to kill one's appetite,' he allowed. 'But try to eat small meals regularly. That often helps.'

Pining for Dio had killed Ellie's appetite, but she kept that demeaning truth to herself.

'You *are* planning to continue with this pregnancy?'

Hearing the edge of concern in that query, Ellie nodded in immediate agreement, but she still didn't look up. She had honestly believed that she was prepared for the news that she was pregnant. Now she was discovering that she hadn't been prepared. She felt shocked, and very scared of the future.

'Excellent,' Nathan Parkes pronounced approvingly.

Ten minutes after that, Ellie stood in the empty waiting room and took several deep breaths to calm herself. From the window, she could see the roof of Dio's Ferrari. As she emerged onto the street, Dio climbed out and strode round the bonnet. His dark, deep-set gaze instantly locked to her pale, strained face.

Ellie stared back at him.

'So we celebrate,' Dio announced, pulling open the passenger door and tucking her back inside his car with hands that brooked no argument.

'Can't you just for once say something *honest*?' Ellie condemned in a tight, taut undertone.

Dio leant in to fix her seatbelt for her. 'We're going to be parents. Personally, I feel that the conception of my first child is a *very* special event. If you have nothing positive to say right now, keep quiet.'

A ragged laugh was dredged from Ellie. Dio swung in beside her and immediately fired the engine into a throaty roar.

Ellie worried at her lower lip. 'How do you *really* feel?' she whispered.

'Shattered…kind of smug…sentimental,' Dio enumerated with husky sibilance, closing his hand over her clenched fingers as they waited at traffic lights.

Her tense fingers loosened beneath the enveloping warmth of his. 'I just feel all shook up.'

'You look very tired. I'll take you back to the apartment and you can sleep.'

'No, I promised Mr Barry that I'd come in as soon as possible…anyway, I need a change of clothes,' she muttered uncertainly.

As the lights changed, Dio released her hand. 'I'd prefer you to remain at the apartment. I have to fly over to Paris this afternoon,' he imparted rather grimly. 'I doubt if I'll make it back before tomorrow evening.'

Dismayed by that unexpected news, Ellie stole an anxious glance at him from below her lashes. His lean, hard profile was taut. But then he had frankly admitted that he was shattered, and he was distinctly pale beneath his Mediterranean dark skin. If she was in shock at the idea of having a baby, why shouldn't he be in shock too?

'I think I'd be more comfortable at home,' she said more firmly.

'When you're my wife, I'll expect you to do exactly as you're told at all times,' Dio murmured without any expression at all.

A stark little silence fell. Ellie's eyes had widened to their fullest extent. She couldn't believe that he had said what he had just said.

'Most especially when I am considering your welfare,' he added gently.

Ellie trembled and compressed her bloodless lips. 'You're not seriously asking me to...marry you?'

'Very seriously,' Dio asserted.

'But we hardly know each other—'

'We know enough. I like you. I respect you. I desire you. What more is there?'

'What about...love?' she prompted, striving for a detached tone.

'What about our child?'

Ellie lost colour.

'I *want* to marry you,' Dio told her with quiet emphasis.

'Not really, you don't. People don't get married these days just because of an accidental pregnancy,' Ellie protested unsteadily, her heart beating very fast.

'People like me *do*.'

Ellie swallowed hard. 'Dio, I—'

'You know it makes sense.'

'Yes, but—'

'We'll get married as soon as I can arrange it,' Dio incised with finality.

'I'll think about it,' she returned unevenly.

Dio shot the Ferrari to a halt in front of the bookshop. Unsnapping her seatbelt, he reached for her, black eyes glittering. 'You should be ashamed of yourself, *yineka mou*,' he told her. 'Just *think* about it? Yet only last night you couldn't *wait* to—'

'*Dio!*' Ellie gasped, with a sound between an embarrassed laugh and a shaken reproach.

'So either you're a wanton hussy who shamelessly used me for sex...or a decent woman with a delightful inability to resist me.'

Ellie went pink, but she was wholly mesmerised by his proximity. Involuntarily, she raised a hand, and with her forefinger traced the surprisingly forbidding curve of his wide, sensual mouth. 'I can't...you know it too,' she acknowledged, utterly desperate for him to kiss her.

But, in spite of their proximity, Dio held back. 'I'll call you tomorrow.'

As he freed her again, Ellie blinked in a daze. Dio wanted to marry her? Dio was *willing* to marry her, she rephrased. 'I can't let you marry me!' she said abruptly.

'I won't marry an argumentative woman.'

'Don't tease about something so serious,' she pleaded.

His strong bone structure set hard. 'You and I...it would work,' Dio intoned, his accent thickening.

'Yes...but could you be happy?' Ellie pressed, her whole being centred on the awful wounding necessity of asking that question when all she really wanted to do was drag him off to the nearest church.

Dio groaned in frustration. 'Obviously I should have proposed over a romantic dinner, with flowers and a ring—'

Ellie winced. 'No, that sort of stuff isn't important.'

'Then my proposal must've been excessively clumsy.' Gleaming black eyes rested on her taut, anxious face. 'I want to marry you, Ellie. The only word I need to hear now is yes.'

'Yes...' Agreement escaped from Ellie before she could bite it back.

'Now that wasn't difficult, was it?' His shadowy smile rocked her heart on its axis, and then he turned away and glanced at his watch. 'Now I'm afraid I have to head straight for the airport. I'll be in touch tomorrow.'

'What's wrong with tonight?' Ellie heard herself ask as she climbed out of the car.

'I'll be tied up all evening.'

Hot-cheeked, Ellie nodded, closed her hands together to stop them reaching out to him and forced a smile. 'OK...I understand,' she said, when she didn't really.

His departure seemed so incredibly low-key that she could not quite believe that he had asked her to marry him and that she had agreed.

Concentrating with a mind in a giddy whirl was far too much of a challenge that afternoon. In the space of an hour she had learned that she was expecting a baby and she had gained a bridegroom. It was too much to take in all at once...

Dio wanted to marry her. Did fairy tales come true? All right, so her father had been a creep, and on that basis she had judged the whole male sex. Only not Dio. Dio had taken her by storm. He didn't love her. But love could grow, she told herself urgently, determined not to pick holes in her own happiness. Happiness was a fragile thing, and Ellie hadn't known much of it. Dio liked, respected and desired her, she reminded herself. All that plus their baby would be enough to build on. She would make him happy. Whatever it took, she would make him the very best wife he could imagine...

At one the following afternoon, a limousine with tinted windows pulled up outside the shop. Ellie grinned, assuming that Dio had got back from Paris sooner than he had thought.

She immediately asked Horace Barry if it would be all right for her to take her lunch break. But a split second later she stiffened in confusion when a female figure emerged from the limousine. A tall svelte brunette sheathed in a pill-box-red suit. Helena Teriakos, she registered in bemused recognition, just as the other woman entered the bookshop.

The Greek woman focused on Ellie with cool dark eyes, her beautiful face expressionless. 'Is there somewhere we can talk in private?' she enquired.

Disconcerted by that disdainful demand, Ellie flushed. 'Sorry, what is—?'

'We can talk in my car.' Spinning round, Helena Teriakos walked back out of the shop, evidently expecting Ellie to follow her.

Ellie hesitated. She didn't like being taken by surprise. Even less did she like being addressed as if she was a medieval serf. But Helena Teriakos was related to Dio, wasn't she? Certainly she had been swanning about that palatial villa on Chindos like a family member of no small importance. There had been that family photograph in Dio's apartment as well. And if Helena had suddenly taken the trouble to seek her out, it could only be because she knew that Dio had proposed and she had something to say on the subject.

Ellie lifted her jacket, slid into it and went outside. The chauffeur ushered her into the rear of the opulent vehicle. Ellie was very tense.

Helena Teriakos studied her with narrowed eyes and slowly shook her beautiful head in apparent wonderment. 'A shop assistant and a cleaner! Dio really *must* have been distraught that night on Chindos! I confess that I wasn't pleased when he showed up with you at his father's funeral, but in the circumstances, I was prepared to overlook that small social indiscretion—'

'Social indiscretion…?' Ellie queried flatly, her skin reddening beneath that derisive attack. She lifted her chin. 'Why should you have to overlook anything Dio does?'

The Greek woman elevated a brow. 'Men will be men. I'm fond of Dio, of course, but I don't have a jealous temperament. I'm not a sexually possessive woman either. I have always expected Dio to have a mistress after our marriage—'

'*Your* marriage?' Ellie interrupted incredulously.

Helena Teriakos appraised her bewildered face and shaken eyes and laughed with sudden amusement. 'You really *didn't* know, did you? Dio and I were practically betrothed in our cradles. We have known all our lives that we would eventually marry—'

'No…' Ellie broke in shakily. '*No*, it's not true! Dio would have told me….' And then her voice just faded away into nothingness as she recalled that conversation on the beach.

'Why should he have told you? You were just one more in a long line of little amusements, none of whom were destined to be of any lasting importance in Dio's life,' Helena retorted drily, watching all the remaining colour drain from Ellie's face. 'Had you belonged to our social circle, you would have been aware that our friends and families have been awaiting an announcement of a formal engagement for some time now.'

The mists of sheer disbelief had now cleared from Ellie's mind. She was absolutely gutted, her sense of betrayal immense. Helena Teriakos, whom she had foolishly assumed to be a mere relative! She felt sick with pain and mortification. An arranged marriage. Only Dio had termed it, 'picking one's life partner with intelligence'. *Of course* Spiros Alexiakis had had a bridal candidate in mind when he'd urged his son to marry! And Dio had said, 'I'm not ready yet.' Too busy having a good time with a variety of gorgeous willing women to settle down into matrimony at the age of twenty-nine. But throughout Helena had been waiting patiently in the wings.

'I just don't understand how you could accept Dio b-being with other women…' Ellie stammered helplessly.

'Dio and I have bonds that you could never hope to understand. We share the same background, status and expectations. We are a perfect match,' Helena informed her with supreme superiority. 'Unfortunately Dio rejoices in a rather touching but very destructive sense of humour. He believes that he has to marry you for his child's sake.'

Aghast that Dio had evidently admitted that she had fallen pregnant, Ellie felt horribly exposed and shamed. 'Dio *told* you—?'

'He flew over to Paris yesterday and spent the entire evening with me. Weren't you aware of that either?' A small scornful smile tilted the brunette's lips. 'Believe me, he was quite devastated by his over-active conscience. However, I am a very practical woman. How much will it cost me to persuade you that an abortion would be in your best interests? Five hundred thousand pounds?'

Ellie gazed back at Helena Teriakos in appalled disbelief.

'One million? I am an extremely wealthy woman and I'm prepared to be generous,' Helena spelt out with icy calm. 'You can always tell Dio you had a miscarriage. I won't even insist that you get out of his life. You can still be his mistress. Believe me, you won't last *five* minutes as his wife!'

'I don't want your money…and I'm not getting rid of my baby,' Ellie asserted strickenly, unnerved by the other woman's total lack of emotion.

'But you can't possibly marry him! Can you imagine the headlines? "Dionysios Alexiakis marries a cleaner"?' Helena suggested with a little shudder of revulsion. 'He's a very proud man. You'll be nothing but an embarrassment to him. And by the time the newspapers have finished hauling out the sordid circumstances of your birth and all your former lovers, Dio will have begun to hate you.'

'What do you know about the circumstances of my birth?' Ellie demanded with a raw edge to her strained voice.

'I know everything there is to know about you, Ellie. Money buys information.' Helena dealt her stricken face a pitying appraisal. 'You're in love with Dio. Thankfully I have never felt the need to indulge myself with such messy emotions. Well, make your choice. If you marry Dio, it'll end in the divorce court. True, you'll get the kudos of being his first wife, but you'll lose him completely.'

'I'm not going to marry him,' Ellie framed numbly.

'Now you're being sensible.' The other woman awarded her a cool smile of satisfaction. 'When you trap a man into marriage, it can only end with him hating you. As for the child—you should learn by your own foolish mother's mistake. It didn't do *her* much good bringing you into the world, did it? All those pathetic years of loyalty, only to be rewarded by the sight of your father marrying a secretary half his age the minute he was free!'

Savaged by that cruel attack out of the blue, Ellie scrambled dizzily up and started to get out of the car. 'I'm not listening to any more of this—'

'The door's locked. I'm not finished yet. I do *not* want you to have this child—'

'My child *is* my business!' Ellie exclaimed in angry distrust. 'Now open this door and stop threatening me!'

With a languid hand, Helena Teriakos signalled her chauffeur. 'Think about what I've said. I make a very bitter enemy, and you will discover that Dio has tremendous respect for me.'

Ellie practically fell out onto the pavement in her eagerness to escape. She hurried through the shop and upstairs to her bedsit. But when she got there the tears didn't come. Instead, the kind of outraged and inexpressible pain which Ellie hadn't felt since her mother's death began to mount inside her.

Dio had not been honest with her. She had been dragged into a situation in which she had no defence but that of her own ignorance. She was pregnant by a man who had been virtually engaged to another woman. She had unwittingly poached on another woman's territory and was now being blamed for the entire ghastly mess which had resulted. As for Dio…as for *Dio*, with his wretched sense of honour and his cold, malicious witch of a future wife—well, Helena Teriakos was welcome to him! And the sooner Ellie told him that, the better she would feel!

CHAPTER SEVEN

ELLIE heard Dio come home. She listened to him exchanging a handful of terse words with his manservant, no doubt learning that she was waiting to see him. Having come over to his apartment the instant she finished work, she had been awaiting his return for almost two hours.

And Ellie now felt like unstable gelignite. The more inconsistencies she recalled in Dio's past behavior, the more she understood, and the deeper her frustrated pain stabbed.

Dio strode into the airy drawing room, his lean, strong face grim, black eyes flat and unfathomable. He emanated stress and tension like a forcefield.

'I understand that Helena paid you a visit,' Dio drawled icily, immediately knocking the ground from beneath Ellie's feet by admitting his knowledge of that fact. 'It was a very generous act on her part, but only what I have learnt to expect from her.'

Thoroughly thrown by that opening, Ellie gasped. 'A generous act? Are you out of your mind or just plain stupid?'

Dio stilled, his darkly handsome features emanating a freezing distaste that cut Ellie to the bone. 'She offered you her support and assistance. You were rude and offensive. I did not enjoy having to apologise for your behaviour.'

'Having to apologise for my behaviour…?' Ellie repeated almost incoherently, registering that she had seriously underestimated the older woman. Support and assistance? The abortion package? Helena had clearly got in first with her own version of events, and Ellie wondered why she herself should even care. 'She offered me a million pounds to have an abortion.'

Dio studied her for a full ten seconds with widening black eyes full of sheer, lancing disbelief. 'If you must lie, strive to come up with something more credible and less melodramatic,' he derided harshly. 'Helena would never sink to such a level.'

Silenced by the level of assurance with which he made that claim, Ellie stared back at him with bitter anger. 'You really do deserve her,' she breathed in a stark undertone, two high spots of red banishing her previous pallor. 'And if she's so blasted special, *why* were you with me?'

Dio froze. 'I will not discuss Helena with you, Ellie.'

'What a pity you couldn't award me the same respect!' Ellie bit out, so mad with rage and pain she could hardly get the words out.

A slight rise of colour burnished the slant of Dio's stunning but rigid cheekbones. 'The very least I owed Helena was a frank explanation.'

'But you couldn't even bring yourself to refer to her existence around me. You must have known that I hadn't a clue *who* she was the day of the funeral!' Ellie condemned in an emotive appeal. 'I thought she was just a relative—'

'We are distantly related,' Dio conceded, tight-mouthed.

'How very cosy. No wonder you didn't introduce me to her! That's some kinky, twisted relationship you two have…and if she was a nicer person, I might have pitied her for being that desperate to hold onto you!'

Dio rested glittering dark golden eyes on her that burned like lasers. 'I will not listen to you abusing Helena. You don't understand what you're talking about.'

A torn laugh escaped Ellie. 'And if it's anything to do with you, I never will, will I? But it really doesn't matter any more. I trusted you. I thought you were a free man. I would never have got involved with you had I known about *her*.'

'Helena and I are not lovers,' Dio delivered grimly. 'Before last night I had never actually discussed marriage with her. But there was a strong understanding between our families that at some time in the future we would marry.'

'Why the heck didn't you just marry her when your father wanted you to?' Ellie demanded bitterly.

'I resented the pressure being put on me. I should emphasise that Helena played no part in creating that pressure,' Dio imparted flatly.

Saint Helena, safe on her pedestal of perfection, Ellie reflected sickly. And what had she herself been but a last little fling that night on the island of Chindos? A physical release, a momentary distraction from his grief? 'That night we spent together…you already *knew* you were going to go ahead and marry her.'

'Ultimately I always expected to marry Helena. No matter how much you resent that reality, I *can't* alter it,' Dio asserted with bleak emphasis.

'But you weren't honest with me. You never gave me a choice. I can't ever forgive that. And now that I do know about her, I find it absolutely disgusting that you were planning to set me up as your mistress before you even married her,' she admitted, with a quiver of repulsion at such naked calculation. 'What's the point of marrying someone you can't even be faithful to?'

Dio threw up both hands in a sudden sweeping gesture of violent frustration. 'The last twenty-four hours have been unadulterated hell for me. I am in no mood to stand much more from you,' he vented rawly. 'Whether you like it or not, Helena is the wounded party in this situation. I have hurt her pride and let her down, but she voiced not a single word of reproach.'

'Yes, she's a very clever woman, much cleverer than I am.'

'*Cristos…*' Dio blazed back at her. 'How can you be so bloody spiteful? It is *you* whom I am going to marry now!'

Ellie stooped to lift her bag with a trembling hand and

then straightened to survey him with eyes empty of all emotion, for she was drained. 'I wouldn't have you as a gift, Dio.'

Dio shot her a look of volatile black fury. 'I swear that I will strangle you before I get you to the altar!'

'I mean it,' Ellie told him quietly, watching a sort of stunned light begin to make inroads into his anger as he absorbed her determination. 'Yesterday I was panicking, and foolish enough to grab at your offer of marriage. But your loyalty is with Helena, not where it should be, and I'm not becoming part of some nasty triangle—'

'You are being totally unreasonable!' Dio condemned harshly.

'No, I'm being very sensible.'

'You are carrying my child—'

'And that's the only reason you asked me to marry you…it's *not* enough.' And, sidestepping him in a sudden move of desperation, Ellie walked swiftly out into the hall.

'There is more than that between us, *pethi mou*,' Dio growled in her wake.

'I can get by without the sex too,' Ellie told him witheringly, although even the sound of that dark, deep drawl pulled at her senses.

'Come back here!' Dio grated. 'This is ridiculous!'

Ellie glanced back at him, her lovely face pale as marble and just about as unyielding. 'No…what was ridiculous was that we ever got together in the first place.'

'Ellie—'

'*Please*, give me some space,' she urged with charged emphasis. 'Don't phone, don't come near me. Maybe when the dust has settled on all this we can talk about the baby…just not now.'

For the next week Ellie functioned on automatic pilot. Locked into the need to conquer her desperate craving for

Dio, even when she hated him like poison for hurting her so much, she felt totally detached from the rest of the world.

In spite of her request that he leave her alone, Dio phoned every day. On each occasion she put the phone straight back down again, refusing to speak to him. The truth was that she didn't trust herself yet, even on the phone. She was far too vulnerable.

Finding out about Helena Teriakos had devastated Ellie with guilt, jealousy and mortification. Discovering that Dio trusted Helena infinitely more than he trusted her had literally torn Ellie apart at the seams. How much in touch with his own emotions *was* Dio? Did he even appreciate how much he already cared about Helena Teriakos? Once he had resented the pressure put on him to marry her. Wouldn't it be ironic if Dio was only now truly valuing Helena because he had had to face the prospect of giving her up?

All she herself could ever be to Dio was a very poor second best. If she hadn't conceived, Dio would never have offered her more than a casual affair. 'A little amusement,' as Helena had so succinctly put it. That had made Ellie feel about an inch tall. It hurt even more to frankly acknowledge herself outclassed by the competition. Helena *belonged* in Dio's elite world. Dio could marry the woman his father had selected and feel very good about doing so. A gorgeous, accomplished, intelligent, rich and classy ice cube, who was *fond* of him and didn't even care if he kept a mistress. Maybe a lot of guys would be happy to marry a woman as understanding as that, Ellie reflected with helpless bitterness.

That weekend, Horace Barry's nephew, Joe Barry, phoned to tell her that his uncle had flu and wouldn't be in. Ellie was run off her feet. On the Sunday afternoon she went to see Meg Bucknall, to explain that she wouldn't be returning to her job at the Alexiakis building again.

Meg ushered her into her small cosy front room with a real smile of pleasure. 'You really do know how to get the gossip going into orbit, Ellie. I think you're making a wise decision, though. I'll miss you, but you'd have to put up with some stick if you did come back. Some of the younger girls are just eaten with envy.'

'If they knew how I was fixed right now, I don't think they would be,' Ellie fielded wryly. 'It's all off, Meg...was never really on, to tell you the truth.'

'He's turning night into day at the office right now. Half the top floor staff are having to work the same hours. They look worn out, and I heard them muttering that he's in a really foul black mood—'

'I don't really want to hear about Dio, Meg,' Ellie shared, having paled at those edifying titbits.

'Just one little question,' Mega almost pleaded. 'Did *you* dump *him*?'

Not having expected so personal a question from the older woman, Ellie stared.

Meg flushed guiltily. 'It's just that's what we're all hoping. The word is he's never been dumped before, but he could do with being taken down a peg or two.'

'Meg...it would take an attack with an axe to dent Dio's ego,' Ellie retorted.

A surprise awaited her when she arrived home again. Her employer's nephew, a portly pompous man in his early fifties, was seated in the tiny rear office behind the shop, going through the accounts. Standing up, Joe Barry smoothed his sparse hair back from his brow. Ignoring her enquiry as to his uncle's state of health, he disconcerted her by admitting that he had come over in the hope of finding her at home.

But it was what he had to say next which really shook Ellie up. He informed her that his uncle had retired and that he was now taking charge of the bookshop.

The bottom fell out of what remained of Ellie's world. Struggling to come to terms with the shock of that blithe announcement, she frowned. 'But you already *have* a job.'

'I'm taking early retirement. I intend to plough a good deal of money into remodelling this place. However...' He paused, pursing his lips. 'I'm sorry to say that your services will no longer be required.'

'I beg your pardon?' Ellie practically whispered.

'I have no need for a full-time assistant.'

The silence hung there.

'Are you aware that your uncle had already agreed to sell me the business?' Ellie asked starkly.

Joe Barry dealt her a rather smug appraisal. 'My solicitor assures me that without a witness or anything written you would find it virtually impossible to prove that such a ludicrous agreement ever existed.'

'But that's *not*—'

'My uncle should've told you weeks ago. You can't blame me for the fact that he couldn't face telling you that he had changed his mind,' the older man told her impatiently. 'Naturally he would prefer to see the shop stay in the family.'

Ellie held her upper body very stiffly, but her legs were trembling. The prospect of buying the shop had been like a life raft, and now she felt as if she was sinking.

'You'll receive everything due to you, of course. I'm giving you a month's notice,' he continued, 'and I'll expect you to move out of that room upstairs at the same time. You've never had a tenancy agreement, and I require that room for other purposes.'

'I'll be out of here sooner than that,' Ellie framed with bleak dignity.

'Well, I must admit that that would suit me *very* well!'

He had the hide of a rhinoceros. Awarding her a relieved look, he closed up the books and departed, humming under his breath.

It was only six o'clock. Ellie sank down at the foot of the stairs. Five years of minimal holidays, low pay and all those extra hours keeping up the accounts. And at the end of it?

One month's notice. What an idiot she had been, dreaming her stupid dreams! There were other businesses out there, but precious few would be within her financial reach. It was time to take stock and make fresh plans. She splayed her fingers over her still flat tummy, thinking about her baby, trying *not* to think about his father.

She was climbing the stairs when the bell went. With a sigh, she turned back. She looked out of the shop's window and simply did not credit the sight of the male grinning at her. Ricky Bolton.

'Come on, Ellie…open sesame!'

Maybe he would give her a laugh. Dio had been notoriously low on giving her a laugh. Ellie unlocked the door. 'How did you find out where I lived?'

Ricky kept on grinning, all white teeth, suntan and bold blue eyes. He exuded a buoyant conceit as powerful as an aura. 'I stole a look at your personnel file before I moved on. I've been meaning to call by for ages, but you know how it is—'

'So many women, so little time?'

'Yeah, well, I can't help being a hot property!' Ricky ran appreciative fingers through his thick blond hair and then grimaced. 'Well, to be honest, I got mixed up with this real terrifying bunny boiler for a while…'

Ellie found herself smiling warmly. 'Tell me more,' she encouraged. 'What did she want? A second date?'

'Could I, like…come inside out of the cold?'

'I'm not feeling *that* friendly, Ricky. You made a real nuisance of yourself on level eight. I also hear you left under something of a cloud? Am I right?'

'Dead wrong!' he contradicted with another hugely self-satisfied grin. 'Good luck came my way and I rocketed up the career ladder.'

'Are you still in that new position?' she couldn't resist

asking, wondering if Dio's forecast that he would be fired even faster had been accurate.

'No way! I got myself headhunted out of there again. It wasn't a safe house, if you know what I mean. Fancy a spin in my company car?'

'I'm pregnant, Ricky.'

His grin fell right off his handsome face. 'You're…*what*? My God, what happened?'

'Well…'

'Flamin' hell, who is this guy? Casanova? Where is he?'

Ellie shrugged.

'It figures. Yeah, well, maybe I'll look you up like…next year or something,' Ricky muttered ruefully. 'Probably never. I'm just not into kids at this stage of my life.'

Helplessly amused, Ellie stood up on tiptoes and kissed his cheek. 'Thank you for being that honest.'

Startled, Ricky laughed and rested his arms down on her narrow shoulders. He lowered his head to murmur with recovering good humour, 'Take it from me, you missed a hell of an experience!'

A split second later, the tall blond was literally wrenched away from her. Ellie stumbled back a step in bewilderment. She was just in time to see Dio throw Ricky up against the wall with a snarled Greek expletive and punch him.

'Stop it!' Ellie screeched, absolutely appalled.

Ricky doubled up, groaning.

'You stay away from her!' Dio roared, hauling him up again. '*You hear me?* You stay away from my woman or I'll rip you apart!'

Ricky focused on his assailant with enlarged eyes full of incredulous recognition.

'You're behaving like an animal, Dio!' Ellie gasped, shattered by his violent intervention.

Dio released Ricky with a volatile gesture of savage derision. He studied Ellie, dark golden eyes blazing condemnation. 'And you ask yourself, whose *fault* is that? I saw you kissing him—'

'On the cheek,' Ricky grunted as he struggled to try and recover his breath. 'You know, I could make a real killing if I charged you with assault.'

'You do what you like,' Dio ground out with magnificent unconcern, still glowering at Ellie full force.

'And an even bigger killing if I went to the tabloids with this extraordinary little set-up,' Ricky mused.

'You deserved a good thump for flogging that tip-off you overheard!' Ellie told him roundly.

Dio froze. His arrogant dark head turned slowly. 'This...*this* is Ricky Bolton?'

'Yeah, you're right, we're definitely evens...' Ricky decided out loud, and displayed his innate survival skills by hurriedly backing into his car. He was gone within a minute.

Ellie shivered in the night air. But even though she was shaken and furious her eyes clung to Dio. His black hair gleamed beneath the street light, accentuating the hard edges of his taut bone structure.

'Ricky Bolton!' Dio suddenly seethed through gritted white teeth. 'What the hell was he doing here?'

'Oh, *please*!' she moaned. 'He just called by. And I don't care what you *think* you saw. You had no business acting like a thug!'

'*Cristos!* How do you think I felt, seeing you wrapped round another man?' Dio growled. 'You told *me* to stay away. You're treating *me* like a leper. I've had just about all I can take!'

Perhaps for the first time since she had learnt that she was carrying his baby, Ellie faced the fact that Dio was under stress as well. Dio had made instant decisions when her pregnancy had been confirmed. Without hesitation Dio had asked her to marry him and had flown over to Paris to explain the situation to Helena. But Ellie had then rejected his matri-

monial solution, refused to see him or speak to him and had
withdrawn to wallow in her own bitterness. But now she felt
guilty. Dio had a right to know where he stood and what was
going to happen next.

'I just don't know what's going to happen next,' Ellie confided raggedly.

'I do…' Dio breathed, reaching for her with determined
hands and raising her up to crush her startled mouth under
his.

That fiery demanding kiss knocked Ellie sideways. His raw
hunger snapped her control, released all the seething emotions she had been trying to control. Her head spun; her heart
thundered. Sexual heat zapped her. She quivered, locking her
straining body to the hard muscle and power of his, a needy
moan sounding deep in her throat as she clutched feverishly
at his shoulders.

Dio flung back his head, brilliant eyes burning like fire
now as he scanned her bemused face. 'You *do* bring out the
animal in me, *pethi mou*,' he husked, backing her indoors
again and setting her back down on her own feet. 'Where's
the alarm system?'

Ellie was still in another world entirely, her body throbbing
with the pangs of denial. 'The…*alarm*?'

Dio located it for himself, set it, and doused the lights.
Stuffing her bag into her hands, he tugged her outside again
and locked up. 'What are you doing?' Ellie finally muttered
in bewilderment.

'We're going to have dinner and talk.'

'But I'm not dressed—'

'You've got clothes on, haven't you?' Dio cut in with very
male impatience.

Ellie frowned down at her skinny-rib cardy, long black
skirt and flat boots.

'You look great,' Dio told her without looking at her as
he pressed her into the Ferrari.

*   *   *

Their corner of the quiet, exclusive restaurant was so peaceful and so empty it was as if an exclusion zone had been set around their table. There didn't seem to be any other diners. Ellie lifted her glass of wine.

Dio looked at her, transfixed. Then he reached across the table and literally snatched the glass right out of her hand. 'You can't have that!'

Ellie gazed back at him in total bemusement. 'Why not?'

'You're pregnant. It's safest to stay off alcohol. Don't you *know* that?' Dio demanded.

'Why should I know that?'

'You're a woman—'

'*So?*'

'You're supposed to know about that sort of stuff,' Dio told her with a frown.

'Well, I don't! I'm twenty-one, single and goal-orien-tated…at least I *was*,' Ellie muttered darkly. 'Why would I ever have been interested in knowing what a woman should and shouldn't do when she's pregnant?'

'As it happens…Nathan dropped this book for expectant fathers in with me.' Dio shrugged, and then shrugged again with exaggerated cool to combat her now widening eyes full of wonderment. 'I just flicked through it.'

Ellie could tell he had read every sentence, down to the fine print. She was touched. He had made more effort than she had and she worked in a bookshop. Maybe he wasn't as squeamish as she was.

'I thought there were things I should know—'

'You really do want this baby, don't you?' she conceded grudgingly.

His dark, deep-set eyes narrowed warily. 'Only if you come as part of the package.'

'What's that supposed to mean?'

'That the way you've been behaving I don't know what to expect any more. You don't want to be pregnant. You don't want to be with me…except in bed,' Dio outlined with a sardonic look of challenge.

An unexpected surge of tears stung the backs of Ellie's eyes. She blinked furiously. 'That's not true…I do want the baby…' she sniffed. 'Oh, for heaven's sake, why am I crying?'

Dio reached for her coiled fingers. 'Your hormones are all over the place right now. It's making you very emotional.'

Ellie reddened furiously and yanked her hand out of his, no longer touched by the prospect of the knowledge he had imbibed on her behalf. 'Did your book tell you I was a brick short of a full load?'

'No, it told me to be understanding and supportive,' Dio imparted piously.

'You haven't got the tact,' Ellie informed him dulcetly.

A slashing smile of amusement curved Dio's beautiful mouth.

Her heart skipped an entire beat. He was so gorgeous she couldn't take her eyes off him.

'I still want to marry you,' Dio delivered. 'But if you've got a better solution, run it by me…just as long as it doesn't entail my baby in a basket behind a shop counter.'

'No, it won't entail that.'

'Leaving him or her to go out to work?'

Ellie squirmed. 'Well—'

'Denying my financial support?'

'Dio, I—'

'No, you listen to me,' Dio asserted forcefully. 'If we don't marry, this child will be an outsider to my family. He won't be a secret. But he's not likely to thank you for making him different from the children I will eventually have *within* marriage with someone else.'

Ellie subsided like a burst balloon. For someone else read Helena. Helena, who would loathe Ellie's child if he or she came visiting. Helena, who would be the ultimate wicked stepmother, determined to humiliate and denigrate the illegitimate outsider. Ellie's tummy curdled, all appetite vanishing. She reckoned even the baby was taking a panic attack at the threat of such a future.

'Something I said *finally* clicked with you?' Dio murmured silkily.

Dredging herself from that nightmare series of visions, pressing a trembling, apologetic hand to her tummy in newly maternal protectiveness, Ellie muttered between gritted teeth, 'Maybe I was a bit hasty saying I wouldn't have you as a gift.'

'That was beautifully put, *yineka mou*. So we're getting married again, are we?' Dio enquired smoothly.

Ellie swallowed hard, humble pie beckoning, and took off defensively on another tack. 'You won't believe what I told you about Helena Teriakos.'

'No,' Dio conceded levelly. 'I could lie to you for the sake of peace, but I won't. Naturally I understand that you were pretty upset that day. You didn't know about Helena but *she* didn't realise that. Had she been aware of it, she would never have approached you.'

Ellie compressed her wobbly mouth. It was obvious he was never going to believe her version. He had known Helena all his life and his trust was absolute. How would she live with that?

'Ellie...the night before you found out that you were pregnant, I made the wrong decision. I didn't think it would be a good idea to start telling you about Helena.'

'You might never had had to tell me.'

Dio left that speaking comment alone, black eyes semi-screened. 'You were under sufficient strain. In any case, Helena was an issue I had to deal with alone.'

'You feel very guilty about her,' Ellie breathed tautly.

Dio frowned. 'How else could I feel?'

Ellie averted her eyes. 'Do...do you love her?' she dared

in a driven whisper, and then sat there in mute terror of his response.

'What does love have to do with it?'

That silenced Ellie. It told her so much and yet it told her nothing. Whether he loved Helena or not, he would marry Ellie because she was expecting his child. But how *long* would he stay with her? Would Helena be proved right? But what did she herself have to lose? She would be Dio's wife, for a while at least. Their child would be born legitimate. These days a lot of people didn't seem to set much store by that, but it meant a great deal to Ellie, whose own father had refused to own up to her very existence.

'We put the baby first. Then we worry about us,' Dio spelt out then, with finality.

It sounded like a leading recipe for disaster to Ellie. But the bottom line for her at that moment was that she loved him, and when he got that brooding darkness in his eyes it scared her and made her feel shut out.

'I'd like to get married in a church,' she announced breezily. 'In a totally over-the-top dress. So if you're planning on a register office, you've got no hope!'

Dio's wide, sensual mouth eased into a smile. She felt like a performing clown, but that smile warmed her like the sunshine and she was defenceless against it.

CHAPTER EIGHT

SIX weeks later, Ellie walked into her local church, where she was a regular worshipper, to become Dio's wife.

She wore an elegant, fitted, off-the-shoulder dress in palest cream, the superb fabric exquisitely beaded and embroidered. In one fell swoop she had virtually emptied her bank account of five years of savings. It had been like an act of faith in their marriage. She had used one of the credit cards Dio had given her to buy the matching shoes and all the other trappings.

She walked down the aisle alone, and quite unconcerned.

'Someone has to give you away,' Dio had told her on the phone from Geneva, where he had been attending a conference.

'Forget that…what do you think I am? A commodity?' Ellie had demanded. 'I'm almost a twenty-first-century woman!'

'Why did twenty-first-century woman say no to me the night before last?' Dio had enquired silkily.

A squirming silence had fallen at her end of the line.

'I want our wedding night to be special. You *said* you understood,' Ellie had reminded him uncomfortably, her face burning.

'When I was standing under a cold shower at two that morning, aching like the very devil,' Dio had growled back in charged response, 'I changed my mind.'

It was with that memory foremost in her mind that Ellie smiled with sheer brilliance on that walk down the aisle towards Dio. She was blind to the assembled guests crowding out the church, impervious to everyone but the very tall, very dark and very, very gorgeous guy waiting for her at the altar with his best man. This was her day, her moment, her guy. *Mine*, she thought fiercely. Well, she adjusted then, for as long as she could hold onto him.

The ceremony was beautiful. Ellie drank in every word, required no prompting when it came to taking her vows, indeed got in there fast. Why? At the back of her mind lurked a no doubt ridiculous but nonetheless enervating image of Helena Teriakos somehow stopping the ceremony in its tracks at the eleventh hour. 'I make a very bitter enemy,' Helena had warned. And even as the wedding ring went on her finger, Ellie's skin chilled at that memory.

Unfortunately, it hadn't occurred to Ellie that Dio would invite Helena to their wedding. So it was a shock when she saw the beautiful Greek woman approaching them outside the church.

A vision of perfection in a stunning white suit, Helena glided up, grasped both their hands and murmured with a rather sad smile, 'I am very happy for you both.' Then she paused. 'Ellie, I hope you don't mind, but I have something I really need to ask Dio.'

That touching air of plucky feminine vulnerability which had taken Ellie entirely by surprise worked like a magic charm on Dio. He was drawn off to speak to Helena and Ellie was left alone on the church steps. As the minutes ticked past, Ellie got paler and paler, her tension rising. Their guests were noticing, stealing covert glances at Dio and Helena, commenting. Ellie just wanted to die of humiliation.

The society photographer finally called, 'Mr Alexiakis...*please*!'

And only then did Dio return to Ellie's side.

'She did that *deliberately*!' Ellie condemned helplessly when the photographer had finished.

Dio raised a questioning brow. 'Who? What are you talking about?'

How could he be so obtuse? Ellie was so furious she could have shaken him. 'Helena!'

A silence as thick as concrete spread.

Dio breathed in deep.

'Helena remains a close friend, a very close friend,' he spelt out with what sounded like twenty-five generations of aristocratic ice and breeding backing up his chilling drawl.

'Oh, I believe I've got that message all right,' Ellie whispered tightly.

'Then understand this too. I will not allow you to embarrass either myself or her in public. That's my last word on the subject. Get used to the idea *before* I lose my temper!'

And with that blunt warning Dio turned away to speak to his best man, Nathan Parkes. Ellie quivered with sheer rage. She couldn't believe that Dio had had the nerve to speak to her as though she were a misbehaving child threatening to cause a scene. For goodness' sake, he'd got the ring on her finger and then he'd started acting like some medieval tyrant! Hadn't he seen how utterly inappropriate and unnecessary it had been for the brunette to demand his attention in the midst of their wedding photographs being taken? Evidently not.

As Dio swung back to her again, Ellie threw back her slim shoulders and lifted her chin. 'You can't talk to me like you just did, Dio—'

'*Ohi*…no?' Dio countered with dangerous quietness, his tone trickling down Ellie's rigid spine like the gypsy's curse. 'You've got a lot to learn about Greek men!'

Frankly, at that moment, Ellie felt she had already learnt quite sufficient. She was fizzing with fury. But before she could respond in kind, Meg Bucknall appeared a few feet from them. 'Freeze!' she begged, and eagerly lifted her camera to take a picture.

'You look just gorgeous, Ellie,' the older woman sighed appreciatively. 'You didn't have to invite me but I'm so glad you did. I'm having a great time.'

'The pleasure is ours, Mrs Bucknall,' Dio responded with a charismatic smile.

'The pleasure has just gone *out* of my day,' Ellie confided as they climbed into the limousine that would take them to the reception at the Savoy Hotel.

'When you're in the wrong, I'll tell you,' Dio countered without a shade of regret.

But I *wasn't* in the wrong, Ellie almost snapped, and then conscience spurred her into questioning that conviction. This was their wedding day. Helena's smooth little power play had embarrassed rather than injured. Possibly in allowing her own insecurity full rein, she herself had overreacted.

'Dio,' she murmured ruefully, green eyes very clear, 'This isn't a very easy occasion for me...'

Dio dealt her a questioning, wary look, her change of approach disconcerting him.

'I didn't realise there would be so many guests and I hardly know anybody here,' Ellie pointed out. 'And all your friends and relatives were expecting you to marry Helena.'

Dio tensed. 'Yes, but—'

'Dio, they wouldn't be human if they weren't wondering *why* you are suddenly marrying me instead...' Ellie coloured. 'And if they're thinking what people usually think at times like this, well, they're dead right where I'm concerned, aren't they? I *am* pregnant! Naturally I feel touchy and self-conscious today.'

Dio closed an unexpected hand firmly over hers, black eyes no longer cool and distant. 'I am proud that you are carrying my baby,' he cut in with roughened sincerity.

'So maybe I went over the top about Helena—'

'No,' Dio sighed. 'Once again I was too quick to judge you, and I apologise. I honestly didn't appreciate how you were feeling.'

It was wonderful what difference a little explanation could make. Ellie watched in wonderment as Dio lifted her hand

and pressed his mouth softly to the centre of her palm. Her heart seemed to swell inside her chest and her pulse-beat accelerated. A simply huge wave of happiness whooshed up inside her, dispelling all anxiety and unease.

'Even worse, you have no family here of your own to support you,' Dio conceded grimly.

'Mum would have loved all this…' Ellie's smile of acknowledgement was rather tremulous at that emotive thought.

With a rueful groan, Dio pulled her all the way into his arms. 'When you said I had no tact, you hit the target!'

Ellie knew better than to remind him of his father. She hadn't the slightest doubt that the late Spiros Alexiakis would have been anything but happy to see his only son marrying someone as ordinary as she felt herself to be. On the face of it, she conceded painfully, Helena would have been so much more suitable. She rested her cheek against his broad shoulder, the warm, intimate scent of him doing the wildest things to her senses.

Dio glanced down at her, dark, deep-set eyes burning gold. 'Have you ever made love in a limo?' he enquired thickly.

Ellie gave him a helpless grin. 'Oh, yeah, Dio…of course I want to walk into the Savoy and greet all these important people with my make-up half off and my hair all messed up!'

'I could persuade you—'

'But you won't. You're going to be a miracle of restraint…until tonight,' she told him unsteadily, her cheeks warming.

Met by Ellie's determined smile as the bridal couple greeted their arriving guests at the hotel, Helena bent to kiss her cheek with cool familiarity, exchanged a light word with Dio and moved on past. The brunette's supreme confidence and control still daunted Ellie.

Dio watched the smile drop right off Ellie's expressive face again. 'Try to appreciate how difficult this must be for her.'

Ellie nodded and flushed, feeling herself rebuked although she had done her utmost to look calm and friendly. She had never been very good at hiding her emotions. And it looked as if she was stuck with the stigma of having lied about what had passed between her and the older woman at their first meeting. But then wasn't it possible that in the heat of the moment Helena *had* acted totally out of character that afternoon? Helena might now regret her behaviour, Ellie thought with sudden hope, resolving to be more generous herself.

Nathan Parkes introduced her to his wife, Sally. She was a bubbly redhead with freckles and a friendly, easy manner. 'I wish I'd got the chance to meet you before the wedding. I did think of asking Dio for your number and calling you. But I knew you'd be frantically busy and I didn't want to seem too pushy.'

'I'd have been delighted,' Ellie told her warmly, since she was beginning to appreciate that the tall, softly spoken gynaecologist was a much closer friend of Dio's than she had initially realised.

'Great. I'm not much good at standing on ceremony,' Sally confided cheerfully. 'And I was really hoping you wouldn't be like—' As she bit back what she had been intending to say, she reddened like mad. 'What I meant to say was… was…we, well—'

Nathan stepped in to rescue his wife from her discomfiture. 'Sally hopes you'll come and stay with us in the country some time soon. We warn our guests in advance—we have a muddy yard, three noisy kids and a manic dog!'

'I'm not a *cordon bleu* cook or anything,' Sally warned rather anxiously.

'I'm not a fussy eater, and I'd be happy to help out,' Ellie said quickly, thinking that their home and family sounded delightful.

Dio glanced at Ellie with a raised brow. '*Can* you cook?' he asked in surprise.

Nathan shot his friend a helplessly amused look and laughed outright. 'Dio, that says it all, it really does! Are you aware, Ellie, that Dio didn't even know how to switch on a kettle when he first came to stay with us?'

'They're a lovely couple,' Ellie whispered when they were eating their meal at the top table. 'Have you known Nathan long?'

'I was in a car smash when I was nineteen. Nathan was doing his stint as a med student in the casualty unit.' For some reason that recollection made Dio's firm lips curve into a surprisingly amused grin.

'What's so funny about that?'

'I only had concussion, but my father was in a highly emotional frame of mind when he arrived.' Dio grimaced. 'He behaved as if Nathan had saved me from certain death and embarrassed the hell out of both of us. I think Nathan agreed to spend the weekend on our yacht just to escape being wept over and embraced!'

'Of course your dad was upset. You were an only child,' Ellie scolded, dismayed even by the mention of a car accident that had happened a decade earlier, simply terrified at the idea of anything ever happening to Dio.

Dio gazed deep into her anxious green eyes and his mouth quirked. 'I wish he'd met you—'

'No, you don't!' Ellie told him roundly. 'He'd have locked you up before he'd have let you marry someone like me!'

'What *is* this "someone like me" stuff?'

'It's my Cinderella complex talking. I certainly don't mean that you're my prince, Dio, so don't be getting a swollen head!' Ellie cautioned. 'You're the guy who first switched on a kettle as an adult…and I was the latch-key kid who got my own tea from the age of seven!'

Dio wasn't amused. 'No damn wonder you find it so hard to lean on me.'

'Most people I've tried to lean on in life fell over!' Ellie joked instantly, hoping to make him lighten up again, wishing she hadn't mentioned her childhood.

'But I won't,' Dio intoned very seriously. 'You have to learn to trust me, *pethi mou*.'

Sometimes men were a tonic, she decided. He had said that without a shade of irony. Yet *he* didn't trust her. At least, her word didn't yet carry the same weight and value as his lifelong friend Helena's, Ellie couldn't help reflecting. But she swiftly suppressed that thought. They were married now, and it was early days yet. Time would take care of that problem. She couldn't see that he would be meeting up with Helena Teriakos very much in the future, and she was too practical to make a running battle of that issue in the short term. A new marriage was a fragile thing. Wouldn't it be foolish to make the beautiful Greek woman a bone of contention?

A few hours later, in the luxurious room set aside for her use, Ellie removed her wedding gown with rueful regret and put on the travelling outfit she had purchased. A loden-green suit, its fitted jacket adorned with snazzy gold buttons and teamed with a fashionable short skirt. It had cost the earth and she had picked it with great care. But the more mature appearance she had initially attempted to strike hadn't come off. Those kind of clothes didn't look right on her yet. She was twenty-one and she didn't look older than her years.

When she returned to the crush of guests awaiting their departure for the airport, she was rewarded by the appreciative gleam that awakened in Dio's expressive eyes the instant he saw her. Her rather anxious smile became downright sunny.

'You look about eighteen. I should be hung,' Dio groaned, but he curved a wonderfully possessive arm round her small thin figure. 'Go on, throw your bouquet.'

'No, I want to keep it.'

'I thought it was tradition.'

'No, I'm having mine preserved and framed…or something,' Ellie told him stubbornly.

The number of people wishing to exchange last words with Dio briefly forced them apart. Ellie watched Dio laughing at some sally, and something akin to pure joy blossomed within her. He really did look happy and relaxed, just as a new husband should look.

And then, from behind her, a cool smooth voice remarked, 'I pity you, Ellie. Playing the whore between Dio's sheets won't hold him for long. And you don't *have* anything else to offer him, do you?'

In shock, Ellie froze, and then she spun round with a jerk. But Helena Teriakos had already moved on to chat to an older couple some distance from her. However, Sally Parkes was standing only a foot away, her mouth wide, her eyes almost as appalled as Ellie's. 'I was just hurrying over to speak to you before you left. Did I *really* just hear what I thought I heard?' she demanded in an incredulous whisper. 'My goodness, I never thought that cold fish had it in her to be that spiteful!'

That surprising comment dredged a nervous giggle from Ellie. 'Now you know.'

'Go and tell Dio right this minute,' Sally urged her keenly.

'No, I'll handle it myself…' Ellie said awkwardly, mortified colour now banishing her previous pallor. 'I did kind of steal her man, so, well…I can't blame her for hating me.'

Sally Parkes frowned. '*Her* man? They weren't even dating, never mind engaged. Surely you don't believe *she's* been sitting home just waiting for Dio to pop the question! If a richer, more powerful prospect had come along, she'd have married him years ago!'

Ellie felt uneasy. She liked Sally, but, although it was comforting to be told such things, she didn't want to discuss Helena with anyone.

'Honestly!' Sally was into full swing now, venting what

were obviously pretty personal feelings about the other woman. 'Helena's all sweetness and light around Dio. I'd just love him to know what she's *really* like! Men can be so blind.'

'Yes,' Ellie agreed, frantically trying to think of a change of subject.

'He's had a real narrow escape. She's the original ice queen and the most awful snob. Nat and I just aren't good enough to share the same room with her!' Sally shared feelingly.

'Who aren't you and Nat good enough to share the same room with?' Dio enquired with amusement. He closed a powerful arm round Ellie as he spoke, only to glance down at his bride in surprise when she jumped in guilty dismay. 'What's wrong?'

'I'm feeling a bit dizzy,' Ellie announced, and right then she genuinely was. Dizzy with apprehension. She was terrified that Sally was about to name Helena and give Dio the impression that they had been enjoying a mutual muck-raking session.

But a split second later she saw that she needn't have worried. Poor, outspoken Sally was hotly embarrassed by Dio's untimely interruption. And, as a distraction, Ellie's plea of dizziness worked a treat. Dio assisted her into the limousine as if she was an elderly lady of at least a hundred and one. Then he climbed back out again to stride over to Sally's husband, Nathan.

From her stance a few feet from the car, Sally made the most comical grimace of relief. She pretended to mop her brow, evidently as aware as Ellie of Dio's high opinion of Helena and grateful not to have caused offence.

Dio swung into the limousine beside Ellie. 'The instant the jet's airborne, you're going to rest,' he informed her with determination, fresh from what appeared to have been an urgent consultation with Nathan in his professional capacity.

'But I'm OK!' Ellie protested in dismay.

'I should never have invited so many people. It's been a hell of a demanding day for you…and I know it sounds crass but I keep on forgetting that you're a pregnant lady!' Dio told her apologetically.

Actually, no news could have pleased Ellie more. Only by the time she heard it, it was too late. There she was, longing to be passionately kissed, and Dio was behaving as if she had turned into some kind of invalid. When she argued, he simply assumed that she was striving not to be a sickly wet blanket. He then told her off for trying to take such an attitude with him, and pointed out that she had to accept the need to take extra care of herself now.

As soon as the jet was on route to Greece, where they were to spend a couple of weeks, Dio stashed Ellie on the bed in the cabin and helped her out of her shoes. He would have helped her out of her suit as well, but Ellie pulled away.

'Go to sleep,' he urged bossily. 'I know you have to be exhausted.'

'I'm *not*,' Ellie groaned in despair.

Dio crouched down lithely by the side of the bed. Vibrant dark eyes swept her mutinous but pale face. 'Don't you want to be awake for our wedding night?' he murmured silkily.

'I thought Nathan might have put *that* on the forbidden list as well,' Ellie said crossly.

Dio gave her a shimmering smile of amusement and smoothed her tumbled hair gently off her brow. 'You're such a kid sometimes.'

Ellie was so annoyed at that assurance she flipped over to turn her face to the wall and presented him with a stiff back.

'And that's really good for me!' Dio protested with a tremor of laughter disturbing his usually even diction. 'Occasionally I now have to think for two people instead of one. For a male who has been extremely selfish and spoilt for most of his life, that's really terrific therapy!'

'Oh, really?' Ellie muttered sniffily. 'I'm so glad *one* of us is having fun!'

Dio burst out laughing. Ellie flipped back over, real temper sparking, and then she collided with his beautiful dark eyes. Her heart skipped a beat and she totally forgot what she might have been about to snap back.

'I promise you, *agape mou*. The fun will include you to-night,' he swore, not quite steadily.

And only when she was free of the undeniable distraction of his vibrant presence did Ellie feel the heaviness of the exhaustion she had rigorously denied slowly creeping over her to weight her limbs.

'Stop it,' Ellie surfaced to mumble in complaint when she sensed disturbance some timeless period later.

'Hush,' Dio soothed.

Ellie slid a sleepily seeking hand beneath his jacket. She spread possessive fingers across the silk shirt separating her from his warm, virile body and sighed with contentment. Dimly assuming he was lying down beside her, she sank back into peaceful sleep.

She finally wakened and stretched, only find to herself under restraint. Her eyes flew open. Dio was carrying her. 'What…where?'

'You've slept well for a lady who wasn't remotely tired. You've been out of it for the whole trip,' Dio drawled, with more than a hint of that satisfaction peculiar to a male who enjoys being proved right.

Ellie focused on the familiar frontage of the vast villa he was striding towards. 'For goodness' sake…put me down.'

'I can't. I left your shoes behind on the jet.'

'How on earth did you cart me through Athens airport?' she gasped.

'The same way.' Dio laughed. 'It did cross my mind that

the fact you're not as staturesque as Helena was a distinct advantage—I'm still fit to carry you over the threshold!'

Ellie froze at his reference to the other woman, the disconcerting comparison which he had unthinkingly made. Dio tensed, closed his eyes and just groaned out loud, evidently registering what he had just said.

Ellie made an enormous effort. 'It's OK,' she stressed with a forced smile intended to soothe. 'She was part of your life for a long time…I understand.'

As he reached the palatial front entrance of the villa, Dio sent a rueful glance down at her. 'Until I met you, I really believed I was a skilled diplomat.'

'It's all that boot-licking that goes on around you,' Ellie told him baldly.

'No, it isn't that. It's *you*,' he condemned with a wry light in his eyes. 'I get so used to listening to you say whatever you like that I relax my guard around you.'

Ellie thought about that. 'That's good.'

Well, sometimes it would be good—even most of the time, she adjusted inwardly. But right now she really could have done without finding out that Dio had been comparing her in even the tiniest way with Helena. Such a trivial little comparison too: Helena so tall and shapely, Ellie so small and slightly built. But still Ellie would have preferred not to have had the confirmation that the beautiful brunette was still so much in Dio's thoughts on *their* wedding day.

But then it didn't take a rocket scientist to work out *why* Helena was on Dio's mind. All his adult life, Dio had assumed that Helena would be his wife. He had had little time to come to terms with the sudden switch in brides. And he certainly *cared* about Helena, Ellie was forced to concede. He praised the beautiful brunette, became angry if she was criticised and hotly defended her. As she faced those hard facts head-on, Ellie was in pain. What if Dio really *did* love the other woman? It was perfectly possible that he had decided to put the needs of his unborn child ahead of his own personal feelings. But if he had done that, time would weaken his resolve, wouldn't it?

As they entered the huge hall, Dio dragged Ellie back to the present by momentarily stilling with a low-pitched groan. 'We have company,' he sighed.

Two tiny old ladies with almost identical creased faces and wide smiles were waiting for them in the hall. Ellie rather thought she had noticed the elderly pair in their old-fashioned black dresses on her previous visit to the villa.

Dio greeted both women in a flow of warm Greek. He settled Ellie down on her stocking-clad feet to introduce her to his grandmother's twin sisters: Polly and Lefki.

'Dio has no mother to welcome you to your new home,' Polly—Ellie thought it was—said in heavily accented English. 'We are here to make you welcome.'

'To make you welcome,' Lefki repeated cheerfully.

'Lefki, I have said that.' Her sister turned to admonish her.

'But we are not staying long.' Lefki gave her sister a decidedly defiant look.

Ellie couldn't help herself. She just grinned.

An abundant supper awaited them in the big drawing room she remembered. Polly and Lefki sat perched on the sofa opposite. They were so small and shrunken that their feet didn't touch the carpet. In between arguing with each other, they urged more food on Dio and shot loaded questions at Ellie.

What did she think of the island? With pride, they announced that neither of them had ever left the island, even for a day. Didn't she think it would be a wonderful place to live all the year round? Did she know how much Dio loved Chindos? Didn't she think that Dio worked too hard and travelled too much? Their love and concern for Dio became more endearingly obvious with each word.

When they finally took their leave in an elderly Rolls

Royce, driven off at a snail's pace by their careful driver, Dio shot Ellie a slightly uneasy glance. 'Sorry about that. Polly and Lefki live at the far end of the island. I can appreciate that some people find them rather eccentric, but they rarely visit.'

'Oh, I hope not. They're absolutely adorable,' Ellie told him. 'What age are they? Have they always been together?'

'Ninety-two and, yes, they're completely inseparable.' Dio smiled warmly down at her and relaxed. He dropped an arm round her as he walked her up the spectacular central staircase. 'I'm glad you like them. I have a soft spot for my great-aunts. When my mother died, Polly and Lefki were a great comfort to me, and I've never forgotten that.'

He drew her into a fabulous bedroom furnished with the same unashamed opulence as the ground floor. Gorgeous flower arrangements scented the still air. Ellie glanced at the magnificent bed and her tummy clenched with anticipation. She looked away, her cheeks warming, embarrassed by the sensual stirrings of her own body. It was hard to credit that only a few weeks ago she had been blissfully ignorant of how powerful sexual hunger could be.

'I could do with freshening up,' she confided shyly.

'So could I,' Dio purred like a big lazy cat, casting off his jacket and tugging loose his tie.

Watching him strip, she ran out of breath and mobility. Meeting those dark golden eyes, feeling their bold, sensual glide over her taut figure, she felt her heart start to beat very fast. Naked now, his lean, bronzed, hair-roughened length a feast for her wakening senses, Dio strode over to her. He undid the buttons on her jacket one by one and eased it from her shoulders.

'I want to drive you wild,' he told her huskily.

'My imagination has already done that for you...' Ellie confided.

Releasing her bra, Dio curved his hands to the new fullness

of her breasts. He smiled with sensual appreciation as she jerked and gasped at the brush of his thumbs over her urgently sensitive nipples. Suddenly intent, Dio pushed her gently down onto the bed. Following her there, he sealed his mouth hotly to a straining pink bud, laving it with his tongue and the edge of his teeth. Fiery response whooshed through her trembling tautness, provoking a driven moan from her parted lips.

Dio raised his dark head again, raw hunger in his eyes. He angled back and skimmed off her skirt. He dispensed with her remaining garments with unconcealed impatience. As he ran his burnished gaze over her pale nudity, she felt as if she was burning all over. 'You are so perfect…I need a shower just to cool off,' he confided thickly.

'Me too…'

In the spacious shower cubicle, she leant up against him beneath the energizing beat of the water. Weak and hungry as her treacherous body was, anxiety still pierced her thoughts. She wouldn't be *perfect* much longer. Her breasts were already fuller. Their baby would soon wreak havoc with the taut, slim figure he liked so much. Her waistline would thicken; her stomach would swell. Would Dio still find her attractive then?

'I'm going to look like a balloon in a few months,' she muttered helplessly, unable to keep her fear to herself.

'Hmm…' Dio sighed, sliding a reflective hand down over her still flat tummy, letting his fingers splay and linger. 'I'm looking forward to showing you off.'

'Showing me off?' Ellie echoed weakly.

Dio sank down on the corner seat and tugged her down on top of him. Angling his handsome head back, he luxuriated in the warm jets of water hitting them from all directions before he looked at her again. A slashing grin slated his wide, sensual mouth then. 'I think it must be a guy thing, *agape mou*. You have my baby inside you. That's a hell of a turn-on.'

'It *is*?' Taken aback by that assurance, Ellie stared at him.

Eyes flaming to molten gold, Dio deftly shifted her so that she sat astride him. With amusement, he watched her register the strength of his arousal for herself.

'Oh…' Suddenly bereft of breath, Ellie found her own hopelessly susceptible body reacting with violent enthusiasm to the sensual masculine threat of his.

Dio cupped her damp cheekbones and took her mouth with a hot, hungry brevity that sizzled through her every nerve-ending. 'So what are we going to do about it?' he husked.

Anything you want,' she whispered, barely able to keep her voice steady.

And, with a hungry groan of satisfaction, he took her at her word. The urgency of his need both shocked and excited her. In the aftermath of her own shattering climax, she was still trembling as he towelled her dry. By then Dio was apologising, and then laughing at the same time.

'Don't you ever tell anyone that our marriage was consummated in a shower,' he breathed. 'I'd never hold my head up again!'

'Why?'

He laid her down on the magnificent bed. 'I should have been more romantic. It's our wedding night,' he reminded her with a rueful glint in his eyes that had so much appeal it tugged at her heart. 'But the thought of making love without contraception for the first time in my life made me rampant!'

'Rampant works like magic with me,' Ellie confided with a giggle, tugging him back down to her with possessive hands, surrendering to her overpowering need to keep in constant physical contact.

Dio smiled, slumbrous dark gold eyes scanning her with

appreciation. 'I like this,' he said softly. 'I like it that we can laugh even in bed. I've never had that before.'

Ellie woke up around dawn. Wandering sleepily back from the bathroom, she paused to study Dio where he lay on the bed, her eyes soft with tenderness and love. The white sheet was tangled only partially round one long, lean, powerful thigh. For a split second she just couldn't believe that he was *her* husband. And then she tossed her silvery fair head back and smiled. The fears she had harboured the night before now seemed remote and rather hysterical.

Right now, her body ached from the hunger of his. He wanted *her*, not just the baby. He wasn't turned off by her pregnancy either. And if he had been feeling trapped into marriage by his own sense of honour, he would surely have been a less keen lover. But Dio had spent the night demonstrating over and over again that he found her very desirable. He had restored her confidence in herself.

Pregnancy had shattered that confidence and hurt her pride. For a while, the status quo had changed, she acknowledged. She hadn't liked that. She had made some mistakes too. Her innate need for reassurance had made her feel dependent and weak, no longer his equal. Now those uneasy feelings were gone and she felt more secure. Sliding back into bed beside him, she sighed. She felt incredibly happy.

A smiling young maid woke Ellie later that morning by opening the curtains. It was after eleven. Dio had gone and she couldn't credit that she had slept so late. Her breakfast arrived on a wicker bed-tray complete with a bud vase. Gosh, this is fun, she decided, resting back against her banked-up pillows feeling like a queen.

After she had eaten, one startled glance at her tousled appearance sent her rushing to the shower. When she had finished drying her hair and had applied a little light make-up, she found that her clothes had already been unpacked and tidied away in the capacious dressing room. She had bought several casual outfits before the wedding, and she put on a cool cotton shift dress in misty pastel shades of mauve.

As she descended the stairs, she heard Dio. Dio…his distinctive voice raised in…*anger*? A short dark young man erupted like a bullet from a doorway at the back of the hall. Awarding Ellie a startled look, he flushed and paused to proffer a strained greeting in Greek before he hurried on past. Ellie frowned in surprise.

Dio was talking harshly on the phone in his own language. He was in an elegant room furnished as an office. His short-sleeved linen shirt and tailored chinos in pale natural colours were a superb frame for his black hair, bronzed skin and sleekly powerful physique. He looked so stunning that for a foolish moment Ellie just hovered on the threshold, watching him stride back and forth like a caged tiger, his every lithe, restive movement screaming ferocious tension.

Ellie's scrutiny finally roamed from the husband she adored to the crumpled tabloid newspaper spread out across the desk. An English Sunday newspaper, she noted, flown out already. Her curiosity was roused as she moved closer.

Slinging aside the phone, Dio swung round and belatedly noticed her. '*Cristos*…what are *you* doing in here?' he thundered in disconcertion.

But it was already too late. Ellie had got close enough to recognise first a photograph of their wedding and then the people in the other smaller photos. Both her parents! There was her father, Tony Maynard, clambering out of his Mercedes, looking hunted and furious. It was the first time Ellie had seen him in over five years. She was paralysed to the spot, the colour draining from her shattered face.

Dio released his breath in a stark hiss. 'I don't think you should read that stuff. It's only going to upset you.'

Ellie stared down at the pages. There was a picture of the shabby street where she had lived as a child. The caption beneath ran, *'From poverty…to wealth beyond avarice. How? The billion-dollar baby!'*

'Oh, *no*…' Ellie mumbled strickenly, her tummy lurching with nausea at the crude shock of such humiliation, in print for all the world to see.

CHAPTER NINE

'SCARCELY the way I would have chosen to announce the advent of our first child,' Dio commented in a charged undertone that fairly screeched with restraint.

'No...' Ellie agreed, trembling.

'But, had you warned me how much scandal there was in your past, I might have been able to bury some of the evidence and protect you.'

Ellie flinched from the censure she could hear in his clipped drawl. And as she read what was in that newspaper article she didn't blame him; she really didn't. It *was* lurid stuff. The barest bones of the truth were there, but sunk beneath a wealth of lies and exaggerations.

'For a start, I had no idea that you and your mother were virtual outcasts in the town where you grew up.'

'Dio...it was a small town. Mum was an unmarried mother when it wasn't at all acceptable.' Ellie cleared her throat of the thickness of tears. 'Her father died owing money to a lot of local tradesmen. Neither of those facts was going to win her any popularity contest. And when my father was seen visiting by the neighbours...well, everyone knew he was a married man.'

'Why didn't you tell me that he ditched your mother to marry his secretary a few months after his first wife died?' Dio enquired drily.

He was concentrating on the revelations about her background rather than the infinitely more damaging and cruel comments about her in the present. She had been branded a cunning little gold-digger, who had seen her chance with a rich man and grabbed it with both hands. She felt sicker than ever.

'Ellie…' Dio prompted curtly.

'Well, to be blunt…Th-that's not one of my favourite memories,' she stammered painfully. 'My father didn't even bother to tell Mum that he had another woman in his life. The first she knew about it was the notice of their marriage in the local paper! She was devastated.'

'Yes, and I would have preferred to have learned from *you* that she took her own life.'

Ellie rounded on him in shaken rebuttal. 'She *didn't*! She was taking medication for depression. She was living in her own little world. She stepped off the pavement at a junction without looking and just got knocked down!'

Dio surveyed her with bleak eyes and his hands coiled into fists which he dug into his pockets. 'You were only sixteen. How the hell did you cope alone at that age?'

'My caring father sent his solicitor to arrange the funeral. He didn't attend himself, of course.'

'Then what?' Dio prompted, looking grimmer than ever. 'Why did you leave school?'

Ellie frowned in surprise. 'What choice did I have?'

'At the very least your father should have ensured that you completed your education—'

'Why would he have done that when he had spent sixteen years trying to pretend that I was nothing to do with him? He was scared his wife would find out about me and throw him out. All the money was hers,' Ellie explained wearily.

'So what did you do after your mother died?'

'Our flat was rented. I sold the household stuff to a dealer and went to London. I stayed in a hostel until I got the job with Mr Barry. The year after that, he offered me the room above the shop. Dio, why are we talking about my background?' Ellie studied him with bewildered eyes. 'I didn't tell you any lies. I may have skipped the messier details, but that's no hanging offence.'

His black eyes flared to smouldering gold. 'At this moment, I want to strangle you,' Dio confessed in a wrathful undertone. 'But if we talk about what doesn't really matter for *long* enough, I have more hope of getting my temper under control!'

Ellie frowned in confusion. Was he blaming her for that scurrilous article? How could he? She asked him, certain she had to be wrong.

'Of course I'm blasted well blaming you!' Dio launched back at her, his pent-up outrage unleashed by what he evidently considered to be a very stupid question.

Ellie turned very pale. 'But why?'

'The trail leads back to *you*, Ellie. If I'm not very sympathetic, it's because your own lack of discretion has brought this on us both!' he condemned with raw impatience.

'Lack of discretion?' Ellie echoed blankly.

'Nathan didn't even tell Sally that you were pregnant! He knows she's a hopeless gossip. And now I know I've got a wife who makes his look as secretive as the CIA!' Dio bit out sardonically. 'How many people have you told that you're pregnant?'

'None!' Ellie's temper rose as she finally grasped why he didn't feel she was entitled to sympathy. He fondly imagined that all that information had leaked from her own foolish lips!

'You must have told someone. I would trust Nathan with my life. The press couldn't have managed to put all this together so quickly *without* assistance from someone close to *you*!' Dio spelt out with emphasis.

Ellie then recalled telling Ricky Bolton that she was expecting a baby, and she coloured hotly.

Dio was watching her like a hawk eager to swoop on a tender prey. 'Who *was* it?'

Ellie was thinking at a frantic pace. Ricky might have

known she was pregnant, but he hadn't known a single thing about her parentage. Then she stilled, an expression of appalled comprehension slowly freezing her eloquent face. She could not believe what a fool she had been not to grasp who was behind such a vindictive attack on her.

'Ellie…I want a full confession. Then possibly I will calm down,' Dio contended, in not the most convincing of promises.

Ellie scrutinised him in agonised silence. She *knew* that he was likely to spontaneously combust if she spoke the name that already lay between them like a mine-filled stretch of enemy territory. But at the same time she had to defend herself.

'Ellie…' Dio grated.

'You really want to know who I think is likely to have been behind this newspaper stuff…?' Ellie swallowed and tilted her chin. 'In my opinion, the most likely candidate is Helena Teriakos.'

Boulders could have dropped soundlessly into the deep, deep silence that fell. She might as well have named a cartoon character. Dio stared at her with wondering black eyes as if she was intellectually challenged.

'It *has* to be her,' Ellie continued valiantly. 'She already knew about my background and she hates me—'

'Have you taken leave of your wits?' Dio demanded in an almost ragged plea.

Ellie jerked a slight shoulder. 'If it's any consolation, Helena has *you* taped too,' she added, no longer struggling to choose her words with care. 'She said that you were easily embarrassed, and she said that you'd turn on me.'

Dio swept a silencing hand through the air. As a gesture, it was highly effective in its intimidating authority. 'You are so devoured by jealousy you can't see straight, never mind reason rationally—'

'Right at this moment, I am certainly not *jealous*, Dio.'

Ellie thrust up her chin as she voiced that reality. 'If Helena came to that front door right now, I'd hand you over without a murmur!'

'That's enough!' Dio growled.

'I'm not finished!' Ellie's anger was shooting higher even as his inexplicably appeared to be on the wane. 'You *deserve* her! I wish you *had* married her. You'd have got frostbite on your wedding night!'

Dio breathed in very slowly and deeply. Then he said, 'I think this could be that stage when the honeymoon phase comes to a sudden very sticky end.'

'I've had enough of you and that malicious vixen,' Ellie announced tremulously.

'Tough,' Dio responded with extreme quietness.

That switch in attitude bemused her. 'What do you mean, *tough*?'

'You're my wife and you're not going anywhere. In fact, while you're displaying this deeply disturbing manic streak where Helena is concerned, you're staying on this island. I have to confess that I literally *cringe* at the prospect of you meeting up with her again. Look at yourself!' Dio invited with a curled lip. 'You're practically jumping up and down with rage as it is.'

'What do you expect?' Ellie screeched so loudly her voice broke.

Dio closed a determined arm round her shivering figure. 'This is not good for the baby—'

'Get your hands off me!' Ellie hissed.

'No, your emotions are running out of control. It has to be your hormone level,' Dio decided, surveying her with extreme gravity but with a definite look of relief at an explanation he evidently liked very much.

'My...hormone level?' Ellie practically whispered.

'In early pregnancy a woman may be prone to emotional changes and may require extra support and understanding.'

Ellie's jaw dropped at what sounded very much like a direct quote from a textbook.

A dark flush scored Dio's stunning cheekbones as he appeared to absorb the meaning of what he had just said. 'I've been far too hard on you,' he added abruptly.

Ellie was disconcerted to find herself being herded over to a sofa and urged to sit down. 'Dio…what on earth are you playing at?' she prompted weakly.

Dio came down beside her, his dark, devastatingly handsome features now stamped with taut discomfiture. 'You were *really* distressed after you saw that article. Even if you had announced your pregnancy to the entire maintenance staff in my building, I should have been more sympathetic towards your feelings.'

Ellie could agree with that, at least. However, she hadn't the slightest wish to shelter behind the excuse of emotional mood swings provoked by hormonal upheaval. 'Yes, but—'

'It just made me so bloody furious to see you being attacked in print!' Dio vented with sudden rawness as he folded a powerful arm round her and drew her close. 'And it was really chilling working out the sort of childhood you must have endured with two such selfish parents. That upset me too, and when I get upset, I blow a fuse. But when you dragged in Helena again, *fortunately* I began to see how wildly out of proportion this was all becoming.'

'I can't live with you not trusting me.'

'Of course I trust you…with one single exception,' Dio extended without hesitation. 'And I don't think we need to discuss that exception *again.*'

Ellie breathed in sharply. All she could taste was her own absolute defeat on the topic of Helena Teriakos. She was shaken and upset. But how did she persist with her accusations? She didn't want to destroy their marriage before it even got going. Helena was already working hard at doing that. Hard *and* successfully, Ellie reflected painfully.

And how could she possibly fight the other woman without evidence? Was she about to sink to the humiliating level of begging Sally Parkes to repeat Helena's malicious verbal attack at their wedding? The sad truth was that no spiteful comment could possibly prove her own infinitely more serious allegations against the brunette.

'As for the newspaper foolish enough to print that rubbish, I shall sue,' Dio continued with chilling cool. 'My lawyers tell me I can hang them out to dry, and hang them I will.'

Involuntarily, Ellie shivered. 'Why bother?'

'When anyone attacks you, they're attacking me. Your reputation is at stake. I will defend it.'

'Well, don't feel you have to on my account,' Ellie muttered limply. 'Sticks and stones and all that—'

'They'll settle out of court and print a retraction. They will also make some worthy charity a most handsome donation.' Dio gazed searchingly at the pale delicacy of her set profile and curved her even closer. 'And before I'm finished with them, they'll also reveal their source.'

Ellie glanced at him in sudden hope, and then her eyes fell again. 'Journalists never do that.'

'You'd be surprised what they do behind closed doors when the pressure is great enough,' Dio asserted wryly. 'How are you feeling now?'

'That…that I want to be on my own,' Ellie confessed ruefully.

Dio tensed.

'I'm sorry. I just do.' Gently detaching herself from him, Ellie rose to her feet. 'I'll go for a walk.'

'I'll come with you.'

Ellie skimmed him a pained glance. 'No.'

She could see his frustration, *feel* it. And she loved him so much. If she didn't she wouldn't be in so much pain. But she needed time to wind down and come to terms with what had happened between them.

Ellie took the path down the beach house. Once she reached the warm soft sand on the beach, she kicked off her shoes and walked along through the surf whispering onto the shore. The sun shone blinding silvered reflections on the sea. It was hotter than it had been on her last visit. But she loved the heat. It seemed to drive out the chill inside her.

Here they were on the very first day of their honeymoon and Helena had already practically torn them apart, she reflected with a shiver. Dio had indeed been outraged by such lurid invasive publicity. And, whether she liked the role or not, Ellie now knew that she had become Dio's Achilles' heel. He *was* a very proud man, and she didn't want him to be any less proud. But they had had yet another violent and destructive argument and she had got precisely nowhere. How many more could they afford to have before Dio decided that their marriage had no future?

Ellie was far along the beach, sitting in the shade of a rocky outcrop, when she saw Dio striding towards her with lithe, long-limbed grace. He was carrying a picnic hamper.

'I did ask to be on my own,' Ellie reminded him gently.

'You've been on your own for three hours, *pethi mou*.' Black eyes held hers levelly. 'Now you need to eat.'

'Did the book Nathan made the mistake of giving you tell you that too?'

His lean, strong face clenched. 'So I want to be with you…is that a crime?'

Involuntarily, Ellie softened. 'No, I want to be with you too.'

'Only not enough to come back to the villa.'

Ellie considered that point and sighed. 'I have to admit that sometimes I really get a kick out of making you run after me.'

Dio looked startled. Then an appreciative laugh escaped him. 'I have never heard a woman admit that before.'

'Don't be slow, Dio. I'm only admitting it because we're married.'

His shimmering smile turned her heart over, and Ellie finally reached a decision. Dio might not recognise Helena's capacity for malice, but men were slow to recognise female cunning and Helena was clever. More importantly, Dio seemed quite happy with the wife he had. He wasn't behaving like a male who had given up the woman he loved. Or was he simply more pragmatic than she was prepared to acknowledge?

A frown drew Dio's level dark brows together. 'What are you thinking about?' he demanded.

Ellie gave him an innocent look. 'You,' she said with perfect truth.

A look somewhere between male pleasure and wariness formed on Dio's bronzed features, sunlight turning his eyes into reflective mirrors. 'Your expression seemed rather hostile—'

'I was just thinking that I want us to hang onto our marriage,' Ellie assured him piously.

The wary edge evaporated. Dio was now free to rejoice in the happy notion that he was at the heart of her every thought. And, yes, she noted with surprise, he liked that idea. She watched the slumbrous smile slowly curve his mouth. Only then did she acknowledge that he was indeed the very centre of her world. Perhaps it wasn't a good idea to let him know that.

'These days you need to work really hard to keep a marriage afloat,' she added.

'But we don't *have* any problems,' Dio stated with a definite aggressive edge.

Ellie busied herself rooting about in the incredibly elaborate picnic hamper and concealed the amused glint in her gaze. He was keen to deny the possibility that they did have a problem. And, having vented her spleen in setting Ellie up for that newspaper article, what, realistically, could Helena possibly do to hurt either her or their marriage in the future?

'My reaction to that squalid newspaper article was unreasonable,' Dio announced with real vigour.

Ellie glanced up. 'Was it?'

'There's scandal in my background too,' Dio assured her.

'Stop trying to make me feel better,' Ellie told him drily.

'My grandfather was temporarily disinherited for marrying my grandmother.'

'Polly and Lefki's sister?' Ellie queried in surprise. 'For goodness' sake, why?'

'She was an island girl. Her father was a…' Dio hesitated. 'Well, he kept goats,' he completed, rather grittily.

'He kept *goats*?' Ellie gasped incredulously.

'Don't say it…' Dio warned.

But for the next few seconds Ellie was quite incapable of saying anything. Recalling the way she had once compared Dio to a goat-herd, she started laughing so hard she flopped back on the sand. 'I'm sorry, Dio…I just love it!' she told him chokily.

'I knew I could rely on you to be tactful.' Leaning over her, Dio gazed down into her beautiful laughing face, black eyes flaring to smouldering gold.

Ellie trembled and raised her fingers to trace his hard jawline. 'How hungry are you?' she whispered unevenly.

And with a ragged groan of very male appreciation, Dio shifted over her. His mouth swooped down on hers in a hot, sensual invasion that spoke for itself.

Having carefully explored the sauna and gym complex in the basement of the enormous London townhouse, Ellie wandered on to study the fabulous indoor swimming pool, her eyes just getting wider and wider.

'I think you like this place,' Dio murmured.

'Hmm…it looks even better than it looked on the video-tape the agent sent out to us,' Ellie confided.

'Then all we have to do is move in.'

Ellie spun round, her eyes lighting up. 'You love it too?'

'It seems to have everything, so we'll buy it.'

'It'll make such a marvellous family home!' Ellie threw both arms round Dio and then she frowned. Tilting back her head, she gave him an anxious, searching scrutiny. 'You're not buying it just to please me, are you?'

'Would I do that?'

'Yes,' she sighed. 'But this is where we're going to live. It's very important that you like it as much as I do. So give me your impressions.'

Dio shrugged. 'It'll make a terrific investment—'

Ellie groaned.

'The location *is* excellent—'

'*Dio!*' Ellie exclaimed in frustration.

He closed his arms round her, a slumbrous smile banishing his gravity. 'You rise to every bait there is, Mrs Alexiakis. I love the house…OK?'

'I'm sorry I made you go and see all the other ones, but I was scared we might be missing something,' Ellie admitted. 'Actually, the minute I saw this house on video I knew it was all my dreams come true, so I saved it to the last.'

Ellie climbed back into the limousine in a state of near bliss. They had been married for over a month now. They had spent three glorious weeks on Chindos, and Ellie had been so happy, she'd felt as if she was walking on air. She had been afraid that their return to London might take some of the magic away, yet, even though Dio was now frantically busy after taking so much time off, nothing had changed between them. They had shared so much more than a bed on the island: visits to Polly and Lefki's cosy little farmhouse, midnight swims, barbecues on the beach and so much laughter.

Now she was amazed that she had got herself in such a twist over Helena Teriakos. The brunette had taken her revenge with that newspaper article. Apart from the odd unavoidable social occasion, Ellie reckoned that the other woman was more or less out of their lives. Indeed, there was only one cloud in Ellie's world, and she knew it was a very selfish and unreasonable one.

She had a guy who would trail round a baby shop without complaint. She had a guy who acted as if the merest breathe of wind might blow her fragile little carcass away. She had a guy who *listened* when she talked, who was still sending her flowers after the wedding, and who phoned her in the mornings even if he was seeing her for lunch. A guy who was caring and supportive and absolutely incredible in bed. She was a really, really lucky woman. So wishing that Dio would fall madly in love with her as well was positively greedy.

Late that night, Dio strolled out of the bathroom in his penthouse apartment, towel loosely knotted about his lean hips, moisture still beading the curling dark tendrils of hair on his muscular chest. 'Ellie…there's something we need to talk about.'

Blissfully engaged in appreciating him, Ellie sat up in bed and smiled before she registered that his lean, dark features had a very serious cast. 'What's wrong?'

'There's nothing wrong,' Dio asserted wryly. 'I'm flying over to Paris to see Helena tomorrow.'

Ellie blinked in sheer shock.

'Naturally I'm hoping that this won't cause trouble between us,' Dio continued levelly. 'Since her father died I have been in charge of all Helena's business interests.'

At that second revelation, an appalled look froze Ellie's fine features. 'Why didn't you tell me that before?' she demanded.

'To be blunt,' Dio murmured steadily, black eyes challenging her now, 'I really don't think that a responsibility I accepted long before I met you is any real concern of yours.'

Ellie turned pale. That wasn't just blunt, that was brutal.

Dio released his breath in an impatient hiss. 'I want you to be rational about the fact that I meet up with Helena on a regular basis.'

'Rational…' Her husband met up with her most bitter enemy on a regular basis. That news was the equivalent of being slugged with a sandbag.

Dio came down on her side of the bed and reached for her hand.

Ellie snatched it back.

'Can't you even try to behave like a grown-up?' Dio censured with stark impatience as he sprang upright again. 'I accept that you felt insecure when we *first* got married—'

Ellie parted bloodless lips. 'Mr Sensitive—'

'But now you've had time to settle down—'

'You think so?' Ellie breathed shakily.

'I think you've got no choice,' Dio delivered with sudden harshness, surveying her with cool dark eyes.

'There's always a choice, Dio.'

'Not on this issue,' Dio contradicted. 'I will continue to oversee Helena's business holdings for as long as she wishes me to do so. Our meetings will also continue. She's a part of my life and you have to accept that.'

'That's not something I can accept.' Ellie lifted her head high, colour burning in her cheeks. Suddenly she was furious with herself. 'What an idiot I've been!' she exclaimed. 'All my life I've stood up for myself, but I wanted our marriage to work and I didn't want to tear us apart.'

'What are you trying to say?'

'You refused to accept that Helena threatened me and tried to bribe me into having an abortion.'

Dio raked long brown fingers through his tousled damp

black hair and groaned out loud. 'Oh, *please*, not that non-sense again!'

'You don't believe me. OK. Right. That's fine,' Ellie said jerkily, punching the pillows and lying down. 'Nice to know where your loyalty lies, Dio. Nice to know that you married me thinking I was a liar—'

'But kind of cute with it,' Dio incised gently.

'Don't try to make a joke out of something this important!' Ellie condemned. 'If you go to Paris tomorrow, I'm leaving you!'

Dio stilled. 'No way would you leave me—'

'Yes, I would! You trust her more than you trust me. So you make your choice,' Ellie told him bitterly. 'You get her out of your life, where she can't hurt us any more, or I'm moving out! If you can't give me one hundred per cent loyalty, I don't want you any more!'

'No problem,' Dio said softly.

Ellie listened to him walking out of the room, and then she leapt out of bed and hauled the door open. 'I *mean* it, Dio!'

Shorn of his towel and magnificently nude, Dio swung round and gazed back at her with outraged dark eyes. 'You do as you like, but I'm going to Paris and I won't be hurrying back.'

All the pain inside Ellie mushroomed. 'Dio...I'm *not* lying. Listen to me—'

Dio stabbed a powerful hand in the air. 'No, *you* listen to me! You don't own me. You don't tell me what I can do, where I can go or who I can be with. Is that understood?'

'That—'

'And when you've got this jealousy jag under control, call me. But don't leave it too long. After all, Helena is a lot of things you're not,' Dio murmured in derisive retaliation.

The angry colour drained from Ellie's complexion.

Dio said something vicious in Greek and strode back towards her.

Ellie slammed the bedroom door in his face and depressed the lock.

'Ellie!' Dio thundered. 'Open that door!'

Tears running down her face, Ellie crawled into bed again and curled up in a tight ball. 'A lot of things you're not.' Well, trust Dio to state the obvious. Only it wasn't a matter of that, was it? In temper, he had revealed his true feelings, and the horribly wounding comparisons he obviously continued to make. Ellie shivered, acknowledging that the furious row that had blown up had drawn more blood than she had bargained on. Her *own*.

Helena was rich, educated, classy, cool, controlled, clever. Her background was identical to his own. Of course, Dio admired and respected her. Unlike Ellie, Helena would have been a bride he could have been really proud of possessing.

'The English rely on love... It's more important to pick a life partner with intelligence,' he had told her that very first night on the beach. But what had intelligence had to do with their shotgun wedding? Ellie muffled sobs in a pillow. For the past few weeks Dio had been *very* good at pretending to be happy. All those years of smoothie womanising, she supposed wretchedly. In his heart, Dio knew she was a very poor but pregnant second best. And Ellie knew that *she* couldn't live with him knowing that...

CHAPTER TEN

SALLY PARKES' anxious face lit up with a hugely relieved smile the instant she saw Ellie walking across the park towards her.

'Thank goodness you didn't stand me up!' she gasped as she flew off the bench.

Ellie dug her hands into the pockets of her jacket. 'I really didn't want to meet up with you like this, Sally. I only phoned you because I need you to pass on a message to Dio. I appreciate now that that was wrong of me—'

'No! No way was it wrong!'

'It was,' Ellie sighed. 'I didn't want to write to Dio because I didn't know what to say…and I didn't want to speak to him personally. But I never should've involved you—'

Sally groaned. 'Ellie…Dio is frantic!'

Ellie frowned. 'Didn't you pass on my message?'

Sally gave her a wide-eyed look of wonder. 'Like telling Dio you were safe and happy and planning on a divorce was going to make him *less* frantic?'

Ellie flushed. 'It's for the best. Did you remember to tell him that I'll let him see the baby as much as he likes?'

'It wasn't quite the consolation you seemed to think it would be,' Sally responded. 'I mean the baby's not due for another six months.'

'Well, I can't help that,' Ellie muttered flatly. 'Is he still in Paris?'

'No, according to Nathan he spent that week looking for you. Then he went off on the most dreadful drinking binge. Nathan dragged him home to sleep it off in our spare room—'

Ellie stopped dead. 'The most dreadful…*what*? Say that again?'

'OK. Sequence of events: Dio wakes up and finds your note…right?'

'I don't know. I'd gone by then. I thought he would have gone on to Paris.'

That very same night Ellie had thrown a few things in a bag and had crept out of the apartment, determined to avoid another harrowing confrontation with Dio. She had lost enough face in that earlier scene. All she'd had left was her pride. And she would only keep her pride by staying at a safe distance from Dio until she'd got her emotions under better control.

'Well, if you'll excuse me for saying so, most husbands wouldn't get dumped and just go on like it was an ordinary day,' Sally said rather drily. 'Even stubborn, macho ones like Dio have *some* feelings.'

'Look, you're on his side because you don't understand and you know him better than you know me—'

'No, to be honest, I've just been totally gobsmacked by the way Dio's been carrying on,' Sally shared helplessly. 'I never, ever thought Dio would be sleeping off a hangover in our spare room.'

'So he spent the first week looking for me…' Ellie was hopelessly hungry for every tiny detail she could glean.

'How do you think we found out you'd gone? He phoned Nathan. He was in a real rage at that point. You were lucky to stay lost,' Sally confided.

'I don't understand him drinking…'

'He just went to pieces the second week. He sat in that apartment just drinking himself into a stupor, and Nathan was worried sick about him. Dio doesn't *do* things like that. You've really gutted him, Ellie…and I think that if you'd decided you wanted out, you could have been a lot more considerate about the way you did it.' Sally gave her a challenging glance.

Ellie tilted her chin, although her colour had risen. 'I told him I was leaving.'

'He didn't think you *meant* it!'

'It just wasn't working for me.'

Sally slowly shook her head with a bemused frown. 'The day of your wedding, I honestly thought you were crazy about him, and when we had lunch the week after you got back from Chindos it seemed even more pronounced. It was "Dio *this*…Dio *that*…"'

'I am crazy about him,' Ellie mumbled ruefully.

Sally fell still. 'Then why the heck are you doing this to him?' she demanded.

'I suppose you've told her absolutely everything, Sally,' Dio's dark growl intervened with sardonic grittiness. 'The big search, the unmanly despair, the buckets of booze and self-pity…'

Both women whipped around. Sally hot-cheeked, Ellie pale as death.

But Dio had eyes only for his estranged wife. As Sally backed away with a guilty grimace, his dark, deep-set gaze welded to Ellie's pinched and shaken face and stayed there. 'I've really messed up, haven't I?'

'Dio…can I give you just a little hint that that is not the right attitude to take?' Sally prompted with a wince.

'No…you don't know what's going on here and you're not going to,' Dio informed the redhead with bleak satisfaction. 'Isn't it fortunate that when I'm drunk I talk in Greek? No, Sally. What this is all about will be one mystery you never manage to solve.'

'Helena…' The redhead murmured with measured female superiority before she drifted off.

Dio flinched, and his bronzed skin lost colour.

'Considering that Sally set me up for you, you weren't

very polite,' Ellie said unevenly. 'I'd never have come to meet her if I'd known you were planning to show up.'

'Sally tortured me with questions when I was at my lowest ebb. And even the worst sinners get their moment to speak on judgement day,' Dio breathed with an attempted lightness that was laced with strain.

Ellie stared back at him, her heart thumping like a hammer behind her ribs, her eyes full of pain.

'Don't look at me like that…it makes it so much worse,' Dio groaned.

Instantly Ellie looked away. Yes, of course he would see how she felt. He always had been able to see inside her. Crushed by the awareness that even her love was obvious to him, she made no demur when he curved a surprisingly tentative arm round her and walked her away. The limousine was collecting a parking ticket beyond the park gates. Dio felt guilty. Obviously he felt guilty. He knew how much he had hurt her. And what was to be gained in trying to avoid a meeting that he was determined to force on her?

In the silence, Ellie stole a glance at him as the opulent car purred through the slow-moving traffic. In two and a half weeks he had contrived to lose quite a bit of weight, she noted. And now it was as if a divide the width of an immeasurable abyss separated them. She had never dreamt that Dio could look as downright sombre as he did now. The end of a marriage. Well, he wasn't so superficial that he was about to celebrate, particularly when she would be giving birth to their child in a few months' time.

'It's OK,' she said flatly.

'Nothing's OK,' Dio countered harshly. 'Where have you been staying?'

'A B&B out in the suburbs. I didn't feel like the hassle of looking for somewhere more permanent yet,' she admitted stiltedly.

'Didn't it occur to you that I'd be going out of my mind with worry?' he demanded with sudden force.

'Why should it have?' Ellie sighed. 'I've been looking after myself for a heck of a long time. I'm not the helpless type.'

The silence seemed to thunder.

'No,' Dio conceded gruffly. 'But you can make *me* feel helpless.'

Her brow furrowed. 'Oh, you mean you looking for me and not being able to find me?' she gathered. 'There was no need for that. I wasn't planning to vanish for ever, or anything stupid like that. I made that clear in my note—'

'*Ne*…yes: "Dio, I'm sorry, but I had to empty your wallet to get some cash."' Dio quoted the opening line of her note flatly. '"Marrying you was a mistake. I'll be in touch. Don't look for me…but then I don't suppose you will, will you?"'

'I don't see why you have to quote the whole thing,' Ellie protested, feeling even more foolish and exposed by that verbatim delivery. 'I was upset and I didn't have much time. You're lucky you *got* a note!'

Instead of exploding at that rather unjust stab, Dio froze in his distant corner of the back seat. 'I guess you're right about that.'

Ellie sent him a slightly bewildered glance, registering the raw tension etched into his bold, dark profile. 'I honestly didn't think you might get worried until later—'

'Much later. It took you eleven days to phone Sally,' Dio reminded her tautly.

'I had some stuff to work out.'

Like how to live without him, how to exist with a ceaseless craving that got more agonising with every passing hour, how to close out the flawed memory of good times that could only have been utterly superficial on his terms. Great sex, she had assumed on their honeymoon, but dared she assume even that now? For her, making love with Dio had been earth-shattering sensational perfection. But how did she *really* know what it had been like for him? He had been flatteringly insatiable, but maybe he was just rampantly oversexed, she reflected grimly.

'So what have you been doing with yourself?'

'I've been making plans.' Actually, she had done nothing but walk around all day, sit in the public library when she got tired, eat for the baby's sake and use up boxes of tissues at night. However, it would have taken torture to force an admission like that from her.

She had climbed out of the limo before she realised that they had not arrived at Dio's apartment building. Her bewildered gaze absorbed the tall, imposing Georgian townhouse they had viewed the same day they'd parted. 'What on earth are we doing *here*?'

'I went ahead and bought it.'

'You did say it would be a good investment,' Ellie recalled as she opened the front door.

'I was joking.'

Had he been? Ellie had spent two and a half wretched weeks picking apart everything Dio had ever said or done, seeking evidence with which to bolster up her resistance level. Waste of time, she now conceded gloomily. One look at him, even in this strange, muted mode he appeared to be in, and she was back where she had been that first night on Chindos. Mesmerised. Poised there in his exquisitely tailored charcoal-grey suit, he was so gorgeous he still took her breath away.

'What did you do with the rest of my things?' Ellie asked to fill the simmering silence.

Dio frowned. 'They're here.'

'Where?'

'In the main bedroom.'

'Oh, right. You didn't tell the staff that I wasn't coming back.' Ellie started up the grand staircase.

'Where are you going?'

Ellie barely glanced over her shoulder. 'I might as well get my stuff packed up while I'm here,' she said briskly. 'It'll save me another trip.'

'Ellie…' Dio began heavily. 'I know I've acted like a total four-letter word—'

'Dio, I don't need to hear that sort of stuff.' Ellie marched on up the staircase at an even faster rate of knots. 'This is nobody's fault. We only got married because I was pregnant, which was just plain stupid…OK? It's no big deal, is it?'

'No big deal?' Dio repeated thickly.

Ellie could not resist the urge to turn and peer down at him from the landing, but he had swung away. 'Look, all I'm trying to say is I don't want to talk about it. There's no need.'

Dio appeared in the dressing room doorway while Ellie was frantically trailing clothes off hangers. Her hands were all thumbs. What on earth had possessed her? In another minute she would either crumple into humiliating hysterical tears or she would seize him by the throat and ask him how he could possibly prefer Arctic Woman to her.

'Helena *was* behind that disgusting tabloid attack on you…'

Ellie stilled, and then suddenly jerked round, eyes very wide.

Dio stared back at her with tormented dark eyes shimmering with strain, his hands clenched into powerful fists by his side. His vibrant skin had a greyish cast.

'I suppose she came off that pedestal you had her on with a real shocking crash…' Ellie's heart felt as if it was cracking right down the middle, and she felt that if she didn't keep on talking she might be at serious risk of starting to sob. Everything she had never wanted to see was etched in Dio's face. His appalled reaction to Helena's true nature.

'I didn't have her on a—'

'I'm sorry, Dio. But you know a woman would have spotted her for what she was a mile off! But then…' Ellie altered direction hurriedly, not wishing to come across as spiteful 'Isn't it comforting to know that she was that determined to get you back?'

'Only because…only because of who I am and what I have.'

'Yeah, well,' Ellie managed with a sickly smile. 'Be honest. You valued those same things in her. All that background and breeding and money.'

Dio just closed his eyes and bowed his proud head. 'I don't expect you to forgive me for refusing to believe you.'

'Good. I wasn't going to make the offer.' Ellie turned back to the built-in units which blurred in front of her eyes. 'I understand that you thought that she was above all that kind of thing, and that you're feeling pretty bad now you know the truth…how *do* you, by the way?' she prompted with sudden curiosity.

'A journalist sang like a canary bird. Helena had had you investigated.'

'I could have told you that.'

'She set up a meeting with a reporter and handed over the file. She gave it on the understanding that the article would vilify and humiliate you.' Dio's dark, deep drawl roughened tellingly. 'She was too arrogant to even *try* to cover her tracks.'

'Maybe she thought it would be more of a risk to trust somebody else with that file.' Tears were inching down Ellie's cheeks, but she kept on hauling garments blindly off hangers as she struggled to get a grip on herself.

'Did you see the interview I gave about you?'

Ellie's wet eyes widened with bemusement. 'No…'

'I hoped it would bring you out of hiding. I knew you had promised to meet Sally today, but she warned me that she'd had to fight to get you to agree,' Dio disclosed tautly. 'And when you would only set a date a whole week in advance…frankly, I thought there was little hope that you would actually turn up.'

'I wouldn't have done that to Sally. She's a nice person.'

'When I faced Helena with what she had done, she kept on lying very convincingly for a long time. Then I mentioned the malice Sally had heard her spitting at you on our wedding day—'

'Isn't it wonderful the way you believed everyone *but* me? That journalist? Sally?' Ellie condemned with tremulous but very fierce bitterness.

'I honestly could never have imagined Helena capable of such behaviour,' Dio framed grittily. 'That is…until two weeks ago, when I confronted her and she finally lost her temper because she realised that she had lost.'

'She didn't *lose*, Dio. She won all the way,' Ellie contradicted flatly, her tears drying on her cheeks now. 'We didn't have much to start out with…and by the time she'd finished we had nothing. But don't you kid yourself that she was the one *most* at fault!'

'I know where the blame lies. I know I let you down and made you very unhappy. You hate me, don't you?'

'Some of the time…like right now, *yes*!' Ellie suddenly snapped as she rounded on him, her green eyes emerald with anger. 'She really scared me that day with her threats. She'd have done anything to persuade me into getting rid of our baby! She sneered at my mother, she insulted me every way possible and you wouldn't even *listen*.'

Dio moved forward. 'Ellie…I—'

'Shut up!' Ellie interrupted furiously. 'I was a total idiot to marry you in the first place! I was very upset that day—'

'You had every right to be. All I know is that I have never been closer to violence than I was when confronting Helena two weeks ago,' Dio revealed with raw force. 'The manner in which she spoke of you almost drove me to assault!'

'Really?' Ellie was quite happy to rein back temper long enough to relish that enervating detail. 'So does that mean that there's *not* going to be a reconciliation?'

Dio stared back at her blankly.

'You're not planning to marry her after me, then?' Ellie rephrased.

'Are you unhinged? *Marry her?*' Dio exclaimed incredulously. 'She's a cold, vicious bitch!'

'Well, it took you a lifetime, but in the end you got there. Congratulations,' Ellie said very drily. 'Could you get me a case?'

'A case?'

Ellie was possessed by the need to keep busy. Dio was getting to her and she had been determined that he was not going to get to her. That five-letter word labelling Helena as beyond the pale, for all her background, breeding and brilliance, had blown a small hole in Ellie's defences. She moved forward and then almost fell over the mound of clothing heaped round her. She looked down in astonishment at what appeared to be a whole heap of Dio's suits.

Sidestepping them, she attempted to brush past Dio. He closed his hand over hers. 'You've got to hear me out!' he grated rawly.

'You didn't hear *me* out, did you? No, when I was trying to state my case either I was insane with jealousy or off my trolley with being pregnant! And shall I tell you something, Dio? Right now, I'm near *my* personal edge!' Ellie vented with ringing honesty. 'Let…go…of…me!'

Dio released her with a jerk. Dark colour scored his stunning cheekbones but it was the savage pain in the depths of his dark eyes that shook her. 'I am more sorry that I have hurt you than you will ever believe,' he breathed raggedly.

Pale and trembling from that charged exchange, Ellie went off in search of a suitcase. It was mad, it was *crazy* to keep on trying to pack in the midst of such emotional turmoil, but she couldn't bear to see Dio in so much pain; she really couldn't! All over the head of that evil witch, who had almost sucked him in like a boa constrictor! Ellie shuddered as she banged through the closets she recalled touring two and a half weeks earlier. Locating the designated luggage storage, she grabbed up a case.

'Let me take that...' Dio took it from her again.

'You know...you don't feel it now, but sooner or later, you'll realise what a lucky escape you've had,' she muttered half under her breath, and hurried back to the master bedroom suite that they would now never share.

'Ellie...please sit down so that we can talk,' Dio urged, sounding almost pathetically humble. 'I need to tell you about Helena.'

Ellie was so appalled by that confession she sank down on the side of the bed before her legs gave out beneath her. If he needed a shoulder, why did it have to be hers? Then she understood. He wanted to make a complete confession. Nothing less would satisfy his over-active conscience. So he was about to drag out personal admissions that would very probably rip her heart out and depress her for the next thirty years.

Dio regarded her warily and very slowly set down the case. He cleared his throat. 'I—'

'Will you keep it short?' Ellie begged without pride.

Dio got even tenser. He looked so absolutely miserable her heart went out to him. She had to face it now. He had really loved Helena. He might now be repulsed, but he *had* loved her.

'My father first told me that Helena would make me a wonderful wife when I was five.'

'*Five*...five years old?' Ellie yelped. 'What age was she?'

'Eight.'

'Five...dear heaven, that's like brainwashing!' Ellie said in disgust.

'My grandparents died in a car accident when my father was still very young. He was brought up by his father's family. You must understand that my father was made to feel very much ashamed of his mother's more humble ancestry.'

'So he was raised to be a real snob?'

Dio nodded.

'And he wanted to be sure you didn't let the side down?'

Dio nodded again.

'So you were indoctrinated from a very early age to believe that Helena was your future.'

'A future I kept putting off.' Dio breathed in deep. 'I could never admit even to myself that I didn't like Helena—'

'You didn't...*like* Helena?' Ellie interrupted in astonishment.

'Did you find her a warm, inviting personality when you first came in contact with her on Chindos?'

'*No*, but—'

Dio's jawline hardened. 'I could never fault her behaviour. Her every accomplishment was continually paraded before me, and she is very accomplished. It was instilled in me that I had to marry her.'

'So you decided you'd marry her and have a mistress to supply the warmth she so conspicuously lacks.'

Recognising her scorn, Dio dealt her a wry look of reproach. 'Such marriages are not uncommon in my world. Until I met you, I didn't realise what I might be missing.'

Ellie sighed. 'I can't believe that.'

'OK...so there have been a few women in my past,' Dio conceded, in distinctly charged understatement. 'But not one of them got to me the way you did. We had that one magical night and then I blew it. But I couldn't stay away from you—'

'So you married me and blew it again,' Ellie slotted in painfully.

Dio crossed the carpet and hunkered down to look up into

her wan face. He tried to reach for her hands. She put them behind her back.

Dio's mouth quirked. 'The night you told me that you might be pregnant, I realised that I was in love with you—head over heels in love.'

'You would tell me *anything* to keep a hold on our baby, wouldn't you?' Ellie mumbled with a sob in her voice.

Dio's beautiful dark eyes shimmered. He unpeeled her hands from behind her back and held them fast in his. 'My biggest mistake was not telling you how I felt that night in my apartment,' he told her rawly. 'I knew then that I would *never* marry Helena, and that's when the guilt kicked in. Then she phoned after we had made love and I felt even worse!'

A little shard of hope pierced Ellie's emotional turmoil. Now she was locked onto his every facial expression, his every word. She remembered the way he had reacted after that phone call that had interrupted them. 'You should have explained about her then!'

Dio released his breath in a rueful hiss. 'I didn't want to upset you. I also didn't feel right talking to you about her at that stage,' he admitted. 'First I needed to see her and tell her that I had fallen in love.'

'Is that what you told her?'

Dio gave her a questioning look. 'What else would I have told her? I knew she wouldn't be too impressed by the announcement, but it was the truth. When you came out of Nathan's surgery, I really was pleased about the baby, but I'm afraid my guilt over Helena ruined what should've been a very special occasion.'

'I can understand how you must've felt.'

Dio grimaced. 'No, you can't. I was very angry with myself for letting that understanding with Helena drift on for so long. I believed that I was letting her down very badly,' he confessed. 'But if I felt bad then, it was nothing to how I felt when I actually faced Helena in Paris.'

Ellie frowned, her hands tightening their hold on his. 'What did she do to you?'

'She played me like a violin,' Dio grated with a perceptible rise of blood to his bronzed complexion as he recalled that meeting. 'She said that she would be a laughing stock, and that no man would ever marry her if I didn't. But she kept on reiterating that of course she understood and forgave me...I was there for *hours*!' He gave a feeling shudder of recollection. 'I felt like a complete bastard. I honestly thought that I had ruined her life.'

'She's a terrific actress...or maybe...maybe she really does love you, Dio,' Ellie suggested unhappily.

Dio gave her an aghast look. 'You've got to be joking!'

'I love you...why shouldn't she? She's known you a lot longer—'

'Ellie...' Dio vaulted upright and carried her with him, his dark eyes ablaze with intense pleasure and relief at that simple confession. 'Ellie, darling, darling, gorgeous Ellie...' he breathed raggedly. 'If I was a poor man, Helena wouldn't give me the time of day. She's obsessed with marrying a wealthy man worthy of her illustrious family tree. She simply could not credit that I could be *wet* enough to start talking about love...she said I could have you if I wanted you—'

'As a mistress—'

'And I said I loved you too much for that.' Dio brushed her hair from her brow with gentle fingers, so much tenderness in his warm dark eyes that Ellie finally believed that he loved her. 'But when I confronted her two weeks ago, she was much more honest. She assured me that if a better matrimonial prospect had come along, she'd have been married years ago!'

'I'm glad she was angry rather than hurt,' Ellie admitted.

'Even after all she's done to you?' Dio demanded with naked incredulity.

Ellie stretched up to loosen his tie in a very proprietorial way. 'I can be very generous when I've won,' she shared rather smugly.

Dio caught her up in his arms and crushed her mouth with hungry intensity beneath his. As he buried his face in her hair, she quivered, feeling as weak as a kitten.

'I never dreamt that hearing a woman telling me that she loved me could mean so much,' he confided with roughened sincerity.

'And to think that if you had told me rather than Helena,' Ellie could not resist remarking, 'that you *loved* me, I'd never have left you.'

'Don't you ever leave me again,' Dio warned fiercely.

'I wouldn't dream of it…' She gave him a teasing glance, rejoicing in this new intimacy of mutual trust which allowed her to do and say what she liked. 'Not if it means you're likely to drown in buckets of booze and self-pity…'

Dio brought her down on the bed and pinned her there, black eyes alight with immense appreciation. 'You are a minx.'

'I've got your number now…you'd better watch out…'

'I adore you,' he husked feelingly. 'But you're not going to boss me around.'

Ellie slid loving fingers into his luxuriant black hair and whispered, 'Kiss me…'

And he did.

Then he lifted his head with a glint of mocking comprehension in his keen gaze. 'Pregnant, barefoot and in the bedroom, *agapi mou*,' he told her slumbrously.

'You're misquoting.'

A slashing smile curved Dio's mouth. 'It was a statement of intent.'

'Well, if we're negotiating, what about all that ''You don't

tell me what I can do, where I can go or who I can be with''
stuff?' Ellie enquired playfully.

'I just knew you would remember every word of that.'

'Because I reserve the *right* to.'

'You could have been a real *agent provocateur* in the
maintenance department.' His brilliant dark eyes roamed over
her and glittered with desire and boundless satisfaction. 'It's
far safer keeping you in my bed.'

'I've got to admit the family cave's pretty comfortable,'
Ellie sighed happily, sparing her impressive surroundings a
look of approval.

And, with a husky laugh of appreciation, Dio kissed her
breathless and proceeded to demonstrate the fringe benefits
of sharing that family cave.

Ellie tucked her infant son, Spiros, back into his exquisite
cradle. At four months old, Spiros was just adorable. He had
hair the colour of silver-gilt and dark, dark eyes—an arresting
combination of his parental genes. When he was sound
asleep, he looked like a little angel.

The past twenty-four hours had been hectic, Ellie acknowledged. Dio had thrown a huge party in London to celebrate
their first wedding anniversary. Then they had flown out to
the island and spent the day entertaining Dio's relatives, who
had now all either gone to bed or travelled home again.

A whole year. Ellie could still hardly credit that she had
been married to Dio for that long. And the magic had not
only lasted but got stronger, she reflected, with glowing eyes
and the slow, steady smile of a contented woman.

Working conditions in the maintenance department of Alexiakis International were now as good as they could get.
Dio had never quite recovered from the sight of Ellie plug-
ging in that floor-polisher and then fainting dead away. Ellie
had had no trouble convincing him that the cleaning staff

deserved more generous remuneration for their rarely appreciated efforts.

Ellie returned to their bedroom to slide into a very sexy confection of gold satin, a special order fashioned along the lines of a flamenco dress. Setting off to the beach house, after having instructed a maid to deliver her surprise note to Dio, Ellie took with her the glossy magazine that gushingly described Helena Teriakos' wedding the previous week. She hadn't had a chance to finish reading the article yet.

The bridegroom was a blue-blooded aristocrat, with a title a yard long. Helena looked positively triumphant. However, it was rumoured that the non-attendance of the groom's powerful family signified their outrage at his choice of bride. On their terms it seemed that Helena was just *not* acceptable. Her family tree only went back a couple of generations, while theirs went back several centuries. But, studying the photo of the bridal couple, Ellie reckoned it would be a successful marriage. Helena's husband looked like Arctic Man, his cold blue eyes, tight mouth and rigid carriage.

Slinging the magazine aside with a smile, Ellie lit all the candles and switched off the lights. Then she began to dance to the music she had put on to accompany her display. This was her private anniversary present to Dio. She loved to surprise him. And when she caught the door opening out of the corner of her eye, she had to work really hard not to be drawn into looking directly at him.

When the music rose to a savage crescendo and ended, then she looked, and just burned beneath the sheer, glittering hunger and appreciation in Dio's stunning eyes.

'You are just *so* easily impressed!' she teased.

Dio hauled her into his arms just like a caveman. She was shivering with excitement. Sensual anticipation ran like fire through her veins, leaving her weak as he slowly crushed her into the hard, muscular heat of his big powerful body. 'So we're back where we started out—'

'Plus Spiros.'

'I never forget our son for a single moment…or the very beautiful, very sexy and wonderful woman who gave him to me,' Dio intoned with impressive intensity. 'I think I love you even more now than I did a year ago.'

Ellie closed her arms round him tightly. 'You make me so happy.'

'That's what I'm here for…' Somewhat distracted by his need to seal his mouth hotly to hers while at the same time backing towards the bedroom, Dio finally contrived the feat and got them both as far as the bed. 'And to give you *this*…before you dare to suggest that I rushed down here in the most uncool manner imaginable just because I could not wait to go to bed with you!'

Ellie gazed down at the exquisite diamond eternity ring he was now sliding onto her finger and she just melted back into him. 'Oh, Dio…it's *gorgeous*.'

'It's engraved with the date we first met.'

'Gosh, you're getting so romantic!' Ellie sighed.

Dio looked exceedingly smug. 'You may have set up the candles and the note, but I brought the champagne and had a rose put on the pillow.'

Ellie's eyes widened and her face fell. 'You mean my note wasn't a surprise?'

Dio winced, registering the error of one-upmanship.

A slow, misty smile curved Ellie's generous mouth and she pushed Dio gently back against the pillows. 'I just love you to death when you drop yourself in a big tactless hole,' she told him helplessly.

'I don't quite follow that.' Dio surveyed her with adoring eyes that had a definite hint of bemused relief.

Ellie arranged herself sinuously round him, knowing he didn't understand. But that anxious look he had worn when he had feared that he had hurt her feelings just turned her heart inside out. 'Great minds think alike,' she whispered soothingly.

'You are just amazing...' Dio curved her so close she could hardly breathe.

But then, at the moment, breathing was not half as important as the urgent need to seal their love in the most intimate way of all. Ellie meant to tell him just how amazing he was as well. But the electrifying combination of passion and joyous happiness now unleashed ensured that she didn't tell him until the following morning.

Jacqueline Baird began writing as a hobby when her family objected to the smell of her oil painting, and immediately became hooked on the romantic genre. She loves travelling and worked her way around the world from Europe to the Americas and Australia, returning to marry her teenage sweetheart. She lives in Ponteland, Northumbria, the county of her birth, and has two teenage sons. She enjoys playing badminton, and spends most weekends with husband Jim, sailing their Gp.14 around Derwent Reservoir.

HUSBAND ON TRUST

by

Jacqueline Baird

CHAPTER ONE

LISA raised her hands above her head, stretched, and yawned. With only a fine cotton sheet covering her body she felt decadent and deliciously languorous, due entirely to the expert administrations of her very new husband last night.

The door to the *ensuite* bathroom opened and Lisa's gaze automatically turned to the man walking into the bedroom. Six feet plus of pure masculine perfection, he was naked except for navy silk boxer shorts hugging his lean hips. He was also strikingly handsome, his strong dark features cast in the classic mould of the Greek male of legend, and he was hers, Lisa thought on a swift, involuntary breath. His thick black hair was still damp from the shower, a stray droplet of water easing its way down his strong throat and lower, to be captured by the curling black body hair that dusted his broad chest.

A lazy smile curved her full lips. 'Alex,' she said softly. Just saying his name was a pleasure. Sometimes she felt like pinching herself to make sure the last few weeks had not been a dream.

In the process of pulling on a crisp white shirt, he turned his dark head and his eyes clashed with hers. 'I know that tone of voice, wench, but forget it. I have to be in London by eight-thirty.' He grinned and continued dressing, stepping into grey tailored trousers.

'Spoilsport.' She pouted, and moved across the bed, allowing the sheet to slip to her waist. 'Do you have to leave so early?' she queried huskily, and was rewarded

5

by Alex's renewed attention. He walked over to the bed and, bending down, brushed his mouth over hers; her lips parted, hoping to prolong the kiss, but abruptly he straightened up.

'Not this morning, Lisa, I have no time.' And, turning, he crossed the room, picked up his jacket and eased himself into it. 'I told you that yesterday, when we drove up here. Today I have meetings lined up in London, morning, afternoon and late into the evening,' he flung over his shoulder, as he picked up his wallet and keys from the dressing table. 'And from what your stepfather said last night, you have a busy day ahead of you.'

Lisa sighed; Alex was right. They had arrived back in England last night and travelled straight to her home in Stratford-upon-Avon. On the death of her mother nine months ago, Lisa had inherited the major share in the family company, Lawson Designer Glass and her mother's job as managing director. Her stepfather, Harold Watson, was the marketing director.

'You're right; I know,' Lisa grudgingly conceded, and, sitting up, she swung her long legs over the side of the bed. She grasped the sheet and wrapped it around under her arms, sarong-style and stood up, flicking a glance at Alex as she did so.

'Amazing! You hide yourself in a sheet.' A dark brow rose quizzically. 'I have seen everything many times, no?' he drawled, and, turning his back on her, he picked up a silk tie, and slipped it under his shirt collar.

Lisa hesitated and, realising how ridiculous it was to cover herself in front of him, she let the sheet fall to the floor. A month ago she would have died if any man had seen her naked, but Alex had cured her of almost all her inhibitions. Her gaze lingered on his broad back; the exquisitely tailored jacket hung perfectly off his wide shoulders, the few tendrils of black hair curling over the collar an endearing dent in a picture of sartorial elegance, she thought with a grin. At that moment Alex turned back round and caught her staring.

His deep brown eyes flared for an instant, as his glance swept her from head to toe. Lisa was a tall girl, five feet nine inches, but perfectly proportioned, with high, firm breasts, a narrow waist, slim hips and legs that went on for ever. The three weeks of their honeymoon, which they had spent sailing around the Mediterranean on Alex's yacht had given her skin a golden glow, the sun adding natural streaks of platinum to her long blonde hair.

'I guess the honeymoon is over and work beckons for both of us,' she said huskily, hiding a smile. She could tell he was rethinking the need for an early departure. From the moment she had met Alex he had awakened a sensuality in her twenty-three-year-old soul that she had not known she possessed. She had taken one look at him in the lounge bar of a local hotel and had fallen in love on the spot. It had been the same for Alex; they'd spent the next day together and by the evening he had proposed marriage. She would have slept with him there and then, so overwhelming was the passion she felt for him. But Alex, with iron self-control, had insisted they wait until they were married. Four weeks later they had been. Her wedding night had been a revelation: Alex was the perfect lover—he had fulfilled all her wildest dreams, and then some!

'I have a feeling our honeymoon will never be over,' Alex declared throatily, and, stepping towards her, he lifted his hand to stroke the soft curve of her cheek. The simple touch was enough to make her pulse race and her stomach clench with excitement. His dark eyes holding hers, his hand trailed tantalisingly down to her shoulder and traced over her breast and waist before hauling her hard against his long length, his head sweeping down to capture her mouth with his own. The kiss was deep and devouring, and when it ended Lisa stared up at him, totally enslaved, her heart bursting with love for him.

'But for today it is,' he added, letting her go. 'We don't have time to discuss it now, but you are going to have to sort something out about Lawson's. I want you with me, Lisa, not tied to a desk.' He paused. 'Well, not unless it is my desk,' he qualified, his dark eyes dancing with wicked amusement.

'Naughty man!'

'It is not me who is stark naked!' he drawled mockingly and, with a swift pat on her derrière, he added, 'Go shower, and I'll go make the coffee.'

Ten minutes later, having showered and wearing a long blue towelling robe, Lisa strolled into the kitchen of the elegant ten-roomed house that had been her home for as long as she could remember. Alex was leaning casually against the worktop, a coffee cup in one hand, a mobile phone in the other, talking in rapid-fire Greek. He glanced across at her as she walked in and indicated the coffeepot with a wave of his cup, but didn't stop talking.

Lisa poured herself a cup of coffee and sat down at the breakfast table, her blue eyes lingering on his rugged profile. His black hair was swept back from his broad forehead; thick black eyebrows arched over deep-set brown eyes; his nose was a straight classic line and his mouth a sensual invitation—perfectly sculptured lips, the bottom one slightly fuller than the top. But at the moment, they were tight with anger.

The honeymoon was certainly over. Alex Solomos the entrepreneur was back. Lisa knew he was the owner of a large company, Solomos International, which his father had started as a small construction firm in Athens. But since Alex had assumed control the company had expanded into a variety of different interests worldwide, all successfully.

Taking a sip of her coffee, it struck Lisa quite forcibly that although he was her husband she did not really know a lot about the man she had married. He was Greek, an only child. Alex had told her that his parents had divorced when he was seven and his father had married again and again, almost wrecking his business in the process. Until Alex had stepped in and taken control after the third divorce, insisting his father must make a prenuptial agreement in any future marriage. Two more marriages had ensued, which was why, Alex had explained, *they* must have a prenuptial agreement. He could not have insisted on his father doing so and then refuse to do so himself. Lisa had agreed, and had quite happily signed on the dotted line.

Lisa had met his mother on her honeymoon, when Alex had berthed the yacht in the harbour at Kos and they had spent the night in a luxurious villa overlooking the sea with the elegant silver-haired woman. In her halting English she had told Lisa Alex was named after Alexander the Great. The old lady had explained her family was partly of Macedonian descent, the same as his namesake, a man who had conquered the whole of the known world centuries ago, including the island of Kos.

A vivid mental image of Alex, his naked body entwined with hers on the large bed in the villa, flooded her mind. She had teased him about Alexander the Great. 'I hope you don't take after the man in every respect, because, according to most historians, although the man was married he was gay.'

Alex had responded with, 'Then I must prove other-

wise, wife,' and had proceeded to make love to her until
they were both satiated by passion. Afterwards she'd quite
happily conceded he *was* great, in at least one department…

Thinking about it now brought a dreamy smile to her
lovely face. She lifted the coffee cup to her mouth and
drained it, her glance straying once again to Alex's long
body. She could easily see the connection. He was a stunningly attractive man, and with the same type of ruthless
energy and drive that conquered worlds. Which, when she
thought about it, made it all the more amazing that he had
fallen in love with her and married her… In the last three
weeks Alex had introduced her to the world of the senses,
as well as to the sophisticated lifestyle of some of his
wealthy friends.

Suddenly he clashed the phone down, and Lisa's eyes
widened at his thunderous expression. 'Bad news?' she
asked.

'My father.' He strolled towards her, running a hand
through his thick black hair. 'But nothing for you to worry
about.' He dismissed her enquiry with a shake of his dark
head. 'I must leave. It is a two-hour drive to London,
providing the traffic is not snarled up. I don't have time
to waste.'

Lisa stood up and slipped her arms around his waist,
the familiar warmth of his body, the husky male scent of
him making her heart flutter in her breast. 'I'll see you
tonight.'

He glanced down at her upturned face, a wry smile
curving his firm lips. 'No. My last meeting is scheduled
for seven-thirty this evening, and tomorrow morning I
have an eight o'clock breakfast meeting. You stay here,
pack what you need, and have it sent to the London apartment. We will make that our base for now. But we will
have to discuss something more permanent. Get your own

work up to date and then I suggest you consider employing someone to take your place. Talk it over with Harold. You seem to be fond of your stepfamily. Something I've never managed to achieve,' he concluded dryly.

'Yes, yes, I am. Harold worshipped my mother, and he has always been brilliant with me. But…' She got no further.

'Good,' Alex cut in. 'Spend the evening with him; he will be glad of your company.' His dark head bent and he brushed the top of her head with his lips, before curving his hands around her upper arms and putting her away from him.

Lisa was not sure she liked the arrangement. The thought of even one night without Alex was hard to bear. Although she knew it made sense. 'Are you trying to get rid of me already?' she tried to tease. But she realised Alex was already gone, if not in body then certainly in spirit.

'No. But I have neglected business long enough. As long as you work, we are going to have to get used to spending time apart. Not desirable, but in the present circumstances inevitable.' And, slipping his hand into his pocket, he withdrew a bunch of keys and removed one. 'Here is a key to the penthouse. I will inform Security to expect you.' He handed her the key. 'I'll see you tomorrow.'

'Yes.' Lisa had only been to his apartment once, on their wedding night, when Alex had introduced her to the joys of love for the very first time. She would have reminded him but he didn't give her the chance.

He glanced at his gold Rolex. 'I must go. Make sure you are in London by six tomorrow night, Lisa. We are dining with my father at seven thirty.' And, with a brief kiss on her open mouth, he spun on his heel and walked out. Lisa followed him into the hall, in time to see him open the front door and disappear through it without a backward glance.

'Was that the door?' a gruff voice queried from the top of the stairs.

Lisa turned around 'Yes, Harold.' She smiled up at the elderly man descending the staircase. 'Alex has just left. Give me ten minutes to get dressed and then I'll get breakfast.' Running lightly up the stairs, she gave her stepfather a little peck on the cheek as she passed him.

Later, when the two of them sat side by side at the breakfast table, the bacon and egg Lisa had cooked long since eaten, they lingered over their coffee, talking about work.

'Mary, your PA, has been wonderful,' Harold said firmly. 'In fact, no disrespect to you, dear, but I think the woman could almost handle your job.'

'Thanks very much. Glad to know I was missed,' Lisa drawled mockingly.

'I didn't mean it like that, Lisa, but you are very much a new bride, and your husband has to come first. You should be at Alex's side, not sitting here with me.'

'Yes, I know. Alex said pretty much the same. As it is, I won't see him until tomorrow—pressure of work…' She shrugged her shoulders and, with a rueful smile at Harold, she pushed her chair back from the table and stood up. 'Tonight I'll be dining with you but right now we'd better get to the office.'

They took Harold's car, a blue Jaguar, and after pulling up in the courtyard of Lawson Designer Glass, Lisa slipped out and viewed her surroundings with a contemplative air. The firm had been the brainchild of her parents. She remembered her mother describing to her how she had met Peter Lawson at a dance in Oxford, and had fallen in love on the spot. He had been the only child of the main partner of the Lawson Lee Glass Factory in Stratford-upon-Avon, a long rambling place that sat alongside the river. Her mother had been an accountant. They had married, and by the time they were thirty, and Lisa had arrived, her grandfather and the silent partner Lee, had died.

Her parents had transformed the factory into one of the leading producers of Tiffany lamps and designer glass in Europe. The Lee heirs had had no interest, other than the twice-yearly dividend, and had made no objection to the change of name to Lawson Designer Glass. Her mother had looked after the financial side, and her father, the more artistic, had simply loved designing. Unfortunately he had died in a car crash when Lisa was nine. Two years later her mother had married Harold Watson, a man who had worked for the firm as sales manager for several years and was a true friend.

Lisa had worked here in the school holidays, and then after graduating from university full time. She loved the place; it had been her whole life so far, but now she had Alex. Juggling a husband and a business would be no easy matter. There were going to have to be some changes.

In fact the changes had already started with the death of her mother last year from stomach cancer. Three short months after the diagnosis her mother had been gone. But when she was dying she'd confided in Lisa; she had loved Peter completely, they had been soul mates, and she had thought it her duty to carry on with his work after he died. Her marriage to Harold, she'd admitted, had not been built on the same kind of love.

Harold had been alone ever since his first wife had left him with a small son to look after years before. That small son had been a twenty-seven-year-old man, with his own

commercial estate agent business in London, by the time
Lisa's mum had married Harold. As her mum had later
confessed, it had been more for companionship than love
on her part, but she had hoped Harold would be a good
father figure for Lisa.

In that respect her mother had been right. Lisa adored
Harold, and the brief visits of his son Nigel had not really
impinged on her life. Except for the year when she was
sixteen and Nigel had made a pass at her. But, as she'd
already been a big girl, she had quickly disabled him with
a hard knee to the groin, and it had not been a problem.
On the subsequent rare occasions they had met they'd
managed to uphold a polite façade.

Smoothing the fine linen of her short skirt down over
her hips and adjusting the collar of her jacket, Lisa entered
the building, a worried frown pleating her brow.

Her mother had died in Saint Mary's Hospice, and her
dying wish had been that five per cent of Lawson's be
gifted to the hospice. She'd had no time to change her
will to encompass this, so Lisa had received fifty-two per
cent of the company, and Harold had got the house. He
also owned thirteen per cent of the company—shares he
had accrued in bonus payments over the years in a scheme
her father had set up. The will had passed probate the
week before Lisa had married and against her better
judgement, she had done as her mother requested the
Friday preceding her wedding. The trouble was, she had
yet to tell Harold, because she knew he would have insisted on making the donation himself. But realistically
she could not see it being a problem as between them
they still controlled the company. Now, Lisa had no more
time to dwell on the subject, as various members of the
staff greeted her return with huge smiles and a few suggestive remarks.

Mary was already in the office when Lisa walked in. A widow of forty with two teenage children, she had worked for the firm for seven years, and as Lisa's PA for the last year.

'Welcome back,' Mary said, looking up from behind her computer terminal. 'I won't ask if you had a good honeymoon; I can see it in your face.' She grinned.

Lisa had invited all the workforce to her wedding. It had been a traditional service in her local church on a Monday afternoon. The reception afterwards at Stratford's leading hotel, apart from the fact that the best man had taken off immediately after his speech, had been a great party. Lisa and Alex had finally left late in the evening to spend the night in Alex's London apartment, before flying out to Athens the next morning to board his yacht at the port of Piraeus. Thinking about it now brought warmth to her cheeks.

'Yes, it was very nice,' Lisa responded primly, and then winked. 'My husband is all that, and more!' Crossing the room, she lingered for a moment at the picture window, glancing at the view of the River Avon and fields beyond. It was a clear, blue-skied June day. A day for lovers to take a picnic and explore the countryside hand in hand. 'And why I am here working when Alex is in London, I do not know,' Lisa said out loud, before sitting down on the chair behind her desk and glancing up at Mary. 'I must be mad.'

'Madly in love,' Mary quipped, placing a sheaf of papers on Lisa's desk. 'Priority messages, okay?'

Two hours later, musing over a cup of coffee, Lisa realised that Harold was right, all the work was up to date except for a few items that demanded her personal attention.

'Congratulations, Mary, you've done a great job in my absence,' she surprised the other woman by remarking.

Mary beamed back at her from her desk. 'Thank you. It's good to know I'm appreciated, but can I ask you something?'

'Sure, ask away.'

'Well, there have been rumours, now you're married…' Mary hesitated. 'Well, rumours you might sell up.'

'I promise you, Mary, the rumours are completely without foundation. In fact, I was about to ask you if you would like to take on more responsibility. A promotion; doing what you have been doing the past three and a half weeks. Obviously we'll hire someone else to take over a lot of your existing work. And it would mean a substantial increase in your salary.' Lisa mentioned a sum more than double Mary's present salary. 'Does the notion appeal?' Lisa asked, grinning at the stunned look on Mary's face.

'Appeal? I would love it.'

'Then get on to the agency and see if you can set up some interviews for Monday, for someone to replace you.'

'But what about you?' Mary asked. 'I mean, you love your work.'

'Oh I'm not giving up all together. But, let's face it, most of the work I have left to do today could as easily be done from my laptop at home, or wherever Alex and I happen to be.'

'Which reminds me,' Mary chuckled. 'Have you checked your E-mail since your wedding? I've had a couple of messages from a Jed Gallagher in Montana on the office computer which were obviously meant for you.'

Lisa grinned from ear to ear. 'Jed! I must get back to him.'

'Don't forget you're a married woman now,' Mary reminded her. 'Alex Solomos might be drop-dead gorgeous, but you know what they say about Latin types. Jealous to the bone. What would he have to say about your on-line romance?'

'You don't understand.' Lisa grinned at her assistant. 'Jed is nothing like that. He's almost like a brother to me. I can remember the first time we linked up. Mum had bought me a new computer for my eighteenth birthday, and I got on-line. One day, whilst flicking through a list of subscribers to one of the chat rooms, I came across Jed. His profile said he was tall, blond, nineteen, and lived on a farm in Montana. I sent him an E-mail and he replied the next day, and that was it. We've been mates ever since. I can confide my deepest thoughts to him and he responds in kind. But it's completely platonic, and as for Alex minding—the man hasn't a jealous bone in his body.'

Something Lisa had been made very aware of the second week of their honeymoon.

They had berthed in Monte Carlo for the night and Alex had taken her to a glittering party on the yacht of a friend of his father's. They had been dancing on the deck to the music of a well-known quartet when a man had cut in and, much to Lisa's chagrin, Alex had agreed with alacrity. Seconds later she'd been in the arms of an overweight man, who had to be sixty if he was a day. And, looking over his shoulder, she had watched Alex talking apparently very seriously to a sultry eyed, black-haired woman, whom Lisa had thought vaguely familiar, until her partner had enlightened her: Fiona Fife, a model, who'd been staying on his yacht till the weekend.

No, if anyone suffered from jealousy, it was herself, Lisa thought moodily.

'Cheer up, girl, it might never happen.' Harold's voice cut into her thoughts as he walked into her office. 'I'm taking you out to lunch.'

'There's no need. I'm having dinner with you tonight, remember?'

'No you're not! I've been thinking about it all morning. You staying here tonight while Alex is in London. It's not natural for a newly married couple.'

'It's pressure of work, Harold.' Realistically Lisa knew she would have to get used to spending days at a time without her husband. His business took him all over the world. He had offices in New York, London, Athens and Singapore. And they had not really discussed yet where they would eventually settle down.

Lisa chewed on her bottom lip, her blue eyes troubled. For three weeks they had done nothing but make love, eat, sleep, and occasionally party, in the few ports where Alex had bumped into friends. Today they were back in the real world, and look what had happened: they were apart.

'Rubbish, Lisa!' Harold remonstrated. 'Mary can manage.' And, turning to Mary, he commanded. 'Get on the telephone and book a seat on the five-thirty train to London.' Then, turning back to Lisa, he added, 'Food first, and then we'll discuss your future working arrangements.'

'Actually, I already have—with Mary. I've offered her a promotion,' Lisa informed him with a smile.

'There you are, then. Give that husband of yours a nice surprise.'

The idea was tempting. Alex had made all the running in their relationship. Only this morning he had teased her about still being shy because she'd had the sheet wrapped around her. Perhaps it was time she showed him she could match him for sophistication. She could let herself into the apartment, slip on her sexiest negligé and seduce him when he got back from his meeting. Just the thought made her stomach tremble, an impulsive action, but why not?

'I'll do it,' she declared firmly, and felt her colour rise at the knowing looks Mary and Harold gave her. Leaping to her feet, she added, 'Book the seat, Mary, and come on, Harold. If you're taking me to lunch let's go.'

After lunch, Lisa did some shopping, and then went back home and packed her bags. Finally, before leaving for the station, she spent half an hour on her laptop, E-mailing Jed. He told her he was back home for the summer after completing his fourth year at college. She was glad for him, because she knew he'd had quite a fight with his brothers to even get to college; they had not approved and had wanted him to stay on the farm. She told him all about the wedding and the honeymoon, and grinned at his last reply.

'Your marriage sounds as if it's made in heaven, as does your husband. I'm only sorry it wasn't me! Only joking. Hey, I'm destined for an even better relationship, I'm sure.'

Lisa sincerely hoped he was.

What was that? Lisa shot off the bed. The sound of a door closing somewhere had awakened her from a light doze. Alex must be back, she thought happily, and, smoothing the white negligé down over her slim hips, she cast a quick glance at her reflection in the mirrored wall and grinned. The astute businesswoman in the smart suit had been transformed into a sexy siren. Lisa hardly recognised herself. Alex was in for a surprise! Barefoot, she left the bedroom and padded along the hall.

'What do you wish to discuss so urgently?' The deep

velvet voice was instantly recognisable to Lisa as she approached the living room door, and sent a delicious quiver along her nerve-endings.

Then the content registered, and she swore under her breath. Damn! He had someone with him. Served her right for falling asleep, she thought ruefully. But what with getting up at the crack of dawn, working all morning, packing several suitcases, and then travelling down to London, by the time she had unpacked, showered, and had anointed her body in aromatic oil, she had lain on the bed for only five minutes before drifting off to sleep. So now what?

Well, he was her husband. She had to stop being so shy. The sitting room door was very slightly ajar and Lisa reached for its handle to push it open. But she stopped her hand in mid-air. She glanced down at herself and grimaced. She had left her long blonde hair loose, to fall in soft curls past her shoulderblades. As Alex liked it... But she doubted he would appreciate the surprise of her presence if she strolled into the living room in her diaphanous white nightgown, the lacy bodice barely covering her breasts, when he had someone with him. Then she heard the other voice and froze.

'Just a friendly chat, old boy. I thought you could give me an update on the riverside project, and a drink wouldn't go amiss.'

Unfortunately, Lisa recognised that other voice, and her heart missed a beat. The nasal tones of Nigel, her stepbrother, were unmistakable.

'Scotch on the rocks?' Alex prompted, and she heard the rattle of ice on glass before Alex added. 'How did you know I was in town?'

'Simple. I rang the old man this morning, and he told me Lisa was back at work and you were spending the night in London. Can't say I blame you. Three weeks with only the ice amazon for company would have tried the patience of a saint—and you're no saint, as we all know!' A nasty chuckle completed Nigel's speech.

Lisa stiffened in anger at her stepbrother's insult, but was slightly reassured when Alex defended her.

'The lady you are referring to, happens to be my wife, and her name is Lisa. When you insult her, you insult me. You would do well to remember that.'

Lisa grinned. That's telling him, she thought, and she almost walked in on the two men at that moment. But still she hesitated. What she could not understand was how Alex knew Nigel so well. To her knowledge they had only met twice. Once at the hotel when she herself had met Alex for the first time, and again at their wedding. Yet Nigel was a visitor in Alex's penthouse, and seemingly was quite at home.

'Hey, no offence, but we're both men of the world. Which reminds me. Does the delectable Margot know you're in town for the night, alone?' Nigel's now slightly slurred tones cut into Lisa's troubled thoughts like a knife. Who was Margot?

'No, and get to the point of this visit. I must ring Lisa soon.'

'Got you on a short rein has she? Don't worry; stick her in front of a computer and she won't notice where you are. The term ''computer nerd'' was invented for the likes of Lisa. I bet she took her laptop on your honeymoon.'

Why, the insulting little toad! Lisa fumed. As it happened, she *had* brought her laptop with her this evening, to use tomorrow, but that did not make her a nerd. Nigel was only jealous because she was computer literate and he couldn't tell the difference between the Internet and a hairnet! Once more she reached out for the door, and stopped again as Alex responded.

'The only lap she was on top of was mine,' he drawled. Lisa felt the colour flood her cheeks and as quickly vanish as her new husband added, 'and that is how it is going to stay. Her working days are numbered, I can assure you.'

Deciding herself to cut back on her working life was one thing, but to have Alex arrogantly say she had to, was quite another! She loved Alex to bits, but she had no intention of letting him walk all over her. As she listened, her anger turned to horror.

'Well, that is really what I wanted to ask. I'm having a bit of a cash-flow problem, and I need your confirmation that the sale of Lawson's will go through as soon as possible. The river frontage is a goldmine, as you and I know; Shakespeare's birthplace is the ultimate tourist trap. The quicker you have the land, and I have my finder's fee and a share of the selling price, the quicker I can invest in your development plans for the site.'

Lisa leant back against the wall, her face grey beneath her golden tan, her legs trembling. She could not believe what she was hearing. Could not bear to believe it. Alex, the man she had fallen head over heels in love with, the man she had married, the man she had thought loved her, was in league with her no-good stepbrother to try and buy Lawson's and redevelop the site. She stifled the groan that rose in her throat and listened, praying it was all a mistake.

'I don't think so. I don't need any investors.' Alex's clipped tone gave her hope. Now he would denounce the whole plan. But she was wrong.

'But your man promised I could have stake in it.'

'I'll need to check, and if that is so, then of course you

can. But could you afford to? Even with your father's share of the sale? It will be *your father's share* I take it?'

'Yes. The old man doesn't need the money. He has a fat pension to look forward to. As I'm his only son and heir, it's immaterial whether he gives me the cash now or when he dies.'

'Has Harold agreed?'

'I haven't asked him yet. But he will, he never refuses me anything.'

'Lucky you. But, as I understand it, Lisa owns fifty two per cent and your father thirteen per cent; the other thirty five per cent is held by the heirs of the original partner in the firm. You're hardly going to get a fortune. In fact...' The deep, slightly accented voice dropped lower and paused tantalisingly. 'My wife is madly in love with me. She may simply give me the company without any necessity on my part to acquire the other forty-eight per cent.'

Lisa bit hard on her bottom lip to stop the cry of outrage bursting forth.

'Why you sneaky devil.' Nigel burst out.

'Enough. I would not dream of accepting a gift of that size from a lady, not even my wife. I don't believe in being beholden to anyone, man or woman,'

'Sorry. No, of course not. But are you sure Lisa will go along with your plan for Lawson's? Her mother flatly refused to sell a year ago.'

'A year ago Lisa had not met me. Now she is my wife, and soon, hopefully, the mother of my children. I can safely say she will not have the time or the inclination to continue at work. She will do as I say. You have nothing to worry about Nigel. You will get yours; I promise you that.'

Lisa closed her eyes, her whole body shivering with

pain and anger. The shocking discovery that her husband
was about to betray her, not with another woman but with
her stepbrother, had cut to the very centre of her being.
It had razored her nerves and turned her into a seething
mass of conflicting emotions.

Alex's love, the wedding, *everything* had been one big
sham. Alex and Nigel were plotting between them to take
over Lawson's. To redevelop the site! Over her dead
body, Lisa vowed.

The week her mother had been diagnosed as having
cancer, an approach had been made to buy Lawson's. Lisa
racked her brains but she could not remember the name
of the company. It certainly had not been Solomos
International and there had been no mention of redevel-
oping the site; developing a partnership had been the impression given. Her mother, Harold and herself had briefly
discussed it at the time. Her mother had decided against
it; Lawson's Designer Glass was to stay a family firm as
a memorial to Peter, and, as it happened a few months
later, also to herself.

Lisa shuddered. The pain was waiting for her, she
knew, but with brutal determination she blocked it out and
allowed rage, fierce and primeval, to consume her mind.
For a second she was tempted to burst into the living room
and confront the two rats who were plotting against her…

Instead, ice-cold reasoning prevailed. She did not need
to hear any more, and silently she returned to the master
bedroom.

CHAPTER TWO

LISA started towards the dressing room, her first thought to get dressed and go. Then she realised the futility of such a gesture. In order to leave she would have to confront Alex, and she was not ready to do that. She doubted she ever would be.

She shivered anew, not with pain but remembered pleasure. Alex, her husband, her lover! He only had to look at her and she went weak at the knees. She and a few million other women, she tried to tell herself. And how many of the other, faceless women had known the wonder of his lovemaking, the seductive power of his caress, his kiss, the magnificent strength of his sleek, hard, toned body?

Lisa groaned in disgust at her own weak will and, swinging around, glanced at the bed. Very soon now, Alex would ring the house at Stratford-upon-Avon and discover from Harold that she had left to join him in London. Panicking, she crossed to the large patio window that opened out on to the balcony and slid it open. Stepping out, she took a few deep breaths in an effort to calm down. Tomorrow was Mid-summer's Day and tonight was clear and light, although it was ten o'clock. A panoramic view of London stretched out before her, tinged with gold as the evening sun slid towards the distant horizon. Much the same as her confidence in her marriage was sliding into oblivion, she thought bitterly.

She squared her shoulders; self-pity was an emotion she despised. She had to think, to do something, but what? It

was still warm; she could spend the night outside. Fool!
Alex was bound to look for her.

Slowly she turned and reluctantly entered the bedroom
again; her eyes slid back to the huge bed, the imprint of
where she had catnapped on the coverlet clearly visible.
Her head jerked up at the sound of a door closing. Nigel
departing, maybe? Any minute now, Alex would make
the phone call and discover her whereabouts. Lisa did the
only thing she could. She lay back down on the bed.
Perhaps if she pretended to be asleep Alex would not
wake her. She prayed he would be fooled, because, if not,
she had no confidence in her ability to resist the magnetic
pull of his virile sensuality. Even knowing Alex had only
married her for a business deal, knowing what a wicked,
callous swine he was, was still no protection against the
force of his potent personality.

Closing her eyes, Lisa feigned sleep, but her mind spun
with images of the past. It had seemed so simple not two
months ago, when she had fallen in love with Alex at first
sight. Fate, Kismet…

It had been Harold's birthday and Nigel had arrived at
their Stratford-upon-Avon home unannounced. He had insisted his father and Lisa had mourned long enough for
her mother and that he was taking them both out for a
meal at the top hotel in the area.

With hindsight Lisa realised she should have guessed
there was something funny going on, because experience
had taught her that Nigel only ever visited his father if he
wanted something, usually money. His appearance in
Statford-upon-Avon on his father's birthday had been the
first time she had seen him since her mother's funeral. For
Harold's sake, she had agreed to the dinner date, and at
nine in the evening the three of them had been sitting in

the hotel's cocktail bar, enjoying after-dinner coffee and Cognacs, when Alex had strolled into the bar.

Lisa would never forget the moment when she had looked up and seen Alex Solomos for the first time. Her body had reacted as if in shock. She'd forgotten to breathe! He was an attractive man, but it had been more than that. Something about him had called out to her innermost being; her stomach had churned and her heart had raced out of control. She'd felt as if she had been struck by lightning.

Wearing a black dinner suit and a brilliant white dress shirt—a perfect foil for his olive-skinned complexion— and standing head and shoulders above every other male in the room, he'd crossed to the bar in a few lithe strides. She'd watched as he'd ordered a drink, before turning around and resting his superbly muscled long-limbed body against the bar. His dark gaze had casually scanned the room his eyes bored.

Lisa, wide eyed and wondrous, had found she could do nothing but stare. Then she'd blushed to the roots of her hair when his deep-set eyes had met hers, and then travelled on down over her body, widening in obvious appreciation on the length of her long legs. She'd been wearing a short black sheath dress and reclining on a low sofa, inadvertently exposing rather more leg than she'd realised. His head had lifted, making eye contact again, before swerving to take in her two male companions. A cynical dismissive smile had twisted his firm lips, and he'd continued his perusal of the room.

Gorgeous, but arrogant with it, Lisa had thought, and, nervously tugging at the hem of her dress, she'd forced herself to look away, taking a swift swallow of her coffee to hide her scarlet face. She had experienced sexual chemistry before, but this was ridiculous.

'Well, I'll be damned.' Nigel had said softly. 'The great man himself, Alex Solomos.' Turning to Lisa, he had added. 'Do you know who he is?'

'I haven't the slightest idea,' she replied coolly, fighting down an urge to ask Nigel to tell her all about the stranger. Along with the urge to mentally strip the man naked!

'You must have heard of Leo Solomos, his father?'

'No, should I have done?' she queried.

Nigel's pale eyes narrowed rather warily on her face. 'Probably not, unless you read the gossip pages in the gutter press. Leo Solomos is a Greek tycoon. But he's rather better known for the number of ladies he has married. The man at the bar is his son. He keeps a much lower profile, but it's well known in financial circles that he's the power behind the throne. The old man would have gone bust years ago, simply because of alimony payments, if it wasn't for Alex Solomos taking control of the company.'

Lisa sneaked a furtive glance back at the man from beneath the mask of her long lashes; she could well believe Nigel. Alex Solomos, with his impressive height and magnificent build, looked every inch the dynamic, powerful businessman.

'Wait here you two, I'm going to introduce myself. This is too good an opportunity to miss.' And, to Lisa's horror, her stepbrother approached the man at the bar, and started to talk.

'Harold, does Nigel know that man?' she asked after a few minutes, only too well aware of her stepbrother's penchant for pushing in where he was not wanted.

'Well, he does now, Lisa.' Harold quipped, with a nod in the direction of the bar.

Lisa looked up, and her stomach lurched. Nigel was returning, with the stunning man in tow. Helplessly, she stared at his face. He was incredibly attractive, with classically sculptured features, a mobile, sensual mouth that was twitching in the beginnings of a smile.

'Nigel suggested I join you for a drink. I hope you don't mind?' He turned all the force of his megawatt smile on Lisa, no trace of his earlier cynicism present.

'You are a friend of his?' she managed to ask, trying not to stare, and wondering how such a superior example of the male species could possibly like Nigel.

'Not really. Apparently he recognised me and took pity on a man drinking alone. But seemingly we do have a mutual business acquaintance.' His voice was low and a little husky, with just the slightest trace of an accent. 'Allow me to introduce myself. Alex Solomos.'

The hand he held out to Lisa was large and tanned, and when his fingers curled around hers, the heat and strength he generated seemed to sizzle right through her whole body. Lisa looked up into a pair of heavy lidded dark brown eyes, and the intensity of his gaze held her mesmerised.

'Lisa—Lisa Lawson,' she stammered, and she did not breathe again until he let go of her hand.

Turning to shake Harold's hand, he said, 'And you are Nigel's father, I believe. There is no mistaking the likeness.'

The three men talked and ordered another round of drinks while Lisa tried hard not to stare at Alex. She was a businesswoman, not some lovestruck teenager, but it was no good. A heady excitement made her blood fizz like champagne in her veins. His hard handsome face, his eyes, drew her gaze like a magnet, and his voice sounded like a caress to her over-sensitive nerves.

Apparently he was in Stratford for the weekend. He had been to see a performance of *Richard III*.

'I confess I left at the first interval. My English is good, but not so good I can understand the language of Shakespeare.'

Somehow his confession that he had walked out on the play rather than pretend he understood it endeared him to Lisa even more, and from that moment on she was a goner...

Alex left half an hour later for a dinner engagement, and Lisa found herself giving him her address. He arranged to pick her up at ten the next morning, in the pretence that she would act as his guide around Stratford for the day.

When he called for her the next morning, casually dressed in blue denim jeans and a black cashmere sweater, she had simply stared.

'You're even more beautiful than I remembered.' His brown eyes darkened with an unmistakable message in their depths, leaving her more flustered than she had ever been in her life. He helped her into the passenger seat of a lethal-looking red sports car and then slid into the driver's seat. But before starting the car, he turned to her with dark, serious eyes.

'There is something I have to tell you, Lisa.' For one heart-chilling moment she thought he was going to tell her he was married. 'I am the boss of Solomos International. Is that going to be a problem for you?'

The relief was so great, Lisa beamed. She was a confident, intelligent young woman, she dressed in designer clothes or snappy casuals, and she could mix in any strata of society. She never gave it much thought, but actually, on paper, she was also wealthy. He had no need to worry; she wouldn't be intimidated by his money. It was in the sexual stakes she was a novice, nowhere else. 'No, of course not. I am the boss of Lawson's, but I never mix business with pleasure,' she said, daringly for her. And she was rewarded by a reciprocal brilliant smile.

'Good. Beautiful and sensible. A winning combination.'

It was the best day of Lisa's life. They walked hand in hand by the river and around the streets of Stratford-upon-Avon and talked about everything and nothing. He insisted on driving out of town for lunch. They shared a ploughman's lunch in the garden of a small country pub, Alex teasingly feeding her a small cherry tomato with his fingers. As Lisa opened her mouth his glance fixed on her face, his eyes dark and hot, and when his fingers touched her lips, she felt a surge of desire so strong she trembled and could not hide it from him.

'It is the same for me, Lisa,' he had told her in a deep, husky voice, and when she blushed, he added with a tender smile, 'The sexual chemistry between us is electric, but have no fear, Lisa, I will not take advantage of you; it's not my style.'

For the rest of the day they enjoyed themselves like a couple of children. By Sunday evening, she was so captivated by him that when he took her into his arms and kissed her, and told her he was going to marry her, her answer was a joyous yes. The following weekend he stayed at her home in Stratford, and formally asked Harold for her hand in marriage. Three weeks later they were married.

Thinking about it now, Lisa cringed in shame at her own naivety. She should have guessed Nigel had had a hidden agenda when he'd introduced her to Alex. But she'd had little experience of men. As a teenager she'd been taller than most of the girls at her school, and had been tormented about being gawky. So when other girls had been dating, Lisa had concentrated on her studies.

Later, she had never seemed to have the time for socialising. In fact her best friend, if she was honest, was Jed,
whom she'd never met in person.

'Lisa, Lisa, darling.' Lost in her own troubled thoughts,
she hadn't been conscious of Alex entering the room. She
heard his deep voice and closed her eyes. How she was
going to get through the night, she had no idea, and for
a fleeting instant she wished she could turn the clock back
to this morning. If she had stayed in Stratford, she would
have been perfectly happy, but by coming to London she
had discovered more than she'd ever wanted to know.

'Lisa.' Alex's deep, husky drawl feathered across her
cheek. She felt the mattress depress and knew she had no
chance of pretending to sleep.

'Alex,' she murmured, turning over on to her back and
blinking her bright blue eyes, as though she had just
woken up.

'This is a surprise.' He gave her a narrow-eyed look.
'Unexpected, but very flattering. When did you arrive?'

Was it her imagination or was there more to the seemingly innocuous question? Did he suspect she might have
overheard his conversation with Nigel?

'What time is it?' She answered his question with one
of her own. Her stomach was churning with a mixture of
distress and desire.

'Ten-thirty.'

'Oh, I got here at eight, bathed and changed, and I must
have fallen asleep an hour or so ago.' She tried to smile,
badly shaken by his close proximity and the proprietorial
hand he curved around her naked shoulder.

Slowly his lips parted over brilliant white teeth, in a
broad smile with just a tinge of smugness. 'Couldn't stay
away from me, hmm?' His gaze lingered on her mouth.

'Something like that,' Lisa whispered, when in reality

she felt like lifting her hand and decking him! She felt furious, and sickened at having been taken in by him so easily. His head lowered and his mouth moved closer and it took all her will-power not to take a bite out of the sensuous lips that closed over hers.

'I need a shower. Come and join me,' Alex husked some moments later.

'What, and waste all the obscenely expensive body oil I have applied for your benefit?' she tried to tease.

'There is something very satisfying about a woman who will go to so much trouble for her man,' Alex drawled, his dark eyes gleaming with an equally teasing light. 'Give me five minutes to shower, and then I am at your mercy. I expect to be thoroughly seduced.'

'Of course. Why else would I be here?' Watching the arrogant set of his broad shoulders as he walked across to the bathroom, she wished she had the courage to tell him to go to hell. Far from seducing him, she felt like strangling him. She was wild with anger, but deep down she knew his lightest touch could send her senses reeling, and his kiss made her ache for more.

As soon as she heard the shower running, Lisa leapt off the bed. No way was she going to be lying there waiting for him like some harem slave! Restlessly she crossed to the patio window and gazed blindly out. How had she got herself in such a mess? She had been fooled by Alex's sophistication, his stunning good looks and the kind of blatant sexuality that had set up an answering need in her own untried body. It hurt so much to discover Alex had not been honest with her. She had given him her trust, completely and unconditionally, and all the time he'd been in league with Nigel.

In one way she thought it might have hurt less if there had been another woman. At least Alex could have claimed to be overtaken by passion. But to have married her in cold blood to pursue a business deal showed a degree of ruthlessness, a contempt for her as a person that she could not come to terms with.

'I'm all yours, darling.' Alex's deep voice broke into her musings and turning around, she gave a strangled gasp. He was totally naked and completely unconcerned as he strode across the room and lay down on the bed, and patted the space beside him. 'Don't keep me waiting, or I might just fall asleep. I've had a hell of a day. But the night is certainly looking better.' He grinned. 'Be gentle with me, won't you?'

It was the grin that did it… Her blue eyes flashed to his, and she saw the gleam of amusement in the deep, dark depths of his brown eyes, along with a glitter of sexual anticipation. The bastard! she thought. I'll show him. Crossing to the bed, she stripped her nightgown over her head and standing proud and naked, she asked, 'Where would you like me to start first darling, top or bottom?'

Without waiting for his answer she draped herself over him, catching his head between her hands. Her mouth fastened on his and she kissed him with all the rage and passion of a woman cheated by love. *Heav'n has no rage, like love to hate turn'd, Nor Hell a fury, like a woman scorn'd.* The quotation leapt into Lisa's mind, and in that moment she knew it was true.

She did not want his tenderness; it was false anyway. Deliberately she nipped his full lower lip between her white teeth, and then dropped lower to bite at his strong neck. She was like a woman possessed in her rage, and Alex's deep, throaty chuckle only incensed her further. She felt his arm close around her waist. His other hand slid between their two bodies to capture one full breast, and rolled her aching nipple between his finger and thumb. She groaned out loud and retaliated by tonguing on his male nipple in a passion of her own, straddling him with her long legs trapping his. She felt his burgeoning arousal and delighted in it.

'So you want to play rough, my lovely Lisa?' Alex husked.

She lifted her head and her blue eyes blazed down into his eyes, which were dark with sexual need. 'You have no idea how rough,' she whispered, the breath exiting her body in a rush as he raised his head and sucked one of her taut nipples into his mouth. Lisa raked his chest with her nails and strained back. Alex laughed, and twisted his hand in her long hair, his lips meeting hers, his tongue delving deep into the hot, moist depths of her mouth while he moved his body against hers. His other arm wrapped around her like a steel band.

Lisa wriggled against him. She was so hot, so furious, and perspiration beaded her skin, but even in her anger, when Alex swung her beneath him, she opened her mouth to give a helpless moan. In a tangle of arms and legs they rolled around the bed, Lisa determined to be the dominant one, but Alex not about to let her.

They battled for supremacy as they kissed, bit and caressed in a storm of unbridled passion, each seeing who could give the other the most pleasure, and finally they came together in a wild, hungry mating that took them both to the heights of ecstasy. Lisa cried out at the intensity of it, and her cries mingled with Alex's as his body shuddered in spasm after spasm of prolonged pleasure.

Afterwards, when Alex lay by her side in total exhaustion, Lisa knew this had been the best ever, and also the worst. The worst because it had revealed her deepest fear:

she could not resist Alex; even in her rage and anger she
felt love.

Alex stirred, and, putting a possessive arm around her
shoulder, he said, 'If I didn't know I am your only lover,
I might be suspicious of your new-found aggressive sexuality.' And with the pounding of his heart almost back
to normal, he added, 'But I knew the moment I saw you
that you had a deeply sensuous nature and it only needed
the right man to reveal it.'

Lisa glanced sideways at him. 'And you're the right
man?' She'd meant to sound sarcastic but instead the
breathless tone of her voice sounded as if she agreed with
him. Filled with shame at her own behaviour, she quickly
looked away.

Alex chuckled. 'Of course.' Tucking her firmly under
his arm, he yawned widely. 'Remind me to leave you
alone more often, if tonight's episode is to be the result,
hmm?' He yawned again.

She stared at him. He looked like some great slumber-
ing lion lying on the bed, his eyes half closed, his broad
chest rising and falling in rhythm to the deep beat of his
heart, his mouth curved in a satisfied smile, content and
assured of his masculine virility.

In that moment Lisa did not know whether she wanted
to hit him, or hug him. Instead, to her horror, she heard
herself ask the one question that had tormented her for
the past few hours. 'Do you really love me, Alex?'

'After what we have just done, need you ask?' he murmured, already half asleep.

But sleep did not come so easily for Lisa. She was
tormented by the thought that Alex and Nigel were plotting together. But, seduced by the warmth of his body and
the protective arm around her shoulder, slowly Lisa felt
her anger began to drain away. Maybe she had been too

hasty in her conclusion. It was perfectly possible her first meeting with Alex had been a set-up, but that did not necessarily mean that what had happened next had been a lie.

Lisa turned on her side and examined her sleeping husband. In repose he looked younger than his thirty-five years, his black hair tumbling in disarray across his broad forehead. She reached out and brushed the offending lock of hair back, but Alex did not stir. Sleeping the sleep of the innocent. But was he?

Sighing, Lisa turned on to her back and gazed at the ceiling. Perhaps she had overreacted. She loved Alex, and up until tonight she had been sure he loved her. He hadn't been able to wait to marry her. Thinking about it now, Lisa decided his haste to marry her could not have been solely for business reasons. He could easily have waited a few more weeks, so it had to have been because he had wanted her. In fact, she probably had nothing to worry about. The solution was in her own hands. If, or when, she was approached to sell her company and asked to agree to flatten it—which was worse—she would simply refuse. If Alex made any comment then, and only then, would she discover the absolute truth.

Her decision made, she closed her eyes and tried to sleep. If she was being honest with herself, she knew she was taking a coward's way out by deciding to wait, rather than confront Alex with what she had overheard straight away. But she was giving herself time. Time to share his life and his love. If tonight had taught her anything at all, it was that she was hopelessly in love with him and could not resist him even when she thought she hated him.

Oh, my God! Suddenly Lisa was wide awake, because she had overlooked one very important fact. From the conversation she had overheard, Alex did not know yet that she had donated five per cent of her shares in Lawson Designer Glass to the hospice! It had never entered Lisa's head that the charity, at some future date, might sell the shares. But with a ruthless operator like Alex on the prowl she had to see it as a possibility.

If the hospice and the Lee estate sold to Alex, that would leave Harold with the deciding vote in the company. Much as she loved her stepfather, she hadn't a lot of faith in his ability to resist the demands of his son. Nigel was his one blind spot. As she actually owned only forty seven percent of the company, she would lose over-all control! How could she have been so stupid?

Finally, with a brief glance at her sleeping husband, she slipped out of bed. A hot drink might cure her insomnia. Pulling on Alex's discarded shirt, she buttoned it up and padded barefoot from the bedroom, along the hall and into the living area. It was a huge room, with a raised dining area, and seating at its opposite end arranged to take full advantage of the view through a wall of glass, with doors that opened out on to a roof garden. Architecturally, it was a magnificent room, but the plain black leather seating, the clean lines of the elm wood furniture and the polished hardwood floor had an oddly sterile look in the bright silver light of the moon. There was nothing personal or homely about it; in fact it looked exactly what it was: a company penthouse.

Lisa walked the length of the room to where double doors opened into a wide hall. At one side of it was the door leading to the kitchen and on the other side another two doors, one of the cloakroom and the other of Alex's study. At the end of the hallway stood a half screen in marble and glass and, beyond that the actual entrance door to the apartment.

Lisa entered the kitchen and switched on the light,

pushing the door almost shut behind her. In a matter of minutes she'd made a cup of hot chocolate and, sitting down at the breakfast table, she cupped the mug in her hands and sipped it slowly, her brain spinning with confusion. Alex and Nigel! If she hadn't heard them with her own ears, she would never have believed it, and yet it seemed they were planning on being business partners, at the expense of *her* business! The mind boggled...

If she felt more secure in her marriage, the sensible thing to do would be to confront Alex and demand an explanation. But it was too late now; she could hardly admit it tomorrow without looking a fool. No, her earlier decision was the best. Wait and see, and hopefully Alex would prove her wrong.

Suddenly an odd noise made Lisa straighten up in her chair. It sounded like a key turning in a lock.

Hardly daring to breathe, Lisa very quietly put the mug down on the table, her back stiffening with tension. Someone had let himself into the apartment. She heard footsteps on the polished wood of the entrance foyer floor. It had to be a burglar! She thought of screaming for Alex, but he was sound asleep at the other end of the apartment.

Glancing frantically around the kitchen, Lisa looked for something with which to defend herself from the intruder. A shelf of bright orange pans caught her eye. They were a well-known French make, and heavy. Silently she got to her feet and, picking up the largest saucepan from the shelf with the utmost stealth crossed to the slightly open kitchen door.

A very feminine giggle stopped Lisa in her tracks. Her blue eyes widened in amazement. A red-headed woman was bent over, and rather unsteadily removing a pair of high-heeled shoes at the entrance to the living room. As Lisa watched the woman straightened, her red lace stole

falling to the floor behind her to reveal a strapless, back-
less, red sheath dress. Then she spoke, before walking into
the living room. 'Alex, darling. Sorry I'm late, and you're
all on your ownsome.'

This was no burglar, Lisa thought bitterly, and for a
long moment shock held her rigid. The woman had a key
for the apartment; the woman knew Alex was alone tonight, or was supposed to be. No! her heart screamed. The
colour drained from her face. Was it only a few hours ago
when she had thought Alex's betrayal with her stepbrother
was the worst that could happen to her? Her soft mouth
twisted with savage irony. She had even thought then that
it would be less painful if Alex had been overcome with
passion for another woman. She had been wrong...

She dared not move, convinced she would splinter like
glass into a million pieces, feeling as if each shard would
pierce straight in her heart. How long she stood there she
had no idea.

Finally Lisa became aware of the saucepan in her hand,
and automatically crossed the floor to put it back where
she had found it. Then, zombie-like, she left the kitchen
and followed the woman as she saw her disappearing into
the corridor that housed the four bedrooms.

She was in time to see the woman enter the bedroom
Lisa herself had only recently vacated. The door was wide
open and bright moonlight flooded the scene. The other
woman was totally unaware of Lisa, all her attention fixed
on Alex, lying sprawled across the bed, the sheet covering
the essentials and nothing much else of him. As Lisa
watched in horrified fascination, the woman stepped out
of her dress. She was not wearing a bra, only a pair of
thong briefs, and as one small hand reached out to lift the
sheet, at the same time one elegant leg was raised.

Lisa could take no more. The frozen horror that had

held her immobile snapped, and she was toweringly, furiously mad. She switched on the central light.

Three things happened at once. The woman in the act of climbing into bed fell back, as Alex opened his eyes and shot bolt upright in bed. 'Margot? What the hell—'

Lisa's face was white, a frozen mask of rage, and the glance she threw at Alex should have burned him to a crisp. But with a glance at the woman leaning against the bed, he returned her look with one of puzzled fury.

'How did she get in here?' he demanded of Lisa.

They said attack was the best line of defence, and obviously that was Alex's strategy, Lisa thought contemptuously. 'The lady has a key. You appear to hand them out like candy bars at Hallowe'en. But don't let me interrupt. I'll just get my things and go.'

Marching into the room, she headed for the dressing room, but Alex stopped her. He had leapt out of bed stark naked, and now grabbed her by the shoulders.

'Don't be ridiculous, Lisa, this is all a terrible mistake. Surely you can see that?'

'I can see everything,' she snorted with a derisive scan of his body, 'and so can your lady-friend. But then there's nothing she hasn't seen before.'

Suddenly made aware of his naked state, between the avid eyes of the woman standing by the bed and the icy cold eyes of his wife, Alex let fly with a string of what could only be curses in Greek, while grabbing the sheet from the bed and wrapping it around himself. Free of his hold, Lisa headed for the door.

'Not so fast,' he growled, and caught her arm. 'You must have seen Margot come in here. Why didn't you stop her? You're my *wife* for heaven's sake.'

Lisa could not believe the audacity of the man. His girlfriend had walked into his apartment, stripped almost naked and had been about to slip into his bed. Yet somehow Alex was making it *her* fault! Not one word of censure to the girlfriend!

'Was,' she said trenchantly, and tried to shrug off his restraining hand. When pulling free didn't work Lisa changed tactics and elbowed him violently in his stomach. It had the desired result as the air whooshed out of him and he let go of her arm. But only for a second. She had barely time to turn round before he had caught her by the wrist again.

'Enough, Lisa,' he growled, spinning her around to face him. Lisa stared at him. He was seethingly angry; she could sense it in the tautness of his features and the cold black depths of his eyes. 'Where the hell do you think you're going?'

'You know the saying—two's company, three's a crowd,' she shot back furiously. 'I'm leaving.'

He shook her arm, his mouth a tight, menacing line. 'You are not going anywhere.' His black eyes held Lisa's in a fierce challenge, daring her to disagree.

'Oops, I seem to have made a mistake.' Margot's voice cut through the electric tension in the air.

Both Lisa and Alex turned to look at the woman with equal degrees of anger.

'Sorry, I must have got the day wrong. I could have sworn it was tonight.'

Lisa took a really good look at the other woman. She had small breasts and a tiny waist, but she was not a natural redhead. On seeing the woman's face for the first time, Lisa's eyes widened in stunned recognition. Her picture had been on posters around Stratford-upon-Avon a couple of months ago. It was Margot Delfont, an up-and-coming Shakespearean actress.

'Margot, get dressed and get out,' Alex commanded. 'I've told you it's over.'

'But after two years I didn't think you meant it, Alex, darling.' Margot replied lightly, though Lisa saw the naked pleading in the other woman's eyes and had to look away. 'I mean, that was weeks ago, and we've had tiffs before, and got over them.'

'How many weeks ago? Seven?' Lisa asked, but she already knew the answer.

'Not now, Lisa,' Alex snapped at her. Then, picking the red dress off the floor, he walked across to Margot and threw it at her. 'Out.'

But Lisa saw it all now. The first time she had met Alex he had said he was in Stratford for the theatre, but had left early. He hadn't been there for the play but obviously to see his girlfriend. Lisa's lips twisted in the travesty of a smile. Alex had had a drink with Harold, Nigel and herself, before pleading a late dinner engagement and leaving, but only after having made quite sure he could see Lisa the next day. The phrase 'killing two birds with one stone' sprang to mind...

A night with his lover and a bid for the property Lisa owned. What a naive fool she had been! Lisa clenched her teeth to stop herself crying out in pain.

'Look, I'm awfully sorry, darling, but really it is no big deal. In fact, it might be rather fun with a threesome,' Margot suggested, smiling up at Alex as she shimmied into her dress. And then, turning her attention to Lisa, she added, 'I'm sorry, we haven't been introduced, but you must be the new wife. So what do you say?'

Lisa shook her head in complete disgust. It was like a black comedy, and she would not demean herself with a response.

'Margot, shut up and get out.' Not by a flicker of an

eyelash did Alex betray his feelings. He simply gave the woman standing by the bed a cold, impersonal inspection. 'And leave the key behind this time.'

Lisa didn't know which one she hated more. Margot, or her arrogant husband. She almost felt sorry for Margot; it was obvious she loved Alex, and would do anything, anything at all for him! But it was equally obvious he cared little or nothing for her; she had been a convenient body in his bed when he had needed a woman.

Alex turned back to Lisa, sliding a proprietorial arm around her waist. 'This is all an unfortunate mistake.'

Lisa glanced up at him. A mistake, he'd said, but it was Lisa who had made one. Alex didn't feel any more for her than he did for Margot. His handsome face was expressionless; he was not at all embarrassed by the ludicrous situation he found himself in. Because he didn't really care for either woman...

The realisation galvanised Lisa into action. With an almighty jerk and a hefty kick to Alex's shin, she broke away, and was out of the door and straight into the guest room across the hall, slamming the door behind her. Luckily it had a lock, and swiftly she turned the key. She flung back her head and took deep, shaky breaths, trying to force the air into her lungs. She saw the light switch and pressed it on. The sudden glare hurt her eyes and she doubled over. Her stomach churned and she knew she was going to be sick. Stumbling into the adjoining bathroom, she bent over the toilet bowl.

CHAPTER THREE

How had she never realised what kind of man she was marrying? Lisa asked herself over and over again. She tore off the shirt she was wearing, she didn't want anything of Alex's near her. Then she crossed to the washbasin and splashed her face with cold water and cleaned her teeth, trying to take the taste of nausea from her mouth. She filled a glass with water and drank it. She was shivering, more with shock than cold, and, glancing around the bathroom, she saw a robe provided for guests on top of a pile of fresh towels by the bath.

Picking up the thick white towelling robe, she slipped it on, tying the belt firmly around her waist. Yet still she was shaking. She had half expected Alex to follow her. She walked into the bedroom and glanced around; it was pleasant, if a bit like a hotel room. A double bed in the centre of one wall. At one side a soft-cushioned sofa and an occasional table, a cabinet that housed a television, video and CD players. Against the wall to the left of the door was a desk and office centre. The three guest bedrooms of the apartment, Lisa knew, were all equipped in the same fashion. Alex had told her this was his base in the UK, so it also doubled as a company apartment. The master suite and his study remained locked when he was not in residence, but the place was occasionally used by visiting executives and for corporate entertainment. A bitter smile twisted her soft lips. Alex had failed to add he also used it for strictly personal, sexual entertainment.

In the distance she heard a door slam. Had the luscious

Margot left? She didn't know and she no longer cared, she told herself. She had no illusions left. She had made a horrendous mistake, marrying a man she hardly knew, but she would get over it—she had to. She closed her eyes for a second and immediately saw in her mind's eye the face of Margot, and the expression in the woman's eyes came back to haunt her. Margot had looked at Alex with slavish, sick desire, and how had Alex reacted? By ordering her out. Yet, for two years, if Margot was to be believed, he had used the woman quite shamelessly.

Lisa opened her eyes, and in that moment she vowed she would never become so enslaved to any man again, especially not her husband. Alex had betrayed her trust, and it hurt. *How it hurt.* But he would never get the chance to do it again… She raised her hands and swept the tangled mass of her hair back from her face and straightened her shoulders. The shivering had stopped and she began to think logically about the night's events.

Dear heaven! She shook her head, appalled at her own stupidity. She could see clearly now. Alex, Margot and Nigel were all alike: immoral, money-hungry, selfish. What sort of fool did they take her for? The only way Margot could have known Alex was going to be alone tonight was if Alex had told her. A harsh laugh escaped her. Her over-sexed husband had made one mistake. In his hurry to let Lisa seduce him he had forgotten to ring his girlfriend and tell her their date was off. Thinking about it now, Lisa supposed she should be flattered his desire for her had overcome his usual controlled efficient self. But she wasn't.

'Lisa, open the door.' Alex's deep voice broke the silence of the night. She saw the handle turn and then he knocked. 'Open the door, Lisa, we have to talk.'

Not in this lifetime, she thought bitterly. She had nothing to say to him.

The banging got louder.

'Please, Lisa, open the door. I really need to talk to you.' The husky, sensual tone of his voice enraged Lisa; it was all an act.

'Get lost,' she yelled back.

'Open the damned door Lisa.' The doorhandle rattled ferociously.

'No.'

'I will count to three and then I will break the thing down,' Alex declared.

It was too much to hope that he would leave her alone. Wiping her damp palms down the soft towelling covering her thighs, she reluctantly turned the key in the lock. She had to jump back as the door swung in and Alex burst into the room.

'Lisa!' His hands grabbed her shoulders and he pulled her towards him. 'What do you think you're playing at, locking me out?' His eyes flared angrily; his fingers gripped her shoulders.

She planted her hands on his chest and shoved hard. 'Let go of me,' she cried, and lifted her knee, her intention plain. He jerked back, but did not release her.

'Lisa, Lisa, calm down and let me explain.' He tried to appease her, but she was having none of it.

'There is nothing to explain. I saw it all. And as for calming down,' she said angrily, her blue eyes like chips of ice, 'I'll calm down when you get out of my sight.'

'You don't mean that,' he growled, pulling her hard against him once more. His mouth swooped on hers with savage anger. She twisted her head—anything to avoid his kiss. But one hand tangled in her hair, as his arm curved around her waist, clamping her firmly to his long body. She tried to wriggle free as he took her mouth with a ruthless passion that would not be denied.

But, even as she felt insidious warmth building inside her she recognised his strategy and was sickened by it. He was blatantly using his sexual prowess to overcome her. Her eyes clashed with his and she saw the implacable intent in their black depths, and she froze in his arms.

'No,' she said flatly, and at her withdrawal Alex lifted his head; what he saw in her face, gave him pause.

'Your response was a bit lacking in enthusiasm. Does this mean the honeymoon is over?' he queried cynically.

'Not just the honeymoon. The marriage as well.' She ignored the burning pain around her heart. Alex had only been able to deceive her so easily because she had wanted to believe in the myth of love at first sight. She felt him tense, and as his hands fell away from her she was free.

'Now you're being ridiculous, Lisa.' he told her curtly. 'The little scene with Margot was embarrassing for all concerned, but there is no reason to be so melodramatic. We will probably laugh about it later.'

She looked at him in the harsh glare of the overhead light. He was standing a foot away. His tall body was covered in a burgundy velvet robe, with satin lapels that fell open to reveal his curling chest hair. The belt was tied firmly around his waist but the garment ended a few inches above his knee, exposing a long length of strong tanned leg.

'You might. I won't,' she bit out, refusing to be intimidated by his towering presence. 'Somehow, finding a woman crawling into my husband's bed not fifteen minutes after I vacated it does not strike me as a cause for amusement.' Turning her back on him, she walked across the room towards the sofa. She couldn't bear to look at him.

'Wait just a minute.' A strong hand wrapped around her arm and stopped her in her tracks. She glanced up at him. He looked dark and dangerous and for a second a shiver of apprehension slithered down her spine. 'Don't you think you're overreacting? It was hardly my fault the woman called here.'

'Hardly your fault?' Lisa almost choked at the gall of the man. She was bitterly angry, angrier than she had been when she had overheard his conversation with Nigel. To be betrayed once was bad enough, but twice in one night! 'Oh, please! Spare me the excuses.'

Alex was silent for a long moment, watching her with narrowed eyes. 'I do not make excuses to anyone.' She saw his face harden 'And certainly not to my wife who, only a few short hours ago, could not keep her hands off me.'

Trust him to remind her. 'But then I didn't expect a few hours later to see another woman crawling into your bed,' she returned with icy sarcasm.

'If you had stayed in our bed, it would never have happened. I'd like an explanation.'

'You want an explanation? That's rich,' Lisa said hotly, backing away a few paces, but Alex followed, until her back came into contact with the wall. 'Especially coming from a man like you.'

'So, humour me, wife,' he drawled tightly, his eyes burning on her. 'Because I have had just about enough for one night.'

She debated telling him to drop dead, but quickly dismissed the notion. He was standing looking down on her, his hands placed on the wall behind her, his body effectively trapping her. His black eyes leapt with anger, and she realised he was in a towering rage. Probably at being caught out, but she had no intention of testing him. She

was hanging on to her sanity by a thread. She simply
wanted him to leave her alone.

'I got up to make a cup of hot chocolate. I was in the
kitchen; I heard the sound of the door, and thought it was
a burglar. I picked up a pan to challenge the intruder with,
and crept to the hall door.' Her eyes flashed with renewed
rage as she added, 'But lo and behold, it was a lady.'

'Why didn't you yell for me, or stop her?' Alex demanded. 'Surely those were the obvious things to do.'

'Because I heard her speak.' And in an exaggerated
voice Lisa continued, '"*Alex, darling. Sorry I'm so late,
and you're all on your ownsome.*"' Her eyes hated him
as she rashly held his gaze. 'The lady could not have
known you were going to be alone tonight unless you'd
told her. My surprise arrival really upset your plan, didn't
it?' She snorted her disgust. 'Now get out of my way.'

'For a girl who avowed her undying love not a month
ago, you certainly have a fine opinion of me,' Alex
drawled sardonically. 'Do you really think I asked Margot
to come here?'

'Who else?' She raised one perfectly arched brow in
query.

'I don't usually explain my actions to anyone, but in
this case I will make an exception.' She looked at him,
and for the briefest of moments he looked away as he
hesitated. Lisa did not need to hear any more. She knew
him for the liar he was.

'It doesn't matter.' Bone weary and sick at heart, she
had neither the will nor the energy to fight with him.

'But it does.' He lifted his hand and cupped her chin
before she could turn away, his breath warm against her
skin, his dark eyes holding hers in fierce purpose. 'Margot
was at a nightclub and spoke to a man I'd had a meeting
with today. I had mentioned I was staying in town tonight

and that he could call me here with some information I required. Obviously in the course of his conversation with Margot he must have let slip the fact. As for her having the key to the apartment—it is true we did have an affair, but I broke it off before I met you.'

'Your poor girlfriend didn't seem to think so,' Lisa said scathingly.

'Don't waste your pity on Margot; she was under no illusion about our relationship. It was never going anywhere; it simply mutually benefited both parties.'

'If you say so,' she responded grimly. 'But, actually, I don't really care.' And at that moment she didn't; she had taken too many shocks for one night, and simply wanted to be left alone.

'That's the whole trouble, you *don't* care,' Alex suddenly erupted, swinging away from her and marching across the room, and then turning back to face her. 'That's what this is all about. Any wife worth her salt would never have allowed another woman to climb into her husband's bed in the middle of the night.' A feral smile curved his lips. 'I am damned sure I would not stand by and let a man walk into your bed.'

She didn't doubt him for a moment. 'But then, as you and I both know, unlike you, I have never invited any man into my bed,' Lisa shot back.

'I'm thirty-five. Few men my age have led a celibate life,' Alex opined with a shrug of his broad shoulders. 'Margot meant nothing to me, though I will admit she should never have got in here tonight. I have spoken to Security, but unfortunately the man on duty this evening has just returned from a rather long absence from work because of ill health. The man knew Margot, and was not aware I had since married. A mistake he will not make again,' he declared. 'I will not tolerate anyone who harms you, directly or indirectly.'

His dark-lashed eyes glittered brilliantly on hers, and he lifted his hand to brush a stray tendril of hair gently back behind her ear. Lisa believed he meant what he said, but sadly she recognised it was not from love, but from his inbuilt male possessiveness. She was his wife, *ergo*, his property.

'You are my wife,' Alex continued huskily, 'and I can safely say from the minute I met you there has been no one else.'

Her blonde head flew back and she shook off his hand. 'Are you sure about that, Alex?'

'Of course. I do not lie.' If she hadn't known better, Lisa might almost have believed he was offended. He lifted his hand towards her again, and she stepped back a pace. His black eyes flared with some indefinable emotion which he then quickly masked, and his hand fell to his side. 'But perhaps now is not the time for this conversation. We are both tired and may say things we will regret. 'Suddenly he had gone all formal on her, his anger held in check. Only the tight line of his mouth betrayed his strict control.

'The only thing I regret is marrying you,' Lisa said bluntly. 'And by the way, Alex, I recognised your girl-friend. She was appearing at the theatre in Stratford on the evening we met. You must have spent that night with her and then called for me the next day.' She watched as a swift tide of colour swept up his face, turning his com-plexion a dark red. 'I'm not a fool, Alex, even if I have let you almost make one out of me. But not any more. Next you'll be telling me you forgot to ask for the key back,' she continued scathingly. 'You are certainly your father's son. Five times married, isn't it? Well, you can mark me down as your first. And start looking for the second. It is over. Finished.'

Alex stared at her in bitter, hostile silence for long moments. Then he stepped back. 'It is finished when I say so,' he informed her arrogantly 'I am not prepared to argue with you any longer. You can stay in here for what is left of the night. We will continue this discussion in the morning, when you have got over your sulk and are prepared to act like an adult.' Turning on his heel, he crossed to the door and opened it.

'As far as I am concerned, the discussion is over. I will be leaving in the morning,' she flung at his departing back.

Alex paused, then turned round and glanced at her, something dark leaping to life in his eyes. Lisa involuntarily stepped back, although he was nowhere near her. 'You are not leaving tomorrow, or any other day. Understood?' And before she could retaliate he walked out, banging the door behind him.

Shock and anger had kept her upright, but with Alex's departure she sank down on the bed and buried her head in the pillow. She wanted to scream and yell out her pain, but the lesson she had learned as a teenager, when her height had made her an outcast from her peer group, gave her the strength to control her emotions. She would not allow herself to show her pain or humiliation to Alex. But anyone glancing at her lying on the bed would have seen her slender body shaking as she wept silently.

All cried out, Lisa turned over on to her back, her throat dry and sore. She wiped her eyes on the sleeve of her robe, breathed deeply and tried to tell herself she would get over it. But she knew she would never recover from the hurt Alex had inflicted on her. She would never trust another man as long as she lived.

Sighing, she rolled off the bed and stood up. There was no point in trying to sleep; the scent of Alex lingered on her skin from their earlier lovemaking—no, not love, *sex*, she amended. Glancing out of the window, she saw it was dawn. She headed for the bathroom, and, slipping the robe off her shoulders, she stepped into the shower stall and turned on the water.

She shivered as the first drops hit her flesh. It was cold. Adjusting the temperature, she flung her head back and let the warm water flow over her. How long she stood like that she had no idea, but slowly a sense of purpose seeped into her tired mind. She shampooed and conditioned her long hair and then, picking up the shower gel, she scrubbed every single inch of her body in frenzied effort to remove every trace of Alex from her. She turned off the water and stepped out of the shower, collecting a large towel from the pile provided and rubbing herself dry.

Dropping the towel, she picked up the hairdryer and, standing in front of the vanity mirror, began blow-drying her hair. She studied her reflection, a grim travesty of a smile twisting her mouth; her skin was red from her efforts in the shower. It was a pity she could not wash Alex out of her mind as easily. But, given time, she would, Lisa vowed.

Grabbing another towel she wrapped it around herself. Her mind was made up: she was going back to Stratford and she was not waiting for another confrontation with Alex. She knew her own weakness too well. Alex was clever; he would talk her into staying and use sex to convince her. She had little faith in her power to resist him and she wasn't hanging around long enough to find out.

All her clothes were in the dressing room of the master

suite, but luckily the dressing room could be entered via the hall as well as the master bedroom. Slipping into the dressing room, she stopped and listened, but everywhere was silent. It took her no more than a minute to withdraw blue briefs and matching lace bra from a drawer and slip them on. Another minute, and she had silently opened the closet where she had hung her clothes and quickly stepped into light blue linen pants. Her head was lost in the folds of a navy cotton knit sweater when disaster struck.

'Lisa, your're not usually an early riser; that is my prerogative.' A deep, husky voice broke the silence, and two arms curved around her waist.

With her arms up in the air, stuck halfway into her sweater, Lisa was in a hopeless position. She felt his hands slide up over her midriff to cup her breasts over the flimsy lace of her bra. She drew in a shuddering breath and managed to wriggle her arms and head free of the restraining garment. 'Let go of me,' she snapped.

A throaty chuckle simmered along her throat as he nuzzled her neck, 'You don't mean that, Lisa. You smell so sweet, so delicious,' he husked, holding her firmly back against his hard thighs.

'And you are an oversexed jerk,' She spat, suddenly aware the beast was aroused, and, twisting around to face him, she splayed her hands over his broad chest and pushed with all her might. But it was like trying to fell an oak tree with her bare hands. Alex simply folded his arms around her taut body and held her pressed tightly to him.

'Now, is that any way to greet your husband?' he drawled mockingly.

'Soon to be ex-husband,' She replied pithily, her eyes skimming over him. He was wearing a white silk shirt, unbuttoned to the waist, and pleated beige pants.

Obviously he had not been lying in bed, as Lisa had hoped. She was uncomfortably aware he was fresh from the shower, his black hair damp, the clean, masculine scent of him filling her nostrils and, to her chagrin, she could feel her breasts swelling against the soft lace of her bra.

He studied her tousled appearance, her long blonde hair tumbling around her shoulders, her hands curled into fists on his broad chest. He took his time looking her over, a glint of devilment in his dark eyes. He knew perfectly well how he affected her. A broad grin curved his mouth, making her vitally aware of the sensuality lurking within his hard body. 'Come on, Lisa, where is your sense of humour? You don't want to leave,' he contradicted softly. His dark head lowered, his lips feathering across hers, and she shivered as the pressure of his kiss deepened, the hard heat of his mouth burning on her own.

Lisa groaned, caught in the trap of sensation much stronger than she was. How could it be? she thought helplessly, while every part of her burned in a fever of need.

'That is better.' Alex eased her away from him with a husky laugh. 'You look more like the girl I married. No more sulks, hmm?' He stepped back, his smile tinged with a glint of triumph.

It was his satisfaction that really got Lisa. Still reeling from the power of his kiss, she was jerked back to reality with a thump. 'I do not sulk, and I meant what I said, Alex. I want a divorce,'

He absorbed her flushed and angry face with arrogant detachment. 'No, you don't. You simply want to punish me for that unfortunate occurrence last night.'

'Unfortunate? I don't think so! Quite the reverse. It was fortunate for me.' Lisa flared. 'It showed me what a low-life I had married. And I want out.'

'Lowlife. Out,' Alex repeated, his eyes narrowed, his jaw clenching. 'No one talks to me like that. Not even you, my beautiful wife.' He told her icily.

'I mean it, Alex.' She defied him.

'Then, if that is so, I will be forced to do something about it.' The illusion of icy control was abruptly cast aside as strong hands curved around her forearms. 'No way are you walking out on our marriage after less than a month.'

'You can't stop me,' she said bluntly, but even so it took all her courage to stare bravely up into Alex's face.

'Oh, but I can.' A hard-boned savagery contorted his handsome features. 'You are mine, and mine you will stay until I decide otherwise.'

'Caveman tactics went out with the Dark Ages, Alex. Or hadn't you heard?' she hit back sarcastically, but inside she was quaking at the force of his rage.

'No.' His fingers held her tight. 'I am not letting you go until I get to the bottom of your outrageous behaviour. What do you take me for?'

He set her free and backed off a few steps, but his angry gaze held hers with narrow-eyed intensity. 'The truth is Lisa, this sudden desire to be single again is not just because of last night. The girl with whom I spent the last few weeks would have laughed off the episode, without a murmur. No. There is a hidden agenda here.'

'I don't know what you're talking about.' But she knew she sounded less than convincing. The thought of Alex's betrayal with Nigel lay heavily on her mind.

A black brow lifted sardonically. 'Oh, I think you do. But if you imagine I am parting with half a million pounds for barely a month in your bed, then forget it. You're good, but not that good.' And, turning around, he collected a jacket from the wardrobe and slipped it on.

Hectic colour tinged her cheeks; she had forgotten about the prenuptial agreement. 'That's a filthy thing to say, and utterly ridiculous.'

Slowly he turned back to face her. 'No more ridiculous than your demand for a divorce,' he whipped back derisively. 'I want the truth, Lisa, and I intend to get it.' With an angry glance around the small room, he added, 'But the dressing room is no place for a serious talk.' Taking her arm, he herded her through into the living area. Lisa was too surprised to object.

He'd had the audacity to suggest she was a gold-digger, when the reverse was true! But then, with her common sense returning, she recognised his ploy for what it was. A way of putting her on the defensive. Well, it was not going to work. When he pushed her down on to the leather sofa, she glared up at him with narrowed eyes. 'Think what you like, but it does not alter my position. I am leaving here today.'

Alex glanced at the watch on his wrist, and then at her flushed face. His dark eyes were calculatingly hard. 'I have a breakfast meeting, and not much time.'

'As soon as you leave, so shall I,' she asserted.

'You love your stepfamily. This I know.' A ruthless smile slanted his sensuous mouth. 'You stay here, or I will ruin them.'

She stared at him, her mind whirling. 'Why would you do that?' From what she had overheard, Nigel was in league with him, and personally Lisa didn't care if creepy Nigel fell flat on his face. But she did love Harold, and it might hurt him. Alex could certainly ruin Lawson's if he discovered she had given away her majority.

'Because, my sweet—' he glanced again at the slim gold watch on his wrist '—I have no more time to argue.'

Lisa couldn't take it in at first. *He had no time*. His

simple reason for threatening to destroy Nigel and Harold was all the more believable when he used that casual endearment. Even after last night, believing Alex had deceived her, she still had not quite believed the man she had married was so utterly and completely ruthless. But, looking up into his hard eyes, she realised he was not only serious but he was perfectly capable of doing what he said without a qualm of conscience. But then the man *had* no conscience.

'Have I made myself clear?' Alex drawled hardily.

'But what you're suggesting is despicable; it's nothing short of blackmail.'

'No worse than what you are trying to do. Our prenuptial gives you half a million for a month. No woman is worth that.'

'But I'm not. I didn't...' Lisa could not believe what was happening. He had turned the tables on her. She felt that she was in some nightmare, and that any second she would wake up and discover last night had never happened, or, better still, she amended, the last seven weeks had never happened.

'I have to return to Stratford today, to work,' she lied. Anything to get away.

'You do not. I had a long conversation with Harold last night. I know your second in command has taken over. There is no hurry for your return, and you have your laptop with you. Use the room you used last night as a study.' And, with another glance at his watch, he bent down and curved a large hand around her chin, and tilted her face up. His dark eyes lit with savage amusement. 'Try not to miss me too much, lover.'

Her furious blue eyes widened to their fullest extent. 'Why, you...you...' She could not think of a word bad enough to describe his sheer arrogance.

'Hush.' A finger was placed firmly across her lips. 'Do not incite my temper any further. You will not like the consequences.' he assured her, and then, as she watched, a wicked smile curved his hard mouth. 'But then again, you might enjoy it, if last night's seduction was a taste of what you are capable of.' With a husky laugh he released her chin.

Lisa blushed to the roots of her hair at his sensual reminder. She leapt to her feet. 'You can't order me around…'

'I can do anything, and don't you forget it,' he drawled his black eyes flashing a warning. 'Be here when I return, or it will be harder for you.'

'Wait.' She grabbed his arm. 'You can't make a statement like that and walk away.'

'Why not? It is no worse than you declaring you want a divorce and walking away.'

'But… But…' she stammered.

Lean fingers enclosed the hand she had laid on his arm. 'Not so nice, is it, Lisa? When the shoe is on the other foot? No?' And he actually laughed.

'You don't mean it,' she said uncertainly, as he slipped an arm around her waist, drawing her inexorably closer into the heat of his hard body. She was not sure if he was teasing or torturing her.

'Neither do you.' Folding both arms around her, his dark gaze steady on her troubled face, he added, 'Think about it from my point of view Lisa. Last night I fell asleep with my wife in my arms. You get up in the middle of the night, and another woman attempts to climb into our bed. Do you really think I am stupid enough to go to bed with one woman while waiting for another?'

She had trouble holding his gaze. His dark eyes bored into hers, and her own innate honesty forced her to admit that, if it had not been for the knowledge she had gained earlier about Nigel's involvement with Alex she probably would have stopped Margot at the door. 'I don't know,' she mumbled.

'Of course I am suspicious of the circumstances. But is your scenario any more valid? I think not,' he declared firmly.

'No,' Lisa conceded in defeat; she had to, unless she told him she knew about his plan to take over her company, and she was not ready to do that. She needed to make some investigations of her own first.

'Good, then let us make a pact, you and I. We will forget last night ever happened.'

'Very convenient for you,' Lisa could not help sniping.

'Come on, Lisa. Do you really want to go back and face your family and friends after a few short weeks, declaring your marriage to be over? Our wedding was reported in the press. Do you want to look a failure in the eyes of the world? More importantly, do you think for one minute I would allow you to make a failure out of me?' he demanded, with silken emphasis on the last question.

Lisa tensed, her slender frame taut as a bowstring, as she searched his darkly handsome face for any sign of weakness. There was none. Did she dare take a chance and defy him? More importantly, did she really want to?

'You are wise not to argue. This was our first fight, probably the first of many; you are a very feisty lady, which is why I adore you. But enough is enough, Lisa. Forget last night, and we start again from today,' he urged softly.

'Just like that?' Lisa shook her head at his arrogant conceit.

His dark head bent and he brought his mouth gently

down on hers. 'No, just like this.' He mouthed the words
against her lips and then parted her lips to the seductive
invasion of his tongue.

Heat coursed through her, and even as she knew she
should resist a muffled whimper escaped her, and the familiar ache of longing arrowed through her body.

Alex only broke the kiss when she was utterly relaxed
in his arms. 'If only I had time,' he murmured throatily,
and raised his head to study her lovely face. His hand slid
down to her buttocks and pressed her hard against his
thighs, leaving her in no doubt about the potency of his
masculine arousal.

Lisa was completely mesmerised by the desire in his
dark eyes. She dragged in a ragged breath, fighting the
pull of his attraction, but she did not need to. He flung
his arms wide and stepped back.

'No more foolish talk of leaving, Lisa. You want me.
I could have you now on the floor, and we both know it.'
His dark eyes met and held hers, mutinously blue. 'And
before you take off in another tantrum, know it is the same
for me, Lisa.' His huskily voiced confession stopped the
expletive she had been about to throw at him.

'It's just sex,' she muttered instead.

'Sex, love—call it what you will. But consider you may
already be carrying our child.'

'I am not,' she shot back curtly. She had discovered
the fact after her shower. 'I found that out as well.' To
her utter astonishment Alex burst out laughing, his dark
head thrown back, the morning sun streaming through the
window glinting in the blue-black of his hair.

'Ah Lisa, now I understand. The wrong time of the
month,' he chuckled, straightening his shoulders, his firm
lips curving back over brilliant white teeth in a broad grin.
'Forget the foolishness of last night, sweetheart; I have.

You were not thinking logically; it is perfectly understandable in your condition.'

'My condition?' She spluttered, almost incandescent with rage. He actually thought her outburst was all down to PMT, the chauvinist. She could see it in his tender, patronising smile.

'Come, I can hear Mrs Blaydon arriving. She and her husband look after this place for me. I will introduce you, and then you go back to bed, rest. Leave everything to me.' With his hand at her elbow he urged her along towards the kitchen, and she was so speechless at his high-handed arrogance she let him!

CHAPTER FOUR

'It is a pleasure to meet you, Mrs Solomos.' The smiling, plump woman extended her hand to Lisa. 'I am so happy for you both, and if there is anything you want me to do for you, you only have to ask.' Smiling at Alex, she added, 'The coffee is fresh; what would you like to eat?'

'Just coffee, Mrs B; I have to dash. But I trust you to look after Lisa for me, and make sure she eats. She is feeling a bit tired today.' After downing the cup of coffee Mrs Blaydon had handed him he settled his dark gaze on Lisa. 'Come, walk me to the door. Mrs B understands. We are newlyweds,' he invited, his voice laced with a cynicism that only Lisa recognised as Mrs Blaydon chuckled with delight.

Alex's hand on the small of her back created a disturbing sensation that held a hidden warning; it also succeeded in fuelling her anger. 'I can walk,' she breathed in an undertone as they exited to the hall.

'So long as you know that you cannot walk out on me.' Alex's lazy reply only served to infuriate her further.

'You've made your point. I wouldn't dare.' Her head tilted fractionally and she met his dark gaze with clear control. 'Can I go and eat now?'

He lifted a hand and caught hold of her chin. 'Eat, yes. Go, no.' He stressed silkily, and his thumb traced a semicircle up her chin, over her full lips and back down to slide to where the pulse beat heavily in her throat. 'Forget last night. Forget our fight. And remember only this appetite.' Alex tapped the pulse-beat in her throat, his head lowered and his lips brushed her cheek and the edge of her mouth. 'This appetite you and I will always share, Lisa.' She looked at him, the tug of sexual awareness impossible to deny. 'But do not underestimate me, Lisa. If I find you have betrayed my trust I can be a ruthless enemy, your worst nightmare.' It was the very softness of his tone that was enough to convince Lisa he was speaking the truth.

'And what of your betrayal?' she managed to retaliate.

Alex's eyes hardened fractionally. 'The question will not arise; you can trust me absolutely.' He caught hold of her hand and raised it to his lips. 'With this ring I thee wed' he repeated softly, and kissed the ring on her finger. 'I keep my promises. Be sure to keep yours, and we will have no more problems.' Dropping her hand, he also dropped a swift kiss on the top of her head. 'Rest. You look tired.'

'Thanks for the compliment.'

'Sarcasm does not become you, Lisa,' Alex opined dryly. 'See you tonight, and remember we are dining with my father.' Turning he opened the door and left.

Deprived of any chance to retaliate, she stood for a moment staring at the closed door. Alex was right in one respect. She did not relish the idea of returning home a failure, her marriage over after only a few weeks. Then there was still the problem of Nigel. It went against her nature to give in to blackmail, but it occurred to her that if Alex actually meant to destroy her stepfamily, that meant Harold. She could not keep Lawson's without Harold, so common sense told her she was better to stay where she was until she discovered exactly what was going on.

Lisa made her way back to the kitchen. Mrs Blaydon was putting toast in the electric toaster, and her smile was warm as she watched Lisa walk over to the breakfast table and sit down. Lisa filled a cup with coffee and took a much needed drink of the reviving brew.

'Scrambled eggs on toast all right for you, Mrs Solomos.'

Lisa replaced the cup on the table. 'Just toast, thanks.'

'Like my Bert; that's all he ever has.'

'Bert is your husband, then?' Lisa asked making idle conversation, as the older woman placed a plate of toast in front of her.

'Yes, married thirty-five years, and for the last fifteen we have worked for Mr Alex. He was twenty-one and still a student at university when he moved in here. He gave Bert and I the apartment below, and we've looked after the penthouse for him. He hasn't been around as much the last few years, but he still keeps us on to take care of all his visitors, and Bert acts as the official Solomos chauffeur when he's needed. Mr Alex usually drives himself, but then the man does everything himself; he's a real workaholic. Of course, that father of his is no help. Always in the newspapers for all the wrong reasons.'

'I haven't actually met Alex's father yet. Apparently I am to have that honour tonight,' Lisa cut in having finished her food.

'Some honour! The man hasn't done a hand's turn in years, and yet to hear the old fool going on in the media, he's a brilliant businessman. Brilliant is as brilliant does, I say,' the housekeeper ended bluntly.

Lisa drained her coffee cup and stood up. 'Well, no doubt I shall discover for myself tonight, but right now I'd better get down to work.'

'Oh, no, you can't do any housework. That's my job.'

'Not housework.' Lisa corrected the housekeeper with a smile. 'But I do run a business in Stratford-upon-Avon.

I've brought my computer with me, and I'm going to commandeer the first guest room for my office, if that's all right with you. Don't worry, Mrs Blaydon, I won't interfere with your work. Why don't you finish up here? It's a beautiful sunny day; you and Bert can have the day off.'

'Well, if you're sure.' Mrs Blaydon's pleasure was evident.

'Yes.' Lisa smiled, getting to her feet. 'But if you'll excuse me, I'd better get to work.'

In a matter of minutes she was seated at the desk in the room where she had spent the night, her laptop on, planning her defence. Buying the Lee shares was her safest option, but it didn't take Lisa long to realise she was paper rich but cash poor. Next, she checked everywhere she could think of to find the name of the company that had made the offer to buy Lawson's before her mother died. If she needed a white knight to help her fight off Alex's takeover attempt, that bidder seemed a good bet. At least that company hadn't wanted to flatten the place. After an hour she gave up in disgust. Perhaps the letter of refusal had never been filed on the computer; given the shock of her mother's illness at the time, it wasn't surprising. It would have to wait until she got back to the office on Monday, it might be in her mother's private papers, and Lisa was the only one with access to them.

As the morning progressed, Lisa fought against recalling last night's events, but she failed. She was mulling over her own ambivalence about the situation when Mrs Blaydon burst into the room, closely followed by two men.

'I was on my way out when these two men arrived. It's for you, from Mr Alex.'

'That's fine, Mrs Blaydon.' She watched the old

woman scurry off with a smile on her face. To say Lisa was astonished was an understatement. Alex had sent her a state-of-the-art computer, and the accompanying card read. 'I hope this will keep you at home.'

Lisa shared a smile with the two young delivery men, and watched with close attention as they installed the new computer. Later, she set about E-mailing Mary, and then Jed. Then she broke off for a coffee. Returning half an hour later, she got the shock of her life when she clicked on and a disembodied female voice declared, 'You have mail.' Her old computer hadn't got a voice facility and she was fascinated by it.

The E-mail was a reply from Mary. *'Congrats: but I still think diamonds are a girl's best friend.'* Chuckling to herself, Lisa spent the rest of the morning thoroughly absorbed in her work. It was only when her stomach rumbled and she glanced at the time in the corner of the screen that she realised the morning had gone.

She couldn't resist one more visit to the Internet, and was rewarded with 'You have mail'. As it was the afternoon in the UK, it had to be early morning in Montana, from where Jed was replying.

'You lucky lady. The computer sounds great, but do I detect a trace of coolness in your attitude to the giver, and so soon??? Correct me if I am wrong. I'll get back to you later. I have to go milk the cows.'

Something in the tone of her message must have given him an insight into her confused state of mind. That was just so Jed. For a man she had never actually met, he had an amazing sensitivity where she was concerned. She sent a brief reply: *'Stick to analysing the cows, farm boy. I'm fine.* A glimmer of a genuine smile brightened her face as she closed down the computer and wandered back through the apartment to the kitchen.

Lisa made herself a cheese sandwich and, filling a glass with milk, she placed it and the plate on a tray and took her late lunch out to the rooftop garden. It was a gorgeous sunny afternoon, and, placing the tray on a Victorian wrought-iron table, she sat down on one of the matching chairs and picked up one half of her sandwich.

She munched her food without really tasting it, her mind awash with conflicting thoughts. She glanced at the gold watch on her wrist; it read slightly after three o'clock. Alex wouldn't be back before five-thirty at the earliest. There was still time for her to leave. But did she really want to? she asked herself. And, much as she hated to admit her weakness, the answer was no. The trouble was, she realised Alex the man she had married, was not the man she'd thought he was. She had never really known him…

She had always recognised Alex had a ruthless streak in him. He wouldn't be a success in the business world without a certain killer instinct to succeed. But, naively perhaps, she had never expected that side of his nature to be turned on her.

Even now she was not convinced he had meant his threat. He had said they would make a pact to start again, and by her silence she had given her agreement.

She could almost forgive him Margot's amazing intrusion last night. Her lips twitched in the beginnings of a smile. Alex's face had been a picture of outraged horror when she had clicked the light on and he had realised it was Margot climbing into their bed! He could not have faked his expression in a million years. He was usually so self-possessed—even in the throes of passion he never totally lost control.

Passion. That was another problem. Lisa had decided to stay, but was she prepared to crawl back into bed with Alex? The next week was taken care of; he wouldn't bother her knowing she had her period.

A deep sigh escaped her and, arching her back to get the tension out of her shoulders, she picked up the glass of milk and drained it, before replacing it on the tray. Then she stood up and carried the lot back to the kitchen. Lounging around the roof garden solved nothing, she told herself firmly. Action was what was needed.

Half an hour later Lisa was standing in the hall, a pile of clothes topped with lacy underwear in her arms, as she tried to push open the guest bedroom door with her rear.

'What the devil....?' Alex was walking towards her discarding his tie in the process, and looking distinctly puzzled.

'You're back early,' she said inanely, and met his dark gaze with a frown, her eyes lingering on the chiselled features and settling briefly on his mouth. Which was a mistake. He was tight-mouthed with anger.

'No, just in time, it would seem. Care to explain what you are doing? Or shall I guess,' he drawled cynically, moving to stand inches from her. His hand plucked a pair of crimson lace briefs off the top of the pile of clothes she was carrying, and swung the offending garment back and forth on one long finger.

He had caught her at a disadvantage, with her back to the door and her hands full. She had nowhere to go. 'Put them back,' she muttered, the colour rising in her cheeks, and she knew her face must almost match the briefs.

'I think that is my line, Lisa.' A faint smile tugged the edges of his mouth, but the expression in his eyes was still totally cynical. 'That room is your study, nothing more. So try acting like an adult instead of a spoilt child and return these.' He dropped the red briefs back on to the pile of clothes. 'Back to where they belong, in the master suite. I thought we had settled our differences this morning. I hope I was not wrong?' Shrugging out of his jacket, he hooked it over one shoulder and with his free hand began unbuttoning the first few buttons of his shirt.

He was too close, his height and wide shouldered frame intimidating. Her gaze slipped to the broad expanse of his tanned chest, and Lisa felt the familiar flood of warmth weaken her defences. She fought against it and, glancing up, her eyes met his. He knew how he affected her, at least on a sexual level, but to her surprise a tender smile curled his mouth.

'Sometimes I forget how innocent you are,' Alex murmured, and trailed a long finger over her burning cheek.

She felt about two inches tall, and totally foolish. She had decided to stay with Alex, but no way was she climbing meekly back into bed with him. 'Not any more,' she said bitterly, 'you saw to that.'

'Hush.' He pressed a finger to her lips. 'Allow me to apologise. You should never have been subjected to what happened last night. The lady had no right to intrude on our privacy, and it was unkind of me to even hint that you were in any way at fault. As your husband, it is my duty to protect you from any embarrassment, and I singularly failed to do so.' With the pad of his finger he flicked her bottom lip before dropping his hand to his side. 'Please forgive me.'

Lisa's mouth fell open and her blue eyes widened to their fullest extent on his serious face. Alex apologising and begging forgiveness? She could hardly believe it.

'Forgive you?' she parroted.

'Yes, ' he said simply. 'I should have realised you, with your lack of experience of predatory females who are all

too common in the world, were in no position to argue
with a woman like Margot. The golden purity that drew
me to you in the first place should have reminded me of
the fact. So, once again, am I forgiven?'

His deep velvet voice flowed like honey over her raw
nerves, and in a voice she hardly recognised as her own,
Lisa said, 'Yes, apology accepted.' In that moment she
would have forgiven him murder. His body moved in
close against her own, his dark head bent and he angled
a kiss across her open lips, a kiss of tenderness and gentle
possession.

Lisa stared up into his sexy, slumberous eyes as he
raised his head and moved back a pace. 'Thank you, Lisa.'
he husked.

Fighting down the urge to fling her arms around him—
an impossible action given she was still holding a pile of
garments, she realised, glancing down at her overloaded
arms—she was suddenly aware of where she was and
what she had been doing, and she stumbled into speech.
'Actually, it is I who should thank you. The computer is
brilliant; it was good of you to buy it for me, but no need.'
She was babbling, but couldn't seem to stop.

'Enough, sweetheart.' Alex grinned, and with a toss of
his dark head he indicated the door opposite. 'After you.'

Her nervous tension dissolved and, taking a deep
breath, she slipped past him and into the dressing room.
Alex confounded and confused her, and retreat seemed
the best option, but that did not mean she was going to
crawl back into bed with him. Moving swiftly, she quickly
placed the lingerie and clothes in the requisite drawers
and the closet. His apology, she knew, was genuine, but
it did not alter the fact he was about to betray her, by
dealing with Nigel. Perhaps that was the difference be-

tween men and women, Lisa thought sadly. Men could separate business completely from their emotional life.

Lisa, unfortunately, could not. By the same token, she knew she would never agree to Lawson's being flattened to make way for something else. It was her parents' memorial. Maybe that made her a poor businesswoman, but she did not care. There had to be more to life than simply the pursuit of riches. But she had a growing conviction her husband did not share her view.

Reluctantly she walked back into the bedroom; she heard the sound of the shower from the *ensuite* bathroom and heaved a sigh of relief. She didn't have to face Alex again just yet; a glance at her watch told her it was five. Time to have a cup of tea and restore her equilibrium before she got ready for the evening ahead.

'Pour me a cup,' Alex commanded, and Lisa almost dropped the teapot. He had showered and shaved and was sporting a pair of well-washed jeans and nothing else.

'I didn't think you drank tea?' she murmured.

Pulling out a chair opposite her he sat down. 'If you do, I do. It is part of marriage, the sharing.' Alex's faintly accented statement had a mocking edge as he reached out and accepted the cup she had automatically filled for him.

'Yes, yes, I suppose so,' she acknowledged.

'Which is why I thought, tomorrow, you and I could spend the day in the countryside. I had my people get on to some real estate agents while we were away, and they have come up with a couple of quite decent looking properties.'

'Properties? You mean houses?'

'But of course.' And with a brief glance around the kitchen Alex returned his attention to her puzzled face. 'This place is adequate in the short term, but obviously we will need a family home. Knowing you as I do the country is the answer, I think.'

Lisa sipped her tea, unsure of how to respond. She had always lived in a large house on the outskirts of Stratford-upon-Avon; she had only to walk out of her garden to take a stroll along country lanes. Alex was right; she did prefer the country. But what of Alex? While not notorious as an international jet-setter like his father, she wasn't sure she could see him as a country squire. 'Do you actually have a proper home?' she surprised herself by asking. 'I mean, apart from here?'

His black eyes twinkled with laughter. 'I hate to spoil my image, but in fact I actually still live with my mother. Officially my residence is the villa on Kos. The yacht is berthed in the harbour there, and whenever I have time I go back home. Otherwise I tend to stay in an apartment the company owns, or a hotel.'

'Of course!' Lisa exclaimed. 'I should have guessed the villa we stayed in when we visited your mother was yours.' She remembered thinking at the time that the sitting room and bedroom of their suite had had a very lived-in feel about them; the pictures on the walls had been mostly of boats—a hobby of Alex's—and there had been a couple of trophies for yacht racing that had borne Alex's name. For a few timeless seconds her eyes locked with his and they shared a mutual memory of a night spent in sheer bliss.

'Yes,' Alex confirmed, his eyes sweeping over her shoulders and the curve of her breast before returning to study the surprised and faintly embarrassed expression on her delicately etched features. A smile quirked the corner of his mouth. 'But now I think I am old enough to own my home,' he teased. 'Don't you agree?'

Lisa couldn't disagree without getting into a morass of

lies. The truth was not an option. She was waiting to see if Alex was going to betray her, along with her step-brother. She gave the only answer she could think of. 'Yes, well,' she qualified, 'we will see.' And, pushing back her chair and getting to her feet, she added, 'But right now I'd better get dressed. What time did you say we were meeting your father?'

Only the slight narrowing of his dark eyes gave away the fact her evasion had been noted and disliked, but, rising to his feet, he said, 'Seven or seven-thirty. I have a few calls to make in my study. I won't be long.'

The bathroom off the master bedroom was almost as big as the bedroom itself. Elegantly designed and con-structed in pale pink streaked marble, it held a large dou-ble shower and a circular spa bath. Plus all the usual fa-cilities. The lingering scent of Alex hung on the air, making her catch her breath.

She did not linger in the shower and, as she had washed her hair that morning, five minutes later she entered the dressing room, a towel wrapped around her slender curves, and selected fresh briefs and quickly slipped them on.

Seated at the dressing table, she twisted the long length of her hair into a high pleat on the back of her head. With the deft use of a few pins, she quickly had a very fash-ionable hairstyle. She pulled a few tendrils of hair loose around her face and the back of her neck and surveyed the finished result. Sophisticated, but not too contrived, she thought, and then began applying her make-up.

Rising to her feet, she crossed to the cupboards that ran the full length of two walls.

Sliding open one of the doors, she withdrew the gown she had hung there the night before, ready for this eve-ning's dinner party. She eyed the dress with dismay.

When she had bought it in a boutique in Stratford she had
thought it was perfect, with stiletto-heeled evening shoes
and a purse dyed to match. The whole ensemble was suitable for a sophisticated lady wanting to seduce her husband. Now she was not so sure. But realistically she had
nothing else; the clothes she had packed were day and
casual wear. So, unless she wanted to meet Alex's father
in trousers or a business suit, she had no choice.

She stepped into the blue gown and pulled the zip up
its side. It was a simple sheath; the bodice had a bra built
in and was cut straight across her breasts in a band of
delicately beaded embroidery, revealing the soft swell of
her breasts. The rest stuck to her like a second skin, to
end some six inches above her knees in another band of
beading. She slipped her feet into the shoes, then quickly
slipped pearl studs into her ear lobes, and fastened the
matching string of pearls around her throat. She dabbed
some of her favourite perfume behind her ears and the
back of her knees. Straightening, she turned towards the
mirror to cast her reflection a brief glance.

'Wow, that is some dress.'

Lisa turned at the sound of Alex's voice, and felt her
breath catch at the image he presented. He was still only
wearing jeans, and his hand had obviously been ruffling
his hair, but there was something about his stance, a sense
of predatory strength as his dark eyes swept down over
her curvaceous body and lingered for an instant on the
long length of her legs before returning to her face. The
deepening gleam of sexual desire turned his eyes to black
as they clashed with hers.

'Maybe we should forget dinner,' Alex murmured,
stepping towards her, his intention obvious.

'You'd better hurry up and get dressed, or we'll be

late,' she retaliated, as she deftly sidestepped around him. He stopped her with a hand on her arm.

'Your're right; I got trapped on the telephone. Be a sweetheart and mix me a whisky and soda. I have a feeling I am going to need it tonight.'

'What about driving?' she murmured.

'Bert is driving us there, and we will grab a taxi back; no need for the old boy to have a late night.'

A few minutes later, she walked back into the bedroom, a glass of whisky and soda in her hand. She stopped inside the door. Alex was slipping on the jacket of his dinner suit, and he turned at her entrance.

'Thanks, Lisa.' He moved to her side and took the glass from her hand; his fingers brushed hers and sent a swift jolt of electricity up her arm. He was devastatingly attractive at any time, but wearing a superbly cut dinner suit, with his black hair slicked back from his broad forehead, he exuded an aura of powerful male magnetism that few men possessed. She watched as he raised the glass to his mouth and drained it. She was fascinated by the way his strong tanned throat moved when he swallowed, and only realised she was staring when he spoke.

'Come on, Lisa, we're cutting it fine as it is.'

At the hotel the doorman opened the car door almost before it had stopped. Taking a deep breath, Lisa alighted with some elegance, and before she could even take a step Alex was at her side, his hand under her elbow to guide her inside…

CHAPTER FIVE

WALKING from the brightness of the fine June evening into the darkened interior of the hotel Lisa was blinded for a second, and she stumbled slightly. Alex tightened his grip on her arm.

'You did not hit the whisky as well, I hope,' he quipped, his dark eyes laughing down at her in easy intimacy.

The charm of his smile squeezed her heart. 'No,' she snapped, scared by the emotion he could so easily arouse in her. 'Though being blackmailed by one's husband is reason enough for anyone to hit the bottle,' she informed him with sweet sarcasm.

'Blackmailed?' His brows drew together in a frown. 'Ah, you mean your beloved stepfamily. I was in a hurry this morning and I said the first thing that came into my head.'

'So you say,' she murmured. 'But it worked. I'm here at your side instead of at home in Stratford.' She didn't know why she was needling him, and as for her stepfamily, Nigel was certainly not her beloved anything...

'Your home is with me,' Alex said, his grip on her arm tightening. 'Now drop this stupid conversation. This evening—' He stopped in mid-sentence. Lisa followed the direction of his gaze and felt her heart sink in her chest.

Some thirty feet away but moving towards them was a tall, overweight, grey-haired man. The family likeness was unmistakable; it had to be Alex's father. By his side was a young woman, dark-haired and beautiful, thirty-something, and moreover someone Lisa had met before.

'Damn, I thought I had frightened the woman off,' Alex swore, his dark eyes narrowing intently on the approaching couple.

Lisa straightened her shoulders and shrugged off Alex's supporting hand. 'Obviously not. Fiona Fife, I believe, another one of your lady-friends.' She was determined to act the sophisticate tonight in front of Alex and his father, but she had a horrible feeling it was not going to be so easy, especially if she was going to keep bumping into her husband's mistresses at every turn!

Alex glanced at her, his dark eyes clashing with her angry blue. 'I do believe you're jealous,' he prompted softly.

Lisa gave a slight shrug, pretending indifference. 'Should I be?' she asked lightly, and held his gaze with difficulty.

'No. You are the only girl for me, darling, plus I am not old enough for that particular lady,' he drawled mockingly, with a brief glance at the other couple. Tilting his head towards Lisa, he added, *sotto voce*, 'It is my father she has designs on. She is hopeful of becoming wife number six. Our Italian friend informed me of that at that party we attended in Monte Carlo. I did try to warn her off, with tales of his weak heart and nowhere near as much money as she imagines, but it looks like I failed.' His firm mouth twisted in a wry grimace. 'Not for the first time, unfortunately.'

Inexplicably, Lisa's spirits lifted considerably at his words. Now she knew why he had danced with the woman when they were on their honeymoon, and somehow it made her feel a whole lot better.

'Brace yourself, here they come.' Alex slid his arm

around her waist and urged her forward. 'Father,' he greeted the older man warmly. 'It's been a while.'

'Indeed it has,' the older man agreed. 'You've met Fiona?' He indicated the woman at his side, and both Alex and Lisa gave a social smile and said hello to the black-haired beauty.

'And this must be your wife.' Mr Solomos senior's dark eyes were so like his sons as he scrutinised Lisa from head to toe, and then he broke out into a broad grin. 'Charming, absolutely beautiful. Though you could have told me, Alex. I thought I was the only one who married quickly in our family. Obviously you have inherited some of my traits after all.'

She felt Alex stiffen at her side but, ignoring his father's comment he simply said, 'Lisa, allow me to introduce you to my father, Leo, and don't be taken in by his charm; it is his stock-in-trade.'

Lisa held out her hand and the old man engulfed it in his. He looked like Alex, though he was a few inches shorter, but he did not have the same aura of compelling dynamism that Alex possessed in such abundance.

'How do you do?' she said formally, and felt the colour rise in her face when Leo laughed out loud.

'So formal, so very English. I hope you are a match for my son's fiery Greek temperament.'

'Lisa is a perfect match in every way,' Alex informed him, subjecting Lisa to a slow, sensual appraisal that left no one in any doubt of exactly what he meant.

His father chuckled again. 'I'm glad to hear it.' Turning to Fiona with a smile, he demanded, 'Shall we tell them?'

Fiona's eyes lifted to Alex, the smile on her perfectly made-up face one of triumph. 'Oh, yes, I think your son and his wife—' she glanced briefly at Lisa, but immediately turned her attention back to Alex '—should be the first to know.'

'Fiona and I are flying to Las Vegas tomorrow afternoon to get married.'

Was the old man aware of the effect he had on his son? Lisa wondered. She felt Alex's fingers dig into her side, and the increased tension in his body, but not by a flicker of an eyelash did he display his concern.

'Congratulations appear to be in order all round,' Alex offered, his eyes narrowing fractionally on his father. 'I trust everything else is in order also.'

Watching him, Lisa actually felt some pity for her husband in that moment. Having met his mother, and seen the love and affection between them, she realised how hard it must be for him when he was about to gain stepmother number five!

'Yes, Alex, I visited Mr Niarchos this morning. He will be in touch tomorrow.'

Lisa felt the tension drain out of Alex, and his hand at her waist relaxed slightly.

'Good,' he agreed urbanely. 'Shall we forgo drinks and go into dinner?'

A slight frown of puzzlement creased Lisa's smooth brow. There was obviously more being said between the two men than the words they spoke revealed. Then it hit her—the mention of the lawyer. Alex was checking his father had made a prenuptial agreement. How sad... But it was nothing to do with her, she told herself, as she walked towards the dining room at her husband's side. She couldn't help being aware of the intense interest their foursome aroused in the hotel's clientele. Mostly down to Alex; she had no illusions on that score. He was an exceptionally impressive man.

The restaurant was filled with customers, but Leo had

booked ahead, and the *maître d'* greeted him with the familiarity of an old friend. They were directed to a table and a waiter appeared at Leo's side in a second, quickly followed by the wine waiter.

The best champagne was requested, and Leo ordered for Fiona without bothering to ask. Alex ordered a Waldorf salad for starters, followed by steak and fresh fruit, but at least he had the manners to ask Lisa what she preferred. She selected the pâté and opted for the fillet of trout garnished with prawns and melted butter. Hiding a smile, she recognized Alex had inherited his chauvinistic traits from his father...

'You're not watching your figure, then, Lisa?' Fiona queried, in the first sentence she had addressed to Lisa. 'But then of course you have never been a model. I have to be so body-conscious; everything must be perfect.' And with a simpering glance at Leo and a hand on his arm she concluded, 'But that is how Leo likes me.'

From the lecherous look on the old man's face as he stared at Fiona's cleavage—she was wearing a white slip dress that plunged to her waist back and front—Leo would have preferred her like Lisa's trout: naked but for a covering of butter, Lisa thought dryly, before responding, 'I'm sure he does.' She paused for a second, stumped for something else to say. She knew she had just been insulted, but she was too polite to retaliate.

The arrival of the waiter with the bottle of champagne was a timely interuption. The waiter filled all four glasses, and Leo raised his first.

'A toast to the newlyweds, Alex and Lisa. And the soon to be wed, Fiona and myself.'

Lisa lifted her glass and sipped the sparkling champagne; she touched glasses with the couple sitting opposite.

'And your husband,' Alex murmured.

It was a rectangular table, with Leo next to Fiona and Alex at her side. She turned her head slightly towards him and touched her glass to his. 'Of course, my husband,' she conceded with a smile, opting for a casual response. There were enough undercurrents of tension in the atmosphere without her adding to it by arguing with Alex.

'To my darling wife.' Alex held her gaze for a few heart-stopping seconds, his eyes darkening sensually with muted desire. She knew he was doing it deliberately, but she still had to fight to control the sudden upsurge in her pulse rate, and hastily took a deep drink of the wine and looked away.

Surprisingly, Leo Solomos turned out to be a witty, convivial host. He asked Lisa about her work and family, and congratulated her on her business acumen. The food was cooked to perfection and Lisa slowly began to relax. In fact she discovered she quite enjoyed the company. Though when Leo tried to fill her glass for the fourth time, she refused.

Three bottles of champagne were consumed, and Lisa couldn't help thinking that for a woman who was so bothered about her appearance, Fiona could certainly down her drink. The only time the conversation flagged was when Fiona spoke. She seemed to have a perfect memory for every modelling assignment she had ever been on, and complete recall of every gown she'd worn. Thankfully, Leo had the happy knack of distracting her by placing a finger on her lips or with a kiss.

Alex on the other hand, played the part of the perfect husband, with reassuring smiles for Lisa or a quick aside to enquire if she was okay. By the time dessert arrived Lisa was happy to concede that Leo was a charming man.

His only fault appeared to be his penchant for young women.

She had just stopped laughing at Leo's tall tale about a donkey that snored, on the island of Kos, and was about to resume eating her fruit salad, when a disturbing realisation hit her like a blow to the stomach. She replaced her spoon in the dish and pushed it away; she could not eat another thing.

'What is the matter?' Alex demanded, turning slightly in his seat, his dark head angled towards her. 'The fruit is not to your liking?' His thoughtful gaze searched her suddenly pale face, and she realised her husband was a very astute man; he saw far too much.

She forced a smile to her lips. 'No, it's fine, but, really, I've had enough.' More than enough, she thought with a heavy heart. It had suddenly occurred to her the friendly smiling Leo opposite was not just Alex's father, he was also his business partner. If Alex was trying to take over her company, then obviously his father was aware of the situation. The older man's good humour and friendly interest about Lisa's work were as false as the marriage vows he kept repeating…

'Are you sure?' Alex insisted, placing a finger under her chin and turning her head to face him. She was unaware of the pain shadowing her blue eyes, but it was apparent to Alex. 'You're tired and not quite yourself; I forgot,' he murmured huskily, as he smoothed his finger down her throat. Her pulse leapt at his touch and he noted the fact with a slight twist to his sensual mouth.

'We can leave now, if you like,' he prompted softly. 'An early night would suit both of us.'

'No, no I'm fine.' Lisa confirmed, forcing a smile.

Thankfully, the waiter arrived at that moment, and Leo demanded quite loudly, 'We will have coffee in the lounge. I don't enjoy a meal without a good cigar afterwards.'

Seated next to Alex on a low leather sofa, his arm casually placed around her shoulders, his fingers on her flesh playing havoc with her nervous system, Lisa chewed on her bottom lip, torn between wanting the evening to end and anxiety about being alone with Alex again. When the waiter deposited the coffee tray on the low table in front of them Lisa leant forward, displacing Alex's arm, and took a cup of coffee from the tray before the waiter had a chance to hand it to her. Lounging on the sofa to the left of her was Leo, a huge cigar clamped between his teeth, and the stomach-curling smell as he blew smoke out was making her feel sick. At least that was what she told herself as she quickly drained her coffee cup and leapt to her feet, excusing her departure with the need to visit the rest room.

In the cool confines of the marble-walled room, she heaved a sigh of relief. But it was short-lived, as Fiona walked in. With a brief smile at the other woman, Lisa opened her purse and withdrew a lipgloss. She eyed her reflection in the mirror; there was nothing in her expression, she thought gratefully, that revealed the fraught state of her emotions. The social mask was still in place, and carefully she outlined her full mouth with the rose gloss.

'Funny to think after this weekend I will be your stepmother-in-law,' Fiona remarked, standing beside Lisa at the mirror, primping her dark hair. Her brown eyes clashed with Lisa's in the mirror. 'And I'm only a year or so older than you.'

More like ten, Lisa thought, but didn't say so. 'Yes, well, I don't suppose you'll want me to call you Mum.' She responded with a tinge of sarcasm. She found it very hard to believe Fiona was marrying Leo for any other reason but money.

'Good God! No! But there's no reason why we can't be friends, you and I, after all, we have a lot in common,' Fiona said with a smug grin. 'The way you hooked Alex was absolutely brilliant.'

'The way I hooked Alex?' Lisa prompted, her blue eyes puzzled. She had not 'hooked Alex'; it had been the other way round.

Oblivious to Lisa's surprise, Fiona carried on, 'So quickly. I couldn't have done better myself. Well, I didn't, did I?' She grimaced. 'But I've got Leo. Though I don't mind admitting when I met the pair of them in March, at Leo's sixtieth birthday in Nice, I had every intention of going after Alex. It was obvious to me—feminine intuition, if you like—that he was fast losing interest in that Margot creature. He was distinctly cool towards her. No, if I hadn't had to go to the Caribbean on a modelling assignment, I would have given you a run for your money over Alex. Still, Leo's not too bad—and, let's face it, they're both as rich as Croesus.'

'But surely you must love Leo,' Lisa prompted. To think a woman was marrying for money was one thing; to be told she was seemed quite extraordinary to Lisa.

'Oh, I do. I love his money, and he's not a bad old stick.' With a last casual flick at her hair she turned to leave. 'Come on, we'd better get back. You can't leave a couple of wealthy men like those two on their own for too long, there are a lot of predatory women out there.'

Lisa chuckled; she couldn't help herself. Anyone more predatory than Fiona would be hard to find. She followed the other woman back to the lounge and her blue-eyed gaze instinctively settled on Alex.

He was the epitome of male sophistication, lounging

back on the deep leather sofa, his long legs stretched out before him in casual ease. The man was sinfully attractive. A tiny shiver of excitement quivered deep inside. And, as she knew only too well, he was a deeply passionate and wickedly sensual lover. Fiona was wrong about the pulling power of the Solomos wealth, she thought, a wry smile curving her mouth as Alex stood up at her approach. He could be a pauper and he would still have women falling at his feet.

'You're smiling; you must be feeling better.' Dark eyes scrutinised her slightly flushed face. 'But I think it is time we left.' He lifted a large tanned hand and let his fingertip trace the purple shadows under her eyes in a fleeting gesture that made her whole body tense. 'Okay?'

Lisa looked up into his eyes, the smile fading from her face. It wasn't okay, but she really had no alternative. 'Yes,' she agreed, and managed not to flinch when his dark head lowered and he pressed the lightest of kisses on her soft lips.

After reiterating their congratulations on Leo's forthcoming nuptials, they said goodnight and left.

Lisa stepped outside into the mild night air, and took a deep breath to clear her head and to steady her wildly fluctuating emotions. She loved Alex; he only had to look at her and she ached for him. To deny him was to deny herself the wonder of his lovemaking, the pleasure she found in his arms. Yet she no longer trusted him.

The doorman was holding open the door of a black cab and Alex, with a hand in the small of her back, was urging her forward. She slid along the seat and Alex followed, casually placing a long arm around her slender shoulders. She immediately shuffled further along the seat. Alex cast her a sidelong glance, one brow arched quizzically, but he made no comment as he simply hauled her back against him. Leaning forward, he instructed the driver on their destination.

The warmth of his large male body, the subtle scent of his cologne all conspired to break down her reservations about their relationship. As Alex sat back, his glance lingered for a moment on the long length of her legs. She attempted to pull the hem of her dress lower and he chuckled, leaning his head back against the seat.

'You did that the very first time I set eyes on you. Not still shy, Lisa?' he teased.

'Not at all,' she denied, but felt foolish. But then most women were foolish where love was concerned, she thought sadly, unless one happened to be like the Fionas of this world; unfortunately for Lisa, she wasn't. Sighing, she let her head fall back; she was tired, and with Alex's warm hand cupping her bare shoulder, his thumb gently kneading the back of her neck, she gradually felt the tension ease from her body. Why fight it? she asked herself. If Alex had married her to get Lawson's, she would find out soon enough. Meanwhile, why not enjoy her marriage while it lasted? After Alex she knew she would never marry any another man. A soft sigh escaped her and she allowed her head to rest on his broad shoulder, and he held her in a comfortable silence as the cab navigated the London streets.

It was only when they entered the private elevator which would take them to the penthouse that Lisa felt the tension returning. She glanced at Alex as he pressed the requisite button and the metal doors slid shut, closing them into the luxuriously carpeted box. 'How do you feel about your father's up-coming marriage?' she asked, more to break the silence than out of any real curiosity, as the elevator whisked them ever nearer the apartment, and the bedroom…

Alex flicked her a glance. 'Don't be concerned; I am not,' he drawled in a dry, mocking tone. 'I gave up worrying about my father years ago.'

'You don't mind he's marrying a woman younger than you.'

'Why should I? We will hardly ever see them,' Alex responded dismissively.

The elevator doors swung open and she flinched as Alex reached for her arm and guided her across the hallway to the apartment. 'But he is your father...' she insisted.

'Drop it,' he snapped as he opened the door and ushered her into the apartment.

'Aren't you worried about him? You must care for him.'

Closing the door behind him, Alex said bluntly, 'It is really not your concern, Lisa. Now, do you want a nightcap, or shall we go straight to bed?'

His response simply confirmed her judgement of the man. Alex did not even care for his father, so what hope had she of him genuinely caring for her? None! She didn't want a drink, but neither did she want to go to bed—at least not with Alex. Or so she told herself. 'I'll have a very small cognac.'

Dropping her purse on the hall table, she kicked off her shoes before following him into the living room. She watched as he crossed to the drinks cabinet and poured a small amount of cognac into a crystal glass, and then twice as much of the liquor into another glass. Turning around, he closed the distance between them, a glass in each hand. He held out the smaller measure to her. As she took it, her fingers brushed against his.

She resented the way a simple touch set her pulse racing, and, glancing up at him, she resented even more the way he knew exactly how she felt. She wanted to rage at him, demand to know about his deal with Nigel. She needed to know the truth. But she could not bring herself to ask.

'You look angry,' he observed with narrowed eyes. 'And there is no need. My father is perfectly able to look after himself.' Lifting his glass to his mouth, he drained it, then placed it on the table. 'But perhaps it is not my father's wedding that has angered you. Perhaps something else,' he mused. 'You're not still thinking of last night's farce? I thought we had settled that,' he declared, eyeing her speculatively.

'No,' she swiftly denied, and in truth Nigel, not Margot, was behind her simmering anger. 'I'm simply amazed you can dismiss your father's marriage so lightly.' Tossing back her head, she swallowed the cognac in one go.' Leaning forward, she deposited her glass on the table. Straightening up, she realised he had moved closer. But he made no attempt to touch her.

'Somehow, I don't think my father is the real reason for all the latent anger that shimmers in your expressive eyes, nor do I think it is because of Margot's untimely intrusion into our life. So, I have to ask myself, what exactly is it that you are hiding?' he queried silkily.

He was too close, in more ways than one. The ease with which he had seen through her attempts to hide the real reason for her anger was worrying. 'I'm not hiding anything.' Lisa paused, then added with a flash of inspiration, 'Unless you consider a conversation with your future stepmother in the rest room a secret.'

He tipped his arrogant head back, a dangerous gleam lighting his dark eyes. 'Fiona? Explain,' he commanded hardly.

'Well, according to Fiona, she and I are very alike, and

if she hadn't had to go on a modelling assignment after your father's sixtieth birthday party she would now be your girlfriend. Fiona congratulated me on how quickly I nipped in and…' She hesitated delicately, the beginnings of a smile twitching her lips. She could see Alex detested the idea of women discussing him in the ladies' room, and she began to enjoy herself.

'Now, let me think. I believe "hooked" was the term she used. Apparently Fiona sensed you were growing tired of Margot and looking for a replacement.'

His snort of disgust was music to Lisa's ears. 'And you'll be glad to know Fiona wants us to be chums. In fact, she said I was almost as good as she at snagging a man, and she bears me no ill will. Mainly because she has hooked your father, and the money is all in the family.'

'It's no more than I expected from her,' Alex declared.

'Yes, well, I have often been mistaken for a bimbo, but if she were blonde Fiona would certainly take first prize. She quite happily admitted she doesn't love Leo, but his money.' Saying it out loud, Lisa couldn't keep her own personal sense of outrage out of her voice.

'Lisa.' He caught her wrist, his thumb idly stroking up her palm. She gave him a stormy look, and tried to pull her hand free. He smiled wryly and let go of her hand, but slid his arm around her waist, pulling her against his length. 'Forget Fiona. I will make sure she never bothers you. Now let's go to bed.'

Lisa's teeth ground together in frustration; her blue eyes flashed with temper. She did not want to go to bed, in fact she hated the idea, but she really had no choice. She supposed she should be thankful he had swallowed the reason for her anger without digging deeper, but she didn't feel grateful, just trapped. 'I suppose so,' she muttered.

Gleaming black eyes held hers and he laughed softly as though he knew exactly what was going through her mind. 'You're very young, Lisa. You still see everything in black and white. Unfortunately, life teaches one there are a dozen shades of grey in between. Don't worry about Leo; he knows exactly what he is paying for,' he assured her with cynical amusement.

She shrugged out of his embrace. 'I'm not that young, and I don't find it in the least amusing, and I bet your mother didn't either, the first time it happened.'

Alex winced. Her barb had hit home. 'All right.' He held his hands up in a gesture of surrender. 'I will say no more. Run along to bed. You've just reminded me, I have a call to make. My mother has to be told before Leo's latest escapade appears in the press.'

Lisa did not hesitate; she spun on her heel and headed for the dressing room.

Quickly selecting a plain white cotton tee shirt, she shot into the bathroom and stripped off her clothes. She completed her bedtime ritual in five minutes flat and walked into the adjoining bedroom. She stopped and stared at the huge bed and a vivid image of Margot standing in the exact same spot last night filled her mind.

It was no good; she could not get into bed with Alex and pretend nothing had happened. She simply could not do it. Turning, she headed for the door.

'I need a shower and shave, but I won't be long.' Alex strolled in from the dressing room, casually rubbing his jaw with his hand.

Lisa stopped at the sound of his voice and glanced at him, her eyes widening on his virtually naked body. Hot colour flooded her cheeks and she was helpless to look away. He was all tanned satin skin, sheathing rippling, hard-packed muscle and sinew, with a smattering of curling black body hair arrowing down over his flat belly to disappear beneath the band of a pair of black briefs that enhanced his masculine attributes rather than concealed them. She breathed in deeply and looked up, her wide blue eyes meeting deep brown.

In one lithe stride he was at her side. 'Why the blush? I am covered, and you have seen me naked before,' he teased.

'Yes, me and countless other women, I'm sure,' she snapped, brushing past him.

'Not so fast.' Alex's hand curved around her arm in a grip of steel. 'Now what is eating you?' he demanded, his eyes narrowing angrily on her furious face.

'Nothing, nothing at all. But I am not sleeping in that bed with you,' she told him bluntly. 'I suddenly realised there is not room on your bedpost for another notch, and I have no intention of being one of the multitude again,' she said with biting sarcasm.

'For heaven's sake, Lisa, it is only a bed.'

'Yes, I can see that, but somehow I had this weird idea the marital bed was something special. You, on the other hand, have shared that one with so many women I doubt you even know the score.' To her intense satisfaction she saw a dull tide of red darken his chiselled features. She realised she had actually managed to get through his arrogant exterior and embarrass him.

'You are far too sensitive for your own good,' Alex snapped, and, dropping her hand, he continued, 'But I take your point. Though for your information I can keep count, and it is nowhere near as many as you imagine.'

'That's the problem, I don't have to imagine,' Lisa responded, her eyes blazing up at him in hurt and anger.

'It's one thing to know your husband has had lovers in the past, but it's quite another to be presented with one of them naked, and by your bed.

'Our bed, Lisa,' he replied with silken emphasis. 'Margot and her ilk belong in the past. Accept it.'

His arrogant command made her blood boil. 'As Margot had to,' she sneered. Why she was defending the other woman, she had no idea, but he made her so mad. 'That woman loved you; I could see it in her eyes.'

'Love.' Alex lifted a shoulder in an infinitesimal shrug. 'Whatever that means, it was not something Margot was ever afflicted with.' His dark eyes mocked her. 'Now money, yes.'

A chill ran over Lisa's flesh and extinguished her anger at a stroke. She felt curiously calm. 'You don't believe in love,' she said softly, the effect of his 'Whatever that means' slicing at the very heart of her.

Alex snorted in disgust. 'With a father like mine, what do you think?' he drawled. 'The man falls in love at the drop of a hat, or maybe the drop of a dress would be more appropriate.' His harsh laugh sounded the death knell of Lisa's hope. 'He compounds his stupidity by marrying them. Substitute sex for love, then you'll be nearer the truth.'

Appalled, she stood glued to the spot. Alex meant what he said; he really did not believe in love. It was several seconds before she could speak. 'Why did you marry me, Alex?' she asked quietly, her blue eyes holding his.

Apparently surprised, he raised his eyebrows sharply above his dark eyes, and, catching her by the shoulders, he drew her against him. 'I married you, Lisa, because I wanted you on sight.' He lifted a strong brown hand and let his fingertip trace the bow of her top lip in a fleeting gesture that made her body tense. 'After spending only one day with you I knew I had to have you. You are all I ever wanted in a wife,' he said softly, his dark eyes smiling into hers. 'Believe me.'

If his words were meant to reassure her, they failed miserably. Something deep down in Lisa shrivelled up under his charming smile. He didn't even realise his answer was an insult, she recognised sadly. Shrugging her shoulder free of his hand, she stepped back. 'Why me, and not Margot?' she asked quietly.

'Really, Lisa.' His dark gaze scanned over her stiff figure, a frown pleating his brow. 'You are not that naive. Margot is an actress.' He said it as if he was talking to a child, the exasperation in his tone clearly evident.

She shook her head in disbelief. The arrogant conceit of the man was absolutely unbelievable, and, raising her eyes to his, she prompted. 'Well, I'm a working girl.' She could not let it go. She was so vulnerable where he was concerned, loving him as she did. She had to know the worst, then maybe she could begin to get over him.

'Don't be so obtuse.' His deep brown eyes clashed with her brilliant blue ones. 'There is a world of difference between a thirty-something ambitious actress, and an intelligent, pure young woman who works and is protected by her family.' Alex's sensual mouth slanted sardonically. 'The first is strictly mistress material, and you, my darling Lisa, are the type men marry.'

'I see,' Lisa murmured, and closed her eyes for a second, fighting back the tears. She had fallen in love with a man who did not believe in the emotion.

'No, you don't see.' His voice tickled her ear and her eyes flew open. Alex had moved, and she stiffened as he slid a large hand around her waist and pulled her in to the hard heat of him. 'I married you because I was desperate with wanting you. No woman has ever affected me the way you do. And, much to my delight, I have discovered you have an endless capacity for enjoyment that perfectly matches my own,' he opined huskily. Lisa shivered as he pressed his lips to the pulse beating frantically in her throat. 'Now, let's go to bed, hmm.'

Afterwards, she would decide it was the softly drawled 'hmm' that had finally caused her to flip her lid...

Lisa curled her fingers into a fist, and swung with all her might, catching Alex a glancing blow on the side of his head. His arm fell from her waist and she turned on him like a mad thing. 'You have the most enormous ego of any man in the world, and you are deaf to boot,' she snarled.

Alex's hand came down on her slender shoulders and held her slightly away from him. 'What the hell was that for?' he demanded harshly.

'I am not sleeping with you in that bed. Got it?' she yelled. How he had dared to suggest it after what he had just revealed beggared belief.

'Enough!' Alex held up his hands, setting her free. 'Sleep in the guest room tonight, if you must. I will have the bed replaced tomorrow.' And with a last grim look at her red, furious face, he strode across the room into the bathroom.

Lisa slipped into the room she had occupied the night before and climbed into bed. She was exhausted, but the thoughts crowding her mind would not let her sleep. For a deliriously happy bride returning from her honeymoon only a few short days ago, confident in herself and the love of her husband, the past two days seemed like a horror story. But they were all too real and she had to face up to reality. Alex had his own reason for marrying her and it was not love.

Alex had taught her a hard lesson. To show one's innermost feelings with total honesty was damaging to one's health. Her marriage was over before it had really begun, though it broke her heart to have to admit it. She remembered all the times they had made love and she had spilled her heart out to him, declaring her undying love; it had never once occurred to her that Alex did not feel the same. More fool her...

She turned restlessly on the bed. Being brutally honest with herself, she admitted, it seemed huge and empty without Alex to share it with her. But she was not going to give in, she vowed. Alex had blackmailed her into staying with him. He had said his earlier threat to keep her with him had been a joke, but she was not so sure. She didn't know what to believe any more. All she knew for certain was she must keep Alex sweet until she found out exactly what he was up to with regard to Lawson's.

With her mind made up, she tried to sleep, but it was no good, she was wide awake. Slipping out of bed, she crossed over to her computer and switched it on. She had never felt so alone in her whole life, but blinking back the tears, she refused to cry. She E-mailed Jed. She needed to talk to someone, and the lonely hours before dawn in England were late evening in Montana; he might be on-line.

To her relief he was there. Within a very short space of time, Lisa was confiding to Jed the whole sorry story of her hasty marriage.

Jed listened and consoled, and his advice was optimistic. He pointed out she had not given the marriage much of a chance. Alex probably did love her, but was not capable of saying the words. She did not know for sure that he meant to take over her company. Why didn't she ask him? There might be a simple explanation. Anyway, she was his wife and was entitled to half of everything he owned. So was she being totally reasonable?

She replied. Was he simply sticking up for his own sex? Jed denied the accusation and reminded her she had been married in church, before God, and her vows were not something to dismiss lightly. They chatted for over an hour and Lisa, completely absorbed in what she was doing, didn't see the bedroom door open, or the tall dark figure of the man watching her. Nor did she see the tenderness in the gleaming black eyes that lingered on her slender body crouched over the machine…

CHAPTER SIX

ALEX manoeuvred his red Ferrari between two massive stone pillars crowned by Lions, past open gates, and gunned the car up a long winding drive.

'Are you sure this is the right house?' Lisa queried irritably. She had overslept this morning, mainly because it had been five in the morning before she had got to sleep. Alex had awakened her with a cup of coffee, looking disgustingly fit in blue jeans and a blue knit polo shirt, ready to go. She had forgotten all about their house-hunting and, glancing at him now, in the close confines of the sports car, she wished he had done the same. But no such luck. Alex pursued everything with a ruthless determination that was impossible to ignore.

Within half an hour of waking up Lisa had washed and dressed in white pleated trousers with a white and blue cropped top to match. She'd grabbed a piece of toast and had only taken one bite before Alex had marched into the kitchen. 'Mrs Blaydon, I have ordered a new bed for the master bedroom. Someone will ring and tell you what time it is arriving. Be here.' And, grasping Lisa's free hand, he had hurried her out of the apartment and into the car.

Alex's voice broke into her troubled thoughts. 'Of course I am sure. I am a brilliant navigator.' His dark eyes flicked her a smiling glance.

The car had breasted the top of a hill, and fifty yards on was the most impressive Georgian mansion Lisa had ever seen.

Alex stopped the car at the foot of stone steps that led to the entrance door, and turned to Lisa. 'You, my darling, should have eaten some breakfast, it might have improved your disposition,' he opined mockingly.

'And whose fault was that?' she prompted. 'You dragged me out of the apartment like you were taking a dog for a walk.'

Alex burst out laughing, his white teeth flashing 'You're certainly no dog!' His gleaming gaze slid over her mutinous face with genuine amusement, dropping to the proud thrust of her breasts against the soft cotton of her top, the slight glimpse of tanned midriff, and came back to her face. 'Though you have been acting like a dog in the manger for the past couple of days.' His dark eyes studied her intently for a long moment. 'I presume it is simply the effect of your period?' he asked quietly.

Lisa felt his intimate glance like a caress, and she trembled inside, but it was what he was *not* saying that worried her. A cynical angry Alex she could handle, but a questioning, analytical Alex was far too dangerous. *She* was trying to discover what deviousness *he* was up to, not the other way around. So she responded carefully, 'Yes, probably.' She managed a rueful smile. 'Sorry.' She had to get her act together and try to behave normally around him.

He leaned forward, his lips hovering within inches of hers. 'You're forgiven.' And he kissed her softly. The warmth of his breath brushed her cheek as he straightened up. She inhaled his clean, masculine scent and knew she would remember it to her dying day. Whatever happened between them.

'Come on, Lisa,' Alex commanded as he climbed out of the car. 'I want your opinion on Stoneborough Manor.'

Lisa slid out of the low seat and followed Alex to the

stone steps, squinting her eyes slightly to look up at the house. At the same time she smoothed her pants down over her hips, then tugged at her cotton top. 'It's a bit big.'

'The house, maybe. But that top is a bit small.' Alex grunted, eyeing the band of bare flesh between her top and pants, and the tantalising indent of her belly button.

'It's perfect for summer. You must be getting old,' she quipped with a grin. 'And you have to admit, it is a glorious summer day.' Weather-wise, at least, she thought privately. In every other respect she wished she was anywhere else than looking over prospective houses with Alex. Jed had tried to convince her to give her marriage a chance, but she was not so sure…

She had not changed her mind an hour later, after wandering around the magnificent Georgian mansion. It was the ideal family home. The interior had been tastefully restored and decorated quite recently. A large elegant hall, with a polished hardwood floor and a magnificent staircase as its centre point, made an immediate impression. The study and five reception rooms were equally as impressive, from the formal dining room to the drawing room, library, and the cosier sitting room at the rear, that opened out into a marvellous conservatory.

Six bedrooms, all with *ensuite* bathrooms took up the first floor. The attic had been converted into an apartment for staff. The master suite was a triumph in interior design. The huge bedroom was dominated by an elegant but massive four-poster bed. A door on one side of the room led to a small sitting room. On the other side, there were his and her bathrooms, and a dressing room. Whoever owned the house had spared no expense; that much was obvious to Lisa's admiring gaze as she walked across the deep-pile carpet and stood at the tall window, staring out at the view. It was breathtaking, like a secret valley, she thought fancifully.

Suddenly Alex's arms slipped around her waist, and the shock of his touch made her jump. She was keenly aware of his casual embrace, of his hands locked across her bare midriff, of his long legs pressing against her thighs, the way their bodies fitted together so naturally. His dark head bent forward, his cheek brushed against her hair, and she could not prevent the trembling in her limbs.

'What do you think?' he prompted softly.

'I think it must cost a fortune. And even more to furnish,' Lisa said jerkily, intensely aware of his powerful body enfolding her and reminding her they were alone in the house. Alex evoked a mixture of hate and love inside her in equal measures, but in the intimacy of a bedroom designed for lovers it was the latter that was threatening her self-control.

Alex's hands tightened on the side of her waist and he spun her round. 'Never mind the price; and as it happens the furniture is included—a lot of it was made for the house.' Cool dark eyes scanned her wary face. 'Do you like it?'

The thought crossed Lisa's mind that he seemed to know a lot about the place. Personally she loved the house. It was perfect, from the magnificent swimming pool and hot tub at the rear of the building, to the more practical kitchen and utilities, and the five acres of beautifully sculptured garden that surrounded the house, with a paddock beyond. But she was not about to admit as much to Alex. Two days ago she would have flung her arms around his neck and begged him to buy it. Not now...

Her blue eyes guarded, she held his gaze. The betrayal of trust in a relationship, she realised sadly, was probably the worst crime, and she formed her answer accordingly. 'Yes, it is a nice house, but it is the first one we have viewed. I don't think we should rush into anything. It is rather a long way from my work, plus it's rather isolated.'

'Hardly isolated,' Alex drawled sarcastically, his hands dropping from her waist, much to her relief. 'Oxford is a mere fifteen minutes away, and it is barely an hour to Stratford-upon-Avon. I would have said it was in a great position, being almost mid-way between London and Lawson's. But—' he gave a slight shrug of his broad shoulders '—if it does not appeal to you, so be it.'

'I just feel we should wait,' she insisted, glancing cautiously from beneath lowered lashes, wondering how he would take her less than enthusiastic response.

'In that case, shall we go?' he slanted mockingly.

'Yes,' Lisa agreed, and preceded him down the stairs and out of the house. She glanced over the building as he locked the huge doors. It would make some lucky family a wonderful home.

During the drive back to London Alex revealed that he had to go to New York on Monday, for a few days, and asked her if she wished to accompany him. Lisa swallowed back a sigh of relief as she refused, with the genuine excuse that she had to go to the office on Monday to begin interviewing prospective candidates for Mary's job.

On their return to the apartment, Mrs Blaydon met them with the information that the new bed had been delivered, and she had left a meal prepared in the kitchen.

Alex glanced at Lisa, a devilish gleam in his eyes. 'Thank you, Mrs B. You can leave now. Lisa and I want to check out the new bed.'

Lisa blushed to the roots of her hair. 'What did you

have to say that for?' she demanded as the housekeeper left in a rush. 'You embarrassed the poor woman.'

'Mrs B was not the one who was embarrassed,' Alex came back in amusement as he studied her scarlet cheeks.

'Oh you're impossible!' she burst out. She had spent all day in his company and she felt as if she had been walking on eggshells. 'And I am not sharing the new bed. I want my own room,' she demanded furiously.

Brilliant dark eyes rested on her defiant face. 'No way, Lisa. This foolishness has gone on long enough. Now, get into the kitchen and see what Mrs B has left for dinner. I am starving.'

Flinching from his blunt statement, and furious at his ordering her into the kitchen, she wanted to slap him. Instead she marched off and set about warming the chicken, mushroom and herb casserole the housekeeper had left.

The meal was a silent affair; Lisa had not the heart to talk, and, picking up on her mood, Alex ate in brooding silence too. When she occasionally caught his eye, she quickly looked away.

Lisa felt the swirling currents of tension building, and finally she could stand it no longer. Pushing back her chair, she stood up. 'I have some work to do on my computer. If you will excuse me.' She spoke to somewhere over his left shoulder.

'So polite, Lisa,' Alex observed indolently, leaning back in his chair and studying her with half-closed eyes. 'Why now, I wonder? When we know each other so intimately.'

As if compelled, she glanced at his reclining form, and the tempo of her heartbeat increased. She met his narrowed gaze with reluctance, her eyes lingering on his high cheekbones and dropping to settle briefly on his mouth, which was a mistake. It wasn't fair; she only had to look at him and the tug of sexual awareness was instant.

'Yes, well, I tend to be that way,' she finally answered. More than anything she wanted to lash out at him, and demand to know why he was plotting against her with Nigel. But she didn't dare. Not yet. If what she suspected was true, she needed to form a plan to defeat him. The fact that she ached for him with every pore she was just going to have to learn to live with.

'I know exactly what you are,' Alex said softly, rising to his feet and moving around the table to stop in front of her. His hand reached forward and captured her chin, tilting it slightly so that he could examine her delicate features. 'You're a very passionate young woman who has suddenly realised the enormity of marriage after playing at it for a few weeks.' His smile was stunningly sensual and she almost groaned. 'And perhaps you are running a little scared. That I can understand. So, go to your computer *agape mou.*' The endearment rolled off his tongue.

Lisa felt the effect to her toes, and his fingers on her chin tightened momentarily. She stared dumbly up at him, noting the glint of what looked almost like tenderness behind his grin. Her shoulders tensed against the potent spell of the fierce sexual chemistry he exuded without even trying. He reached out to brush a stray tendril of hair from her brow. She shivered, and his hard lips thinned. 'Suddenly I frighten you, Lisa, and I don't know why. Care to tell me?' he queried silkily.

Lisa took a deep, steadying breath. 'You're imagining things, Alex.'

'If you say so.' His expression did not change, but she could sense his anger. 'I have work to do myself,' he said casually, but something hardened the depths of his eyes.

'However, do not make the mistake of thinking you can avoid our bedroom tonight. You have no excuse.'

There was no mistaking the silent warning in his gaze, and it took all Lisa's considerable control to reply lightly, 'As if I would, Alex.' and she even managed a chuckle. She was discovering she had quite a talent for acting, smiling on the outside when inside she wanted to rage at her arrogant husband.

'Good girl.' And before she knew what was happening his dark head swooped down and his mouth caught hers. Warmth coursed through her veins, and helplessly she opened her mouth to accept his kiss. When he finally raised his head she stared mutely up at him.

'See you later, in our bed.' Alex said, his chiselled mouth curving in a confident grin at her all-too-obvious surrender to his kiss.

As it happened, Lisa did not see him again that night. At midnight she crawled into bed, and the effect of the last forty-eight hours finally caught up with her. She went out like a light, and when she woke up in the morning the only hint that Alex had shared the bed was the indentation of his head on the empty pillow beside her.

Sunday was a repeat of Saturday; the only difference was that the house they viewed was on the outskirts of Banbury. Luckily for Lisa, this time she did not have to pretend uninterest in the property, because she hated it on sight. A huge, very new redbrick mansion, from the outside it reminded Lisa of a supermarket. It did have one saving grace: it was so horrific, Lisa found herself laughing with Alex over the various rooms. Consequently she managed to get through the evening without the tension that had marred the past two days. They watched a video of the latest blockbuster film, and when Lisa went to bed

Alex simply said he would join her in a while; he had a few calls to make.

Lisa closed the bathroom door behind her and crossed to the bed. She pulled back the covers, and climbed into bed, tugging down the bottom of her crisp white cotton nightshift, and closed her eyes. She felt the light brush of warm lips against her own and sighed; she was in that hazy period before sleep, and lazily she opened her eyes. A naked Alex was bending over the bed.

'What are you doing?' she asked stupidly.

'Hush, Lisa,' he murmured, lifting the coverlet and sliding in beside her. She edged back along the bed, but a long arm reached out and curled around her waist. 'I simply want to hold you.' Drawing her against his hard body, he covered her face with countless little kisses.

Her startled gaze met a pair of amused brown eyes. 'But...'

'Hush, I know,' He whispered with mocking humour, continuing to press kisses to her cheek, the curve of her ear. His fingers brushed the pulse at the base of her throat and she sighed. Her lips parted and finally his mouth claimed hers.

The trouble was he knew her too well. She was helpless to resist the tenderness of his embrace, the curling of his tongue against hers, the delicious pleasure as his hand trailed down to cup the underside of her breast. He had a magic touch, Lisa thought dreamily.

A second later he lifted his head, 'What on earth are you wearing?' he demanded with a chuckle.

With the dim glow of the bedside light illuminating the room, Lisa stared up into his shadowed face. She had succumbed to him so easily she was ashamed. His dark eyes smiled down into her own, deep and lazily humorous, and his hand lifted to trace the soft contours of her breasts again, over the soft cotton of her nightshift. She felt a needle-sharp quiver of delight pierce her body, and she burst out, 'Get off,' and brushed his hand away. 'This is a genuine Victorian antique I bought in Bath.'

His roar of laughter would have wakened the dead.

'You can laugh, but it was very expensive. I had to search…'

'Shh.' He brushed his thumb over her lips. 'I'm sure it is lovely.' She could hear the lingering trace of laughter in his voice. 'And I know you're not well. But later, when you know me better and you are not quite so shy, I will teach you ways to make love that know no boundaries, ways you've never dreamed of.'

His deeply evocative words made the heat flood through her body, even as she reminded herself he did not love her, it was only sex on his part.

'But not now,' Alex husked, noting the flush of embarrassment on her lovely face. Replacing his hand with his mouth, he nipped at her lips, and she opened her mouth in ready acceptance of his tender, possessive kiss. 'I simply want to kiss you goodnight,' he whispered against her lips. 'We have had our first argument as man and wife.' His lips trailed to her throat and he laved the pulse that beat frantically in her neck. 'It should not have happened.' He raised his head and brushed her lips briefly with his own. 'And we will never argue again.'

It was so Alex! So arrogant. *We will never argue again.* He said it as if it was a done deal, Lisa thought, a wry smile curving her mouth.

Alex's dark eyes narrowed on her face. 'What is so amusing?'

'You… ''We will never argue again.'' Some hope,' she jeered.

'You don't agree? But there is no reason to fight. To build a good marriage one must learn to compromise.'

'You sound like you are quoting from a marriage guidance book. Some people like to fight.' Alex being one of them, she privately thought.

'Rubbish. It's a ridiculous waste of energy.'

'Alex, are you arguing with me?' Lisa asked sweetly, and her smile broadened at the look of exasperation on his handsome face.

'You're a witch. Close your eyes and go to sleep before I change my mind and ravish you.' And with one hard kiss on her laughing mouth, he rolled over on to his back and hauled her into his side. With his free hand he switched off the bedside light.

In the darkness, curved into Alex's large body, the warmth and comfort of him enfolding her, Lisa closed her eyes, and within minutes was fast asleep.

It was *déjà vu*, she thought lazily, the brush of warm lips against her own. But the voice shouting, 'Wake up, woman,' was not. Her eyes flew open and rested on Alex. He was standing by the bed, shaved and dressed in an immaculate grey silk suit with a white shirt and conservative grey and blue striped tie, apparently ready to leave.

'What time is it?' she demanded, dragging herself up into a sitting position.

'Coffee time.' He indicated with a tilt of his dark head the bedside table, where a large cup of steaming coffee was standing. 'Also time I left for the airport.'

'Oh, well, thanks for the coffee. I have to get going myself. I said I would be in Stratford by ten.' Lisa tried for a light tone. Which was no mean feat, considering for the first time since their marriage, she had just spent the night very comfortably in Alex's arms without making love.

'It is not too late for you to change your mind, Lisa, and come with me to New York,' he offered casually. 'I could, at a pinch, put off going until tomorrow.'

Lisa looked at him carefully. She could not believe he had said it, and for a second she was tempted, but quickly she squashed the idea. 'No. No, really. I have far too much work to catch up on.'

'As you like.' He leant down and pressed a brief kiss on the top of her head. Lisa looked up in surprise.

'Try not to miss me too much,' he commanded, a gleam of mocking amusement glinting in the dark eyes above her own.

The trouble was, Lisa realised with a sinking heart, she would miss him. 'I won't have time,' she returned brightly, ignoring her innermost feelings.

His dark gaze sharpened on her cool face. 'Hopefully after this week your work will no longer be a problem. It is not that hard to hire a secretary. Or you could consider selling the company.'

Lisa glanced away from his penetrating gaze, the word *selling* echoing in her head, her worst suspicion confirmed. Her eyes fixed on the folds of the coverlet, an icy chill penetrating her heart. 'I have no intention of ever selling, and finding a secretary for Mary will be no problem, I can assure you.'

'I certainly hope so. I have no desire to have a part time wife,' Alex countered with devastating frankness, and left.

So now she knew. He had suggested she sell the company. Her fingers curved convulsively in the coverlet. How long before he put himself forward as a buyer, or suggested razing the factory to the ground? she wondered on a shaky breath. And what could she do about it when he did?

*   *   *

Turning the key in the drawer which held her mother's papers, Lisa found what she was looking for. The offer to buy had been made by Xela Properties with no mention of changing the business. She debated ringing them, but decided to display caution. She searched the Internet instead and found Xela Properties, only to discover to her horror that Solomos International was the parent company to it and a host of others. Starting in alphabetical order: Alexsol Cruises, Alomos Financial Services, and, of course, at the end, Xela Properties.

Switching off her computer, Lisa stared at the blank screen. In a way it was her own fault. She could have checked to see if Solomos International had a web page ages ago, but it had never occurred to her to do so. So much for her idea of a white knight helping her. It had been Alex who had tried to buy Lawson's out a year ago…

The telephone rang, and Mary answered it. She listened for a second, then covered the mouthpiece with her hand. 'It's for you, Lisa. Your husband.'

Reluctantly Lisa reached out to take the call. 'Alex. What are you calling for?' she asked calmly, when she really felt like shouting every obscenity she could think of at him. He had been planning for over a year to get control of Lawson's and destroy it!

'I was not aware I needed a reason to speak to my wife,' his deep voice echoed down the telephone.

Sarcastic, devious devil, Lisa thought furiously. 'Yes, well, I am rather busy, so unless it was something important…' She paused.

'Not really. I thought you might like to know I have arrived in New York.'

'Oh, yes, great. But I haven't time to talk; ring again some time.' And she clashed down the phone.

Lisa spent the rest of the day interviewing people for a job she was not sure was going to be available if Alex had his way…

Over dinner that evening with Harold, she was surprised when he had asked her quite seriously, 'You do love Alex, don't you, Lisa?' His cherubic face was rather grim.

'Of course I do.' She forced a smile. 'What makes you ask?'

'Well, your mother expected me to take care of you, and I just wanted to make sure you were happy.'

For an instant Lisa was tempted to confide in him her fears for the company. As long as Harold voted his shares with hers, there would be nothing to worry about. He loved her like a daughter, and he loved the company and his job. But Lisa knew his one weakness was his son, Nigel. If Nigel asked him to sell, he might agree.

'I miss her.' Harold sighed wearily.

Looking at his sad face, she hadn't the heart to trouble him. No! She had to solve the problem herself, and, rising to her feet, she walked around the table and pressed a swift kiss on the top of his head. 'I know you do, Harold, we both do. But life must go on.'

'Yes, yes, you're right.' he declared emphatically.

Lisa's eyebrows rose in surprise at the determination in his tone, and what looked like relief on his round face. 'Well, goodnight,' she murmured, and went upstairs to her old bedroom. But it was hours before she slept, and when she did she dreamed of Alex.

Tuesday was even worse. Mary reminded her. 'You're taking Mr Brown from Beaver Pine to lunch today.'

Lawson Designer Glass sublet two work units, which provided extra income for the business.

Lisa looked up from scanning the references of the girl

they were considering employing and smiled. 'Yes, I know. Keep your fingers crossed he renews his lease.'

Two hours later when Lisa returned to the office, her face was set in a worried frown. 'What happened to you?' Mary asked. 'You look like you lost a pound and found a penny.'

'I have. Mr Brown was very polite, but he is not renewing his lease. He's moving to bigger premises on the new industrial estate. He also let slip that Curly Cane is thinking of expanding elsewhere as well. I'm meeting Mr George, the boss, tomorrow for lunch. I can just see it now. Both leases run out at the end of July. Come August, the height of the tourist season, we'll be the only firm operating; two boarded-up premises will not make a very good impression on our customers.'

'No,' Mary murmured. 'But it shouldn't be too hard to find other tenants.'

Lisa hoped she was right. Picking up the references she had been reading before lunch, Lisa scanned them one more time. At the interview, Miss Clement had come across as perfect for the job. The woman's references were excellent, but Lisa was in a dilemma. Last week she had been all for leaving Mary in charge and looking forward to a long and happy life with her husband. Now she didn't trust her husband and she had an uneasy feeling she might not be able to hang on to the company.

'Mary, get in touch with Miss Clement.' She had to think positively, and, standing up, Lisa crossed to Mary's desk. 'Offer her the job.'

Then she called Mr Wilkinson, her lawyer. She was going to ask him to put in an offer for the Lee shares. She would find the money from somewhere. Unfortunately he was on holiday until Thursday. Lisa explained to his secretary what she wanted, and the woman promised to inform Mr Wilkinson as soon as he returned. Lisa could do no more.

Thankfully, the next day, her lunch with Mr George went well. He had looked into moving but had decided against it. He took the new lease she offered.

Lisa returned to the office in a much happier mood than the day before, and it improved even further when Mary said Miss Clement had agreed to start on Monday.

By Thursday, Lisa came back from a visit to her bank manager, with a loan agreed and a genuine smile on her face, to find Mary standing by her desk. 'Good, you're back. Wilkinson and Morgan just called. Mr Wilkinson said, would you call him back?'

Lisa grinned. Her problems would soon be over. Five minutes later, she carefully placed the telephone receiver on its rest, her face pale beneath her tan. She didn't see Mary's concerned look. Her whole vision was centred internally. Mr Wilkinson had called to tell her the Lee estate had sold their thirty-five per cent holding in Lawson's to Xela Properties. Apparently Mr Wilkinson had tried to get in touch with her to ask if she wanted to make an offer for the Lee shares, but she had been on her honeymoon and he hadn't been able to contact her. So had Alex been honeymooning, she thought bitterly but that hadn't stopped him buying them, the sneaky, conniving, lying bastard!

'Are you okay?' Mary's voice cut through her rage.

'Yes, yes, I'm fine.' But she wasn't. She wanted to scream her fury out loud. Instead, when the telephone rang on her desk, she picked it up and yelled, 'Yes, who is it?' It was Alex. His timing could not have been worse. 'What do you want?' Apart from my company, she felt like adding.

'Not a very lover-like greeting. I simply wondered if

there had been any developments at your end. Have you managed to find a replacement for your PA yet?'

Developments! What a nerve. He knew damn well what had happened. She wanted to confront him with his duplicity, but instead she simply replied, 'Yes everything is fine.' Her mind was made up—she would fight him every inch of the way. She might have fallen into his arms like a ripe plum, but no way was she going to allow Lawson Designer Glass to do the same...

'Good,' Alex said. 'I will be back in London tomorrow afternoon. Bert is meeting me at the airport, and I will see you at the apartment.'

'Right, goodbye.' She didn't trust herself to say more, and she replaced the phone with rather more force than was necessary. She glanced at Mary. 'I'm leaving now and I won't be in tomorrow.' She said, and walked out of the office, out of the building, and slid behind the wheel of her red BMW—her one indulgence—drove out of the car park and straight home.

On Friday afternoon, Lisa sat on the train to London, outwardly a beautiful, elegant young woman, but inside a mass of conflicting emotions. To say she felt mad was an understatement; she was blindingly furious! She had E-mailed Jed before she left home. But even his words of wisdom had not calmed the rage in her heart. He had advised to simply confront Alex and demand the truth. To explain to Alex that absolute honesty was a prerequisite for a good marriage. She had laughed out loud at Jed's message. How come a young man almost the same age as herself had more insight into relationships than the older, arrogant swine she had married?

By the time the train was pulling into the station Lisa had calmed down somewhat. She had done a lot of soul-searching last night, and had analysed her behaviour, and reached a conclusion. She had allowed herself to be completely overwhelmed and overawed by her husband. Probably because it had all happened so quickly, and because Alex was her first and only lover. Or maybe because he was older and she had not considered herself an equal partner in the marriage. Obviously neither had he. He had bought shares in her company without even telling her. But he wasn't getting away with it...

The train stopped and Lisa stood up. She had dressed carefully in a smart, double-breasted, button-through navy blue linen dress, its wide belt accentuating her narrow waist. She smoothed the skirt of her dress down over her hips and picked up her brief case and laptop before leaving the train. In minutes she was in the back of a black cab and heading for the penthouse. Alex Solomos had a lot of explaining to do. She was going to confront him, something she should have done a week ago.

Lisa fitted the key into the lock and pushed open the door, and walked into the apartment. She didn't know what time Alex was due back, but it was now four p.m., so he couldn't be much longer. She walked straight through to the inner hall and disposed of her briefcase and laptop in her so-called study and, turning, walked back out.

'A bit late, Lisa.' Alex's deep voice held a mocking edge, and she spun around as he strolled out of the master bedroom.

'You're back.' Her startled gaze focused on his tall, hard-muscled frame. He had obviously not long stepped out of the shower. Incongruously, on such a masculine man, a pink towel hung low on his hips; another was slung around his neck, and his black hair was ruffled and wet, as if he had just been rubbing it. Her mouth went dry. It had only been a week, but the familiar rush of awareness curled her stomach.

'Not quite the response I hoped for,' Alex revealed as he walked towards her.

'You surprised me,' Lisa got out. Her blue eyes clashed with his, and what she saw in their darkening depths sent a jolt of sexual excitement quivering along every nerve in her body. She couldn't move, and she watched mesmerised as he closed the distance between them.

'I surprise myself,' he murmured enigmatically, and, raising his hands, he closed them over either side of her head, his long fingers raking through her hair, sending pins flying in every direction.

'Don't.' She tried to shake her head but his dark head dipped and his mouth crushed down on hers, stopping the words in her throat as he ravished her mouth with deep, hungry passion that she was helpless to deny.

A tiny voice of reason told her she must stop him. Lisa reached out to push him away, but it had been so long. When her hands came into contact with his bare chest she felt him shudder, and that was her undoing…

CHAPTER SEVEN

FLAT on her back on the bed, the skirt of her dress bunched up around her hips, Lisa drew a shuddering breath and gazed up at Alex, looming over her. She glanced frantically round the room and wondered how on earth she had got there. A few minutes ago she had been in the hall. Her stunned gaze returned to Alex. His night-black eyes traced the long length of her bare legs to settle at the juncture of her thighs. 'Alex,' she gasped breathlessly, taken aback by the fierce sexual hunger in his burning gaze.

'Yes, Lisa,' he rasped harshly, casting aside the towel, magnificently uninhibited by his aroused state. Her heart began to pound, and, to her shame, her traitorous body responded instantly to his aggressive male virility. He leant over, his fingers fumbling with the buttons down the front of her dress. The belt frustrated him and he simply tore the front of her lace bra, freeing her breasts to his avid gaze, then he reached down, kneading the creamy softness of them with his hands. She could not disguise her need, and when one hand reached for her briefs, she instinctively raised her pelvis to help him whisk the scrap of lace from her body.

'I want you,' Alex admitted fiercely, coming down on the bed and curving strong hands around her hips. Nudging her legs apart, he eased his strong thighs into the feminine cradle of her hips, his awesome body trembling against her.

Lisa, reeling from the speed of his seduction, still might

have made some effort to protest. But his firm lips fell upon her mouth and he kissed her with such ferocious need all thought of denying him was wiped from her mind.

'I have to have you; I can't wait,' Alex declared in a deep growl, his dark head dropping to press his mouth to the slender curve of her throat, mouthing dark husky words in Greek against her tender skin with an eroticism that made her heart shake. He trailed one hand up over her thigh, expert fingers seeking the fold of tender flesh that masked her femininity. Lisa trembled, a fierce primeval heat racing like wild fire through her veins, consuming her mind and body.

'You want me. You are so ready,' Alex grated with satisfaction. His long fingers discovered the hot moist core of her, teasing and tormenting her ultra-sensitive flesh until she became a slave to the agonising pleasure his touch evoked.

'So sweet, so hot…You've been aching for this all week,' Alex murmured huskily, lowering his mouth to tease and lick her nipples with delicacy until they were hot, hard peaks. 'I know I have,' he mouthed against her silky skin.

Lisa twisted and squirmed against him, consumed by a desire so fierce it was almost painful. She clutched at his broad shoulder, her misty blue gaze clashing with his as he raised his head. She stared up into his handsome face and his dark eyes burned black with the effort he was making to control his passion, a question in their glittering depths.

'Yes, yes!' She pleaded for his possession, and relief from the primeval passion that consumed her. His mouth descended on hers, parting her lips with a hungry sensuality she more than matched. She cried out when he moved, his strong hands lifting her hips, and she felt him glide, hard and urgent, into the velvet heat of her body. Her whole being centred on Alex. She clung to his broad shoulders, her long legs wrapping around his waist as he forced himself deeper and deeper with each stroke. Her body met each thrust, the raw power of his possession filling her with spiralling desire, until the familiar fierce wild pleasure swamped her, and her whole body convulsed in frantic release. Alex reared back, the tanned skin pulled taut across his high cheekbones, his black eyes unfocused, as Lisa's inner muscles contracted around him, and with one final thrust his great body followed hers into a shattering climax.

She felt his full weight relax on her, but she did not care, languorous in the aftermath of total physical satiation. She stroked her hands softly up his broad back with feline delight. He was hers. The thought registered, and with it reality. He was not hers, never had been. His reasons for marrying her were varied, but love was not part of the equation. She dropped her hands to the bed, suddenly chilled.

Alex rolled off her, breathing hard, then as his breathing steadied he turned towards her, his head propped on one elbow, and contemplated her rosy face with a lazy smile playing around his sensuous mouth.

'Now that is what I call a homecoming,' he drawled. 'In every sense of the word.'

Immediately on the defensive, Lisa avoided his amused gaze and tugged at the bodice of her hopelessly crushed dress. 'You could have waited until I was undressed,' she said, smarting at the inelegant picture she must present and heaving a sigh of relief when she finally got the offending garment down over her hips.

'Such modesty.' He chuckled. 'But totally unnecessary.' And, skimming one hand down over her stomach, he followed the line of her hip and thigh, smoothing the fabric until he reached the hem. 'Here, let me help you.' On the pretext of straightening the top of her dress, his teasing fingers sneaked across her breast.

Lisa swallowed hard and hastily sat up. Flinging her legs over the side of the bed, she stood up. 'I need a shower,' she muttered, and dashed for the bathroom, Alex's husky laughter ringing in her ears.

Lisa dragged the remains of her clothes off and stepped into the shower stall. 'Damn you, Alex,' she mouthed as she turned on the shower tap and lifted her head to the powerful spray. Alex was back, and she could not believe how easily she had fallen into his arms. Where was the cool, sophisticated image she had decided to adopt? The cutting questions she had for him regarding her company? Gone the same way as her dress, she thought bitterly, crushed to bits by her inability to resist the potent sexuality of her husband. Sighing, Lisa closed her eyes and, shaking her head, allowed the water to soothe her turbulent emotions.

'Need any help?'

Lisa's eyes flew open and she spun round on the wet tiles. Only Alex's long tanned arm curling around her waist stopped her from slipping to the floor. 'No, I can manage,' she spluttered.

'But it is much more fun my way,' Alex pronounced. With the water cascading down over both of them, his eyes were dark, slumberous as they slowly traced over her slim curves. 'You are so perfect,' he whispered throatily, his hand lifting to cup the underside of one breast, his thumb delicately scraping over the pert tip. 'So responsive.'

The slow ache deep within her began to spread, rekindling a flame of desire so potent she had to bite her lip to stifle the groan that threatened to sound her surrender once again. It wasn't fair. No man should have this much power over her. Throwing back her head, her blue eyes clashed with brown. 'I want…' to talk, she had been going to say, but at that instant his other hand curved around her waist and, lifting her up, he swung her out of the shower.

She clasped his wide shoulders, his tanned skin wet and smooth as satin beneath her fingers. She trembled when her naked body brushed in intimate contact against his as he gently set her on her feet. She swallowed hard, shamed by her body's swift response. She lifted angry eyes to his impossibly handsome face, humiliated by the strength of her passion for the man.

'I know exactly what you want.' Alex slanted a brilliant smile of masculine satisfaction over her warm cheeks. 'The same thing I do,' he declared throatily, flicking a glance over the proud thrust of her breasts and back to her face.

It was the smile that did it. Shame was submerged by sheer, ungovernable rage and she told him the truth as she saw it. 'You have taken me for a fool long enough, Alex,' she breathed.

'I've taken you many times, but never as a fool.' Alex surveyed her with the disturbing light of amusement in his eyes.

Without even thinking about it, Lisa swung her hand and tried to hit him. Instead, shocked by the speed of his reaction, she found her wrist caught and her naked body pressed hard against him. 'No.' Alex controlled her easily with his superior strength. 'This has gone far enough. I explained about Margot, she is no longer an issue, but something else has been eating you since last Friday. I made allowances because of your condition, but you no longer have that excuse.' His black brows drew together in a frown. 'I want the truth. What supposed sin have I committed in your mixed-up female mind?'

His tall, muscular frame towered over her. She stared up into his black questioning eyes, her own wild with fury. 'I know you own Xela Properties.' Lisa planted her free hand on his chest to put space between them. This time she was not going to be seduced by his body, she vowed, adding scathingly, 'Need I say more?'

'So?' One dark brow arched sardonically. 'What's new about that?' He demanded, releasing her in a cool, almost careless manner. Catching a towelling robe from the back of the door, he slipped it on before handing her a matching one. 'What is your point?' he queried, his firm mouth quirking in amusement. 'Presuming you have one, that is.'

Lisa almost choked on his patronising words. She felt like screaming in frustration. Instead, she pulled on the plain white robe and fastened the belt firmly around her waist. He thought it was a joke. She probably was a joke to him—the naive innocent, to be used when and how he wished. Lisa curled her fingers tightly into her palms, fighting to control the rage boiling inside her. But she needed all her wits about her to confront Alex, because he had the uncanny ability to turn off his emotions with the flick of a switch.

'Well, I'm waiting. I suppose waiting in bed would be out of the question?' he said, a wicked gleam in his eyes.

She swept her wet hair back from her face. 'You've got that right,' she snarled, and with a defiant toss of her head she glared at him. What the hell? she thought. He might as well have the whole truth; he couldn't hurt her more than he already had. 'I know you were behind the offer to buy Lawson's long before we ever met.'

'An oversight on my part. If I had known, the first and only time I visited the site, that the owner's daughter was such a beauty, I would have insisted on meeting you,' he informed her with a sexy grin.

She couldn't believe the audacity of the man; he still thought it was funny. He really was a heartless beast and the anger drained out of her. 'Don't pretend, Alex. You know exactly what I mean. I do not appreciate being married for the property I own,' she said bitterly.

The amusement vanished from his eyes; his mouth hardened in a thin, ominous line. 'If that is what you really think, then perhaps it *is* time we talked.' Turning, he walked back into the bedroom.

Lisa had no choice but to follow him. He had stopped in the middle of the floor and now moved around to face her. She glanced at him, a tall, dark giant of a man with cool, remote eyes, and then quickly looked away. She saw the rumpled bed, her mouth twisting in disgust at the evidence of her own weakness where Alex was concerned. What was the point of talking? Alex hadn't denied marrying her in an attempt to gain control of the company. There was nothing more to say...

She half turned, but long tanned fingers closed over her shoulders and wheeled her back to face him.

'You can't throw out an accusation like that and walk away, Lisa.' His dark eyes raked over her hostile face. 'When I married you, the company you owned was the last thing on my mind.' His deep husky drawl feathered along her taut nerves as smooth as silk. 'And, if you remember, the first day I took you out I told you I was the owner of Solomos International and asked you if it would be a problem. You said no.'

'But you never told me you were Xela Properties.' Lisa snorted. 'A very sneaky omission on your part.'

'I naturally supposed you knew. It is all there on our web site, and with your love of computers I find it amazing you're now telling me you never bothered to check it out. Any businessman worth his salt, when presented with a buy-out, would naturally investigate the company making the offer,' he said with cool reasoning.

Lisa stared up at him, appalled. What he said was true, but at the time her mother had just been diagnosed as terminally ill. The offer had been refused and banished from their minds. But he was right, damn him! Yet she was still convinced that if he had really wanted her to know he would have come straight out and told her. 'Very plausible, but I don't believe you,' she countered with a disdainful shake of her head. 'I know everything.'

'Not everything.' His sensual mouth twisted in the shadow of a smile. 'You are so young, so impulsive, Lisa, but life is rarely black and white, as I have told you before.' His long fingers kneaded her shoulders.

But Lisa wasn't fooled. He used his powerful masculine sensuality as a weapon to control her. Call me an idiot, why don't you? she thought furiously, incensed anew by his superior, patronising air.

'Please spare me your platitudes. I know you have already bought thirty five per cent of the company. But understand this: I will do my damnedest to make sure that that is all you get.' Lisa let fly with all the pent-up fury of the last week. 'You disgust me. You are the most devious, despicable man I have ever had the misfortune to meet, and my sincerest wish is that I never have to set eyes on you again.' And with one great effort she pushed him away.

'Believe me, Lisa. I would never hurt you,' Alex said softly.

'Trying to take over my company is not supposed to

hurt?' She eyed him bitterly. In his own way, Alex probably saw nothing wrong in what he had done. He was a businessman first, last and always.

'I am not trying to take over anything. I have bought out the other shareholders, that is all,' he asserted.

'That is impossible.' She knew he had bought the Lee shares, but Harold's? Never! 'I don't believe you.' Her stormy blue eyes clashed with his. 'You're lying. Harold would never sell without consulting me.' She saw a flash of what looked like pity in his dark gaze, and a peculiar sense of foreboding rose up inside her.

'I'm sorry to disappoint you, Lisa. Andrew Scott, my London manager, completed the deal last Tuesday. But it was for your own good.'

Nothing was more calculated to stiffen Lisa's backbone than her most hated phrase in the English language: *For your own good.* Invariably, it meant the exact opposite. 'And how did you persuade Harold to betray me?' she asked flatly.

'I didn't have to; he loves you. Apparently you convinced him it was time to move on.'

With a rising sense of inevitability, she cleared her throat, determined to go down fighting. 'Now you're going to tell me it's for my own good that Lawson Designer Glass will be razed to the ground to make way for some poxy redevelopment,' she prompted sarcastically. 'Well, it won't work; I still have overall control.' She was lying, but she was banking on Alex not knowing that.

His firm mouth quirked at the corners. 'Actually you do not have a majority; the Hospice sold their shares yesterday.'

Shock held her rigid. Her anguished eyes roamed over his arrogant dark head. 'Oh, God!' Lisa exclaimed. Alex now owned fifty-three percent of Lawson's. He had done it. Bought her company from under her. 'You really are the devil! You used sex to blind me, while robbing me blind.' How could she have fallen in love with a man so lacking in any moral fibre? A man who had played on her innocence of the male sex to manipulate her into marriage and, cruellest of all, to rob her of her birthright. Easily, she thought sadly. She had recognised the dark power of his personality the moment she had met him. But love had blinded her to the ruthlessness inherent in the man.

'I seem to recall, not so long ago, your body welcoming mine with an eagerness you could not hide. Far from being the devil, I am your guardian angel,' Alex offered tautly, his narrowed eyes colliding with hers. 'I bought the shares so you could keep your company.'

A harsh laugh escaped her. 'Excuse me, but it was already mine,' she reminded him bitterly, ignoring his crack about sex.

'If I had not bought the shares, somebody else would have done.' Alex shrugged. 'Solomos International is an incredibly wealthy company, Lisa. We invest in many and varied projects all over the world. Do you really think it matters to me if we have one more site?' he said, exasperation lacing his tone. 'In fact, I have decided to cut *back* on my workload since meeting you.' He glanced at her lovely proud face, and something very like compassion moved in his dark eyes. 'I know it's not your fault you ended up in the position you have, Lisa. Grief can do funny things and make fools of us all. It was an admirable gesture in memory of your mother to donate those shares, but it did put your business in a vulnerable position. You're an intelligent woman, but you are very young and lack experience. Have you any idea how quickly you would have been out on your ear if any other firm had bought into your company?' Not waiting for an answer, he added, 'You were a sitting duck when you made that gift to the hospice.'

'And you shot me down.' But it was slowly dawning on her that there was an awful lot of truth in what Alex said. Had she made a terrible mistake?

'The hell I did,' he said savagely, reaching out and grabbing her shoulders. 'I saved it for you.'

'Oh, so how do you work that out, pray?' she enquired sarcastically.

Alex's hands tightened for a moment on her shoulders, and then he released her, the expression on his handsome face bleak. 'Trust me, Lisa; you don't need to know.'

'But I don't trust you,' she said bluntly. 'Not any more.'

He stared hard at her for long, tense seconds, the line of his jaw taut. She thought she saw a flicker of something like pain in his black eyes, but she must have imagined it, because he turned and walked away, to stand looking out of the window. He came back round to face her. 'You'd better sit down; you are not going to like this,' he said curtly, and indicated the small satin-covered sofa that rested against the wall with a wave of his hand.

Her first thought was to refuse, but something in his expression made her hesitate to defy him. With a nervous tug on the belt of her robe, she crossed to the sofa and sat down. She tilted her chin, her eyes cold as they met his. 'So fire away. But try for the truth this time.'

His dark eyes flared briefly with anger at her slur on his honesty, and then he sighed. 'A year ago Xela Properties—one of my companies as you so rightly said— was approached by a broker with an investment opportunity. Lawson's Designer Glass was ripe to be taken over and the site developed more profitably.' He glanced down at Lisa. 'But then you know all this.'

'There was no mention of redevelopment in the offer my mother received,' Lisa snapped.

Alex simply arched one dark brow sardonically. 'No one shows all his cards to his opponent.'

Lisa frowned. Her mother had been dying at the time, and that made it somehow worse. She looked back at Alex; was he the sort of man to prey on a dying woman?

He read her mind. 'No. I did not know.' He began pacing the floor in front of her. 'Andy Scott investigated the feasibility of the deal, and approached me for permission to proceed, which, after visiting the site, I gave. The offer was turned down. The whole project was shelved and would have stayed that way.'

'And that was when you decided to use more devious means, like marrying the owner,' she cut in, hurting from the way he had tricked her.

'Don't be ridiculous, Lisa, I did not even know you then,' Alex snapped. 'And I could buy and sell your company a million times over. I certainly did not marry you to persuade you into parting with it.'

Put like that, it did make her fears seem a bit groundless, but it did not alter the fact she had overheard him plotting with Nigel. 'So you say,' she mumbled, still not prepared to believe him.

He stared down at her for a moment, his dark eyes cold and angry. Then he renewed his pacing. 'I walked into the bar of a hotel in Statford-upon-Avon and I saw a beautiful elegant blonde with legs to die for. Then I saw her two companions—older, shorter, fatter and dark—nothing like the girl. I concluded they must be her sugar daddies.'

Lisa gasped in outrage. 'You've got a nerve, especially with your record with women.' Then she remembered his dismissive glance at the time and realised why.

'Yes, cynical of me, I know, but true. Then Nigel, your

stepbrother, introduced himself to me, claiming Andy Scott as mutual acquaintance. I'm sorry to have to be the one to tell you, Lisa,' he said with unaccustomed gentleness, 'but Nigel was the commercial property broker who first brought Andy Scott's attention to Lawson Designer Glass.'

'How could he?' Lisa whispered to herself. But, knowing Nigel, she believed it.

Alex heard her. 'Quite easily, I'm afraid. I know you consider him family. But he couldn't wait to inform me I was missing out on a great deal. He suggested I raise the offer and it would be second time lucky. He could guarantee delivering Harold Watson's thirteen per cent—and if I wasn't interested, he told me, he had another company lined up that was. I wasn't particularly keen. The Lawson family was still left with fifty-two per cent—not a very viable proposition for Xela Properties.'

'But if that's true, if you really did think like that, why did you go behind my back and buy the shares?' Lisa asked quietly.

He stopped pacing and stood in front of her, a deep tide of colour darkening his handsome face. 'Because Nigel pointed you out on that night in Stratford as the owner and was quite effusive about your...' he hesitated. '...character, shall we say, and the relationship between you. He suggested a man of my experience should have no trouble talking you round.' He had the grace to look ashamed for a second. 'I would like to think my intentions were noble at the time. It was immediately apparent to me that Nigel was a rogue. I could barely remember the deal he was talking about. I had to ring Andy later that night to refresh my memory. But, to be honest, at the time I simply saw a beautiful girl, who was not the freeloader

I had first thought, and jumped at the chance of an intro-
duction.'

Flattering though it was to be called beautiful, Lisa
wasn't fooled, and, leaping to her feet, she cried, 'I was
right all along. You and Nigel *are* in it together!' Spinning
on her heel, she stormed past him.

'Stop.' His hand caught her arm and pulled her around.
'Don't you dare walk away from me.' His hard, angry
eyes roamed over her face. 'You are going to hear me
out, even if I have to pin you to the bed to do it. So make
your choice.' Suddenly she was very conscious of his
large tanned body. His robe hung open to the waist, revealing his broad hairy chest, and when she glanced up
at his angry face he met her look with hard, mocking eyes.

'All right,' she muttered, and sat down on the sofa. But
this time Alex sat down beside her.

He caught her hands in his. 'To prevent you lashing
out,' he said grimly, 'I have had enough of your histri-
onics.'

He continued as if he had never stopped. 'When you
agreed to marry me, your company was the last thing on
my mind. But I did tell Andy Scott to keep a wary eye
out for any developments, and also to watch Nigel
Watson. I did not trust the man. You were shortly to be
my wife, and I naturally wanted to protect your interests.'

'Don't you mean your own?' she sneered.

'No, damn it, I don't! The third day of our honeymoon
I received a fax from Andy Scott. He had some disturbing
news. Nigel had approached another property company
with the proposed deal, and they were interested enough
to put in a bid for the Lee shares. I instructed Andy to
string Nigel along with the promise of a finder's fee, and
put in a counter-bid for Lee's shares, whatever it cost.
That only left Harold's. Then, last Thursday, Andy made

the amazing discovery you had given some shares to the hospice. I had no choice but to buy them.'

'You could have told me straight away,' Lisa said fiercely. 'I could have bought the shares myself. But, no, you had to be in control. I am telling you now, I will fight you every inch of the way if you try to close Lawson's down.'

Alex shook his head, frustrated as well as angry. 'For heaven sake, Lisa, we were on our honeymoon. I would have to have been the most insensitive man on the planet to have worried you with business at such a time. And I do not want to close Lawson's down. I might wish it had never existed, the trouble it has caused,' he opined dryly, 'but in fact you should be thanking me for saving it.'

'You don't want to demolish the place?' she queried, lifting wary blue eyes to his.

'I still think in the long term redevelopment is the best way forward, but I am perfectly happy for you to run the business as you like. I bought the majority share simply to protect you. You're my wife, and if it suits you to work I won't deprive you of the privilege. I meant to tell you last weekend, after checking the state of affairs with Andy on Thursday. But with the fiascos that night and the rest of the weekend turned into somehow I never got round to it. Perhaps because whenever I look at you I forget everything but this.' Alex wrapped an arm around her shoulders and his dark head bent towards her.

'No!' Lisa put a restraining hand on his bare chest. 'I am not going to be diverted by sex. Not again,' she said, quickly appalled at her own weakness. 'You see, Alex, I know you are lying. I overheard you and Nigel last Thursday in this very apartment. I heard you telling him he could invest in your development.' She still burned at the memory, and the tone of her voice reflected her feelings. 'The slimy rat. And you're no better.'

'I thought you loved your stepbrother. You told me you did.' Alex jerked back, his arm falling from her shoulder, his voice hard and accusing.

'You've got to be joking.' Lisa stared at him in genuine astonishment. 'I can't stand the man. I wouldn't give him the time of day if it weren't for Harold, and the feeling is mutual. Ever since he made a pass at me when I was sixteen and I made my feelings plain.'

Alex sucked in a deep breath, his black eyes glittering with some fierce emotion. 'I wish I had known that last week; I would have flattened the bastard.' He shook his dark head in a gesture of utter disgust with himself, and, grasping her hands in his hands, he asked, 'Why did you not tell me last Thursday what you had overheard? Am I such an ogre you could not talk to me?'

She shrugged wearily. 'What difference does it make? I heard enough to know my husband and stepbrother were plotting behind my back.'

'Exactly what did you hear, Lisa? I need to know.' His voice was flat, devoid of any emotion, only the tightening of his hands on hers told her he was nowhere near as calm as he appeared.

She stared unwaveringly for a moment into his taut face. Her teeth worried at her bottom lip. She remembered every word, they were carved on her brain but she wasn't sure she wanted to tell him.

'Tell me, Lisa,' he prompted curtly.

'All right.' And with complete honesty she told him. 'I heard Nigel say that after three weeks with the ice amazon he didn't blame you spending a night on your own. Then he asked you if the delectable Margot knew you were in town.'

'It was Nigel who told Margot I was in town. She confessed as much before she left,' Alex said flatly, and Lisa winced. She had misjudged him badly. 'But I did not want to disillusion you about Nigel.' He laced his fingers with hers, as if to give her some of his strength. 'Go on.'

'There was a comment about a computer nerd.' It was Alex's turn to wince. 'Then he asked for your confirmation that the sale of Lawson's would go through. You teased him about getting my shares for nothing. And finally you said Nigel would get what he wanted.'

'What I actually said, Lisa, was that he would get his... And I did not mean it in a friendly way. But I was labouring under the impression you loved him like a brother, so I had to put up with him, while making sure he did not harm you. I was stringing him along that night because, thinking ahead, I realised if anything happened to Harold, Nigel would end up with a share in your business. There was no way I wanted Nigel to have anything to do with you, so I had to keep him sweet until I had done a deal with Harold.'

'You still could have told me. I never thought Harold would ever sell without consulting me first. Until you came along.' She glared at him, but her heart wasn't in it. What Alex said made sense.

'Blood is thicker than water, Lisa. Harold is always going to be weak where his son is concerned, and I realised it that night when I spoke to Nigel. Suffice to say, after Nigel left the apartment I had a long talk to Harold.'

'Yes, you said so at the time.' Lisa knew that was true. Was it possible Alex was telling the truth and he really was not the villain she had painted him?

'I believe I did. Just before you seduced me.' He stopped, an arrested expression on his handsome face. 'Now I understand,' he declared, a sensual, reminiscent smile lighting his brown eyes. 'Your sudden aggression in bed last week was more fury than a fever of passion?' he queried softly, lifting their joined hands to his mouth and kissing her fingers.

'Never mind that.' She wasn't going there for anything! 'What did you say to Harold to get him to sell his shares?'

'I promised to pay off Nigel's debts.'

'What!' Lisa exclaimed. 'Are you mad?' She pulled her hands free and eyed her husband with stunned disbelief.

'I am now,' Alex said with wry amusement. 'When I learn he laid a hand on you. But it is too late. It is done. Harold loves his son, and would do anything for him, though he is not entirely blind to Nigel's faults. Harold and I agreed that the money I paid him for his shares would go into a trust to give Nigel an income from the interest. But Nigel can't get his hands on the capital.'

'And you did this for me?' Lisa said, feeling her way through what felt like a minefield. 'You bought the Lee shares first, to protect the company from a hostile bid set up by Nigel?'

Alex gave her a considering look. 'No,' he said and, rising to his feet, he stared fixedly down at her.

'No? But—' She raised confused blue eyes to his, and suddenly she felt the strong grip of Alex's hands on her arms, pulling her up against his body.

'I bought the shares for you, and only you. I don't give a damn about Lawson's, except as it affects you. You're my wife, my partner, and if you had shown a little more trust in me, talked to me, you could have spared us both a lot of unpleasantness,' Alex declared, with a disturbing intensity in his voice that left Lisa in no doubt he was telling the truth.

'I'm sorry, but it's not that easy to trust a husband when you think he's plotting behind your back, and then you're

confronted in the apartment you share by an almost naked
ex-mistress all in the same night,' Lisa retorted dryly. She
believed his explanation; she had to. Alex was the majority stockholder now, whether she liked it or not, and
did that matter if he was prepared to let her run the company as she wished? More than that, she loved him, and
eventually she might persuade her cynical husband to fall
in love with her.

'Okay, so there were mistakes on both sides,' Alex conceded. 'Mine being I should not have brought you back
to this apartment in the first place. I know you don't like
it.'

Lisa had to smile. 'Oh I don't know.' Placing a hand
in the open vee of his robe, she felt his hot satin skin
beneath her fingers. 'I seem to remember our wedding
night was not that bad.' Rising up on her toes, she pressed
her lips to his; his arms tightened around her and he took
over the kiss with a passionate thoroughness that had her
melting in his arms.

Suddenly Alex pulled back, his hands falling from her
waist. 'No, Lisa, I am not going to give you the chance
again to accuse me of manipulating you with sex.'

'I wasn't going to,' she teased, suddenly feeling light-
hearted.

'Good, then get dressed. We are leaving. We have to
learn to communicate better and here is not the place to
do it. Too many bad memories,' Alex insisted.

'I'll send you an E-mail from my laptop. Is that communication enough for you? Though I do remember over-
hearing you tell Nigel something about your lap.'

Alex stiffened, and she watched with laughter in her
eyes as his brow furrowed and he tried to remember, then
he disconcerted her completely by roaring with laughter.
Sweeping her up in his arms, he carried her to the bed.

'You're right. Who needs to talk when we have this?' And, with a wolfish smile, he dropped her on the bed. Falling down beside her, he deftly eased her out of her robe, shed his own, and drew her in to the hard heat of him. Lisa trembled violently, and wondered how she had ever been dumb enough to even consider forgoing such pleasure.

A long time later she lay with her head resting on his broad chest.

'Are you okay?' Alex queried softly. She felt the vibration of his words against the wall of his chest.

'I'm speechless,' she sighed.

'I'm surprised,' Alex murmured. 'You are usually such a verbal lover.'

'Yes, well, for once I am struck dumb.' But she knew what he was getting at.

Before she would have cried out in the throes of passion and declared her love in gushing terms. Not any more... She had accepted his reason for buying the shares in her company the same way she had accepted the fact that Alex did not believe in love. She told herself she didn't care, that the pleasure she found in his arms was enough...

'Good.' He rolled her on to her back and, propping his head on one elbow, he grinned down at her. 'How about a long weekend in Kos? Or perhaps you would prefer house-hunting again?' he ended less than enthusiastically.

Lisa pretended to consider. 'Well, a house is important...' She saw the flash of disappointment in his dark eyes. It was time to take a chance, and her lips parted in a purely feminine smile. 'But I doubt we'd find anything better than the first one we saw last week. So Kos it is.'

'You little witch.' Alex surveyed her with a disturbing light of understanding in his dark. 'You wanted the house, but you had so little trust in me you could not admit it, hmm.'

'Something like that,' she agreed.

'Hardly flattering, but understandable, I suppose.' Slipping off the bed, Alex picked up his robe and put it on. 'I have a few calls to make, so why not get up and get packed?' He glanced down at where she lay on the bed, her blonde hair spread in a tangled mass over the pillow, her body relaxed in the aftermath of passion, and his firm lips curved back over his brilliant white teeth in a blatantly sexy grin. 'And hurry, wife, or I might just change my mind!'

CHAPTER EIGHT

THE flight from London took a little over three hours and, allowing for the time difference, it was midnight when the jet touched down at Kos airport. They had travelled in the Solomos company jet, Alex explaining his father had been using it at the time of their wedding.

'Are you sure your mother won't mind our arriving in the middle of the night?' Lisa asked Alex, as he helped her onto the Tarmac.

Alex gave her a surprised glance and tucked her hand under his arm. 'You don't know much about Greek custom if you think midnight is late. In my mother's house we do not dine before ten, and quite often later.'

Two cars drew alongside them. In minutes, passport and customs details were accomplished, and Alex was ushering Lisa into the back seat of the second car, a chauffeur-driven limousine, and sliding in beside her.

'You must be famous?' She prompted. 'Not for you the queue at Customs!' She slanted him a sidelong glance. Dressed casually in jeans and a short-sleeved white shirt, he looked totally relaxed.

'Famous no, but local, yes. The population of the island is only twenty-five thousand, and most people here know each other. Actually, I had forgotten the first weekend in July is one of the busiest of the year. For the next two months the island will be heaving with tourists and the population swells to more like a million. For which I should be grateful.'

'Why?' Lisa tipped her head back to look up at him, intrigued.

'Because my father came here on holiday, met and married my mother, an island girl, and for the next few years built many of the hotels and apartments. In fact—' he looked down at her warily '—we are in the process of constructing a large holiday complex at the other end of the island, beside Paradise Beach. I thought I might take a look at it while we are here, see how it is going.'

'I might have guessed, you con-man,' she mocked. 'This is no holiday, but a business trip.'

'And who slipped their laptop in the side pocket of their holdall?' He asked drolly.

'Force of habit.' Lisa grinned at being caught out.

His dark eyes gleamed appreciatively down at her. She was a vision of loveliness, her blonde hair loose and curling around her bare shoulders. Her dress was a simple pale cream sheath in knitted cotton, the strapless bodice moulding her high, full breasts like the hands of a lover, the skirt ending a few inches above her knees. She had no idea how desirable she looked. Alex bent and placed a swift, hard kiss on her parted lips. 'So was that,' he said huskily.

At one in the morning, sitting on the terrace of the villa, sharing a soft-cushioned sofa with Alex and content in the curve of his arm, Lisa sighed blissfully. With the warm night air caressing her skin, the blue-black sky showered with sparkling stars above, and below, in the distance, the brilliantly lit shoreline and the sea beyond, she had rarely felt so relaxed.

'If you two young ones don't mind, I will say goodnight. I am so glad you are here, but at my age I need my beauty sleep.'

'So do we, Mamma.' Alex grinned and, rising to his

feet, took Lisa with him. Without releasing her he bent and kissed his mother's cheek. 'Goodnight.'

'Your mother is a lovely lady; I'm surprised Leo ever left her,' Lisa murmured as they watched the older woman enter the house.

'He didn't; she threw him out,' Alex said bluntly.

'Well, I can't say I blame her from what I've heard and seen of Leo. He can't keep his hands off women.'

'Life is never that cut and dried, Lisa,' Alex remarked, and, placing his other arm around her, he linked his hands lightly at her back. 'Women have a tendency to jump to conclusions, as you know,' he mocked her lightly, but the expression in his brown eyes was strangely reflective. 'I suppose nowadays medical science would have solved my parents' problem, but on an island like this thirty-five years ago, postnatal depression wasn't always recognised.'

'All the more reason for your father to stand by her, if she was ill,' Lisa argued.

Alex sighed. 'That is how I thought until a few years ago, when I had a fight with my father about his third divorce, and what it was costing, and he told me his side of the story. I don't condone his behaviour, but I do feel sorry for him.'

'I wouldn't,' Lisa murmured.

'No, but then you are not a man, thank God!' He gave her a quick squeeze that set her heart beating a little faster before continuing. 'Apparently, for two years after I was born, my mother would not let him anywhere near her. He loved her quite desperately and he was nearly out of his mind. He went to Athens on a construction project and while he was there my mother finally got over her depression. For the first time in her life she travelled to Athens by herself. Unfortunately, when she got to my father's hotel, he wasn't in. She waited in the foyer and saw him return, drunk and with a lady in tow. He swears it was the first time he had ever picked up a girl. I am inclined to believe him. My mother wasn't. She confronted him, threw her wedding ring at him, and got the next boat back to Kos. She has never left this island since.' Alex let go of her and, turning abruptly, caught her hand in his. 'End of story. Time for bed.'

She cast a sidelong glance at his harsh face as they walked into the house. 'And she never forgave him?' Lisa asked.

'No. One betrayal was one too many in her book.'

Lisa wondered if the same applied to Alex. In character was he like his mother or his father? She didn't know. But for her own sake she hoped it was the former.

Walking upstairs with her hand in his, Lisa wondered how Alex had felt as a small boy about the break-up of his parents' marriage.

They had reached the door of his bedroom suite, and, opening the door, Alex curved an arm around her shoulders and drew her inside, closing the door behind them.

She looked around the comfortable sitting room, and, suddenly nervous, she slipped from under his arms and walked out on to the balcony that ran the length of the building. 'It's hot.'

She felt Alex's hands close around her waist and his breath stir her hair. 'And it's going to get a lot hotter,' he husked. Awareness flared as his hands moved up to cup her breasts. 'This dress has tormented me all night.'

The breath caught in the back of her throat as he reached for the zip fastening and freed it. Lisa let her head fall back against him and made no protest as with deceptive ease he turned her to face him, the dress falling at her feet. Something vital leapt in his eyes and Lisa responded. Willingly she moved into his arms, and the kiss they shared was like no other. It was passionate, but tender, saying without words promises of hope, happiness, and need. Was it love? Lisa didn't know about Alex, but on her part it was, so why fight it?

'Bed, I think,' Alex opined huskily. His dark eyes gleamed down into hers. 'And I can guarantee no other woman but you has ever shared this bed.' Swinging her up in his arms, he carried her the short distance to the bedroom.

With an arm around his neck, her eyes level with his, Lisa's lips curved in a sympathetic smile. 'Poor Alex,' she mocked, 'would your mummy not let you?'

'Cheeky! But true.' And, sliding her slowly down the long length of his hard body, he let his hands drop to her hips, his fingers curling round the top of her briefs, her last remaining garment. He dropped to his knees on the floor, and with slow, delicate deliberation he slid her briefs down over her hips, at the same time covering her navel with his mouth. Lisa jerked and tried to pull back, but his hands would not let her. He pressed a kiss into the hollow of her hipbone She looked down and the trembling started in the pit of her stomach. Never had she seen anything so erotic as Alex's dark head against her thighs. He flicked a brief upward glance from beneath his thick lashes.

'I used to think I was a breast man,' he husked as he trailed his hands down the back of her thighs and followed with his mouth, pressing tiny kisses on her heated flesh. His hands continued their downward journey, curving her calves. 'But since meeting you, my sweet wife, I've decided I am a leg man.'

Lisa almost tumbled over when his hand lifted one foot, the trembling in her limbs was so great.

'Steady.' Alex chuckled as he helped her step out of her briefs. Slowly straightening up, a primitive glitter in his dark eyes, he let his hands sweep up her thighs and hips adding throatily, 'But then again...' his hands stroked up to her breasts '...your breasts are perfection.' His long fingers teased the sensitive peaks. 'I am spoilt for choice.'

Lisa groaned deep in her throat and focused on his darkly handsome face. She was shivering with excitement and involuntarily swayed towards him. He stopped her with the flat of his hand across her collarbone.

'No, Lisa, now it is your turn to undress me,' Alex declared roughly, but the fire in his dark eyes belied his apparent control.

Her heart thudding in her chest, Lisa raised her hands and slowly unfastened his shirt. She put both hands on his flat stomach and stroked up over his chest, her fingers tangling in his crisp curling body hair and grazing his taut male nipples. She eased the shirt off his broad shoulders, leaning forward to do so, deliberately brushing her breasts against his muscular chest. A secret smile curved her lips as she felt him shiver. It was an empowering feeling, knowing Alex was as susceptible as she was.

She let one hand drop to the fastening of his pants, and unclasped the top. Slipping her hand beneath the material, she was instantly aware of the strength of his arousal. Lisa glanced up at him through lowered lashes; his eyes were half closed, his lips pulled back across his teeth, and she had a daring idea. 'I'm not very good at this,' she said quietly, and turned guileless eyes up to his.

'I wouldn't say that,' Alex almost groaned. 'Go on.'

Her fingers finding the zipper, Lisa very slowly began to free it, pressing against his aroused flesh with her knuckles. 'I don't want to damage you,' she said breathlessly, and with both hands she slid his pants and briefs halfway over his hips and stopped. 'You're so powerful.' She edged one hand across his belly, her blue eyes gleaming with devilment and desire as they met his. Her fingers curved around him and gently squeezed, her thumb stroking the velvet tip.

Alex groaned for real. 'You little tease, Lisa.' And, pushing her hands away, he stripped off his pants in a second and tumbled her on to the bed. He caught her wrists above her head and, his lips, gentle as wild silk against her skin, trailed kisses over her eyelids, the soft curve of her cheek and finally her lips.

His tongue stroked the roof of her mouth, and then her own tongue curled around his in a welcome caress. Lisa ached to put her arms around him but he wouldn't let her.

'No, Lisa.' Alex raised his head; his night-black eyes met hers, a glint of mockery in their depths. 'Take turns— it's only fair.'

She arched against the hard heat of him as his lips blazed a trail of fire down her throat, lingering where the pulse beat wildly in her neck. Then he went lower, until his mouth closed over the tip of her breast.

'Alex.' She groaned his name as he suckled hungrily at her aching breasts, first one and then the other. Her skin tingled as if a million nerve-ends had suddenly come alive at his caress. 'Alex, please!'

He released her wrists and immediately she reached for him, her slender arms moving around his broad back. He captured her mouth again, and kissed her with an ever deepening hunger, and she kissed him back, one hand slipping around his neck, her fingers tangling in his hair to hold him to her, a fierce hunger, a need so great, exploding inside her. But Alex was not about to be rushed. With incredible control he led her to the brink of fulfilment over and over again. Soothing and enflaming her pliant body even as he fought to withstand her feverish intimate tactile exploration of his magnificent form. His strong features were taut and intent in passion, his black eyes flaring triumphant at her husky plea for release, and when she thought she could take no more he tipped her over the edge, and with a deep, rasping growl of release he followed her there.

Locked in his arms, his skin hot and damp against her own, Lisa stroked her hands lovingly over his shoulders and down his broad back. What did it matter if Alex didn't believe in love as long as they had this? He had shown her he wanted and needed her with a fierce and tender passion that touched her soul. Turning her head slightly, she pressed a soft kiss against the hard line of his jaw.

He eased his large frame to one side, and, leaning over her, he gently stroked a few strands of hair from her wet brow. 'All right?'

Her lips parted in a slow, wide smile. 'Never better.' She sighed, her brilliant blue eyes lingering on his darkly flushed face.

'Lisa, I...' Alex hesitated, his eyes widening on her delicate features almost in surprise. 'Meeting you was the luckiest day of my life,' he said huskily, and she had the distinct impression he had meant to say something else.

Midday Saturday, Lisa, hot and tired, gratefully took the hard hat off her head and handed it to Alex. Her hair was pulled back in a ponytail and she was wearing the minimum of clothing—brief white shorts and a sleeveless shirt knotted under her breasts—but still she had to wipe the perspiration from her brow. 'Do you visit all the construction sites your company is involved in?' she asked. 'It must take an awful lot of your time.'

'No.' Alex handed the hats to his site manager and said something in Greek, then, catching Lisa's hand in his, he added, as they walked off the building site, 'I employ a very efficient staff to do it for me. But as I was born here I do take a particular interest.' They had reached where he had parked the car and after opening the passenger door for her he walked around to the driver's side, and stopped when he saw she had not got in the car. 'Something wrong?' Not waiting for her answer, he tagged on, 'Sorry if you were bored.'

'Not bored. The view alone is incredible; the complex is bound to be a success.' She glanced at Alex. The blue cotton shirt fitted tautly across his broad shoulders, the first few buttons open to mid-chest. His black hair shone sleek as a raven's wing in the brilliant sun, and somehow, over the past few hours, he'd seemed more Greek to her than before. Looking at him, so cool while she was melting, she decided to get her own back.

'But you did promise we could go for a swim, Alex.' The maid had woken them that morning with a breakfast tray. She had set it on the table on the balcony and quickly withdrawn. They had made love for the fourth time. Then, when Lisa had been trying to get dressed, with a lot of interference from Alex, he had suggested she put her bikini on under her clothes and they could go for a swim later.

'So I did,' Alex drawled, a reminiscent smile curving his firm lips. 'But do you really want to join the tourists on the beach?' She eyed the wide sweep of Paradise Beach and the sparkling sea, a smile curving her generous mouth, her eyes gleaming with mischief as they met his over the top of the car. Sophisticated, arrogant Alex on Paradise Beach with hordes of tourists held great appeal. 'Yes, why not? It's so hot I'll melt.'

They spent the next half-hour playing like children in the warm clear waters, and then they dried off in the sun. Later still they returned to the villa and went to bed for a siesta, at Alex's instigation, insisting it was the Greek thing to do!

A sigh of pure pleasure left Lisa's lips as she sat down on a comfortable padded chair, one of two, set either side of a small table on the balcony of their suite and looked around her. Alex was downstairs talking with his mother. Apparently his mother had arranged a party for them to-night—a delayed wedding reception and a chance for Lisa to meet friends from his boyhood, she had said.

Lisa had left them talking and now, having showered and changed into a plain blue satin slip dress, she opened her laptop on the table in front of her and began composing an E-mail to send to Jed later. Enthusiastically she described the island, the history and the beauty of the place, and she smiled to herself when she thought of how green with envy Jed would be when he received it. Poor Jed had never been outside his state, let alone his country.

That was how Alex found her, smiling to herself, her fingers racing over the keys.

'Now who is working?' Alex prompted as he sat down opposite her, placing two glasses and a bottle of champagne on the table. 'And I was hoping to seduce you with champagne.'

'I wasn't working; I was writing to a friend,' she said simply, raising humorous eyes to his.

'A friend?' One dark brow arched quizzically.

'Yes, Jed.' She returned her attention to the keyboard. 'Usually I write down all the things I've been doing of interest. I compose my E-mail off-line and send it later, which is much more economical.' She didn't see the dark frown that creased his brow, or the slight narrowing of his deep brown eyes.

'Forget the economics.' Alex reached out a hand and brushed the back of her hand. 'Close that, and join me in a glass of champagne before the rabble arrive.'

'The rabble?' She grinned, closing her laptop. 'Not a very nice way to describe your friends, Alex.' She glanced across at him, struck by how vibrantly attractive he looked, wearing a cream open necked polo shirt and matching chinos, his handsome face tanned a deeper brown from a day spent in the sun.

'You haven't met them yet.' One brow lifted and his mouth twisted in an amused smile. 'Unlike your cerebral friends, mine are all too physical.' And, deftly popping the champagne cork, he filled two glasses and handed one to Lisa.

'That sounds ominous,' she replied, sipping the champagne.

His intense gaze caught and held hers, and for a second something hardened the depths of his eyes and she had the ridiculous notion she had angered him.

'Well, I will have to watch you like a hawk. No hardship in that dress,' he teased, allowing his dark gaze to skim across the soft curve of her breasts, revealed by the low neckline of her dress. 'Given half a chance they will throw you in the swimming pool, a favourite initiation rite, left over from boyhood.'

Alex was right about the party. It was a riotous affair. Yet Lisa couldn't help thinking that her arrogant, autocratic husband appeared much younger and much more open with his Greek friends than he had with the business friends they had met on their honeymoon. And she said so, when they finally got to bed at three in the morning. Alex's response was to laugh and to make love to her.

On Monday they left Kos. It had been a wonderful weekend, and Lisa watched through the aeroplane window as the island disappeared from view with a tinge of sadness.

'When do you think we'll come back?' she asked turning in her seat. Beside her Alex, immaculately dressed in a light suit and snowy white shirt, once more the consummate Greek tycoon, didn't hear her. His briefcase was open on his lap, his whole attention on the document he was reading. With a slight sigh Lisa returned to looking out of the window. Their dream weekend was well and truly over…

CHAPTER NINE

LISA signed off her computer and, with a contented sigh, sat up straight and stretched her slender arms above her head, easing the kinks out of her shoulders. That was her last job completed.

She glanced around the room, a soft smile playing around her full lips. It was hard to believe, but in the five weeks since they had returned from Kos Alex had bought the house at Stoneborough and three weeks ago they had moved in. Bert and Mrs Blaydon had accompanied them. A girl from the village had been hired to come in daily to help with the cleaning, and last Saturday they had had their first dinner guests.

Jake, who had been Alex's best man at their wedding, but who had vanished immediately after his speech, and his wife Tina had joined them for dinner. Apparently they lived a mere five miles away. Lisa had also discovered the reason Jake had exited the wedding reception so quickly. Tina had gone into labour that morning, but had insisted Jake could not let Alex down. Luckily Tina hadn't given birth until late in the evening, to a little girl, their second child.

Now, it seemed, they had a near perfect marriage, a beautiful home, a fantastic sex life. Alex made love to her until she didn't know if she was on her head or on her heels. She drove to Stratford-upon-Avon and Lawson's one or two days a week, and the rest of the time she worked from home.

They could spend hours talking about books and music,

politics, even business. But for all that, Lisa felt beneath the surface of the relationship a certain tension, and she was incapable of doing anything about it. If she was honest she knew it was her own fault. But she could not forget Alex didn't believe in love. The fact that he seemed perfectly happy with their marriage simply added to her confusion, because she wanted it all.

Sighing at her own stupidity, she glanced at her watch. Almost nine; about time she thought about eating. Mrs Blaydon and Bert had gone to visit friends in London and were staying overnight, so she was alone in the house. Alex was in Singapore on business, and was due back tomorrow, Friday. Lisa couldn't wait to see him; she had missed him dreadfully.

She placed the cover on the computer's keyboard and reached to the printer, picking up the E-mail she had printed from Jed. It gave the address of the hotel he was staying in the following weekend. He was actually coming to London with a group of students from his college; they were on a guided tour of Europe: London, Paris, Madrid and Rome. Lisa had arranged to meet him at his hotel on the Saturday afternoon, the only time he was free. She was really looking forward to seeing the man who had been her confidant for so long. But she had never heard of his hotel, so she had taken the precaution of printing out the address. A taxi driver would have no problem.

'I thought I'd find you here.' Alex's deep melodious voice feathered along her nerves.

Lisa spun around on the swivel chair, the sheet of paper falling from her hand to the desk. 'I wasn't expecting you back until tomorrow.' She smiled, her blue eyes drinking in the sight of him. He was leaning against the doorframe, his tie pulled loose, his shirtsleeves rolled up to his elbows and the top three buttons of his shirt unfastened. He had discarded his jacket and his black hair was rumpled. He looked rakishly handsome and infinitely sexy…

'Yes…' He moved towards her and Lisa got to her feet, wishing she was wearing something more glamorous than an old pair of white Lycra shorts and a blue vest. 'I missed you, so I cut my visit short.' Alex's dark eyes swept over her slender body with a blatant sexuality that made her pulse beat heavily. His hands reached out to close over her shoulders. 'Dare I hope you missed me?' And he studied her face with a narrow-eyed intensity that for a moment arrested the smile on Lisa's lips.

'Of course I did,' she freely admitted. If only he knew how much! She wanted to fling her arms around him, but it wasn't necessary, as his dark head bent and his mouth captured hers. His strong arms encircling her, he kissed her with all the pent up passion of what seemed like years.

'I needed that,' Alex husked some minutes later, holding her loosely in his arms. 'I have had one hell of a trip. I need a shower.'

Aware of him with every nerve in her body, she let her luminous blue eyes roam over his darkly handsome face. He did look tired, and she ached with love for him. She linked her hands behind his head and pressed her face into the curve of his throat, nuzzling him with her mouth.

'Hmm, you do seem a bit ripe,' She commented, and with an exaggerated sniff lifted mischievous eyes to his.

'You will pay for that, woman.' Alex grinned, and, swinging her up in his arms, he carried her out of the study.

Later, after they had showered, they didn't bother to dress, but simply slipped on towelling robes. Lisa made a quick meal of scrambled eggs and tossed salad, and they washed it down with a glass of Chablis.

Seated next to Alex on one of the two comfortable sofas

in the conservatory, she looked out over the garden, and the trees beyond, and leant her head back against his shoulder, completely relaxed.

'You do like this house?' Alex asked idly, his breath stirring her hair.

She chuckled. 'Yes, Alex, I love it, and I also know you had every intention of buying it anyway because Tina told me you had viewed it the week before we were married.' Lisa had met Tina for lunch in the village pub on Monday, and had discovered quite a lot about her husband.

'For a tiny woman, Tina has a big mouth,' Alex said dryly.

'She also told me you play golf on a Saturday afternoon with Jake, whenever you are in England, and, surprise, surprise, the golf club you both patronise is two miles down the road.'

'All right. So you found me out. I am suitably chastised and, to show you the depth of my regret, I will take you shopping tomorrow.'

'Can't, I'm afraid.' Lisa turned her head and looked at him. I have a meeting tomorrow with a Mr Bob Burnett. Apparently he's a potter, and he wants to expand from selling to a few private galleries into leasing Lawson's unit and selling direct to the public.'

'What do you know about the man?' Alex asked, his hand slipping over her shoulder, his long fingers edging open her robe and then, seemingly idly, stroking the curve of her breast.

Lisa swallowed hard, her pulse quickening. 'Not a lot really, only the information Mary faxed me today: a copy of his application and a brief outline of his intentions. The fax is on my desk. I'll go and get it, and you see what you think.'

A gentle restraining arm tugged her back against the sofa. 'No, I'll go.' Alex stood up, his lips brushing the top of her head. 'You work too hard and I want you completely rested for later.' His dark eyes sparkled with amusement and a sensual promise that told her he knew exactly how he affected her.

A wide smile curved her generous mouth and she watched as he strolled out of the conservatory, her husband, her lover. With a deep sigh of contentment Lisa snuggled back against the soft cushions. Life could not be better. She was now totally convinced Alex had told her the truth about buying the shares for her protection. He had proved it in the last few weeks. Although he was the major shareholder, he took no active part in Lawson Designer Glass. He was quite happy for her to remain the boss. But he was perfectly prepared to listen and discuss any problems that arose. For Lisa, that was a pleasure which had been missing from her life since the death of her mother. To be able to discuss and debate her work with Alex was an added bonus to the intimate relationship they enjoyed.

She was a very lucky girl, and, curling her feet beneath her, she brushed her long hair, now almost dry, behind her ears. She couldn't believe she had actually thought of divorce a few weeks ago. She shivered. She had so nearly made a huge mistake, but then, didn't the cliché say that the first six months were the worst in a marriage? Lisa's eyes filled with latent laughter. In her case, it had been the first six weeks!

'Something amusing you, Lisa?' Alex's deep, melodious voice echoed in the silence.

She turned her head, her eyes unerringly finding his. He filled the conservatory with his presence and her heart did its familiar leap in her breast. 'No, I was just thinking. What took you so long?'

He lifted the fax in his hand. 'This. I read it.' He waved the paper in the air. Whether he thought it was good or bad, Lisa couldn't be sure. His dark face was curiously expressionless. Restlessly he prowled around the room, while Lisa watched him with lazy, loving eyes.

'And?' she prompted.

'I think your man appears to have been pottering at pottery, excuse the pun, using his garage as a studio. He needs that unit more than you need him,' Alex drawled cynically. He glanced down at her, his brown eyes assessing her sun-kissed features. 'Don't make a decision tomorrow. Have the man investigated first.'

'You have no faith in human nature,' Lisa teased.

Something bleak moved in the depths of his eyes, and then it was gone. 'I've lived a lot longer than you, Lisa. People are rarely what they seem.'

Her eyes held by his, Lisa shivered, suddenly chilled. 'Sorry, I forgot you're heading for your dotage,' she quipped, dismissing the shiver in her mind.

'Dotage, indeed! I'll have you know I am in my prime,' Alex informed her. He reached down and tilted her head back with one hand. His brown eyes darkened and she trembled in anticipation; she knew that look so well. 'Come to bed now, and I will show you,' he purred as he bent over her and his lips took hers in a long, lingering kiss.

The following afternoon, Lisa let herself into the house and dropped her briefcase on the hall table. The weather was scorching hot, and the drive back from Stratford-upon-Avon had been horrendous. She walked wearily upstairs to the bedroom, and kicking off her shoes, slipped out of her clothes. A shower or a swim in the pool? She couldn't decide. Grimacing, she walked into the bathroom and turned on the shower. Maybe her determination to keep on running Lawson's was not such a great idea. At the height of an exceptionally hot summer there was a lot to be said for being a lady of leisure. Especially with a husband like Alex.

Five minutes later, when Alex joined her in the shower, she almost told him as much. Except he diverted her very effectively from all normal thought by a gentle but thorough assault on her senses until she could only stare into his deep dark eyes, her own hazed with mindless desire. She hadn't even realised he was home...

Jake arrived midday Saturday, and whisked Alex off to play golf. Lisa spent a lazy couple of hours at the poolside before retiring to her study, and her E-mail, and that was where Alex found her on his return from golf.

'Talking to friends again?' he growled. 'I might have guessed.'

'You don't look very cheerful,' Lisa commented, swinging around to face him. 'Bad golf day? She arched one delicate brow enquiringly. He had a face like thunder.

'You could say that,' he muttered. 'I need a drink.' And walked out.

Lisa chuckled to herself. Tina had told her that Alex and Jake were fiercely competitive on the golf course, although they were the best of friends. Personally she couldn't see the fascination in knocking a little white ball around all afternoon. But it gave her some satisfaction to know her arrogant husband didn't win at everything.

The following Saturday Lisa glanced at the bedside clock and, pushing Alex's arm from around her waist rolled off the bed. 'Jake will be here in an hour for you, and I'm going up to Town.' She glanced back at his reclining form and caught a look of such terrifying anger in his eyes that she stopped. 'Alex?' she queried uncertainly. Surely he wasn't upset because she had got out of bed? They had made love already this morning, and last night. In fact for the past week Alex had made love to her every night and morning with a hungry intensity, a driven passion, that if she had not loved him so much she might have found disturbing.

'Lisa?' he mocked, one dark brow arching sardonically. 'I understand; less than three months and our honeymoon is definitely over.' And rolling off the other side of the bed, he stood up. 'I am collecting Jake today. So I'd better get a move on.'

Reassured, Lisa blew him a kiss from her open palm, and, turning with a deliberate wiggle of her hips, she sauntered into her bathroom.

A quick shower was followed by a laborious twenty minutes drying and styling her long hair. She walked back into the bedroom, but there was no sign of Alex. Hardly surprising, she thought, with a tiny smile playing around her mouth. The only occupation her husband lingered over was lovemaking, much to her delight. Everything else in his life he achieved with a speed and efficiency that left lesser mortals standing.

Lisa took her time. She slipped on a pair of cream lace briefs, and then, seated at the dressing table, she applied the minimum of make-up. She selected a cream soft cotton dress from the wardrobe, and slid her arms into its tiny cap sleeves. Pulling the edges together, she deftly fastened the tiny buttons down the front, from the low scooped neckline to the hem that flared out jauntily a few inches above her knees. Slipping her feet into a comfortable pair of cream canvas sandals and picking up a matching canvas shoulder bag, she surveyed her reflection in the mirror, flicking a long curl back over her shoulder.

'Very nice.' Alex appeared behind her.

Spinning around, a broad smile lighting her face, she bobbed a curtsey. 'Thank you, kind sir.' Her eyes roamed over him; dressed in black trousers and a black knit polo shirt he looked so vibrantly masculine she wanted to reach out and touch him, and he knew it.

His brown eyes darkened. 'I could give golf a miss and we could, perhaps, find something more interesting to do. Does the notion appeal?'

Any other day Lisa would have said yes, but not today. She was meeting Jed in London and they only had three hours together—not much for five years of friendship.

'Jake would never forgive you standing him up, and I have to meet my friend in London,' she said with a rueful smile.

'Forget I asked,' Alex drawled lightly. But his eyes glittered hard as they flicked over her. 'How are you getting there? I don't want you driving into London on your own. Get Bert to take you.'

'There's no need. I'm driving to the station and taking the train.'

'So be it,' he said curtly, and left.

What had rattled his cage? she wondered with a frown as she followed him downstairs a few moments later. Alex had been angry last week when he'd returned from golf. This week he was mad before he started! For a sport that was supposed to be relaxing it didn't seem to do much for Alex. Still, it was not her problem, though she winced as she heard the screech of tyres on the gravel drive…

The taxi stopped outside a large building, left over from the era of the grand London townhouses. This one had been converted into a modest hotel. Paying the driver, Lisa leapt out of the cab and ran up the steps. She walked between the two massive columns that supported the portico and into the hotel's foyer, and glanced around with interest. To one side was the reception desk, and in front a grand staircase, a couple of sofas and a table with a few magazines on display, across the wide hall an arch opened into a lounge bar. She still couldn't quite believe she was going to meet Jed in the flesh. She had his photo, and all his confidences, but meeting him after so long was a thrill.

Excited anticipation put a spring in her step as she walked into the lounge bar and glanced around. Apart from the barman, it was empty.

'Lisa, is that you?' a deep voice enquired, with a noticeable American drawl.

She turned, and a broad grin split her face. 'Jed!' She recognised him immediately—looking older than in his photo, and totally out of place next to the shabby but comfortable very English décor. He was tall, long-legged and narrow-hipped, his faded blue jeans fitting him like a second skin and his half-unbuttoned shirt seemed to be straining the remaining buttons over his massive muscular chest. His attractive face was tanned a deep golden brown, and was in sharp contrast to his sun-streaked blond hair. But it was his eyes that really captured Lisa's attention. Deep sapphire-blue, with a light of such piercing brilliance in their depths, they reflected a tenderness that could not be disguised.

For long moments they simply stared at each other.

'Damn, but you're beautiful enough to make a man change his mind, Lisa.' A deep tide of red surged up Jed's face. 'Sorry for the language.'

Lisa chuckled. Though a year older than her, it was good to know Jed could still blush. 'No apology needed,' she said, with a broad smile that illuminated her whole face. 'And you look like a cowboy,' she added, having noticed his boots.

Two great arms curved around her and swung her off her feet, and a deep chuckle rumbled from the bottom of his chest.

She clasped his neck and he gave her a great bear hug, before setting her back on her feet. 'A part-time cowboy, as you know.' He grinned down into her face, still holding her. Staring into each other's eyes, a look of complete understanding passed between the two of them.

'You have no idea how much your friendship means to me,' Lisa said, suddenly serious, her blue eyes filling with tears of joy.

His blond head bent and he pressed the lightest of kisses on the curve of her cheek. 'It works both ways. Without your support and understanding, I would never have got this far.'

Neither of them saw the tall, dark man standing in the archway observing the tender scene, but suddenly all hell broke loose.

Lisa stood rooted to the spot as Jed's arms fell from her waist and he went flying backwards in a blur of movement, to land flat on his back a few feet away. Caught off balance, he'd had no chance. Lisa stared in horror, at Jed's assailant: Alex! His dark eyes gleamed like the coals of Hades in the blank mask of his face as he stood over the floored Jed.

Galvanised into action, Lisa dropped to her knees beside her friend and tenderly brushed the hair from his brow. 'Are you okay? I'm sorry, so sorry.'

'Hush.' Jed managed a grin, and, leaning up on his elbows he added 'I'm fine.'

'How touching,' Alex grated, his lips drawn back against his teeth in a malevolent sneer. 'My wife and her boyfriend in a seedy hotel for a seedy affair.' He took a step forward, towards Jed.

Lisa, shaking with fury, leapt to her feet and grabbed Alex's arm, terrified he was going to grab Jed again. 'You great brute!' She didn't know how Alex had got here, or why. And she didn't care. 'Are you mad?' she demanded, her blue eyes flashing fire.

'Look, buddy you've got it all wrong. Let me explain,' Jed said, trying to cool the situation.

Alex turned to look down at the younger man, his black eyes pitiless. 'You want her, you're welcome to her.' And, turning on his heel, he walked out.

The colour drained from Lisa's face. She could not believe what had just happened. She closed her eyes and shook her head.

She felt the warmth of a protective arm around her shoulders and sagged against Jed, who was now back on his feet. 'Are you okay, Lisa?' Jed's husky tones got through to her.

Lisa turned her head to look up into his face and gasped, lifting her hand to stroke along his cheekbone, where the swelling was already evident. 'I should be asking you that. I can't begin to apologise.' She shuddered again at the image of Alex grabbing hold of Jed.

'Shh. It's okay. It takes more than that to anger me. My brothers have tried for years to get me going and failed.'

Lisa's lips quirked in a tiny smile; she knew what Jed meant.

'I guess that was your husband. Pity you didn't have time to introduce me; he seems quite a man,' Jed observed laconically.

'More beast,' Lisa answered, a desolation in her voice that she could not hide as the full horror of what had happened sank into her mind.

'Don't be too harsh on the guy. He loves you; that

much is obvious,' Jed sighed. 'I guess this is the end of our meeting. You better go after him.'

'Go after him? Never,' Lisa said adamantly, her shock giving way to righteous anger. 'He had no right to follow me, and no right to call me names, and he most definitely had no right to grab you, the savage swine that he is.'

'He was jealous, Lisa, give the guy a break. It's not all his fault. Did you tell him you were meeting me?' Jed asked quietly.

'I told him I was meeting a *friend* in London.' The more Lisa thought about it, the angrier she got.

'Anger is a waste of emotion, Lisa. And, be honest, did you actually tell him you were meeting a man?'

'Since when did you become my conscience, Jed?' she queried with a wry grin.

He grinned back, but didn't answer the question. 'He's your husband. Go after him and explain.'

She looked up into Jed's handsome face, so open and honest. 'No, Jed, this afternoon is for us. I don't know why or how Alex appeared like he did. But he is not going to spoil our afternoon together.' And, clasping his hand in hers, she added, 'It's a glorious day. We are going to have our walk in Hyde Park, sit in the Italian Gardens and take a boat on the Serpentine; everything I promised you.'

'If you're sure, Lisa.' The expression on Jed's young face was incredibly grave. 'But promise me when you get home you will explain to your husband the truth—that we're friends, nothing more.'

Lisa felt overwhelmingly protective of this man she had met for the first time today. She knew Jed had not a cynical or nasty thought in his head, money didn't interest him, only people, and he would never understand a ruthless predator of a man like Alex.

'Of course I will, Jed, and don't worry. Alex and I will be laughing about this by dinnertime.' Forcing a brilliant smile to her lips, she tightened her fingers around his calloused palm. 'Now, come on, cowboy, you can watch the horse riders on Rotten Row and tell me how they compare to Montana.'

At six in the evening, Jed helped her onto the train. She turned and leant out of the window, and brushed a gentle kiss on his tanned brow. 'Till the next time, Jed.'

His brilliant blue eyes glistened with something remarkably like tears. 'I've had a wonderful afternoon, Lisa. Never mind the rocky start. Know that I will always be there for you.' The guard sounded his whistle and the train moved off... Lisa waved until the platform was out of sight.

CHAPTER TEN

LISA stepped reluctantly out of her BMW just as the heavens opened. She walked up the stone steps to the front door to her home and got thoroughly soaked in the process. Great! Just great… That was all she needed.

It was only her promise to Jed to explain their relationship to Alex that had brought her back to Stoneborough tonight. Was she destined to be a fool all her life where Alex was concerned? She had forgiven his escapades with Margot and Nigel. She had even convinced herself he loved her. But his behaviour with Jed had finally shown her the truth. Alex did not love her.

How and why he had followed her today, she had no idea. But he was not talking his way out of this latest episode, she vowed silently. Much as she loved him, she had no intention of being a doormat for any man. Her pride would not let her. With her dress plastered to her body by the rain, she pushed open the front door and walked into the hall. She didn't see Alex until he spoke.

'I'm amazed you had the nerve to come back. Like living dangerously, do you?'

Her head lifted, he was striding towards her, wearing the same black pants and shirt he had donned for golf that morning. He looked incredibly sexy, and a wayward leap of her pulse told her she was not immune to him. But whatever game Alex had been playing today it certainly had not been golf…

Dropping her purse on the hall table, she shrugged. 'I live here, and I need to change.' A confrontation with

Alex was inevitable, but not yet. Because she knew if she did confront him now, her anger would get the better of her and she would say something she might regret. Brushing past him, she headed for the stairs, but he was faster than her and blocked her way.

'Don't you walk away from me!' he bit.

That was the last straw for Lisa. No way was any man going to talk to her like that, especially not an arrogant devil like Alex. She flung her head back, her blue eyes spitting fury. 'Get out of my way, you great brute, you Neanderthal numbskull,' she raged, swiping at him but missing, as he caught her flailing hand.

'A Neanderthal? A brute, am I? You dare to call *me* names?' An expression of cold derision tautened his handsome face. 'This from a woman who has spent the afternoon in the arms of her toyboy.'

'Don't be ridiculous! Jed is not a toyboy; he's a year older than me,' she snapped.

'And that makes your betrayal all right?' Alex enquired silkily.

'Betrayal?' she threw back, her eyes warring angrily with his. 'That's rich, coming from you. I went to meet an old friend, and what happens? You appear like some demented dervish, knock him flat, and whirl off. And *I* am in the wrong? Oh please…'

'What kind of fool do you take me for?' Alex rasped.

'The kind of sneaky, devious fool who spies on his wife because he thinks everyone's morals are as low as his own,' Lisa shot back hotly. 'The kind who conveniently forgets to retrieve the key of his apartment from his mistress.' She was on a roll and could not stop; she was so incensed by the injustice of Alex's attitude. 'The kind of man who thinks the only relationship between a man and a woman must be carnal.'

His hand released hers to snake around her waist and bend her back over his arm before she had a chance to move. He captured her mouth in a ravishing kiss. His mouth searched, teased and tormented with a devastating thoroughness, until she whimpered in despair at her own frailty and lifted her hands to cling to his broad shoulders.

'What happened Lisa?' he demanded softly, his mouth close to her lips and brushing sensuously over their swollen fullness. 'Tell me?' He kissed her eyelids and the small curve of her ear, and her hands with a will of their own slid from his shoulders to his nape, twining in his silky black hair. His kiss, his caresses plunged her into a sensual sea of need, which overrode all her good intentions.

His dark head lifted. 'No answer?' Lisa stared up at him in frustrated desire, not able to trust herself to respond.

'After cyber sex with your boyfriend, the physical reality a bit of a letdown was it?' Alex demanded mockingly. 'The young man not quite as experienced in the flesh, as you would have liked?'

The import of his words hit her like blows to the heart. She could not believe he could be so cruel. She stared at him. His dark eyes were as cold and hard as a block of ice. Her hands fell from his shoulders, her fingers curling into her palms, her nails digging into her flesh as she fought to control the agony of frustrated desire. What was it about him that made him irresistible to her? While she was tormented by aching passion, he was as contained and remote as Antarctica. A frozen waste—a very apt description of their marriage.

'You're disgusting,' Lisa said in a raw voice, but, worse, she disgusted herself.

His arm fell from her waist and he stepped back. 'Liar.'

His smile mocked her, his narrow-eyed gaze triumphant.
'I could take you now…'

Lisa went red, then white. It was one insult too many.
She stared at him with bitter, hostile eyes. Tall, dark and
strikingly handsome, but she must have been mad to
imagine she had loved him. He didn't deserve to be loved.

'You're a stunningly sexy woman, Lisa, but I have
never taken another man's leavings and I am not going to
start now. I may have married you, but that is easily rem-
edied.' He cast her one long, derisory glance. 'Pack your
bags. I want you out of here within the hour. Anything
you leave can be sent on to Stratford. My lawyer will be
in touch next week. Personally, I never want to set eyes
on you again.' Spinning on his heel, he crossed the hall
into his study, slamming the door behind him.

Shock held her rigid. She squeezed her eyes tightly
closed. Alex was throwing *her* out. The arrogance, the
sheer hypocrisy of the man took the breath from her body.
For a second rage engulfed her. She took a step towards
the study, and then stopped. Alex was not about to listen
to anything she had to say, and, in all honesty, she no
longer had any desire to explain about Jed.

Alex did not love her, and never would. He was not
capable of the emotion. Let him think she had betrayed
him with Jed. He would anyway. This way at least she
kept her pride. He would never know how much she loved
him.

Several weeks later Lisa sat at her desk, fingering the pile
of mail the office junior had just delivered. The recent
past had taken its toll on her fresh-faced beauty: Her
golden tan had faded, and deep purple shadows framed
her large blue eyes.

Lisa picked up the first letter, a bill, and dropped it in

her in tray. Opening the next letter, she scanned it, her eyes widening in horror. As a major shareholder in Lawson Designer Glass she was requested to attend an extraordinary board meeting called by Xela Properties—in the other words, Alex—on Friday the twenty-third of September. The subject for discussion was the future direction the company should take. The meeting was scheduled for twelve noon in a private suite at a local hotel.

Lisa read the name and blanched. The same hotel in which her wedding reception had been held. She dropped the document on the desk and let her head fall back on the slender column of her neck, closing her eyes. Why was she surprised? She had been waiting for the axe to fall for weeks. Though she would not have believed one man could be so unrelentingly vindictive.

Moisture glazed her eyes, and she blinked hard. She was not shedding another tear for Alex Solomos. When he had thrown her out she had returned to live with Harold. The first night her anger had kept her going—but by the next she had cried herself to sleep. On the following Tuesday she had swallowed her pride and telephoned Alex at Stoneborough, only to be told by Mrs Blaydon he did not wish to speak to her, and all further communication between them must be conducted through his lawyer, Mr Niarchos.

Lisa had heard nothing more until a week later, when she had received divorce papers in the post. But once she'd read the divorce petition, she'd seen red... Any last lingering hope of reconciliation had vanished from her mind. All her old feisty spirit had returned... No way was she letting Alex get away with naming Jed Gallagher as the co-respondent in their divorce. If he wanted to play dirty, Lisa vowed she would do the same. She had

instructed Mr Wilkinson to cross-petition, citing Margot.
There had been an ominous silence ever since.

Wearily, Lisa brushed a few stray strands of hair from
her brow, and looked once more at the document in front
of her. Even knowing it was only a matter of time before
Alex would make a move to dismiss her and put his own
plan into action, it had still come as a shock. Alex had
won. But then she had been naive to think she'd had a
chance against the man. He was an arrogant, merciless
adversary, a powerful man who always got what he
wanted, and she should have recognised it the night she
met him.

She recalled that first Sunday when she had gone out
with him and when he had asked her to marry him. Then
she had thought his proposal the most romantic thing in
the world. But he hadn't asked, he had told her. She could
hear his voice now. *'I am going to marry you, Lisa. You
are going to be my love, the mother of my children.'* She
had thought he was telling her he loved her. What a joke!
He had recognised the overdue sexual awakening in her
eyes and had used it for his own ends. He had secured a
very lucrative business deal, and an innocent girl as his
wife and mother of his children.

Alex was a throwback to the Dark Ages, a pure male
chauvinist. His reaction when she had met Jed was understandable, given his flint-hearted nature. Like Caesar's
wife, Lisa had to be above reproach, and the slightest hint
that she was not, had been enough to cast her out.

The door opening broke into her bitter musing. 'Lisa?'
Harold walked into the office and frowned. 'What's up?
You look dreadful.'

Silently she handed him the letter and watched while
he read it.

'Good, good.' He visibly relaxed. 'I'm delighted you're

going to meet Alex. I know he loves you. It's obvious this meeting is a ploy so you can get back together again.'

'You think so?' Lisa responded dryly. Harold didn't know about the divorce; she hadn't the heart to tell him. He thought they had just had a fight.

'Of course. It couldn't be anything else. He knows you hold the majority of shares in the company anyway.'

'Yes,' she lied. And watched Harold leave happily. She still hadn't told him about her donation to the hospice, and obviously neither had Alex when he'd convinced Harold to sell. Poor Harold would be devastated if he knew that by selling to Alex, he had destroyed any chance Lisa had of keeping Lawson's. Let him be happy for a few more days; he would know soon enough after Friday.

The scales had fallen from her eyes and she could see it all clearly. Alex had manipulated and deceived from day one. It wasn't enough for him that he had broken her heart; now he was intent on grinding her into the dust beneath his feet, along with Lawson Designer Glass.

But not necessarily… Lisa mused, the light of battle sparkling in her blue eyes. She spent the next half hour on the telephone to her lawyer. The following day she spent walking around Stratford-upon-Avon until she had found what she was looking for…

At five minutes to twelve, Lisa parked her car in the hotel car park and slid out. With trembling hands she smoothed the short black skirt of her fine wool suit down over her hips and adjusted the bright red collar of her blouse over the lapels of her tailored jacket. She had taken special care with her make-up, and had swept her long hair back off her face and into a knot on the top of her head. On her feet she wore black stiletto shoes coupled with sheer black silk stockings that accentuated the length of her legs.

Tightening her grasp on her briefcase, she walked into the hotel.

Lisa crossed to Reception, and enquired of the male receptionist directions to the Oberon Suite. He responded with a broad, admiring smile, and told her it was on the first floor.

Her stomach churning with nervous tension, she glided across the lobby, a tall, stunningly attractive and elegant woman, totally unaware of the admiring glances of every man in view.

Ignoring the lift, she ascended the stairs to the first floor. The Oberon Suite. Wasn't Oberon the king of the fairies in *A Midsummer Night's Dream*? she mused, as she walked along the wide hall reading the door signs. It hardly suited Alex's macho image, but she needed a touch of magic if she hoped to survive the next hour with her pride intact. She had to face Alex one last time and let him see she didn't give a damn!

Her eyes flicked over a name-plate and she stopped. Taking a few deep breaths, she lifted her hand and knocked firmly on the door; straightening her shoulders, she composed her face into a cool, polite smile and opened the door.

Two sofas covered in blue velvet were set either side of an elegant fireplace, at the other end of the room was a large rectangular table set with the accoutrements for a business meeting. But the model building placed in the centre of the table confirmed her worst fear: the proposed redevelopment, no doubt. Lisa moved into the centre of the room. She glanced again at the table, and as she did so a large black leather high-backed chair that had been facing the window suddenly spun around.

'You came. Brave of you. I had a bet with myself you wouldn't.' With the sun behind him she was not able to see his face clearly, but it made no difference; she knew that slightly accented voice as well as her own. It was Alex…

'And on time as well. Would you like to take a seat and we can begin?'

Her legs trembled, and it took an enormous effort of will to walk to the table and sit down on the nearest chair. 'Good morning.' She gave the conventional greeting without looking at him, and, placing her briefcase on the table in front of her, she clasped her hands tightly in her lap and waited.

'As the only two shareholders, in what is really a family business…'

Alex began to speak, and at his mention of 'family business' Lisa's head jerked up, her eyes narrowing angrily on his dark face.

His black hair was longer than when she had last seen him, but the tanned handsome face still wore the mask of derision she remembered so well. He was enjoying this, she realised bitterly. Not content with discarding her like so much garbage, he wanted to watch her be destroyed. Why else would he mention that Lawson's was a family firm, other than to rub in her failure to retain it? Well, he was not going to get away with it if *she* had her way.

His black eyes caught hers and she immediately looked away, unable to stand the intensity of his gaze. 'I have had my architect prepare a model to show you how we envisage the finished complex.'

Lisa's glance skimmed over the model, but she didn't see it. She wasn't interested.

'What do you think, Lisa?' The strident question had her glancing at Alex once more. He was watching her, a wary anticipation in his dark eyes. Why, she had no idea. Alex knew damned well that she couldn't oppose him. In fact, she had decided she was not going to try. She wouldn't give him the satisfaction.

'I think you've said it all. Do you want to go through the charade of taking a vote?' She could almost taste the tension in the air. The hairs on her neck were standing on end; it was sheer bravado that enabled her to hold his gaze. 'All in favour say aye,' she announced facetiously, and lifted her hand.

'Lisa, you haven't even looked at the model.'

'What's the point? You own Lawson's, have done for months. It's yours to flatten to the ground. I wish you luck with it.' Her gaze roamed over his perfectly chiselled features and she felt the beat of her heart quicken, knowing it was time to have her say and get out.

'The only reason I am here is to tell you I am prepared to sell you my forty-seven per cent stake at the same rate as you paid Harold. But, in return, I want the right to retain the name Lawson Designer Glass. So, do we have a deal?' she asked firmly.

His dark brows rose and she could see she had surprised him. 'Why?' Alex settled back in his chair, his narrowed eyes fixed on her face.

'Does it matter? You've got what you want—the land, the river frontage…that was all you were ever interested in.' She made no attempt to hide the edge of bitterness in her tone.

'You malign me, Lisa. Not a good idea when you are asking for a favour.'

'I don't want a favour from you. I want what is mine: my name.'

'I thought your name was Solomos.' The taunting softness of his comment made her anger rise. But she refused to give in to it.

'Not for much longer, and you know perfectly well what I mean.'

'Humour me. Tell me why.'

'I have found alternative premises for the glass foundry. I intend relocating and starting again. That way none of my employees need to suffer because I believed all your lies. They will all keep their jobs.'

'I might have guessed.' Alex's sensuous mouth quirked in a smile of reluctant appreciation. 'Very noble. But then you always were far too noble for your own good.'

'Not something you have ever suffered from,' she snorted, suddenly fed up with the whole mess. Pushing back her chair, she stood up. 'If you have no objections, I'll expect your lawyer to be in touch about the financial details as soon as possible.' And, picking up her briefcase, she walked round the table and headed for the door.

But she didn't get far. Suddenly she was stopped from behind and held against Alex's muscled length. The air whooshed out of her and she dropped her briefcase. 'Let go of me!' She was sick of playing the sophisticated businesswoman; she just wanted to get away.

To her surprise, Alex released her immediately. She bent down to pick up her briefcase, and before she had time to straighten up he had crossed the room and locked the door.

'What do you think you're doing?' she cried. Locked in a hotel suite with Alex was the last place she wanted to be.

'You will soon see,' was his enigmatic reply as pocketing the key card he walked towards her.

Lisa swallowed nervously. Suddenly what had appeared to be a large, elegant room at first sight now took on the proportions of a bird-cage as far as she was concerned. Her blue eyes skated warily over Alex. He was wearing a black pin-striped three piece suit, the jacket fitting perfectly over his wide shoulders; with a grey silk shirt and matching tie, he looked devastatingly attractive and infinitely dangerous.

He stopped a foot away from her, but he made no effort to touch her. There was a curious stillness in his stance. But his dark eyes strayed restlessly over her, from the top of her head to her toes, and back to her face. 'You're looking very beautiful, Lisa.'

'Thanks. But your opinion means nothing to me,' she said curtly. 'Open the door and let me out of here.'

'You really don't like me, do you?'

Like him? Her heart lurched. Not so long ago she had loved him more than life itself. 'No,' she snapped, banishing the unwanted memory from her mind. But just looking at him was having a disastrous effect on her senses.

'Are you afraid of me, Lisa?'

'No. I am simply surprised you asked me here at all. I distinctly remember you saying you never wanted to set eyes on me again.'

'I lied.' He smiled tightly, and his hand reached out, but she quickly took a step back, not wanting him touching her. She remembered the last time all too vividly. His hand fell to his side. ' How is Jed, by the way?' he queried softly.

'The last I heard, he was in Rome.' Alex had a nerve asking, but she refused to be riled, and answered him conversationally. 'He managed to E-mail me from an Internet café. He's due back in Montana this weekend.' But she could not resist adding, 'I might go and stay with him for a week or so while our lawyers work out the finer points of our deal.' Let Alex think she was going to her lover...

'I think not, Lisa.' He moved a step closer, and Lisa took another step back, and another until she bumped into the table. 'Because there is not going to be any deal. I am not buying you out, and I am keeping the trade name.'

Her face went ashen. For sheer malevolence Alex had no equal. 'You bastard!' she swore. 'Why did I ever marry you?' She shook her head. 'Our divorce can't come quickly enough for me.' Lisa had been functioning on adrenaline for the past half-hour, but suddenly the enormity of what had happened finally hit her. This man had taken her company, and now he was holding her captive. What more did he want? Her life's blood? She felt her knees weaken, and with Alex towering over her she was glad of the table to support her.

'No, we are not.' A black brow lifted and a ruthless smile slanted his sensuous mouth. 'Because I have decided to take you back. So stop playing games.'

Lisa's mouth fell open in shock. She was powerless to utter a word. He wanted her back! It didn't make sense.

'No more pretending Jed is your lover.' He lifted a hand and tilted her chin with his finger, his dark eyes intent on her face. 'I had Jed investigated. He is in his final year at the seminary and will very shortly become a priest. According to all accounts, he is only one step away from an angel, and according to his brothers he has never had sex in his life.'

Fierce colour flooded her cheeks, and she wasn't sure if it was because of the warmth of his hand on her face, or her sheer anger at his daring to investigate Jed. 'You didn't tell his brothers your disgraceful assumption?' she demanded, finding her voice. 'Jed had enough trouble convincing his family to allow him to study for the priesthood. The last thing he needs is you accusing him of adultery.'

'No, I didn't, but no thanks to you. You could have told me he was a priest.'

'I seem to remember you never gave me a chance,' she bit out.

'I'm sorry, Lisa. Forgive me.' Alex's hand dropped from her chin and he stood with his arms hanging loosely by his sides, an air of vulnerability about him that Lisa had never seen before. 'You can't begin to imagine how deeply I regret the way I behaved, but if you would just let me explain.'

'Why should I? You never afforded me that courtesy.'

'Because I love you, damn it! He forced the words out between gritted teeth, and for a second her heart stopped. Then she remembered.

'Now who is playing games?' Lisa prompted, willing her voice to remain steady. At one time she would have given anything to hear him say he loved her. But not now; it was too late. 'You married me for a bit of real estate, remember?' She declared, but it was more to remind herself. She was not falling into Alex's clutches again. Her marriage had been a rollercoaster ride to hell, and she wasn't paying twice. 'In fact, I seem to recall you telling me you did not believe in love. So what *are* you after, Alex?'

She was on the defensive. She couldn't help it. Her awareness of Alex was such that it was agony for her to be in the same room with him, and to compensate she lashed out, 'You already have my property.' She waved her hand in the direction of the model.

Alex visibly flinched. 'I deserved that,' he said with unnatural humility. 'But if you would only look at it!' He forced her to turn and face the model complex. His humility hadn't lasted long, she thought dryly.

The building was long and low, only four floors, with

gardens leading down to the river and to one side more buildings forming a courtyard. 'Lawson's.' She read the tiny blue lettering on the front of the model and fury enveloped her. 'You've called your hotel Lawson's?' she cried, spinning around and glaring up defiantly at his face, only inches from her own. 'Why did you do it, Alex? A sop to your conscience? But then we both know you haven't got one.'

'Even now, you really don't see, do you?' Alex asked flatly, slipping his arm around her shoulder and turning her back to face the table. 'If you look closely—' he stretched his other hand across in front of her, one finger pointing to the courtyard and the low buildings '—you are not going to lose Lawson's Designer Glass. The architect has incorporated the glass house, with a viewing area for the general public, into the overall design. So you see, you have nothing to worry about. It is quite common to have a few selected attractions in the grounds of a hotel.'

Stunned, Lisa stared down again at the model, her blue eyes widening in wonder, and then she lifted her puzzled gaze to Alex. 'But…but… Why…? I mean…' She stammered to a halt, completely gobsmacked.

Tentatively, he slid his hand to her waist and turned her fully to face him, locking his hands loosely behind her back. Lisa was too shocked to offer any resistance. 'I never thought I would see the day when I would bare my soul over a conference table.' His lips twisted in a self-mocking smile. 'But you deserve no less after the way I treated you.'

Baring his soul. A minute ago Lisa would have argued that the man did not possess a soul. She couldn't take it in. Lawson Designer Glass was saved. Alex was confusing her yet again.

'I know I have hurt you in the past, Lisa.' He'd got that right. The ache in her heart was a constant companion. 'But it was never my intention.'

Lisa swallowed nervously, unsure where Alex was leading. But deep down inside a tiny flicker of hope unfurled. 'No?' she queried.

'No. Believe that if you believe anything, Lisa. From the second I set eyes on you I wanted you,' Alex began in a deceptively quiet tone. 'But you were right; the night I met you in Stratford I was there to see Margot. Though only to tell her it was over. And I didn't spend the night with her. We had separate rooms.' His voice became cynical. 'But it did not stop Margot trying to persuade me into her bed. Which is why I never got the key back. I left in rather a hurry in the end.'

'I see,' Lisa said shakily.

'I hope you do.' Alex's eyes bored into hers, dark and oddly pleading. 'I could hardly wait till ten the next morning to see you. Then when we spent the day together, and I discovered you were feisty, and fun and yet innocent, I decided your credentials were perfect for a wife, and that I was going to marry you. I deliberately rushed you into it.'

That wasn't strictly true, Lisa silently acknowledged. She had been no slouch herself. She had wanted him and found it hard when he'd insisted they wait until their wedding night.

'I would like to say that business had nothing to do with it, but I want to be totally honest with you. I don't know.' His hands tightened behind her back, pulling her slightly nearer, as though he was frightened she would try to break away. 'When Nigel approached me at the bar, it might have crossed my mind that I could have the woman

I wanted *and* a lucrative business opportunity. But within a day of knowing you all I was interested in was *you.*'

She didn't know what to believe. He need not have admitted he hadn't been sure of his own motive that first night. Warily, Lisa tilted her head back and looked up at him. What she saw in the depths of his deep brown eyes made her heart skip a beat as warmth flooded though her veins, and she was tempted to give him the benefit of the doubt. His arms tightened a fraction more and her legs brushed against his, making her vitally aware of the electric tension between them. In a last-ditch attempt to control her crumbling defences, she murmured, 'But I did overhear you talking to Nigel.'

'Ah, yes, Nigel. When I came back from New York, and you knew I had bought the shares, everything I told you was the truth, Lisa. I did it to protect you.'

She had believed him at the time, but after Jed she'd been willing to discredit his every move. Now, after seeing his plan for the complex, she had to believe him again. 'I believe you,' she conceded, but she was still not sure where he was leading.

'Thank you for that.' He eased her into the hard heat of his body and pressed his mouth to her brow.

Lisa raised her hands and palmed them on his broad chest, whether in resistance or simply because she ached to touch him she did not know. She was powerless to utter a word. She felt as though she was on the brink of some great discovery.

'It is more than I deserve.' Alex's eyes caught and held hers. 'Because what I have to say now shows me in a very unfavourable light.' His sensual mouth turned down in a grimace. Lisa held her breath, the hope that was slowly growing in her frozen.

Alex kept an arm around her waist, and as though in a

gesture of comfort he lifted his other hand and caressed the soft curve of her cheek, his dark eyes kindling as he registered the slight dilation of her pupils. 'I had it all, and in my conceit, my arrogance, I did not know it. Of all the lovers I have ever known…'

Lisa stiffened imperceptibly. The last thing she needed was a rundown on his women. 'No, there were not that many, Lisa.' He read her mind with ease. 'But you were the most passionate, the most generous, giving… And I took everything you had to give and took it for granted.' His eyes clouded with what looked suspiciously like remorse. 'I could make excuses. I did not believe in love because of my parents. My mother loved my father, still does, but would not forgive what she saw as a betrayal.'

Lisa suddenly saw the parallel in their relationship. Alex had caught her in the foyer of a hotel and had thrown her out of their home. He was more like his mother than she had thought, and she listened with mounting hope as he continued.

'But that is the easy way out. In reality I had reached the age of thirty-five without experiencing the emotion, and was cynically convinced it did not exist. Until I met you. But even then I refused to recognise it.'

Her blue eyes widened to their fullest extent on his serious face. Was he implying again that he loved her?

'Even after the fiascos with Margot and Nigel were sorted out and we went to Kos…' Their eyes met and clung for a long moment with memories shared. 'Even then I could not admit to myself that I loved you. In my conceit I didn't think it mattered, because I knew you loved me. On our honeymoon, you delighted me with your unabashed enthusiasm, both physically and verbally. But after I returned from New York it slowly dawned on me you no longer said the words. You became a silent lover. I told myself it did not matter, but it did,' he admitted with a self-mocking smile.

Alex was right; she had withdrawn slightly, out of insecurity, but she hadn't thought he'd noticed. The hope expanded to every part of her as he went on.

'I found myself growing more and more suspicious. I was jealous of the time you spent E-mailing your friends. Then, on the night I got back from Singapore, I went into your study to get the fax from the pottery chap.' Pain clouded his expression, and involuntarily Lisa's hands stroked comfortingly up over his chest.

He gave her a crooked smile. 'I found a printout of an E-mail with the address of a hotel in London and it was like a knife in my gut.' He paused. 'I have absolutely no excuse for following you, or grabbing your friend Jed. It was sheer rage, primitive male jealousy; the man was touching my woman.' He said it with such possessive arrogance Lisa had to mask a smile. It was so Alex… He could not remain humble if he tried.

'In that moment I knew the sheer agony of love and betrayal.'

'Not betrayal,' Lisa interjected swiftly.

'You were close to Jed mentally. Is a betrayal in the mind any less harmful than a physical betrayal, Lisa?' he asked, and she did not know how to answer him. His eyes never left her face as he bent his head, and brushed her lips gently with his own. 'Forget I said that. Just know I love you, Lisa. I think I always have, but I was too arrogant to admit it,' he murmured against her mouth.

'But you still insisted it was over…'

'Hush, Lisa.' Alex lifted a finger and placed it over her lips, and she marvelled at the slight tremor in his touch. 'I will regret to my dying day the way I behaved. You are my wife, and I will love and treasure you in this world and the next, if you will let me.' His dark eyes gleamed with the fierce burning light of love. There was no mistaking it, and Lisa's lips parted in a brilliant smile of pure joy, her shimmering blue eyes reflecting the love she found in his. 'Will you?' He repeated huskily.

Lisa had a million questions to ask, but they could wait. Swaying towards him, she moved her hands up to his wide shoulders, and then trailed her fingers through his hair, bringing his head down to hers. 'Yes, I will. In fact, I will insist,' she teased, and placed her lips on his. Delicately probing with her tongue, she initiated a kiss that was tender and passionate, loving and giving, a kiss like no other they had shared. Finally, so he would be in no doubt, she looked up at him through her thick lashes and murmured, 'I believe there is a bedroom next door. It would be a shame to waste it. After all, you have paid for it, partner.'

Alex's husky laugh contained an element of relief, and he bent and curved an arm beneath her knees and lifted her high against his chest. 'Your wish is my command,' he groaned, as her hands slid around the nape of his neck and she nuzzled his neck.

They fell on the bed, clothes discarded haphazardly, and finally, when they were both naked, Alex reared up over her, his eyes dark and feverish as they roamed over her slim curves and the luscious fullness of her breasts. 'I do love you, Lisa.' She felt her breasts grow heavy beneath his gaze.

'Then love me,' she whispered, and he did...

Kate Walker was born in Nottinghamshire but as she grew up in Yorkshire she has always felt that her roots were there. She met her husband at university and she originally worked as a children's librarian but after the birth of her son she returned to her old childhood love of writing. When she's not working, she divides her time between her family, their three cats, and her interests of embroidery, antiques, film and theatre, and, of course, reading.

CONSTANTINE'S REVENGE

by

Kate Walker

CHAPTER ONE

It HAD begun with a knock at the door.

Such a simple thing and yet it had changed Grace's life for ever. It had taken her happiness, her dreams of a future, and ripped them into tiny shreds. And as a result, even now, two years later, she still had to nerve herself to answer any summons from someone on the outside of the house.

'Gracie, sweetie!' Ivan's voice reached her from the kitchen, where he was busy creating his own devilishly intoxicating version of a fruit punch. 'Are you going to answer that or just stand and stare at the door all day?'

'Of course I am!'

She hadn't even been aware that that was what she had been doing, Grace realised as, with a fierce little mental shake, she pushed herself into action. It was stupid to react in this way. After all, it was fully twenty-four months since that appalling day. This wasn't her father's house, the place she had used to call home, but the elegant Victorian building where Ivan had the ground-floor flat. And nothing could be more different from the careful preparations for the elaborate society wedding of the past than the casual, noisily crowded atmosphere of the party her friend was giving to celebrate his thirtieth birthday.

'I didn't know we were expecting anyone else!' she tossed over her shoulder, using laughter to disguise the irrational uncertainty that still clutched at her stomach as she hurried to answer a second imperious knock at the door. 'Just how many people have you invited? The place is bursting at the seams already.'

'A party isn't a party until you don't have room to breathe!'

Grace barely heard Ivan's response. Joking hadn't helped. If anything, the crazy feeling of apprehension had grown worse. She felt like some nervous cat, scenting the approach of an aggressive intruder into its territory, every fine blonde hair lifting at the back of her neck, her soft grey eyes clouded and shadowy.

Lightning couldn't strike twice! she told herself. At least not the sort of lightning she had in mind.

White teeth digging sharply into the softness of her lower lip, she dragged in a deep, fortifying breath before grasping the handle firmly and pulling at the door.

It came open far more swiftly than she had anticipated, flying back towards her with a force that almost knocked her off balance, so that she staggered slightly, struggling to keep upright.

'Steady…'

A deep, drawling voice, rich as honeyed cream, was the first thing she registered. Then two other facts hit home at the same time, with the force of a devastating blow in the pit of her stomach.

Two frighteningly significant facts. Two disturbingly familiar and shockingly vividly remembered details about the man before her that made her thoughts reel, her head spinning sickeningly.

Deep, dark eyes. Eyes black as jet, and every bit as hard. Their stunning colour and blazing intensity had been etched into her memory long ago, impossible to erase. And that sensual voice, exotically accented, seemed to coil around her nerves, tightening and twisting them until they screamed.

Other images bombarded her. Smooth olive-toned skin, a strong jaw, a beautiful mouth with a surprisingly full lower lip. Hair black as a raven's wing, cropped uncompromisingly short in order to subdue a rebellious tendency to curl. Suddenly it was as if some cruel hand had reached out from the past, snatching hold of her and dragging her back into the tumult of emotions she had experienced then.

'Are you all right?'

Strong hands had fastened over her arms, supporting her, and only when she was secure on her feet did the tall, dark man actually look into her face.

'*You!*' he said sharply, his expression changing instantly from one of concern to a look of pure contempt that seared over Grace's already rawly sensitive skin. 'I didn't recognise you, looking like that.'

Every vital function in her body seemed to have shut down in shock. She had to tell herself to breathe, her heart to beat. Lightning *could* strike twice, it seemed. Certainly Greek lightning could. Because the force of the most violent electrical storm had always been the effect that this man had had on her.

'Constantine!'

Her tongue felt clumsy as it tangled around the name that she had refused to speak for so long. The name she had promised herself she would never, ever use again if she could help it. But now sheer shock and a sense of unbelieving horror had forced it from her against her will.

'What are you doing here?'

The look he turned on her burned with cynical disbelief. Only an idiot would have had the stupidity to ask that question, his lofty disdain declared. And if there was one thing that Constantine Kiriazis was quite unprepared to tolerate then it was the presence of any sort of a fool.

'I was invited,' he declared, his voice as curt as his movements as he belatedly became aware of the way that he was still holding her, long, tanned hands on her arms, the immaculately manicured fingers incongruous against the shabby, well-worn leather of her jacket.

With a fastidious gesture that communicated only too clearly the feeling that simply to touch her had somehow contaminated him, he abruptly let her go and stepped away from her side. The move spoke eloquently of a mental distance that was far, far greater than the few centimetres that actually separated them.

'This *is* where the party's being held?'

With a brusque nod of her head Grace dismissed the unnecessary question. The sheer volume of noise behind her, the music and laughter, the loud buzz of fifty or more different conversations made a nonsense of the fact that he had even asked it.

'But Ivan wouldn't have invited you!'

The cynical lift of one black, straight brow mocked at her vehemence, shaking the certainty of her conviction without a single word.

'Tell me, my sweet Grace, do you really believe that I would appear here, dressed like this…?' An arrogant sweep of his hand swept down the powerful length of his body, drawing her clouded grey eyes unwillingly after it. 'Without the excuse of your crazy friend's theme party to justify it?'

Silently Grace cursed herself for being every sort of a fool. She hadn't wanted even to *look* at him. But with that single haughty gesture he had forced her to do just that. And, having looked, she found herself incapable of turning away again.

She didn't want to be reminded of the lean power and strength of Constantine's body. Didn't want to recall the honed muscle and hard bone that she had once known so intimately. It hurt just to remember how it had felt to be held in those arms, to be crushed close to the wall of that chest, feel that sensual mouth on her own.

'I don't think you've exactly understood the theme of tonight.'

Furious control gave her words a biting coldness, and her clear grey eyes were like shards of silvery ice as she let her gaze run back up the length of his tall frame in an expression of disdain that matched his own of only moments earlier. Matched and outstripped it as she let her full mouth curl derisively.

'The idea is that this is a Turn Back the Clock party. Ivan's painfully aware of the fact that at midnight he'll be thirty, that he'll have left his twenties behind for ever. Everyone is to dress in the sort of clothes they would have worn ten years ago, so that just for tonight he can pretend…'

'Do you think I don't know that?' Constantine snapped, his accent deepening as anger marked his voice. 'I do not need you to explain what I already understand perfectly. And if I had any doubts then the distressingly unflattering outfit you are wearing would erase them once and for all.'

'At least I entered into the spirit of things!' Grace flashed back at him, her chin lifting in angry defiance.

She didn't need to be reminded that what she was wearing was so very different from the way he was used to seeing her. The way anyone was used to seeing her. Ten years ago she had been a mere fourteen, and then the skin-tight denim jeans worn with a white sleeveless tee shirt and a leather biker jacket over the top had been her ideal of relaxed weekend clothing.

Dressing to come to the party tonight, she had actually thought her chosen costume was quite fun. That the uncharacteristic way she had done her hair, tousling the blonde sleekness into wild disarray, together with the use of much more make-up than usual, particularly around her wide grey eyes, made her look younger and more relaxed. She had smiled to see herself looking totally unlike the elegant, controlled Grace Vernon her workmates at the advertising agency would have recognised.

But now, faced with Constantine's obvious censure, she felt the bubble of euphoria that had buoyed her up burst painfully sharply, leaving her limp and miserably deflated. What had seemed light-hearted and fun now seemed gauche and unsophisticated in the extreme, making her shift uncomfortably from one foot to another as once more Constantine's jet-black gaze seared over her in a way that brought a burning rush of colour to her pale cheeks. How she longed for the protection of her usual refined way of dressing.

If she had known he would be here tonight she would have worn something that oozed sophistication and would have knocked him dead. Something that would have shown him just what he was missing. What he had discarded so brutally when he had tossed her aside, declaring that she wasn't fit to be his wife.

If she had known he would be here...!

Who was she kidding? If she had even so much as suspected that Constantine Kiriazis was in England, let alone in the capital, where she and Ivan lived, she would have turned and run, putting as much distance as was possible between herself and the man she had once loved so desperately.

'I bothered to dress up, while you...'

'And what, precisely, is wrong with what I'm wearing?' Constantine enquired with a silky menace that sent a sneaking shiver down her spine.

'It's hardly *fun*, is it? I mean, it's so...'

Words failed her. The only ones that sprang to mind were

such that she clamped her mouth tight shut on them, refusing to let them out.

The truth was that his outfit was pure *Constantine*, somehow displaying outwardly the very essence of the man.

The long black cashmere overcoat he wore against the unexpectedly bitter winds of the last evening in March had to have been handmade and superbly tailored into its perfect fit on his athletic form. It spoke of wealth, more wealth than the average person could even begin to dream of, but an affluence that was very definitely old money. Riches that had been in the family for so long that they no longer even registered on their owner's mind. And they certainly needed no show or ostentation to draw attention to their existence.

Constantine Kiriazis had never flaunted the trappings of the fortune she knew he possessed, both from having grown up as the son of a very rich man and from having earned a second, equally huge amount in his own right. His clothes, like the rest of the man, were always exquisite but severely restrained, the heavy, square-faced gold watch he wore on his wrist the only ornament he ever indulged in.

Underneath the luxurious overcoat he wore equally stark black and white: a pristine shirt, bow tie, close-fitting black trousers and, unexpectedly, a tailored waistcoat, but no jacket. In contrast to the weird and colourful assortment of clothing worn by the other guests in response to Ivan's choice of the theme for his party, he looked polished, sophisticated, totally disciplined, not at all in the mood for a party.

'So…?' Constantine echoed, a dangerous edge to his voice.

'So—controlled, so…'

She was only too well aware of the way that her own complicated feelings were setting her nerves on edge, making her take exception over what was in fact very far from her real preoccupation. She wanted—needed—to drag her thoughts away from their wanton fixation on the very masculine body beneath the fine clothes, the devastatingly sexual male animal that she knew Constantine to be.

'You look like nothing so much as a waiter.'

Something violent flared in the depths of those stunning eyes at her tone, and she actually heard his strong white teeth snap together, as if he had bitten back the furious outburst he had been about to make. She knew her remark had caught him on the raw, stinging the fierce pride that was so much a part of his character.

'It runs in the genes,' he had told her once. 'The ancient Greeks were cursed with it—the *hubris* that so often brought about their downfall. These days we call it *perifania*, but the feeling is exactly the same.'

'It might interest you to know, my sweet Grace,' he said now, 'that that is exactly how I am supposed to look.'

His tone was surprisingly soft, but laced through with a thread of darkness that revealed only too clearly the ruthlessness with which he had reined in his volatile temper.

'Ten years ago, when I was twenty-one and fresh out of university, my grandfather insisted that I learn about every aspect of his business empire—from the bottom up. I spent my first six months working as a waiter in one of the hotels owned by the Kiriazis Corporation.'

'Oh…'

It was all she could manage. Her lips were suddenly painfully dry and she moistened them nervously with her tongue. The movement froze as she saw those intent black eyes drop to fix on the small action that betrayed the chaotic state of her thoughts, and at the same moment the significance of what he had said came home to her on a rush of shock.

'Then—then Ivan *did* invite you?'

'Ivan invited me,' he acceded, moving at last into the small hallway and kicking the door shut behind him. The thud it made slamming home into its frame had such a sound of finality that Grace shuddered on a feeling of irrational dread. 'You didn't know that?'

Grace shook her head, sending her blonde hair flying.

'I didn't know.'

How could he? How could Ivan have done such a thing and not told her? He must have known how Constantine's appearance would affect her, the pain it would inflict. Ivan of all people would know how far from being fully healed were the scars of the past, and yet he had behaved in a way that was the emotional equivalent of ripping open the old wounds.

'But believe me, if I had known—if I'd had so much as the faintest suspicion that you might be here—then I wouldn't have come. I would have gone anywhere rather than here—anywhere at all. After the way you behaved, I never wanted to see you again...'

Constantine's beautifully carved mouth twisted in an expression of scorn that was heightened by the flare of fury in the inky depths of his eyes.

'After the way *you* behaved...' he returned silkily '...the feeling is entirely mutual. The question is, where do we go from here?'

'You could turn round and walk out.' Grace made the suggestion with little hope that it would be taken up, her fears confirmed as she saw the uncompromising shake of his dark head. Constantine Kiriazis would have known she must be here, and would have had his strategy worked out well in advance. He had never backed down before anyone. She had never really expected that he was going to start now.

'Then...'

'Gracie?' It was Ivan's voice, coming from very close behind her. 'Are you—? Constantine! You made it! So tell me…how is my favourite Greek tycoon?'

'I am well.'

Grace watched as Constantine submitted to the exuberant hug Ivan gave him with resigned patience. But one dark, straight brow did lift in questioning amazement at the other man's costume of a school uniform, complete with two-coloured cap.

'Ivan, my friend, were you truly still at school ten years ago? I thought that at the age of twenty you were actually at university…'

'Strictly speaking, that's true.' Ivan laughed back. 'But I was much happier at school, so I went for that. And if that's bending the rules, who cares? After all, this is my party, so I can do as I like.'

'Fair enough.' Constantine's amusement was evident in the warmth of his tone. A warmth that had been distinctly lacking when he had talked to her, Grace registered miserably.

This was one of the ways he had surprised her in the past. She had never expected that such a blatantly macho male as Constantine was would ever tolerate her friendship with the other, openly gay man. But Constantine had not only accepted it, he had apparently warmed to Ivan himself too.

In that, at least, he hadn't behaved at all in the way she had expected. But in other ways, she reminded herself bitterly, he had been pure arrogant Greek male through and through. And when that pride had been turned on her it had savaged her life, ripping it apart.

'I wasn't sure if you would make it,' Ivan was saying. 'I thought you might be somewhere the other side of the world.'

As if that would stop Constantine going anywhere he wanted to be. This was a man who used his private plane to fly from country to country with the casual ease that other, lesser mortals might take a bus or the Tube. And wherever he was he always had a fleet of chauffeur-driven cars at his disposal. He had probably expended less effort to get here tonight than Grace herself.

But her thoughts had distracted her from what Constantine was saying. Too late she registered his words with a sense of horrified shock.

'...major problems in the London office. I expect they will take three months or more to sort out.'

No! Grace barely caught back her response before the single word revealed her feelings. The only way she had coped over the past two years was by knowing that Constantine was thousands of miles away, in his office in Athens, or the family home on Skyros. The thought of him being practically on her doorstep for the next few months was a prospect that appalled her.

'So we can hope to see more of you,' Ivan continued, blithely ignoring the look of alarmed appeal Grace shot him. 'Can't be bad. Now, let me relieve you of that *gorgeous* coat.'

But as Constantine shrugged himself out of the elegant garment the sound of a buzzer from the kitchen brought Ivan's platinum blond head swinging round.

'The food! I'm sorry, darlings, I must dash or it will all be ruined. Gracie, you'll see to this for me, won't you?'

And, dumping Constantine's coat in the arms she had no option but to hold out—it was either that or let it fall to the floor—he turned and with an airy wave in their vague direction hurried away again.

'I see Ivan hasn't changed.' Constantine's tone was dry. 'Outrageous as ever.'

'That's Ivan…'

Grace prayed that her response didn't sound as shaken and upset to Constantine as it did in her own ears. She was having to struggle to control the unexpected reaction that had assailed her simply as a result of holding the coat. It felt too personal, somehow, too intimate.

Soft and sensuous, it was still warm from the heat of Constantine's body, and the tangy scent of the cologne he always wore still clung to the material, agonisingly familiar. It was impossible not to recall how in the past, when she had been held close to him, that fragrance had always filled her nostrils, intoxicatingly blended with the more subtle, personal aroma of his body. If she closed her eyes she could still feel the heat of his skin under her fingertips, the brush of his black hair against her cheek…

'Grace?'

Constantine's husky-voiced question intruded into the torrent of sensual memories that had flooded her mind, snapping her back to reality with a painful jolt. Wide and startled, her eyes flew open to clash sharply with his frowning black ones.

'Where did you go?'

'Nowhere!'

Her sharp response was too fast, too spiky, arousing his suspicions instead of subduing them. She saw his dark brows draw together swiftly and hastily set herself to covering her tracks.

'I—I'm just a little tired,' she invented hastily. 'It's been a difficult week at work. We've been having problems with a new campaign…'

'You are still at Henderson and Cartwright?'

'Yes…'

That was better. Her voice was back under control, calm and even.

'I was promoted recently. Now I'm in charge of... But you don't want to know this.'

She didn't want him to know it. She didn't want to let him know anything about her life or what was going on in it. He had relinquished that right when he had turned his back on her, and she had no intention of ever letting him in again.

Constantine's shrug dismissed her comment as irrelevant.

'I thought you were making polite conversation,' he drawled indifferently. 'It is something you are so good at here in England. It is so very civilised, especially in an uncomfortable situation.'

'I'm not uncomfortable!' Grace snapped defensively, grey eyes flashing defiantly.

'Perhaps I meant myself,'

'Oh, that I can't believe!' With a wave of her hand she dismissed Constantine's silky murmur. 'I've never seen you fazed by anything. You wouldn't have got where you are if you let anything get to you. And you've been trained by an expert—your father.'

But she was on dangerous ground there. She knew it from the way his proud head went back sharply, the flare of something menacing in his eyes. But when he spoke no trace of his inner feelings shaded his tone.

'Nevertheless, this could be somewhat...' He hunted for the right word. 'Awkward for you.'

'That's something of an understatement.'

Biting her lip, she wished the careless words back as she realised the advantage she had thoughtlessly given him.

He was quick to pounce on it, of course, that sensual mouth curving into a sardonic smile at her discomfiture.

'You are clearly at a disadvantage here—Ivan gave you no warning of the fact that he had invited me, and I presume that some people here will know what passed between us.'

He knew only too well that almost everyone Ivan had invited would be aware of the fact that two years ago she had been about to marry this man, but that the wedding had never taken place. They might be unclear on the gruesome details, but after that final, appallingly public scene in the foyer of the agency, no one could be in any doubt that Constantine had tossed her aside and walked out of her life, ignoring her pleading for a second chance.

The fact that she had also been at fault in the beginning brought the additional complication of a guilty conscience to an already volatile mixture of emotions roiling inside her. Under the cover of the coat, her hands clenched tightly, crushing the expensive material.

'That was two years ago, Constantine,' she told him coldly. 'Two years in which I have got on with my life, as I presume you have with yours.'

His nod of agreement was curt to the point of rudeness.

'I'm over it,' he declared bluntly.

'And so am I.' Grace wished she could sound as assured as he had done. 'People have short memories. You and I might once have been a nine-day wonder, but now we're stale news. Neither of us can leave—it would upset Ivan too much. So we're just going to have to make the best of things. Don't you agree?'

The look that seared over her was icily assessing; black eyes narrowed thoughtfully for a moment.

'It should be easy enough,' he said at last, his tone a masterpiece of indifference. 'I shall simply do what I have done every day for the past two years, and that is to wipe your existence from my mind, forget I ever met you.'

'In that case, why come here at all? You must have known...'

'Obviously I knew you'd be here, but the wish to please Ivan on his birthday was strong enough to overcome the repugnance I felt at the thought of seeing you again.'

It was meant to hurt, and it achieved its aim with all the ruthless efficiency for which Constantine had achieved his reputation in the business world. Grace was deeply thankful for the protective concealment of the coat she still held as she crushed it close to her, feeling almost as if she needed to stem some agonising internal bleeding that had sprung from the wound he had deliberately inflicted on her.

'But I don't have to spend any more time with you. There are enough people here to distract us...' An autocratic wave of one hand encompassed the crowded room at the far end of the hall. 'And the room is quite large enough to keep us apart for some time.'

'I couldn't agree more.' She had to force herself to say it. 'If we're really lucky, we won't even have to see each other again.'

She would do it if it killed her, would rather die than let him see just what it was doing to her to have him here like this. Constantine nodded slowly, his gaze already drifting away towards the other room where other, obviously more attractive company awaited him.

'That would make it possible to salvage something from this appalling evening.'

'Then don't let me hold you back!'

Her tartness drew that black-eyed gaze back to her for one more of those uncomfortably probing stares, a faintly cynical smile playing around Constantine's firm mouth.

'To be honest, my dear Grace, I sincerely doubt that anything you could do would ever affect me again.'

Was it possible? Grace asked herself as he strolled away without so much as a backward glance. Could he really feel nothing for her, not even the dark anger she had seen blazing in his face at their last, cataclysmic meeting? Did she now mean so little to him that he could dismiss her from his thoughts in the blink of an eye? What had happened to the love he had once declared so eloquently, the passion he had been unable to hide?

It was dead, she told herself drearily, dead and gone, as if it had never existed. Which seemed impossible when her own feelings were in such agonised turmoil that she felt as if there was a raging tornado where her heart should be, a monstrous tidal wave of shock and distress swamping her stomach. She could only pray that she was enough of an actor to hide her misery from Constantine. That she would be able to get through what remained of this evening without giving herself away completely.

CHAPTER TWO

IT WAS impossible.

There was no way at all that she could pretend, even to herself, that she was oblivious to the fact that Constantine was there in the room with her. His presence was like a constant dark shadow, always hovering at her shoulder, following her everywhere she went.

If she paused to talk to anyone she felt him there, just out of sight, driving all thought of what she had been about to say from her mind. If she tried to drink some wine, or taste some food from the extensive buffet Ivan had laid on, her throat closed over what she was trying to swallow, threatening to choke her.

And the worst thing was that, for some private reason of his own, Constantine hadn't kept to his declaration that he was going to wipe her existence from her mind. She had only to glance across the room to meet the intent stare of his watchful black eyes following every movement she made, every smile, every word she spoke.

In the end she sought refuge in the kitchen, privately admitting to her own cowardice as she used the excuse of the mounting pile of washing up to keep her there, hidden away. She was filling the bowl with hot water for the second time when Ivan wandered into the room.

'Uh—oh! I wondered where you'd got to. Does this mean I made a mistake?'

'In inviting Constantine?' Grace turned a reproving look on him. 'What do you think? Ivan, how could you?'

'No chance of you two making it up, then?'

'Was that what was in your mind when you asked him here? If that was the case, you couldn't be more wrong. It's over, Ivan, and has been for years.'

'Are you sure? He was pretty keen to accept. I thought perhaps—'

'Well, you thought wrong,' Grace inserted hastily, as much to squash down her own foolishly weak heart as it leapt on an absurd flutter of hope as to disillusion her friend. 'Whatever reasons Constantine had for coming here today, seeing me wasn't one of them. I mean, does he look like a man who can't let me out of his sight?'

'He looks like a man with something on his mind, if you ask me,' Ivan returned, with a nod towards the open door.

Reluctantly Grace followed the direction of his gaze, her eyes fixing immediately on the tall, muscular figure of Constantine leaning against the wall. With a glass in one hand, he had his attention firmly fixed on the woman in front of him. Small and curvaceous, with long dark hair, she was wearing a nurse's uniform with a skirt so indecently short she would never have been allowed on to any hospital ward.

'And what he has on his mind is very definitely not me,' she said, unable to erase the bitterness from her voice.

Her stepsister Paula was dark and petite, she recalled on a wrench of pain at the memory. And Constantine had always admitted to being attracted to small, curvy brunettes, so much so that Grace had never quite been able to understand just what he had been doing with *her*.

'Are you sure?'

'Ivan, *leave* it!' Grace pleaded, unable to take any more.

The words had barely left her lips when Constantine looked up suddenly, deep-set eyes meeting Grace's clouded grey ones. For a fleeting, tormenting moment their gazes locked, and she shivered before the cruel indifference in their ebony darkness. Then with a cold travesty of a smile Constantine lifted his glass in a grim mockery of a toast, one that had her biting down hard on her lower lip to keep back an expression of pain.

Swinging round so that she no longer had to see him or his companion, she squirted washing-up liquid into the bowl with a force that made bubbles boil up wildly.

'Constantine has no thought of any reconciliation on his mind,' she said through gritted teeth, blinking hard against the burning tears that stung her eyes. 'Just get that into your head, will you?'

And just who are you trying to convince? her conscience questioned reproachfully, distracting her so that she was barely aware of Ivan leaving her alone again.

Was it true? Was it possible? Had she really been fool enough to harbour even the faintest hope after all this time? Oh Grace, Grace! You fool! You crazy, weak-minded fool!

How could she ever have been so stupid? Hadn't Constantine made his feelings, or rather his lack of them, brutally clear? Had she spent so many long, lonely nights lying awake with that final callous dismissal still sounding in her thoughts, and yet not been convinced by it? She had to be out of her tiny, crazy mind if that was the case.

We have no future together... The words Constantine had flung at her, the coldly contemptuous voice in which they had been spoken lacerated her soul all over again, making his feelings for her patently clear.

Clear enough even for the most foolish, naively besotted heart, Grace told herself miserably. In spite of being blinded by love, as she had been then, she had heard the conviction in his voice, recognised the finality of the emotional life-sentence he had been handing her. So why should she allow herself to dare to question it now, when surely the two years' silence, two years' distance on

Constantine's part, was added evidence of just how much he had meant what he'd said?

'If you wash that plate any more, you will erase the pattern from it.'

The dryly amused voice, instantly recognisable as Constantine's, broke into her reverie with such unexpected suddenness that she started violently, dropping the plate into the washing-up water in a plume of spray.

'Don't sneak up on me like that!'

'I did not sneak. You must have a guilty conscience to jump like that. Or perhaps you were daydreaming. Is that it, *agape mou*? Were you thinking of some man—someone deeply important to you, to judge by the look on your face?'

'I wasn't thinking of anyone!' Grace objected, terrified that he would suspect the true nature of her thoughts. 'And don't call me that! I'm not your love any more!'

'So you remember the Greek I taught you?'

She remembered *that* particular phrase! How could she ever forget it? Her thoughts skittered away from memories too painful to bear. Memories of tenderly embracing in the warm darkness of a mild early spring evening on Skyros, her head pillowed on the strong frame of his chest, hearing that softly accented voice whispering those words in a way that resonated with barely suppressed desire.

'Oh, yes, I remember that, and so many other valuable lessons you taught me.' Grace laced the words with vinegar, deliberately taking them miles away from the sort of lessons he had originally had in mind. 'And believe me, I don't ever intend to forget them. I— What are you doing?'

She flinched back as Constantine moved suddenly, one hand coming out towards her face.

Her instinctive panic earned her a sharp-eyed glance of reproof, Constantine's mouth twisting cynically.

'You have soap bubbles on your nose...' A long finger gently flicked the froth away. 'And on your brow... They might have gone into your eye.'

'Thank you.'

It was muttered ungraciously because she was struggling with the shock waves of sensation, the recollection of other, very different feelings that this man's lightest touch had once sparked off inside her. Times when it had seemed that those long, square-tipped fingers might have been made of molten steel, so intense had been the force of her reaction. She had felt as if the path they had taken was scorched deep into her flesh, branding her irrevocably as his.

'It was no trouble,' Constantine returned, the elaborate courtesy deliberately mocking at her stilted response. 'Would you like some help in here?'

It was the last thing she wanted. Standing so close to her, she was sure he must sense the unevenness of her breathing, hear the heavy pounding of her heart. Just when she most wanted to appear unmoved and totally indifferent to his proximity, her traitorous body seemed determined to go into sensual overdrive, responding to the nearness of his with all the hunger of a famine victim suddenly presented with the most tempting banquet.

'Won't that rather spoil your plan to behave as if I don't exist?' she demanded, hiding her unsettled feelings behind a show of aggression. 'Anyway there's no need. There's nothing left to do.'

To demonstrate the fact she removed the last plate and plonked it down on the drying rack before upending the bowl in the sink so that the soapy water drained away with a faint gurgling sound.

'Then shall I fetch you a drink?'

Nerves on edge, Grace swung round suddenly to glare into Constantine's unreadable black eyes.

'Just what game are you playing now, Constantine? What exactly are you doing here?'

'No game, I assure you. Perhaps a compromise…'

'Compromise!' Grace scoffed. 'I thought such a word didn't exist in your vocabulary. You wouldn't know a compromise if you came face to face with one.'

'I am trying to be reasonable here.' Constantine's careful restraint was obviously slipping slightly, traces of the barely reined in temper escaping his ruthless control. 'I do not feel comfortable being at a party where the woman who is one of the host's best friends spends all her time hiding in the kitchen, especially when I suspect that—'

'Suspect what?' Grace broke in, definitely rattled. 'That you're the reason I'm "hiding" away in here? I always knew your ego was excessively healthy, but…'

'Grace, this *is* meant to be a Turn Back the Clock party. Surely it should be possible for two mature, civilised adults to abide by the theme of tonight.'

'And turn back the clock until when, precisely?'

It was scary to realise how much she wanted to do just that. Frankly terrifying to admit that her heart had leapt in anticipation of the prospect.

If only they could! If only they really could go back to the time when he had been her life and she had believed herself his. The time when they had been so much a couple that they had thought, acted, almost even breathed as one. The time before Paula's lies and her own fears had ripped them apart, driving a chasm between them that it seemed nothing could bridge.

'Well, the idea of the party is that everyone comes as they were ten years ago, but I'm afraid I have problems trying to imagine you at fourteen.'

Constantine's sudden brief flash of a grin was devastating in its impact, winging its way to Grace's already vulnerable heart like an arrow into the gold at the centre of a target. In spite of herself, she couldn't hold back a faint sigh of response, regretting it at once as soon as she saw those brilliant black eyes narrow in swift calculation.

'So what if we settle on half of that time? Five years ago we would have been complete strangers. We'd never even met.'

The faint flame of hope that had lit inside Grace's heart flickered briefly then abruptly went out. If she had needed any warning that their thoughts were running on entirely different lines, then he couldn't have given it more clearly.

Turn back the clock. She had taken that phrase to mean going back to the beginning of their relationship, to the time when their love had been fresh and new, intoxicating in its heady delight. To Constantine, the idea was that they should act as if they had never met, as if they were total strangers to each other.

'All right,' she managed, swallowing down the burning disappointment that seemed to eat at her like acid. 'That should be okay.'

Gravely she held out her hand to him, schooling herself to make sure it showed no betraying tremor.

'I—I'm Grace Vernon. Pleased to meet you.'

Constantine fell in with her pretence with an intuitive ease that made her heart ache with the memory of how it had once been, when that easy understanding had been used on other, far more important matters.

'Constantine Kiriazis,' he replied, taking the offered hand and executing a small formal bow over it. 'Can I get you a drink?'

'W-white wine, please.'

The last thing she wanted was anything alcoholic. Already she felt as if every one of her senses was on red alert, hypersensitive to the sensual force of his physical presence, and she needed no stimulation to add to the sensations that were sizzling through her.

But what she *did* need was a brief time to herself. A few moments in which to draw breath, try to slow the frantic, erratic pulse of her heart. Constantine had only to touch her and she felt as if she had foolishly grabbed at the exposed end of a live electrical cable, violent shocks running up her arm, along every exposed nerve. Instinctively she cradled the hand he had released against her breasts, nursing it as it if had actually been burned.

Just what was he up to? Because he had to be up to something. Less than an hour ago he had declared his intention of ignoring the fact that she was at the party. Now, he was actively seeking out her company.

'White wine...'

Far more quickly than she had anticipated, and certainly long before she was mentally ready, Constantine was back, two glasses in his hands.

'Dry white, of course,' he added with a wry twist to his mouth. 'Though I suppose that technically I shouldn't have known that and should have asked what you'd prefer. This isn't going to be as simple as I thought.'

'Not if we're going to play it strictly by the rules.'

Rules? What rules? Precisely what rules came into play in this sort of situation?

'I think we can allow a little leeway,' Constantine was saying, his words coming dimly through the fog of misery dimming her thoughts. 'After all, I've already asked you about your work, so there's really no need for the "And what do you do?" conversation. One thing I did wonder, though...'

'What was that?' Grace asked, swallowing a much needed sip of the cool, crisp wine, and feeling the effect of the alcohol spread through her body with unnerving rapidity.

She must be much more on edge than she had realised. Better take it steady. Or perhaps her response was to the brilliant smile Constantine had turned on her, and not the wine at all. In that case, she needed to be even more careful. The last thing she wanted was to end up tipsy and not fully in control.

She had to keep a clear mind and all her wits about her if she was to cope with Constantine at his devastating social best. She had seen him turn on the charm so many times, seen far more sophisticated, more blasé personalities melt underneath its potent warmth not to be wary of the powerful spell he could weave with the force of his personality.

'Did you really dress like that when you were fourteen? I find it hard to believe that the elegant Grace Vernon ever deliberately chose to appear in public looking...'

'Such a sight?' Grace finished for him when he seemed uncharacteristically uncertain of how to finish his sentence. 'I think that was the idea.'

In spite of herself a small, wry grin surfaced as she looked into the darkness of his eyes.

'I was rebelling as hard as I could. Going against everything my mother wanted. She insisted on my dressing smartly, as she did. She hated me in trousers, and jeans were anathema to her. So, naturally, I took every opportunity to annoy her by wearing them.'

'Your mother was still married to your father ten years ago?'

'Just. The marriage was already on the rocks, though. She'd already had more than one affair and my father had just met Diana. Mum and Dad separated very soon afterwards.'

'And you went to live with your father. Isn't it more usual for the child to live with her mother?'

'I wasn't exactly a child, Constantine.'

They had never talked about this when they had known each other before. Perhaps if they had things might have been different. He might have understood about Paula. But, no, she couldn't let her thoughts go down that path. It led to too much pain.

'I was old enough to have some say in the matter. I chose to live with my father and, deep down, I'm sure my mother didn't mind. She already had her sights set on a new life in America, and a teenage daughter would just have held her back. My school was here in London, all my friends, naturally I wanted to stay.'

'Even when he married Diana?'

'Even when he married Diana!'

Grace moved to deposit her glass on the worktop with a distinct crash. They were getting into dangerous territory. Talk of Diana led inevitably to thoughts of Paula, her stepmother's daughter.

'I was really happy that he was getting married again. I thought that...'

But she never completed the sentence. At that moment their private haven was invaded by a bunch of laughing, joking party guests.

'Come on, party poopers! You can't stay in here all night! Ivan's going to cut the cake, and he says that instead of it just being him who gets a wish, we can all have one too!'

Grace could only watch and follow as Constantine was led away into the next room, her friends urging her after him. It was as if a sheet of glass had come down between her and the rest of the people in the room. She could see them, hear their voices and their movements, but the sounds were blurred and incomprehensible so that she felt completely cut off from reality.

A wish. If she had been offered a wish by some fairy godmother only a couple of hours ago—less—she would have said that what she wanted most in the world was to make peace with Constantine. That if she could just come to some sort of accord with him, it would be enough to satisfy her. She had truly believed that if they could come to an understanding where they could be on civilised terms, she could be content.

But they had achieved that truce, those civilised terms, and all that it had taught her was that it was *not enough*. It could never be enough. She didn't want *peace* with Constantine; she didn't want *civilised*. She wanted so much more.

'Happy birthday, dear Ivan...'

All around her Ivan's guests joined in the traditional singing of 'Happy Birthday', and Grace forced herself to open and close her mouth along with them. But no words would form, her tongue seeming to have frozen, her lips as stiff as board.

There was no backing away from it. No avoiding the realisation that had hit her hard, like the splash in her face. The two intervening years might as well have not existed. They had had no effect on the way she was feeling. No effect at all.

'Grace?'

'W-what?'

Somehow she dragged her thoughts out of the shocked daze in which they were hidden, forcing her eyes to focus on the man who had come to her side.

Constantine. Hastily she veiled her eyes, hiding her feelings behind her lids, her heart jerking into a rapid, jolting beat at the thought that he might be able to read what was in her mind. The cake-cutting ceremony was over, and the party had moved on, the pulsing music starting up again.

'Dance with me?'

Say no! Every instinct screamed the warning at her, every nerve instantly thrown into panic mode. Say no—back away—just turn—run! Anything other than expose her already weakened defences to the potent onslaught of his sensual appeal. She already knew how vulnerable she was to the sight, the sound, the scent of him. How her body reacted to just the slightest touch. She couldn't risk…

'Yes, okay.'

How had that happened? Just what was she doing? Grace could find no answers for her outraged sense of self-preservation. She was acting on a far deeper, more primitive level, responding purely on instinct, unable to force her mind into any form of rational thought.

So she let Constantine take her hand and draw her towards the part of the room that had been cleared for dancing. And when the music changed just as they started to dance, turning from a rhythmic beat to a slow, seductive number, she made no objection to the way he turned to her and took her into his arms, drawing her close to the warmth and strength of his body.

She fitted into his arms as if she'd been born there. And it felt like coming home. The rest of the room, the noise and all the people around her, blurred into one indecipherable mass. There was no one in the world but herself and this man, whose strength enclosed her, whose heart beat under her cheek, the strong wall of his chest rising and falling with every breath he took.

'Grace…' he murmured softly, her name just a sigh against her hair.

'Don't talk…' Grace heard herself whisper back. 'Just hold me…'

She had no idea whether it was simply one dance that seemed to last for ever, or if there were many such dances, impossible to count, while she was lost in a dreamy haze of sensual delight. She only knew that when at last the music faded into silence and the world around her righted itself again she was no longer in the big main room where the party was centred, but had been subtly manoeuvred out into the hall beyond.

'Where…?' she began in confusion.

As her eyes focused again she discovered that she and Constantine were in the shelter of the wide flight of stairs up to the next floor, hidden from everyone.

Immediately the dream world that had enclosed her vanished, evaporating swiftly like a mist before the sun. Reality came rushing back with a speed and force that rocked her on her feet, made her shiver convulsively.

'What are we doing here? I can't—'

'Grace…' Constantine silenced her by laying strong tanned fingers across her mouth. 'I want some time alone with you.'

'You!'

Grace wrenched her head away from the gentle pressure of his hand, grey eyes blazing up into his black ones, seeing the way that the heavy lids came down over them, concealing his feelings from her.

'You want! You *want*! Isn't that always the way with you? What you want comes before everything else. ''Dance with me…'''

Deliberately she mimicked his own words of earlier, emphasising the autocratic note, the lack of any 'please' that had turned the phrase into a command rather than a request.

'''I want some time alone with you.'''

'I got the impression that was what you wanted too.'

'And how, precisely, did you come to that conclusion?'

Constantine's proud head bent until his mouth was level with her ear, and his voice was softly husky, his warmth breath caressing her skin as he whispered, ''Don't talk... Just hold me.'''

His echoing of her own foolish reaction was uncannily accurate, making her head go back in shock.

Had she really been so stupid? Had she really let her feelings get the better of her? Had she been so weak as to put that pleading note into her voice, the one that Constantine had just reproduced with merciless exactness? How could she have betrayed herself in that way?

'I—I was enjoying the dance,' she blustered frantically, desperately trying to cover her tracks. 'But that doesn't mean I wanted anything more.'

'No?'

The lazy lifting of one dark brow questioned the truth of her spluttered declaration.

'You must forgive me if I don't believe—'

'You can believe or not as you want!' Grace tossed back at him, ignoring the ominous thread of warning that shaded the softly accented voice. 'I don't care. I know my own mind, and I don't want anything more to do with you! As a matter of fact, what I really want right now is to go home.'

'Then I will take you,' Constantine returned smoothly.

'No!'

That was definitely not what she had in mind. Desperately she shook her head, so that her fair hair flew out wildly.

'I can make my own way home. It's just a short walk.'

'You no longer live with your father?'

'No.'

Living at home would have meant living with Paula, and that was something neither of them could have handled.

'I have my own place now—about ten minutes away from here. I can walk.'

'And I will escort you.'

Grace groaned inwardly. She knew this mood of old. When Constantine set his mind on something like this, he was immoveable. A dog with a bone had nothing on him. But she couldn't give in to him. If she did, then he would only take it as evidence that his own interpretation of events was the real one.

And wasn't it? her own unforgiving conscience threw at her, refusing to let her off the hook, no matter how much she mentally squirmed. Hadn't she admitted to herself that she wanted...'

But what she wanted and what was *safe* were two very different things. She might dream of more time with Constantine, of letting him know her feelings for him, but to do any such thing would be emotional suicide.

Whatever feelings he might once have had for her, they were obviously now all dead. All, that was, except for the burning sexual attraction that had once flared between them, and which time had not dimmed at all. Weakly, stupidly, she had let Constantine see that it was still there, and with characteristic opportunism he had decided to turn that fact to his advantage.

'Grace, I have never in my life let a woman walk home alone at this time of night. I don't intend to start now. Get your coat. I am coming with you.'

'Do I have any choice?' Wearily she accepted that, short of creating the sort of scene that would have everyone at the party talking for weeks to come, she had no option but to do as he said.

'None at all,' Constantine returned on a note of satisfaction that sounded rich as a tiger's purr. 'I know that we've only just met, but I must insist that you humour me in this.'

Only just met. What…?

It took Grace a moment or two to realise exactly what Constantine meant.

Grace, this is *meant to be a Turn Back the Clock party.* His words sounded inside her head like a lifeline as she went reluctantly to fetch her coat from the bedroom. *Five years ago we would have been complete strangers.*

So Constantine was still playing according to the rules they had laid down earlier that evening. They were still pretending that they were complete strangers who had met for the first time tonight.

That being so, perhaps she could cope with letting him take her home after all. Surely even Constantine wouldn't pounce on what was supposedly their very first meeting?

It was little enough comfort, but it was all that she had. And Constantine wasn't about to back down, so she could only pray that it was enough.

CHAPTER THREE

'OVER there.'

Grace lifted a finger to point, then immediately dropped it again when her hand showed a worrying tendency to shake in a way that revealed her inner turmoil.

'It's the last house on the right. The one with the blue door.'

Constantine's nod of acknowledgement was curt and silent as he steered the car to a halt precisely opposite the door she had indicated. Perhaps, like her, he was already regretting the impulse that had pushed him to insist on taking her home. Perhaps he too had found what stiff and hesitant conversation there had been during the brief journey so uncomfortable that he was glad their time together was almost over.

Which suited Grace fine. All she wanted was to get out of the car and get inside, into the safety and privacy of her small flat. If she had to sit next to Constantine for a moment longer, listen to his stilted, one-word responses to the few remarks she had managed to force herself to make, she was going to scream with frustration.

'That's perfect. Thank you.'

Already she was fumbling with the seatbelt, even before the powerful vehicle had fully come to a halt at the side of the kerb, anxious to be out of the car and away from his unsettling presence.

'It was kind of you to see me home… What did you say?'

The question was jolted from her in response to something Constantine had muttered. Something incomprehensible in Greek that had sounded rough and impatient, stilling her nervous movements suddenly.

But even as she asked the question, she saw the change in his mood. With an obvious effort he smoothed away the frown that had drawn his brows, the cynical twist to his carved mouth.

'I'll see you to your door,' he said, his voice retaining nothing of the disturbing intonation of moments before.

'There's no need.'

But she was talking to thin air. Already Constantine was out of the car and moving round to open the passenger door for her.

It was only a few yards from the edge of the kerb to the threshold of her house. Just a few short steps, but they seemed to take an eternity, every sound of their feet on the pavement ringing unnaturally loudly in the midnight silence of the street. At her side, Constantine was a dark, silent figure, his long stride outstripping hers so that she had to hurry to keep up with him.

To her intense annoyance she found that her inner tension had communicated itself to her hands, so that she fumbled clumsily as she tried to insert her key in the lock. Supremely conscious of Constantine's eyes, dark as the night sky, watching every awkward move, she cursed herself silently under her breath, trying again. Luckily this time she succeeded, and turned back to face him, relief evident in her smile and her voice.

'Well, here I am. Safe and sound, as you can see. Thank you again for seeing me home.'

If this really had been a first meeting, she would have added something about having enjoyed her evening, perhaps even a suggestion that they could do it again some time. But of course the idea that they could turn back the clock in that way was a pure fiction, throwing her mind

into total confusion as she hunted for a way to say goodbye
that fitted the circumstances.

'I—I'll say goodnight, then.'

'Is that all?'

'All? You— I mean, what else is there? After all…' She
aimed for flippancy and missed it by a mile, her voice becoming high-pitched and shrill. 'We've only just met tonight.'

'So would it be too forward to ask for a kiss goodnight?'

The question sounded light, friendly even. The way he'd
been earlier in the evening, in the kitchen, when they'd
been pretending that they really had just met.

A goodnight kiss; nothing more. She could cope with
that.

But underneath all the carefully rational, logical reasoning lay something darker, something more disturbing.
Something that lurked like the jagged rocks at the bottom
of a still, calm sea, just waiting to catch at the base of her
thinking and rip it apart, laying open the real truth. The one
she hardly dared acknowledge to herself. The fact that she
wanted this, wanted Constantine's kiss more than she
would ever admit.

'Okay.' She nodded—casually, she hoped. 'One kiss
goodnight…'

Constantine's head lowered, blocking out the light from
the nearby streetlamp, and instinctively her lips parted
slightly.

But it was her cheek that his mouth made contact with,
the kiss brushing against it warm and soft and so painfully
familiar. And heartbreakingly brief.

'Goodnight.'

Before she even had time to think, even as she was
steadying herself for the real kiss, the one her lips were
aching for, the one that had already quickened her heartbeat
in anticipation, he had stepped back.

'Goodnight,' he said again, his voice harsh and flippantly dismissive. 'See you around.'

Grace couldn't believe it. She shivered inside as pain, raw and cruel, ripped through her, lacerating her heart. She had actually let herself believe—had hoped... Bitter tears of humiliation burned in her eyes, blinding her.

'G-goodnight.'

She forced herself to say it. Forced herself to turn the handle and open her door. Felt the rush of warm air from the hall out into the coldness of the night.

But she couldn't make herself step over the threshold and into the house. Even now she couldn't turn and move away from him.

It was *not enough*! She wanted more, so much more. That one kiss had sparked off all the need, the hunger, the passion she had once felt for this man and which she had thought was safely buried, out of sight.

But it seemed that Constantine had spoken nothing more or less than the truth when he had said so casually, 'I'm over it.'

'I—I'll...'

Go! Her mind screamed at her. Out of here *now*, before it gets any worse!

But, *no*, her heart pleaded. Let me have just a little bit more. Just one moment longer in his company. After these two long, empty years, let me have one more chance to hear his voice, see him smile.

Before she knew she had even formed the thought she had acted impulsively. The aroma of Constantine's cologne and the warm, clean scent of his body reached her nostrils as she leaned towards him, making her head swim with the force of its sensual impact. His eyes were deeper, darker pools in the shadows of the night, and she could hear the soft, regular sound of his breathing.

'Goodnight,' she said on a very different note as, taking

her cue from him, she pressed her lips to the hard, lean plane of his cheek. The warm satin of his skin was slightly roughened by the result of a day's growth of beard that brushed abrasively against her mouth.

'And thank you...'

But that one unthinking act proved her undoing. With a phenomenal speed of reaction, Constantine turned his head so that her lips were forced to move. Unable to do anything but slip over the bronzed skin, as if on ice over a frozen pond, they found themselves sliding inexorably towards the heated softness that was his mouth.

'Grace...'

He muttered something thick and rough in Greek against her lips before taking them harshly, urgently, crushing her mouth under his.

'You should have gone—headed for safety—while you had the chance. Now it's much too late.'

Too late! Grace echoed inside her head on a note of disbelief. It had already been too late in the moment that he'd kissed her. Even such a desultory peck on the cheek had told her all she needed to know.

No, it had been earlier than that. It had happened in the moment when she had opened Ivan's door and looked into the black depths of his eyes and known that, no matter what had happened, Constantine was still the only man in the world for her.

'Sweet Grace...'

A cold sneaking wind wound itself around Grace's legs, but she was beyond noticing it. The bulk of Constantine's strong body protected her from the cold, and the heated race of her blood through her own veins warmed her skin until she felt as if she was on fire. Her heartbeat was staccato with excitement, the coming and going of air in her lungs feverishly erratic.

'You really *should* have gone in.' Constantine's

breathing was every bit as uneven as her own, his voice hoarse and jerky. 'Now there's no turning back. Grace, *agape mou*...invite me in.'

Invite me in. It was a command, not a request. She knew exactly what was behind it, what was uppermost in his mind.

So why wasn't she saying no? Why wasn't she telling him to get out of there and out of her life? The thought slid into her mind very briefly, but then, just as swiftly, slid straight out again.

'D-do...?'

Her voice failed her, drying painfully, so that she had to moisten her lips before she could speak again. In the light from the hall she saw Constantine's black eyes drop to her mouth, to follow the tiny, unconsciously provocative movement with an intensity that made her heart jerk convulsively against her chest.

'Do you want to come in?'

'*Do* I...?' It was a shaken, husky laugh. 'Grace, I swear to God that if you don't let me in with you right now, I'll—'

'There's no need for that!' Grace broke in hurriedly, shaken, breathless, half terrified of what he might be about to say. 'Come in, out of the cold.'

It seemed to her that the slam of the door behind her, shutting out the world and closing them in together, was a sound of decision, defining a moment that would change her life for ever. It was now too late to go back, to even think of changing her mind.

And she didn't want to. All she wanted was right here, with her, at her side. His arms enclosed her. His heart beat under her cheek, and she felt as if she had come home.

But once inside the mood changed sharply. She had barely closed the door before Constantine released her so abruptly that she felt as if she had been dropped from a great height, landing, stunned and disbelieving, on a very hard floor.

She could only watch as he pushed his way into her flat and prowled around it like some caged wild beast, scenting out the borders of its new territory.

Slowly, deliberately, he turned on his heels so that his dark-eyed gaze could take in the comfortable living room with the pale cream armchairs—the room was too small to take a settee—peach velvet curtains, and softly polished pinewood dresser. On the far wall, opposite the big bay window, was a Victorian style cast-iron open fireplace set in a tiled surround.

'It's not very big...' he murmured at last, his survey completed.

'It's all I could afford!' Grace protested indignantly. 'We can't all have homes on every continent and a private plane to ferry us between them.'

'Half of the houses are owned by my parents,' Constantine pointed out, his tone coolly reasonable. 'I only have the use of them.'

'But what you do own my poky little flat would fit into a hundred times over.'

'Did I say it was poky?' he murmured smoothly, continuing his exploration.

He didn't need to, Grace was forced to reflect, ruing her foolish tongue. What she had really meant was that now she saw him in her flat it was as if his tall, imposing presence so dominated the room that it appeared it had shrunk around him, becoming impossibly small and claustrophobic.

'W-would you like coffee?' Belatedly she remembered her role as hostess.

'No.'

Stark and uncompromising, it was tossed over his shoulder at her as he studied the collection of paperbacks on her bookshelf.

'Tea, then?'

'No…'

'Something stronger?'

The question was high-pitched and uneven, coming from a throat that had tightened uncomfortably over the question she knew she was really asking. This was his opportunity to say no, he couldn't drink any more because he was driving.

'Some wine, perhaps?'

An autocratic gesture dismissed the question; Constantine's attention was still fixed on her book collection. But then a moment later he shook his dark head.

'Perhaps—yes…'

'Oh, for heaven's sake, Constantine!' Grace exploded, more on edge than she had allowed herself to admit. 'Yes—no—perhaps… Which is it?' she added, braving his swift frown. 'Make up your mind.'

'*Cristos*, I am trying to be civilised, that is all! But I feel—'

'You feel?' Grace echoed when he broke off abruptly. 'What do you feel?'

Unexpectedly those black eyes avoided her questioning grey ones. It was such a shock to see the confident, self-assured Constantine Kiriazis so uncharacteristically at a loss for words that it gave her the determination to go on, push him a little harder.

'Constantine? What do you feel?'

For the space of another heartbeat he still hesitated. But then, just when she was sure he was going to ignore her completely, or change the subject, a dismissive lift of the broad shoulders under the elegant coat shrugged off whatever restraint he was imposing on himself.

'I feel totally uncivilised,' he muttered, his voice thick-

ened and rough. 'If you want the truth, I feel wild, pagan—
primitive.'

Well, she'd asked!

'And why…?'

'You know why!'

Constantine flung the words at her as if he hated having
to speak them. Yellow flames of emotion flared in his eyes,
burning away the control he had been imposing so ruthlessly up until this moment, and his proud head went back
in a gesture of defiance.

'I feel this way because of you. I *want* you! I've wanted
you all night! I've always wanted you—and I doubt if I'll
ever be cured of this need. The two years we've been apart
have been hell. Not having you has been like an ache in
my gut, always there, always reminding me of how it used
to be.'

'Me?'

She couldn't believe what she had heard. It wasn't a
declaration of love, but right now it was enough. He wanted
her. He had missed her. He had hurt being without her.

'Grace.'

Her name was a raw, rough-voiced sound.

'Grace, come here!'

Common sense screamed at her to be careful, to hesitate,
to allow time for second thoughts. But her heart brushed
aside such foolish considerations impatiently.

She wasn't even aware of having moved before she was
across the room and in his arms, feeling them close around
her, holding her tight.

His mouth claimed hers in the same second, shocking in
its wild, hungry demand. And Grace responded in kind, all
the pent-up longing, the loneliness, the agony of the past
two years exploding into a white-hot, raging conflagration
of need. She kissed him back with all the force of her
emotions laid bare for him to see.

'Grace, *pethi mou*…beautiful Grace…' Constantine muttered against her mouth. 'You are mine. You always have been mine. I will let no one else…'

'There is no one else,' Grace managed breathlessly, dragging in air in a brief respite from the calculated assault upon her senses. 'No one now, no one—'

Some sixth sense had her snatching back the final word before she spoke it. She wanted Constantine to know that there was no other man in her life right now. Whether she also wanted to admit that there had been no one else since he had walked out on her was quite another matter entirely.

Oh, there had been plenty of interest. She had even been out on a few dates. But they had been short and not particularly sweet. No matter how hard she'd tried, she'd found it impossible to put on even a show of an interest she was very far from feeling.

And now she knew why. For the past two years she had been slowly starving inside, wasting away emotionally without a sight or sound of Constantine to nourish her. She had been in suspended animation, like Sleeping Beauty, waiting only for his kiss to bring her alive again.

And she never wanted to go back to those empty days. Never wanted even to think of them. Particularly not now, with Constantine's arms enclosing her, his hands caressing her body, his mouth following a heated trail from her lips, across the soft skin of her cheek and down her throat to where her heightened pulse beat frantically in the scooped neckline of her tee shirt.

'I lied, you know…' he muttered against her hot skin.

'What?'

Adrift on a warm sea of pleasure, Grace only registered that he had spoken. But then the true import of that *lied* hit home, slashing into her delirium.

'You *what*?' Fear clutched at her heart. 'Constantine?'

His laughter feathered over her tightly stretched nerves, softly reassuring.

'I lied. When I said I didn't like what you were wearing.'

'"Distressingly unflattering" were the words you used, I believe,' Grace managed, the words sounding strangled and uneven as long-fingered bronzed hands smoothed over the offending outfit, making her writhe in responsive delight.

'Distressingly *provocative* is more like it!' Constantine growled. 'Do you know what it does to me to see the way those jeans hug your pert little backside, the sway of your breasts underneath your tee shirt?'

'I never wore a bra when I was fourteen.'

Her reply broke in the middle, cracking noticeably as those wickedly knowing fingers found the small gap between the bottom of her shrunken tee shirt and the tight-fitting waistband of the denim jeans. Shuddering in response to the tiny electric shocks of pleasure his touch sparked off along her sensitised nerves, she caught her lower lip between her teeth in order to hold back the cry of delight that almost escaped her.

'And every time you moved, this tiny patch of skin could just be seen...tormenting me, tantalising, just begging to be touched.'

He was touching it now—with a vengeance! Making her shiver and writhe against him in a way that made the heated force of his desire only too obvious through the fine fabric of his well-cut trousers. Her blood raced through her veins, making her heart pound, her thoughts swim.

'Grace...'

'No. Shh!'

Gently she silenced him by laying soft fingers over his mouth, stilling what he had been about to say.

'No words—for now.'

There had been too many words between them in the

past. Hurtful, destructive words that had shattered the love they had once shared, smashing it into tiny pieces.

'Don't talk. Let's just let our lips…'

She kissed him softly on the forehead, the bridge of his nose, the burning eyes that closed under the gentle caress.

'Our hands…'

Her fingertips slid through the silky black hair, down over the strong muscles cording his neck, and under the soft cashmere of his coat. With only a little urging she was able to lift it and slide it from the powerful shoulders, letting it fall in a heavy pool on the floor at their feet.

'And our bodies do the talking.'

Deliberately she inched closer, circling her pelvis over his, a teasing smile curling her lips as she heard the groan of response he could not hold back.

'Lips, hands and bodies… Suits me.'

With a rough, husky laugh deep in his throat, he echoed her own movements, sliding the leather jacket from her shoulders, down her arms, and discarding it somewhere, tossing it disdainfully aside without caring where it fell.

His mouth was everywhere, on her face, her throat, tugging at the scooped neck of her tee shirt in order to gain access to the soft, sensitive skin of her shoulders. And his hands trailed paths of fire under the white cotton, across the slender contours of her waist, the fine bones of her ribcage, and slowly, irresistibly upwards, towards the aching, waiting peaks of her breasts.

When she had dreamed of it so often, longed for it so many times in the loneliness of the past years, the feel of the heat of his palms against her sensitised flesh was so devastating that she twisted against him, shaken by the convulsions of sensual need that sizzled through her fine-boned frame like lightning across a storm-dark sky. And lower down, deep at the most feminine core of her being, an answering pulse of hunger began to throb in a primal, basic rhythm that would allow for only one possible appeasement.

'This will have to go…'

Constantine wrenched the white tee shirt from her with such force that she heard the worn material rip. But she couldn't bring herself to spare the abused garment more than the briefest passing thought as it too was discarded, Constantine's strong brown fingers caressing her skin, leaving her no time to feel cold.

'And these…'

As he dealt with her belt and the clasp at her waist with brusque efficiency, his hot mouth seemed to everywhere on the upper part of her body, kissing, licking, nibbling, even taking tiny playful nips at her skin that didn't hurt but only fuelled the spiralling storm of hunger roiling up inside her.

She wanted Constantine every bit as much as he had made clear that he wanted her. She felt that she would die if he didn't make love to her, right here and now, without a thought for the future or their unhappy past. Without Constantine she *had* no future. The present, this room, this man, and the wild electrical storm he had sparked off inside her were all that had any reality for her.

'The bedroom…'

Constantine's voice was thick and rough in her ear, and as she struggled to focus on his carved face she saw the febrile glitter in his eyes, the streak of burning colour along the broad cheekbones that betrayed how close he was to losing control completely.

She had barely time to make a wild gesture vaguely in the right direction before she was snatched off her feet and carried bodily across the room. Constantine kicked open the door, crossing the oatmeal-coloured carpet in three swift strides before depositing her on the cream cotton of the duvet cover with scant ceremony. She had scarcely time to draw in a ragged, uneven breath before he came down beside her on the bed.

'Undress me, Grace,' he ordered. 'I want to be naked, like you. I want to feel your skin against mine.'

It was what she wanted too. Wanted with an urgency that made her fingers clumsy, driving her to fumble with the buttons on his shirt, impatient tears stinging her eyes as she made a complete hash of the simple task.

'Here…' Long fingers stilled her increasingly frantic attempts. 'Let me.'

In just a few seconds the shirt and waistcoat were stripped from his strong body, his trousers following with equally swift efficiency, and when he came back to her again he was totally, proudly nude, completely unselfconscious and blatantly, magnificently aroused.

'Now,' he said, sliding his long body down on the soft cotton beside her. 'Now we can do this properly.'

Pushing her back against the pillows, he subjected her to a sensual onslaught that made the breath catch in her throat in a strangled moan of hungry pleasure. There wasn't an inch of her quivering body that he didn't kiss, the tiniest spot on her burning skin that didn't feel the calculated caress of his knowing hands. His lips were like fire on her breasts, blazing a trail to the tight, stinging nipples and closing over first one and then the other, toying softly before suckling hard, sending shafts of white-hot fire searing down the nerves between her thighs.

Muttering in a mixture of agonised delight and screaming tension, Grace couldn't keep her own hands still. She wanted to touch him anywhere, everywhere, her fingers clutching, stroking, skimming over every part of the powerful body she could reach.

One moment they tangled in the black silk of his hair, another they were smoothing the taut, straining muscles of his shoulders and back. And then, as excitement made her bolder, they slid between their bodies and explored the soft dark hair that curled at the base of his erection, the hot, hard shaft itself.

'*Theos*, Grace!' Constantine muttered thickly. 'You are like wildfire—so hot—so eager! You never used to be so responsive.'

Never used to be… No, in the past she had had foolish, naive ideas that clinging on to her virginity mattered more than showing how she felt about this man. She had wanted everything. The perfect wedding, church flowers—and to be the virgin bride as well!

And as a result of wanting everything, she had very nearly lost everything too. But not now. Now she had been given this unexpected second chance, and she intended to take it. Grasp it with both hands and never let it go.

'Grace, I need to know something…are you protected?'

'Protected?'

Grace's teeth worried at her bottom lip as she struggled to find a way to answer him. But Constantine needed no words, she realised, as she felt his immediate withdrawal and the obvious cooling of the heated passion that had gripped him.

'I don't—' he began, but she couldn't let him finish.

'And do you think I care?' she cried sharply. 'It *will* be safe, Constantine. It's the wrong time of the month for it not to be. And don't you dare think of stopping now!'

'Grace, I'm not sure…'

'But I am!'

She had never been more sure of anything. Never wanted anything so much in all her life. Constantine had said that wanting her was like an ache in his gut, but he had gravely underestimated the truth. What she felt wasn't so much an ache as a sharp, burning pain of need. Every inch of her body craved his like a drug to which she had become ad-

dicted but had been denied for far too long. She felt she
would die if he left her alone now.

And so she writhed against Constantine's long, hard
body, shifting her slim legs in an invitation that was more
blatant than anything she could say.

'Don't talk, Constantine!' she whispered against the coil
of his ear. 'You promised action, not words.'

His groan was a sound of surrender, of excitement, of
delight, all blended as one. And as his mouth took her lips
hard once more, those tantalising hands slipped lower,
smoothing over the flat plane of her stomach before sliding
between her legs, stroking the soft skin of her inner thighs.

'Action? Like this?' he whispered as his sure touch found
the most feminine spot of all and caressed it gently.

The choked cry that escaped her was the only response
Grace was capable of making, and she clutched him to her,
fingers digging into the hard muscles at his shoulders as
she arced her body up to meet his in yearning hunger. The
need for him now was like a scream inside every nerve,
the sexual hunger he had awoken sharp as a pain deep
inside.

'Or like *this*?'

The final moment of possession, the fierce, wild thrust
of his body into hers, was so much what she wanted that
her head swam in a delirium of pleasure. But at the same
time some small, residual instinct she couldn't control made
her stiffen faintly underneath him, halting him suddenly,
his head going back in shock, glazed black eyes staring
down into her wide grey ones.

'*Still?*' he managed, in a tone that left her in no doubt
as to his state of mind.

Forcing herself into some degree of consciousness in order to face that appraising stare, Grace managed to move
her shoulders in what she hoped was a careless shrug.

'It doesn't matter.' And then, when he remained frozen

into immobility above her, 'It *doesn't matter*, Constantine!' she repeated more forcefully, moving her hips under his with deliberate, calculated provocation.

'Grace…' Constantine began, but another of those sensual movements took whatever he had been about to say from his tongue and turned it instead into a groan of ecstatic surrender. The shock in his eyes turned to a glittering hunger *'Grace!'* he sighed on a very different note as he shifted slightly, thrust almost gently.

With that first movement all the careful, almost brutal control he had been exerting splintered, shattering into tiny, irreparable pieces. As one they gave in to the fierce primal rhythm, slowly at first, then faster, faster, faster. Together they clung closer, clutched tighter, reached higher and higher.

To each powerful thrust Grace returned a response of her own, passion answering passion, heat building on heat, harder, fiercer, wilder. Until at last, with the force and starburst brilliance of an exploding meteor, they broke free of the last bonds holding them in time and soared into the formless, dazzling dimension of ecstasy.

Still clinging to Constantine's sweat-slicked form, hearing the breath rasp into his lungs, the shuddering of his muscles as he returned, unwillingly, to reality, Grace could neither think nor feel. She was only aware of the pounding of her heart, still sounding like thunder inside her head, the lingering aftershocks of pleasure that sizzled through her, growing slowly, gradually fainter as a languid sense of repleteness moved along her veins like warm, thick honey.

Stirring slowly, Constantine rolled away from her to lie at her side on the rumpled covers. With a deep, contented sigh, he half opened heavy-lidded eyes, stretching indolently, lazily luxuriating in his own satisfaction.

'I knew it would be like this,' he muttered thickly. 'Knew you…'

'Knew I what?' Grace asked when his voice trailed off.

But Constantine's eyes had already closed, sleep claiming him even as she lifted her head to watch.

Her sigh exactly matching his in deep gratification, Grace shrugged off the momentary confusion.

It didn't matter. Nothing mattered, she told herself as, with an effort, she pulled up the quilt to cover them both before nestling down into the warmth of Constantine's totally relaxed body.

For two years she had lived a sort of half-life, going through the motions, acting on autopilot, putting one foot in front of the other, eating, sleeping, breathing, because she had to. But at the centre of that life there had been an empty core, big and dark as a black hole, taking the real meaning out of living because Constantine was not there.

But now he was back in her life. He was here, beside her, in her bed. He had just made her his finally and completely, by making love to her with the sort of mind-blowing passion that spoke so eloquently of how he must feel. Perhaps they still had a long way to go, but they would travel that road together, and she had no doubt that together they'd reach the happiness she had once been so sure of.

Constantine was back, she repeated inwardly, a blissful smile curling her lips as heavy waves of sleep rolled over her, claiming her. Constantine was back and so everything was right in her world.

CHAPTER FOUR

THE shrill sound of the alarm clock broke violently into the deep, deep sleep that enclosed Grace, jolting her roughly into wakefulness. Groaning wearily, she pushed a hand through her hair, brushing it back from her face so that she could see the clock on her bedside table.

'Seven thirty!' It couldn't be. It still felt like the middle of the night.

But then she had not exactly had a normal night's rest!

It was impossible to hold back a small, contented smile as she recalled just how she had spent the hours of darkness. Her softened eyes went to the side of the bed where Constantine had lain, one hand smoothing over the pillow that still bore the imprint of his dark head, the faint scent of his body.

The end of the night had been a long time coming. They might have dozed, but that first frantic coming together had only temporarily appeased Constantine's appetite for her, and hers for him. He had soon woken again, waking her in her turn with enticing kisses and caresses.

She had lost count of the number of times they had reached for each other, satiation fading into interest, interest sparking into hunger all over again. So that now, as she stretched wearily, she found that her body ached in unexpected places, and there were tiny tender spots to prove that the force and urgency of her lover's desire had been totally unrestrained.

Her lover. Just to frame the words inside her head made her mouth curve into a dreamy, cat-that-got-the-cream smile. Constantine was her lover. He had come back to her, and, to prove it, he had made love to her all night long.

But he was not at her side, where she had expected him to be. His half of the bed was empty, though still warm from the heat of his body. Blinking dreamily, she managed to focus enough to realise that Constantine had slipped from the bed and was quietly hunting for his discarded clothes.

'What are you doing?' Still only half awake, she found it a struggle to force the words out.

Constantine's dark head swung in her direction, his hands still busy with the buttons on his shirt.

'Places to go; people to see.'

His response was curt, almost sharp, certainly totally un-loverlike, so that Grace frowned in sleepy petulance.

'At this time of day!'

'At any time of day. I have a breakfast meeting first thing—a meeting I cannot possibly attend wearing the clothes I had on last night. Then at nine I have to—'

'Okay, okay, I get the message!'

Realising from the impatient way he stamped his feet into his shoes that she was using quite the wrong approach, she hurriedly changed tack completely.

'It's just that I'm disappointed,' she murmured in a soft, enticing tone, accompanying the words by a sensual wriggle of her body under cover of the downy quilt. 'I had thought we could wake up together…start the day properly.'

'Grace!' The look he slanted at her was partly amused, partly reproving, and tinged with what she fervently hoped was a strong thread of regret. 'I am in England to work, remember.'

'Oh, yes,' Grace sighed disconsolately. 'The problems at the London office.'

She should be thankful for them, really. After all, weren't they what had brought Constantine back to her so unexpectedly? But right now she didn't feel at all thankful. All she knew was that her bed was starting to feel very cold and empty, and the man who could remedy that situation was now heading for her sitting room in search of the coat he had discarded all those passion-filled hours ago.

'The problems at the London office,' he confirmed, coming back into the room even as he shrugged himself into the expensive garment that seemed to have suffered no ill effects from its night on her lounge floor. 'They're what I came here to deal with, I never expected to get...sidetracked in this way.'

His glance at his watch was swift, impatient, telling its story only too clearly. Grace knew him in this mood. Determined, unyielding, his mind totally fixed on the matter in hand; there would be no moving him, however hard how she tried.

She might as well give in now in order to avoid any unpleasantness.

'All right, so you have to go. But when will I see you again?'

'I could be tied up all day...'

He moved to drop a kiss on her sleep-flushed cheek. But his lips had barely made contact with her skin before he was straightening up again, checking his watch once more.

'I'll call you.'

'I'll look forward to that...' Grace began, but the words faded from her tongue as he strode from the room, only acknowledging her with a vague gesture of his hand.

It hadn't been the sort of awakening she had anticipated, Grace reflected as she forced herself to go through the everyday motions of showering, dressing, preparing for work. That particular daydream had involved a long, slow start to the morning, with Constantine's arms around her, his mouth pressing kisses all over her face.

But all the same it had been a much better beginning

than she had ever imagined. Constantine was here, back in her life—in her bed—and she couldn't be happier. Just the thought of it was enough to make her feel like dancing as she made her journey to work.

'Someone looks as if all their birthdays have come at once,' Ivan commented when he stopped by her desk later that morning. 'Could this have anything to do with a certain tall, dark, devastating Greek who took you home from the party last night?'

'You know it has!' Grace smiled. 'After all, wasn't that exactly what you had planned right from the start?'

'What I *hoped*,' her friend corrected. 'But only if it's right for you. I wouldn't want you hurt again, Gracie, not like you were the last time.'

'Constantine isn't going to hurt me. When he left this morning he promised he'd ring me tonight and... Oh!'

Her hands flew up to cover her burning cheeks as Ivan's exaggeratedly rounded eyes told her just what she had given away.

'When he left this morning!' he echoed archly. 'Gracie, sweetie, are you sure about this?'

'Couldn't be surer. I remember when I first started dating, the one piece of advice my dad gave me. He said that it wasn't sleeping with someone that was the problem—the problem only arose when you woke up the next morning. So he told me always to stop and think, to ask myself if I'd feel embarrassed waking up beside this person.'

'And I take it Constantine passed Daddy's embarrassment test?'

'Absolutely. I didn't feel anything but happiness at waking up next to him. In fact it was quite the most wonderful feeling of my life. It couldn't have felt more right.'

'Then I couldn't be happier for you. When's the wedding?'

'Wedding? Oh, Ivan, don't rush things. We've only just got back together.'

'But he loved you enough to want you as his wife before. If you ask me, Constantine doesn't let grass grow under his feet. When he wants something, he goes for it, and nothing gets in his way. It's my bet that he'll have you hauled before a priest and a ring on your finger before you have time to say, "I do."'

'That would be wonderful.' In spite of her determination not to build up her hopes too quickly, Grace admitted to the dream she prayed would come true. 'Oh, Ivan, I hope so!'

'So do I, sweetie. Because you know I've always wanted to be there on the day you become Constantine's bride.'

Constantine's bride. Constantine's *bride*. Grace hugged the words to herself throughout the rest of the day.

Was it possible? Could it really be true that the whole nightmare was over and that she was really going to have a fairytale happy ending?

Certainly, from the way the day went, it seemed it might be so. Everything appeared to have been touched by the same magic that had brought her and Constantine together. Her work progressed effortlessly, a new campaign she had thought up for a particularly difficult and picky client won instant approval, and even the notoriously unreliable English spring weather decided to put on a show of mild sunshine and blue skies.

So it was with a light heart and a sense of breathless anticipation that she pushed open the door on her arrival home that evening.

The first thing she checked was her answer-machine. There was bound to be a message from Constantine. He would have had time in between his so important meetings. If she knew Constantine he would have *made* time, no matter how difficult it was.

But the glowing red letters on the machine obstinately recorded the number nought, and when she pressed the relevant button the mechanically flat tones of the recorded message informed her blankly that she had no messages.

No messages. For the first time that day a hint of doubt assailed her, sending an apprehensive shiver creeping over her skin.

I'll call you.

Constantine's voice sounded inside her head, but this time she subjected the words to a more intense scrutiny and analysis.

She had been so sure that he meant what he'd said. That he had every intention of phoning her just as soon as it was possible. But now a nasty, sneaking doubt made her frown uncertainly, white teeth worrying at the skin on her bottom lip.

I'll call you.

How many times had that phrase been used to cover up the fact that the speaker meant the exact opposite? Hadn't she and every other woman she knew been assured that someone would call, only to find, after long nights spent in waiting for the phone to ring, that they had had no interest at all in furthering the relationship? That in fact they were already seeing someone else?

No! She couldn't believe it! She *wouldn't* believe it! Constantine didn't make promises he couldn't keep, and if he gave his word, he stuck to it.

No, he must just have been every bit as busy as he had anticipated. He had been caught up in the problems he was here to sort out and hadn't been able to snatch a single minute to himself.

But he would ring. All she had to do was wait. She would get herself something to eat. Maybe even have a long, scented bath—with the phone handset carefully within reach, of course. She would linger in the warm water until she felt completely relaxed, then she would use the perfumed body lotion she had bought the previous week-end…

Hot colour suffused her skin at the thought of just why she was indulging in this way, the final end towards which all this luxuriating and pampering would lead when Constantine finally arrived. If she was lucky, he might not pause too long between 'Hello' and 'Let's go to bed', and that was just the way she wanted it.

But by the time she had carried out her carefully planned programme, dawdling over her meal, lingering in the bath until the water was almost cold, before pulling on a soft peach towelling robe, and still there was no sign of Constantine, her mood changed yet again.

'Oh, where *are* you?'

She spoke the words aloud, unable to keep them in any longer.

'What's happened to you? Surely you can't be still at work at this time?'

But of course he could, and often had been in the past. Constantine was the archetypal workaholic: totally absorbed in what he was doing, and prepared to devote all the hours in a day to it if that was what it took to achieve the result he wanted. As his fiancée, she had often complained about feeling neglected, that she'd resented the little time he could spare to devote to her at the end of his business commitments. And he had appeared repentant. He had promised to change once they were married.

Once they were married.

Grace took the mug of tea she had made into the sitting room and curled up in one of the armchairs, her feet tucked underneath her, her mood suddenly flat and reflective. They had never married. Paula's lies; the wicked, malicious stories she had made up had seen to that.

It had begun with a knock at the door.

From nowhere it seemed that the past had reached out

to enclose her. That it had taken her back to the time, exactly two years before, when her whole world had fallen apart.

She had spent the day at Constantine's apartment. The apartment that, in less than a week, was to have become her home too. It had been a Sunday night, and on the following Saturday she and Constantine were to have been married. This was to have been her last weekend as a single girl.

They had shared a long, intimate meal together, lingering over a bottle of wine, until at last, reluctantly, she had decided it was time to leave.

'Don't go,' Constantine murmured, one long hand toying softly with the strands of her hair. 'Stay tonight.'

'Constantine, you know I can't! You agreed to wait, and there's only another week to go. That's not so very long.'

'True,' Constantine conceded, getting reluctantly to his feet. 'But I have to admit that this old-fashioned idea of yours of insisting on holding out until the wedding night has made the waiting to make you mine even harder to bear.'

'But think how special that first night will be.'

Grace had to struggle not to show how his use of the phrase *holding out* had disturbed her. It made her actions sound almost perverse and selfish, not the carefully thought out beliefs they actually were.

'I have done nothing *but* think! If you only knew how I lie awake at night—alone in my bed…how I long to come to you…'

His footsteps silent on the thick pile of the rust-coloured carpet, he came towards her, black eyes fixed on her face.

'To take you in my arms…'

Suiting action to the words, he gathered her up, lifting her clean out of her seat.

'Kiss you here…and here…and here…'

Grace's breath caught in her throat as his warm mouth caressed her cheeks, her lips, her softly closed eyelids. Her senses swam, her blood firing immediately in frantic response to his caresses.

'Kiss you until you're senseless with wanting, aching with hunger as I am, until you're—'

'Constantine!' With an effort Grace forced herself to control the raging pulse that throbbed through her veins. 'No!'

With more force than was strictly necessary she pushed him away when he tried to kiss her again. It was either that or succumb to his sensual enticement right here and now. On this settee, or even the floor; she doubted if she'd have cared. Constantine wasn't the only one who had found her decree of celibacy difficult to live with.

Constantine drew in a deep, ragged breath, obviously fighting for control.

'You are a cruel woman, Grace Vernon,' he told her with mock severity. 'Cruel and hard, and a wicked tease.'

If only Constantine knew, Grace thought to herself. If only he realised just how difficult she found it to say no to him, then he would never think her hard, or cruel, for imposing such restrictions on him.

He might think her crazy, though. Because although he had tried to understand and appreciate her wish to hold back on the physical consummation of their relationship until their wedding night, he wasn't averse to applying a little pressure, just enough to test her resolve.

And there had been so many times that she had been tempted. After all, this was the man she loved, the man she wanted to marry. She wasn't exactly indifferent to him! Quite the opposite, in fact. He had only to smile at her and she melted inside, to touch her and her heart started to race, kiss her and she went up in flames. She wanted him so much it was like a constant nagging hunger. But she also wanted their first time together to be so very special.

She knew it was unusual, definitely unfashionable. But, having grown up watching her mother's casual attitude to sex and the ideal of faithfulness in a marriage, and the pain it had caused her father, she had always known she wanted something very different for herself. When she married, she had vowed, it would be for ever, and that for ever would begin with the very first time she had ever made love.

But she hadn't reckoned with the reality of the physical desire she felt for Constantine. When she had first met him she had been knocked completely off balance. He had left her feeling as if she had been picked up by a howling tornado, whirled high into the air and deposited somewhere that looked like the world she knew and yet was so very different from that comfortable place. Every light seemed brighter, every colour sharper, every sound intensified, and all her senses were on red alert, hypersensitively attuned to him.

Those thoughts were still in her mind when she reached her home, lingering in her head as she made herself a cup of coffee before going to bed. Her father and Diana were out, having dinner together, and Paula was away, staying with a friend. She was heading for the stairs when the knock came at the door.

'Who on earth...?'

The words shrivelled on her lips as she saw the identity of the late caller, and the state she was in.

'Paula! What are you doing here?'

Concern paled her face, shadowed her eyes, as she took in her stepsister's ragged breathing, her glittering eyes and the evidence of tears down her colourless cheeks.

'What is it? What's wrong?'

'Grace...' Her stepsister ran into Grace's arms with a choking sob and a cry of, 'Oh, Gracie, I'm so sorry!'

'Sorry?'

Grace could only frown her confusion, her heart jerking inside her chest in some intuitive premonition of horror, of something that was terribly wrong, but she couldn't even begin to guess what.

She had never seen her stepsister in such a state before. Normally Paula was full of the confidence of youth, bubbling over with self-assurance. At nineteen, almost twenty, she had the sort of dark-haired, blue-eyed voluptuous prettiness that had men buzzing round her like bees round a honeypot. But today those brilliant sapphire-coloured eyes were red-rimmed from weeping, her pale skin blotchy and marked.

'Paula, darling...' Grace smoothed a soothing hand over the long deep brown hair. 'What is it? Look, come and sit down and tell me everything.'

'I—I can't...' her stepsister managed unevenly. 'You— you'll hate me!'

'Hate you?' Had she heard right? 'What do you mean, Paula? I could never hate you. You're my sister.'

They had first met when she was fourteen, Paula just a schoolgirl of eleven. Grace had always longed not to be an only child, and she had taken the younger girl, lost and alone following her father's early death and her widowed mother's move to London, very much under her wing. Later, when Grace's father and Paula's mother had married, Grace had opened her heart to her new stepsister, and at first her affection had seemed to be reciprocated.

But just lately the younger girl had been mixing with a rather wild crowd from the office where she worked; she had become rebellious and defiant, and she regarded her older sister as dull, too conventional and altogether boring. As a result, the friendship had become rather strained, almost to breaking point. But Grace had always had a special place in her heart for Paula.

So, now, 'You can tell me anything,' she told her. 'Anything at all.'

'Even if it's about *him*? About Constantine.'

'What about Constantine?'

Paula caught hold of her sister's hands, clutching them so tightly that Grace winced in pain.

'Grace, darling, I'm so sorry about this—but I just couldn't live with myself if I didn't tell you. I can't let you delude yourself any longer.'

'Delude myself... About what?'

'About that pig of a man you're engaged to. You can't let things go any further. You can't marry him! He's totally promiscuous—hasn't got a faithful bone in his body!'

'No...' Grace shook her head firmly, refusing even to consider the idea. 'No, Paula. I don't know where you've got this idea from, but you have to be mistaken. Constantine would never...'

'Oh, wouldn't he? You say you don't know where I got this idea from, but I didn't *get it* from anyone. I didn't need to—I know all the facts I need from personal experience. Because, you see, the woman your fiancé was unfaithful with—one of the many, for all I know—was me. He slept with *me*.'

'*No!*'

It was a cry of pain, the sound of a heart breaking.

'*Yes,*' Paula insisted. 'Yes! Yes! Yes! He's been after me for weeks—pushing, pushing, pushing! I told him I wasn't interested—that you were my sister—but he just laughed...'

Grace's shadowed gaze was concentrated on Paula, seeing the distress in her eyes, the way her hands clenched and unclenched nervously.

'I tried to resist him, Grace, I really did! But then that weekend in February, when you were away seeing your mother, everything came to a head. I was alone in the house and he turned up. I thought he'd come to see you, but he said—he said that of course he knew you weren't there, that while the cat was away the mice could play.'

Paula drew a long, shuddering breath and straightened her shoulders.

'He'd brought a bottle of wine, and he asked me to share it with him.'

'He got you drunk?' Grace couldn't conceal her horror.

'Not exactly—just a bit tiddly. But then he started coming on to me again. He was insistent, forceful. I said no; he said yes. I retreated; he followed. And then he caught hold of me and kissed me. He—he said that he knew it was what I really wanted, that I was only playing hard to get. That all he did was think about me when he was alone in his bed. He told me that I was a wicked tease—a cruel, hard woman...'

All he did was think...a wicked tease...a cruel, hard woman. The words reverberated inside Grace's skull, making her head reel as if from actual physical blows.

Less than an hour before, Constantine had used those exact words to her when he had tried to seduce her, to entice her into making love with him. And now to hear them repeated, quoted as they had been used to another woman...! Were they, then, the lines of a practised seducer, a man who churned out exactly the same lines for each new conquest? The thought was like bitter acid inside her, eating away at her heart.

'And he said he was frustrated as hell. That the other women in his life hadn't kept him dangling like this. That your insistence on holding out until the wedding was more than he could take. He wanted a real woman, someone who knew her own mind, not a—'

'That's enough!' Grace couldn't bear to hear any more.

'Oh, Grace, I'm sorry! I wish I hadn't had to tell you this! But please believe what I've said—for your own sake.

If he's done it once, he'll do it again—probably has, for all I know. Grace—think about it!'

Think about it! She couldn't do anything else! She knew she couldn't go to bed now. She couldn't rest, couldn't sleep, couldn't do anything until she had confronted Constantine.

And the terrible thing was that all the way to Constantine's apartment she could see how it might have been. She knew so well the cold force of her fiancé's single-minded determination, the steel-hard ruthlessness that drove him. When he was set on something, he could sweep aside anything he considered irrelevant, trampling any foolish, feeble objections under the soles of his highly polished handmade shoes.

So had that merciless power been turned on Paula? And if it had been combined with the potent sexuality, the devastatingly carnal appeal that Constantine also possessed, the seductive eloquence of his silken tongue, then what woman could have resisted?

Paula was so much younger. Fresh out of school and naively impressionable—though she'd be the first to deny that description—she was no match for a sophisticated, experienced man of the world like Constantine.

Hadn't Grace herself been tempted so often by his huskily whispered enticements, their sensual appeal heightened by his beautifully accented deep voice, until she had come close to succumbing, to abandoning her long-held and deeply felt principles?

'How could you?' The words burst from her as soon as she was through the door. 'How could you do this to me? How could you even believe that you'd get away with it? That I wouldn't find out and...'

'Hold on a minute.' Constantine's tone was almost as harsh as her own. 'Precisely what is it I'm supposed to have done?'

'Oh, don't give me that! You know—Paula has told me everything…'

She had to force the dreadful story out, finding it unbearable even to tell it, hating the way the words felt on her tongue.

'It's a lie.'

It was too quick, too pat. Feeling raw and distraught, her heart just an anguished, burning pain, as if someone was pulling it to pieces bit by bit, she needed more. So much more.

'That's it? "It's a lie" and I'm supposed to believe you?'

'Grace, nothing happened. This is all some crazy story that Paula's made up.'

'And why would she do that?'

'She has some fantasy—'

'Fantasy!' Grace couldn't believe what she was hearing. 'This wasn't any sort of fantasy! You didn't see her! You didn't see the state she was in!'

'No, I didn't, but it wouldn't change anything. She lied.'

'And why would she lie about something like this? She's my sister! And besides, some of it she didn't have to tell me—some of it I already knew. Like the fact that there have been other women in your life. Sophisticated women with no hang-ups about the physical side of a relationship. And are you going to deny the fact that you've been finding it hard to wait for our wedding night?'

Constantine raked both his hands through the darkness of his hair, his expression grim as he shook his head.

'I'd be the liar if I did!'

'And you've always admitted to a weakness for petite, curvy women with black hair and blue eyes.'

'So now I'm tried and condemned because of some innocent remark I made months ago?' Constantine's tone had changed noticeably, and something dangerous sparked in his eyes. 'If you're not prepared to believe me, is there any point in continuing this conversation?'

'I need the truth! Did you do this?'

Constantine's arrogant dark head lifted even higher, nostrils flared, jet-black eyes blazing.

'I have already answered that question. Can you have any doubt—?'

'Quite frankly, I have nothing *but* doubts!' Grace flung at him. 'And, feeling like this, there is no way I can go ahead with our marriage!'

'You're cancelling the wedding? Over *this*!'

He made it sound as if it was the proverbial storm in a teacup. This wasn't what she had expected. She had thought—had hoped—that he would take her in his arms and tell her that he adored her, that he worshipped the ground she walked on, and he would rather die than let anything hurt her.

'Postponing it, certainly. I need time to think.'

'No, you don't.'

'I *do*! Constantine, you have to—'

'Have to!' Constantine repeated on a note of pure scorn. 'You're on quite the wrong track, my sweet Grace, if you think I'm obliged to do anything at all! I've said all I'm going to say. The ball is in your court, and nowhere else, my darling. It's your move.'

Her move! Grace couldn't even think what the words meant, never mind do anything about them.

'Constantine…'

And then it happened. Just as she looked into the hard, set mask that was his face, just as ebony eyes met grey, locking and…

The room spun sickeningly round her. Grace had to put out a hand to clutch at the nearest chair for support. It couldn't be! Dear God, please let it not be true!

Because impossibly, unbelievably, suddenly Constantine's

gaze was not quite steady. It was his stare that wavered, just for a second. And that second was enough to reveal another, very different expression that had lain hidden until now. Underneath the confident pride, the arrogant self-assurance, lurked something she could only describe as fear and…and…

And *guilt*, her unwilling mind supplied, her heart stopping dead in horror.

A moment later he blinked and it was gone. But she had seen it, and it was enough to shatter her belief that he could still convince her all was well and she would fall into his arms on a wave of heady relief.

'I want to go home,' she said drearily, all life, all feeling stripped from her voice so that it was as flat and dead as her thoughts.

And the truly frightening thing was that Constantine didn't argue. She had been nerving herself for a fight, struggling to dredge up enough emotional strength to resist him, only to find it wasn't needed. Instead, he turned without a word, reaching for the telephone.

'I'll ring for a taxi,' he said, not a flicker of regret or any other reaction showing on his face. 'I'd offer to drive you, but I very much doubt that either of us would want to be alone with the other any longer tonight.'

But it didn't end there. Because eventually Paula admitted that she had lied. Somehow Grace's father managed to work on her stepsister's conscience until at last Paula owned up to the terrible jealousy she had always felt for Grace.

'You were always so damn perfect! So tall and slim and blonde—and a real male-magnet! No man ever gave me a second look when you came into the room. And if I brought a boyfriend home, he was guaranteed to lose interest the minute he set eyes on you. It was always, ''Is *she* your sister? You're not at all alike, are you?'' until I was ready to scream.'

'But, Paula, that wasn't my fault.' Grace was shocked to realise the thoughts that Paula had been harbouring all this time, the resentment she had let grow into something more dangerous. 'I didn't know it was happening.'

'Oh, sure you didn't!' her stepsister scorned. 'Little Miss Perfect just didn't realise that she was flirting with every man I've ever liked! Well, I knew—and I didn't like it. And I vowed that I'd get even. That one day I'd steal a man from you as you did from me.'

And the man she'd set her sights on was Constantine. Waiting and watching, letting her jealousy fester deep inside, she had finally made her move just at the point where it would have the most deadly effect.

But somehow Grace couldn't bring herself to care about Paula's behaviour. Her heart was soaring, excitement bubbling up inside her. She couldn't wait until she could speak to Constantine again and tell him that his name had been cleared. That with Paula's confession there was nothing now to stand in the way of their wedding. She loved him, and she couldn't wait to be his bride. They could be married within the month.

But Constantine didn't react in the way she had expected at all.

CHAPTER FIVE

A SOUND from the street brought Grace suddenly wide awake, throwing off the world of the past and its unhappy memories. A car door slamming and hurried footsteps coming towards the house.

In a rush she got to her feet and dashed to the window, pulling back the curtains so that she could see out.

Constantine, his strong figure outlined by the street lamps, a huge bouquet in one hand. He was obviously as impatient to see her as she was to see him and he mounted the steps to the door two at a time, reaching the top before she really had time to register he was truly there.

Delight put wings on her feet as she raced to let him in. So what if he was late? He was here, and that was all that mattered.

'At last!'

She couldn't hold back the exclamation as she flung open the door, her heart doing a tap dance of joy inside her chest as her eyes feasted on the wonderful sight of him. With his tall frame sheathed in a superbly tailored suit in charcoal-grey, immaculate white shirt and discreet burgundy tie, he was no longer the trainee waiter he had claimed to be last night, but every inch the city man. Constantine Kiriazis of the Kiriazis Corporation. The man who had companies like the agency she worked in for breakfast.

'I'd just about given up on you.'

Not the most auspicious of beginnings, she realised as she saw the swift frown that drew his black brows together. She had meant to imply that she had been impatient to see him, but had only succeeded in making it sound like a reproof.

'It is—what…?'

A swift glance at the clock stunned her. Perhaps she had meant to reproach him after all.

'It's ten-thirty, Constantine! I was starting to think about going to bed.'

'So I see.'

Brilliant black eyes seared over her body in the cosy but hardly glamorous towelling robe.

'That's fine by me,' he drawled insolently.

'Fine…'

Grace found she was actually struggling to speak. The audacity of the man! Okay, she was glad to see him, but that didn't mean he could turn up as he liked, when he liked, and expect her to fall straight into bed with him.

'You could have phoned. I don't like to feel taken for granted.'

'Grace, I have been working,' Constantine explained with an exaggerated patience that expressed more of the annoyance he was trying to keep in check than any true equanimity.

'All this time?'

'I had dinner with a client. That ended…' He consulted his watch briefly. 'Half an hour ago. It took some time to get over to this side of London, and I had to make a minor detour on the way. And as for feeling taken for granted, perhaps this will help.'

The bouquet he held out would have taken anyone's breath away. Lilies had always been Grace's favourite flowers; not that she ever had enough spare cash to indulge herself. So to be presented with this profusion of the glorious blooms—three dozen at the very least—was absolutely overwhelming.

'Oh, Constantine, thank you! They're beautiful—gorgeous!'

And what mattered most was that he had found time in the middle of what had obviously been a very busy day to think of her and arrange to have the bouquet made up. Okay, so men like Constantine didn't do the ordering and suchlike themselves; they had teams of minions to perform such tasks for them. But he must have specified exactly what type of flowers he wanted. Which meant he remembered her personal likes and dislikes.

'But I wasn't really cross. Honestly, you didn't need to…'

'I usually give my women flowers. Particularly on a first date.'

Grace was suddenly thankful for the way that her head was bent to the flowers, the fall of her hair concealing her momentary reaction, the flicker of pain across her face that she couldn't quite suppress.

'Your women,' she echoed when she felt she could manage to sound as if it didn't matter. 'I hope I'm more to you than that.'

His unexpected silence brought her head up in a rush, just in time to catch the expression on his face. With the memory of the freezing lack of emotion he had displayed when she had cancelled their wedding still vivid in her mind, she found the similarity between the two made her blood run cold.

But then, as swiftly as it had appeared, the look was gone. In its place was a glance of sexually devastating significance slanted at her from gleaming eyes.

'Right now, you're everything I want,' he told her huskily. 'Grace, for God's sake, come here and say hello properly.'

It was like a salve to the smart of uncertainty she had

felt. Willingly she went into his arms, holding her face up for his kiss.

His lips were still cold from the night air outside, but the heat of his passion soon erased any lingering chill. As his mouth crushed hers in urgent demand she felt her own blood heating in response, her own lips parting under his, allowing the practised invasion of his tongue.

'You smell delicious,' Constantine eventually murmured against her hair. 'And you feel wonderful. But *this*...' arrogant hands plucked contemptuously at the peach towelling robe '...is hardly the most flattering of garments.'

'It's the only one I've got. Remember, I never even expected that I would be entertaining you tonight.'

'I shall buy you a better one. What would you prefer—silk—satin?'

'Constantine, you don't need to buy me presents.'

'No?'

A dark eyebrow winged upwards in exaggerated surprise.

'I thought all women liked gifts—the more expensive the better.'

There was an edge to his voice that made Grace frown uneasily, reminding her of the almost dismissive *my women* he had used earlier.

'Oh, I like them... Which reminds me—I'd better put these flowers in water before they start to wilt. I just hope I have enough vases. Constantine, you've been hopelessly extravagant.'

Constantine's shrug as he followed her into the kitchen was a wordless reminder that a bunch of flowers, however large and lavish, was hardly going to make even the slightest dent in his personal fortune.

'I thought they would please you.'

'Oh, they do!'

Suddenly and inexplicably she felt anxious and uneasy. Inside the confined space of her small kitchen,

Constantine's lean, powerful frame seemed impossibly big and strong, totally dominating the room. She felt as if every cell, every nerve-ending was sharply attuned to the potent sexual magnetism of the man behind her. So much so that her skin heated under the robe, all the tiny hairs on the back of her neck lifting in instinctive response at the sound of his breathing, the tiniest movement.

'Oh, this is ridiculous!' she muttered to herself.

'What is ridiculous?'

To her consternation Constantine's sharp hearing had caught the mumbled comment, his soft question making her jump so that the water in the vase she was filling went everywhere.

'I haven't offered you anything to...to drink,' she amended hastily.

Anything to eat she had been about to say, only recalling just in time that he had been at dinner with a client only an hour before.

'Would you like coffee? Wine?'

'Oh, Grace...'

Constantine's laughter was unexpected, bringing her whirling round to study his face in order to try and understand the reason for it. Her heart lurched sharply in uncontrollable response to the sudden softening of the strongly carved features, the new warmth in his eyes.

'Grace, *pethi mou*, I believe we played out exactly this scene last night. And my response now is precisely the same as it was then.'

'You don't want anything to drink?'

'No.'

'And you're not hungry?'

'No—not for food anyway.'

He didn't need to elaborate. It was there in his eyes, in the sensual curve of his mouth. He had said he wasn't hungry, but there was no denying the raw need that was stamped on to his strong-boned features, drawing the skin tight over the broad cheekbones.

As she watched, her mouth drying painfully, she saw the warmth fade from his eyes to be replaced by another, very different form of heat. A blazing, scorching fire that made her feel as if she was in the path of a laser beam, one that had the power to strip a layer of skin from her body, leaving her deeply vulnerable and exposed.

'Grace,' he said on a very different note from before. 'Come here.'

Without quite being aware that she had moved, she was suddenly in his arms, being held close against the hard lines of his body, hearing the heavy beat of his heart against the strong wall of his chest.

'Grace, my sweet, beautiful Grace, there is one reason and one reason alone that I came here tonight. And that was not for food, or wine, or anything but this...'

The gentle sensuality of his kiss took her breath away, making her head spin. It soothed all the ragged feelings of moments before, driving every nervous thought, every uncertainty from her mind. He was here for her and for no other reason, and that was what made her heart sing.

She'd been thinking about the past; that was the problem. Remembering how it had once been. And those memories had coloured her thoughts, darkening them and making her irrationally fearful. She had to put that past behind her, far, far behind, and move forward into the bright new future that had dawned so unexpectedly.

'Constantine...' His name was just a sigh on her lips, a sound of pure pleasure blending into a longing that he heard, and laughed at in soft triumph.

'I know, sweetheart, I know. I feel exactly that way too. Today has felt like a lifetime. I couldn't work, couldn't concentrate. All I could think of was getting through the hours and getting back here so that I could kiss you...'

He suited action to the words, his former gentleness changing swiftly, moving into a hungry demand that had Grace responding with eager enthusiasm.

'So that I could touch you…' Constantine managed, his voice thickening noticeably when at last, reluctantly, they had to break apart to draw in a much needed breath.

It was only when his hands slid underneath the cotton towelling that Grace realised he had tugged at the tie belt that held her robe closed, letting it fall open, revealing the simple white nightdress she wore underneath.

'Now this is better,' he murmured, pushing the towelling robe down from her shoulders and pressing his mouth to the smooth flesh exposed by the narrow shoestring straps. 'Much better…'

'Constantine!' Grace gasped as firm white teeth closed around one strap, tugging it gently until it slid over her left shoulder and hung loose over her arm.

With her hands and forearms imprisoned by the confining folds of her robe she could only stand immobile as that tormenting mouth inched its way across her shoulder and back towards her throat. Making a momentary detour along the fine lines of her neck, Constantine marked out a trail of burning kisses along her collarbone and across to the other side. The right-hand strap went the same way as the left, the loosened top of her nightdress sliding downwards to reveal the smooth slopes of her upper breasts.

His lips followed its path, his hot tongue occasionally flicking out to taste the creamy flesh he had exposed. The sizzling pleasure of his caresses made Grace shift restlessly, arching her neck, her head flung back in delight, an uncontrolled moan escaping her.

A moment later she was catching her breath in her throat as that proud dark head moved even lower, to the tightness of her breasts where her nipples thrust against the soft cotton of her nightdress. First on one side and then the other he took the throbbing peaks into the heat of his mouth through the fine material, moistening each with his tongue before he sucked hard. Stinging pleasure radiated from that one, devastating focus point, and arrowed with white-hot force straight to the point between her thighs where her hunger centred, pulsing fiercely.

At the same time, hard, warm hands were sliding under the hem of the short nightdress, pushing it upwards, higher and higher. Bronzed fingers slid over the slender length of her thigh, over the curve of her hips, and then angled down to the most intimate spot of all, sliding deep inside her, stroking rhythmically.

'Constantine!'

Grace shuddered wildly, thrusting herself against him, hungry, demanding. The need she felt was too intense, the delight too close to pain for her to say any more. She could only whimper in ecstatic response, her hands clutching at his shoulders, supporting herself with difficulty.

'Steady, sweetheart…' Constantine's voice was raw and husky, as if it came from a painfully tight throat. 'Easy now…'

Easy! She didn't want to take things easy! The only thing that would *ease* the way she felt was the feel of his possession, of his hard, strong body blending with her own. She wanted him to take her, take them both to that devastating, brilliant place where the world and everyone in it ceased to be and there was only the two of them and the blazing consummation they created between them.

But already Constantine was moving his hands away, depriving her of the caresses that had so excited her. His mouth moved up the fine lines of her throat, kissed her mouth briefly as he smoothed down her nightdress with almost matter-of-fact control.

'Constantine…' The name broke in the middle, her voice ragged, uneven, pleading. 'Constantine, please.…'

His laughter was soft against her hair.

'Grace, honey, be realistic. There isn't enough room in this kitchen for two consenting mice, let alone a couple of fully-grown adults. I think we'd better continue this somewhere more comfortable.'

The idea of continuing reassured her. And so when he held out his hand she put hers into it willingly, following him like a sleepwalker.

He led her not, as she had expected, to the bedroom, but to the darkened living room, where the only light came from the fire in the grate, now burning low, the coals glowing red-hot. Standing before it, he eased the cotton robe from her body, arranging it on the floor at their feet.

Gently he laid her down on the makeshift rug, pausing only to strip away his own clothes before he came down beside her.

'This will have to go,' he muttered, taking the white nightdress in two strong hands.

With one powerful movement he ripped it in two and tossed it aside, exposing the pale flesh underneath, the soft curves coloured by the glow of the fire.

'So, now, where were we?'

Like the fire, Grace's desperately aroused body had not actually cooled, but only quietened. And just as the fire would have needed only a moment's attention before it once more burst into flames, so she too only needed the slightest touch of his hands and lips to be once again at fever-pitch.

Within a couple of heated seconds she was reaching for Constantine, pulling him over her, even sliding her hands between them, closing over the slick, hot hardness of him, guiding him into her in her urgency to know his possession.

Holding him tight, with her arms clamped around his narrow waist, her legs tangled with his, she abandoned all restraint. Lifting her hips in the sure, instinctive rhythm that she knew would pleasure them both, she took control, driving him onward with every move, every touch. Above her, she felt his muscles tighten, heard his muttered curse as he abandoned himself to her lead, taking the secondary role for once.

A bubble of triumphant laughter burst from her as the pace mounted higher and higher. With her own body burning in electric sensation, she was supremely aware of his, and the response she was drawing from it. Constantine Kiriazis, the man who was always in control, always the epitome of restraint, was lost, adrift on a sea of sensuality, and it was all because of her. It was more than she had ever dreamed of, and she couldn't hold back a wild cry of ecstasy as with one final thrust she took him with her into the blazing consummation they were striving for.

The scene that Grace woke to on the following morning was almost a carbon copy of the previous day, except for one thing. This time Constantine was already dressed when she finally forced her heavy lids open, and he was leaning over the bed, placing a small gift-wrapped parcel on the side-table.

'What are you doing?'

'Going to work.' As before, it was short to the point of rudeness.

'But…'

There was something wrong with that, if only she could get her head round it. Once again, it had been hours before they had slept, and exhaustion was catching up on her.

'But it's Saturday!' she pronounced at last on a note of triumph at having forced herself to think.

'I have a lot to do. I am here to work…'

'Not at the weekend! Oh, Constantine, please…' she pleaded. 'No one gets up this early!'

'At home, I rise early all the time,' he contradicted her.

'That way I can get more done before the day really heats up.'

'In Greece, perhaps, but I really doubt that it's going to get too hot to work in April in London. Constantine, I had plans for today…'

'And so do I,' he returned shortly, running a hand over his hair to smooth it.

She could still remember how it had been to feel that jet-black silk under her touch, Grace thought hungrily. In the height of passion she had clutched at it, fingers twisting, tugging, until she was sure it must have hurt. But never once had Constantine complained.

Instead he had actively encouraged her.

'Grace, *pethi mou*,' he had whispered in the darkness of the night, his accent sounding so much stronger to ears made sensitive because she couldn't see. 'I wouldn't know you for the same woman. I never guessed it could be like this—that you could be so exciting, so passionate…'

And she had wanted to turn to him and tell him that her response shouldn't surprise him. Didn't they say that absence made the heart grow fonder? Two years before, she would never have believed that she could have loved him any more than she did then. But, having spent two long, lonely years believing that she had lost him and that she would never see him again, she now knew the truth. And that truth was that what she had felt for him then had been like the tiny, flickering flame of a candle compared to the wild, blazing fire that was her love now.

But even as she opened her mouth to speak Constantine had blocked off her words with an urgent, demanding kiss. The hunger that she had thought was satiated proved instead to have simply been temporarily appeased, dampened down, not obliterated. Within the space of a couple of heartbeats she had been in the grip of it once again, words becoming totally superfluous as she'd found other, more satisfying ways to declare her love.

'But your plans won't be as much fun as mine.'

Deliberately she stretched lazily, letting the quilt that covered her slide provocatively low, exposing a large amount of creamy flesh, flushed pink from the warmth of the bed. A heady rush of very female triumph mixed with a hot flood of sensual awareness as she saw his brilliant black gaze drop to follow the slight movement, the convulsive swallow he could not control.

'I thought we'd wake up more slowly than this…'

A sensual little wriggle of her hips made it plain exactly how she had hoped to be woken.

'That we'd breakfast together…having showered together first, of course. Which might just mean that breakfast would turn into brunch.'

He was tempted, she knew. Just his silence told her that. The fact that Constantine, confident, assured Constantine, who was never at a loss for words, could find nothing to say told her that her suggestions had hit home.

But not hard enough. And Constantine wasn't as tempted as she had hoped. Because the next moment he had shaken his dark head resolutely, destroying her hopes in a second.

'No,' he declared, coolly inflexible. 'Not today.'

Grace's full mouth formed a soft moue of protest and disappointment.

'Then when?'

'When the time is suitable. Grace…'

Her name sounded an ominous warning note as she tried to speak again.

'You must learn not to make demands. I will be here when it is possible. But I cannot dally with you all day long. My work is important.'

'I think I got that message,' Grace muttered petulantly.

I cannot dally with you... I will be here when it is possible. When he could fit her in, it sounded like.

'But I also think I deserve better than that.'

'And why is that, *pethi mou*?'

It was low and dangerous, fiendishly soft. But Grace was past heeding.

'You can't just come round here when it suits you, stay for just as long as it suits you...'

Constantine's sigh was a perfect blend of resignation and irritation, something in the sound flooding her with apprehension.

'I left you a gift.'

'What?'

It was such an unexpected change of tack that it threw her completely. She could only blink in confusion as Constantine reached for the parcel he had placed on the bedside table and held it out to her.

'I thought you would find it when you woke.'

There was something wrong here, Grace thought uneasily. Every instinct she possessed screamed at her that things were not as she'd thought, not as she wanted. And yet there was nothing concrete on which she could pin her feelings, no grounds for the suspicion that buzzed along her nerves like uncomfortable pins and needles.

'Look,' Constantine continued with careful patience when she could only stare at the gold-wrapped gift box he held, unable to find the strength to bring herself to reach out for it, 'I'll stay while you open it...'

The carved mouth curled slightly at the corners.

'Then you will be able to thank me properly.'

Her movements as stiff and jerky as some wind-up automaton, Grace held out a hand and he let the little box fall into it.

Slowly, carefully, almost as if she feared she might find some deadly snake or spider underneath the pretty paper,

Grace peeled away the wrapping, eased off the lid and finally lifted the cotton wool padding that protected the contents.

'Oh…'

It was all she could manage. Her mind seemed to have blown a fuse.

She knew what her reaction *should* be. She should make some sound of delight. Say, Oh, Constantine, it's beautiful! just as she had said about the flowers last night. And he obviously expected that she would fling her arms around him, rain kisses on the lean, hard planes of his cheeks. That she should *thank him properly*.

Which she would have done normally.

Because the delicate gold bangle that the box contained *was* beautiful. And under normal circumstances she would have been happy to receive it, delighted by such a generous present.

So what was it that changed this moment from normal circumstances into something that froze her tongue and kept her eyes fixed on the opened parcel, unable to look into Constantine's face for fear of what she might see there?

'It—it's very nice,' she managed shakily.

'Nice!' Constantine exploded. '*Theos*, Grace, *nice* is for chocolates, a card, or a pen, perhaps. What is wrong? I thought all women liked jewellery.'

And that was when the truth dawned on her. When she realised just why this situation was ringing warning bells loud and clear in her mind.

I thought all women liked gifts—the more expensive the better. From her memories of the previous night, his words came back to haunt her.

I usually give my women flowers. That was what he had said as he'd handed over the ridiculously extravagant bouquet of flowers.

My women…. All women.

Her head came up sharply, tossing her blonde hair back.

'But I'm not just one of "all women"!' she declared angrily, grey eyes flashing defiance. 'I think I'm rather more than that!'

He didn't move, didn't say a word, but she suddenly knew that she was on very dangerous ground indeed. It was there in the tightening of the muscles in his jaw, the cold, obsidian stare, his very stillness.

'And what, precisely, gives you that impression?' he asked, each word seeming to be formed in letters of ice, so that Grace shivered violently, as if they had actually landed cruelly on her exposed skin.

'Well, I—I'm more than just any woman...'

Nervously she glanced at him, expecting some response. But Constantine didn't even blink, his eyes opaque, revealing nothing.

'I mean—I'm...'

That dangerous stillness was beginning to affect her ability to speak. It reminded her of nothing so much as the unmoving crouch of a savage hunting cat, waiting, watching, judging the precise moment at which to pounce. Her already taut nerves tightened even more, as if in anticipation of the brutal claws, the cruel teeth.

'Surely when we are married you won't...'

That got a response.

With a sudden, unexpected movement, Constantine uncoiled lithely from his place on the bed and got to his feet to stand towering over her, black eyes blazing a terrible rejection of her words.

'"When we are married",' he echoed, giving each word a freezingly precise enunciation. 'And what, my sweet Grace, makes you think that that prospect is on the cards?'

There was a sound inside Grace's skull like the buzzing of a thousand frantic, angry bees and her eyes blurred so that she could no longer see Constantine's dark face. Her head swam sickeningly and she fell back against the pillows, painfully aware of the fact that if she had been standing her legs would no longer have supported her. She felt as if all the blood had been drained from her body, leaving her limp as a puppet with all its strings cut.

'But I thought…'

Her voice failed her, croaking embarrassingly, and she had to swallow hard in order to be able to speak. And all the time Constantine just stood there, his cruel glare burning into her skin so that she feared she might actually be scarred where it touched.

'I mean—we—we were going to be married before, so naturally when we got back together again, I assumed…'

'You assumed wrong.' Brutally sharp, it slashed into her stumbling explanation with the force of a steel blade. 'Nothing was further from my mind.'

'Wrong?'

He couldn't have said that. She couldn't be hearing right! Somehow they'd got their wires crossed and she'd become confused. She hadn't really taken in what he'd said.

Drawing a deep, fortifying breath, she sat upright, straightening her shoulders. It was time she got this sorted out.

'Don't mess me about, Constantine, this is too important for that. You know what I mean. We were engaged before. You loved me and I loved you, so it's natural that we'll want to take up where we left off. Since you came back to me, it's obvious that you still want to marry me.'

Her words fell into a silence so deep and profound that she could almost feel it drawing in around her, closing her throat so that she found it impossible to breathe naturally. Her heart was beating frantically inside her chest, making the blood pound against her temples with a sound like distant thunder.

'It is not obvious to me at all,' Constantine said at last.

'Nothing in what you have said has any bearing on this matter at all. I'm afraid you have been totally deluded in your assessment of the situation.'

His tone took that *I'm afraid* to a point light-years away from any real concern.

'But just to ensure that there is no misunderstanding between us, let me make myself perfectly clear. I came back to you because I wanted you. Nothing more. Once I had seen you again, I found it physically impossible to live without making you mine. That is the sum total of my feelings, and anything else you have come up with is pure conjecture—the product of your over-active imagination. And one final point...'

When he paused, obviously to emphasise the importance of what he was about to say, Grace had to bite down hard on her lower lip in order to hold back a desperate, fearful cry of, Don't!

She had to fight a nasty, painful struggle with herself in order not to give in to her impulse to lift her hands and press them over her ears, blotting out the words that she sensed intuitively were going to taken her new-found happiness and destroy it as effectively and callously as Constantine had when he'd rejected her two years before. She didn't want to hear him speak, and yet she didn't have the strength to even try and stop him.

'If you have any foolish ideas in that pretty head of yours—dreams of weddings and rings and happy ever after—then I strongly recommend that you forget them. We tried that one, remember. It didn't work out. But whatever else may happen between us, there is one thing I am sure of, and that is that you will never be my wife.'

CHAPTER SIX

YOU will never be my wife.

The words were like a knife in her heart.

She had been so sure, so happy. She had thought...

No. Admit the truth. She had never actually stopped to *think*. She had just reacted on instinct, on emotion, and hadn't stopped to consider whether what she was doing was actually wise. And she certainly had never even considered that Constantine might have any motivation other than the love she had naively attributed to him.

Well, now she knew. And although what she really wanted to do was to scream, to let out her pain in a tirade of abuse, a strong sense of self-preservation made her impose a ruthless control over her face and voice in order to hide what she was feeling.

'Might I ask your reasons for that statement?'

The look Constantine turned on her was icily contemptuous, scathing in disbelief that she even had to ask the question.

'You know my reasons. Nothing at all has changed in the past two years. My opinion of you is no different now from what it was when you came crawling back to me the last time.'

'Crawling...!'

Oh, this was better! With the help of a much needed rush of anger at the scornfully insulting words he had tossed at her, Grace was able to straighten her back, lift her fair head proudly, and meet those cold black eyes head-on.

'I did not *crawl*! As I recall, I came to apologise. I had made a genuine mistake, and I wanted to put things right.'

'A mistake!'

The bitter cynicism with which he flung the word at her had the burn of acid on her soul.

'I doubt if you really know what the real "mistake" you made actually was!'

'Of course I know!'

Indignation brought Grace fully upright to glare at him furiously. But she regretted the impetuous movement as soon as she saw Constantine's appraising gaze drop to survey her naked torso, exposed by the way the quilt fell back to around her waist.

'Cover yourself up,' he commanded harshly.

For one wonderful, mindless second, Grace was sorely tempted to defy him. She even considered letting the covers fall even lower and flaunting her nudity just to show how little his presence affected him. But no sooner had the thought formed than it shrivelled again, all her confidence leaching away in the face of that baleful, cold-eyed stare.

But what finally destroyed her self-assurance completely was Constantine's voice. It was as cool and analytical as a knife, leaving her in no doubt that if she had hoped to incite a sexual response in the man before her, and so reduce his ability to think clearly, she had failed miserably. He was as unmoved by her appearance as he would have been by a dead salmon on a fishmonger's slab.

'I said, cover yourself up. You look ridiculous sitting there like that.'

'I would if I could!'

Grace struggled against the temptation to clutch the quilt up close to her. She had never felt so defenceless, so vulnerable, so thoroughly exposed, but she was damned if she was going to let him see that.

'But, if you recall, my robe is still in the other room.'

The thought of exactly why it was still in the living room, the memory of their impassioned lovemaking before the fire, almost destroyed her. She had to swallow hard to force down the sudden thickness in her throat. Refusing to let the hot tears that stung at her eyes even have a chance of falling, she forced herself to go on.

'And I'm sure that if I got out of bed in order to go and fetch it, you would find some other, even more insulting description of my behaviour—accuse me of parading my nakedness in front of you like a...'

'*Christos!*' Constantine muttered furiously, but she was relieved to see that he turned on his heel and marched out of the room, returning only seconds later with the peach towelling robe dangling from one finger.

In a gesture of haughty disdain he tossed it on to the bed beside her, discarding it swiftly, as if he felt that to touch it any longer might contaminate him.

'Put it on!' he commanded arrogantly. 'Then perhaps we might be able to continue this discussion rationally.'

'You weren't so quick to cover me up last night,' Grace retorted, struggling to pull on the robe without revealing any more of her naked body that she absolutely had to.

Even though it was crazy after all that had happened between them on the past two nights, she still wanted to scream at him to turn his back, give her some privacy. But she knew what his reply would be. That there wasn't a single inch of her body that he hadn't seen, caressed, and more during their lovemaking.

But then last night, and the night before, he hadn't made her feel so ashamed, so humiliated. Then he had treated her body as something beautiful, something to be revered and cherished. Now he was looking at her as if she was something particularly sordid and unpleasant that he had found dumped in the dustbin.

'Then you were only too keen to take my robe *off* me and keep it off.'

'Last night was last night. I had other things on my mind then. Are you ready to talk now?'

What she really wanted was to tell him to go to hell and never come back, but instead she contented herself with getting out of bed and drawing herself up to her full five foot ten, knotting the tie belt of her robe extra firmly round her slim waist as she did so.

'If we have to talk, then, yes. I suppose so. But if you don't mind I would prefer to continue this conversation in another room.' And if he did mind, she couldn't care less. 'It really doesn't seem at all suitable for a bedroom.'

With her head held high she marched past him out of the bedroom and into the sitting room, leaving him with no option but to follow.

'Now,' she began, turning to face him. 'I believe you were about to tell me just what sort of a mistake I made—in your opinion—two years ago.'

'Love requires absolute trust,' he pronounced inexorably, severe as a magistrate pronouncing judgement. 'As I told you at the time. When your trust was challenged you broke immediately. You actually believed I had done those appalling things. You had no faith in—'

'Constantine...'

Unable to bear the distance between them any longer, Grace moved forward, reaching out to take hold of his hands. With her shadowed grey eyes fixed on his face, she gripped his fingers firmly, as if by doing so she could will him to believe her.

'Paula was my *sister*!'

'And I was your *fiancé*!' Constantine flung at her, snatching away his hands as if her touch had actually burned him.

Swinging away from her, he strode to the other side of the room to stand, staring out of the window at the street, still silent and unoccupied at this early hour of the weekend. The tension in his back and shoulders, the way his hands

were pushed deep into the pockets of his trousers told their
own story of the struggle he was having to bring his black
temper back under control.

At last he turned back again, and Grace quailed inwardly
at what she saw in his face. Anger and contempt etched
white lines around his nose and mouth, marking him outwardly with the feelings that burned deep inside.

'You couldn't trust me completely then, and I cannot
trust you now. And that is why you will never be my wife.'

Well, she'd asked for it, Grace told herself unhappily.
She'd insisted that he told her, and he had done just that,
coldly and concisely.

She'd admitted that she'd been partly to blame, but
Constantine's insistence on seeing everything in black and
white—that she should have believed him, and only him—
was every bit as uncompromising now as it had been then.
And he obviously wasn't about to change his mind.

If she had felt terrible at their last meeting two years ago,
now she felt a thousand times worse.

'So that's it,' she said drearily, thinking that this must
be what it felt like to stand in court and hear your death
sentence pronounced. 'That's all there is to say.'

'Not entirely.' Constantine surprised her by coming back
swiftly. 'The question is, where do we go from here?'

'Go? Is there anywhere to go?'

'Of course.'

He sounded stunned that she should have doubted it.

'But—but you don't love me. You don't trust me. So
what sort of basis do we have for any sort of relationship?'

'The perfect basis for the sort of relationship I have in
mind.'

'How could you call anything that's based on the way
you obviously feel about me a *relationship*?'

Constantine shrugged off the question as if it was just a
petty matter, not worth consideration.

'You don't trust me, but you *want* me,' he declared with callous indifference to the distress in her eyes. 'And I don't want to feel anything for you, but I find that I'm addicted to you—physically at least. I need you; I can't live without you. You're in my blood, in my soul, and I can't get free.'

'You make me sound like some particularly nasty virus,' Grace muttered bitterly. In his blood, and in his soul—but never, apparently, where she most wanted to be: in his heart. 'I take it this "relationship" you have in mind is not meant to be permanent?'

Another of those careless shrugs indicated that he neither knew nor cared.

'I have no place in my life for a wife right now, but that doesn't mean that I want to live without a woman and all the pleasures that involves. It seems to me, *pethi mou*, that the faults that mean you are not the sort of wife I am looking for are such that would make you the perfect mistress.'

'Careful, Constantine,' Grace snapped back, using deliberate satire to hide the pain that was wrenching her heart in two. 'If you sugar-coat your proposition like that I might not fully understand exactly how sordid it is. So what, precisely, makes for a perfect mistress in your book?'

'You,' he returned, casually succinct, moving to throw himself down into one of the cream armchairs.

Leaning back easily, his hands linked together behind his head, he looked for all the world as if he actually believed that the matter had been settled, the subject closed. The arrogance of the man! Grace stormed inwardly. Did he think that all he had to do was to snap his fingers and she would fall in with whatever he had planned?

'Wouldn't you be more comfortable sitting down?'

'I don't want to sit down! I'm quite comfortable exactly where I am!' Physically at least. Mentally was quite a different matter. 'And you can't call that an answer. I want to know exactly why I would be what you term ''the perfect mistress''.'

'Isn't it obvious?' Constantine drawled lazily. 'You're a beautiful woman. You turn me on just by looking at you...'

Last night she would have taken those words as the greatest compliment; now she was no longer so sure. Hating the feel of those darkly sensual obsidian eyes on her, Grace tugged at the neckline of her robe, pulling it closed over what little skin was actually exposed.

'And you have to admit that we're sexually compatible. We only have to touch and it's like a nuclear explosion. Add to that the fact that you're bright, intelligent, classy. You have a natural style which makes you the sort of woman I would be proud to have act as my hostess, or meet my friends or business colleagues.'

'Well, thank you kindly, sir.'

Grace couldn't stop herself from dipping a mocking curtsey.

Stretching indolently, he ran one hand through the crisp darkness of his hair, looking up at her through narrowed, assessing eyes.

'We will both know exactly where we stand from now on. You understand just what it is I want from you—that and no more. And I will know that the way you feel about me, that fundamental lack of trust you have for me, will always keep you just a little on edge. Because you can never be completely sure of me, you will always feel a touch insecure. You will always be afraid that I might leave you, drop you as easily as I picked you up, and as a result you will be prepared to go to great lengths to make sure I'm happy and keep me by your side.'

'You arrogant pig!'

'And of course...' Constantine cavalierly ignored her outburst '...I shall have the peace of mind that comes from knowing that, no matter what length of time we are together, as long as you mistrust me I shall be free from the possible complications of having you fall in love with me.'

Now Grace did want to sit down. If she stayed on her feet, she strongly suspected that in another moment her legs would give way and she would collapse into the nearest chair. Far better to subside into it more elegantly while she still could, and so not reveal her feeling to the cold-eyed monster sitting opposite.

'You seem to have it all worked out.'

Pain made her voice cold and tight. She could only thank God that she hadn't weakened and opened her heart to him earlier. She shuddered inside to think what might have been the repercussions of telling Constantine that she was still in love with him.

'But there's one thing you haven't taken into account in your careful calculations.'

'And that is?'

'You claim that I don't trust you, but if that's the case, how do you explain the last couple of nights? Why do you think I went to bed with you? Why did I make love with you?'

For the life of her she couldn't call it having sex. She didn't care if her use of the more emotive term 'making love' gave too much away. That was what it had been to her and she couldn't describe it as anything else.

'Why did I give—give you…?'

'The gift of your virginity?' Constantine finished for her when she floundered desperately, unable to complete the sentence. 'I was honoured—what man wouldn't be? But, oh, Grace, don't delude yourself. That wasn't trust. Trust had nothing to do with it. Instead, it was the result of another, very similar-sounding word, with many of the same letters but a very different meaning.'

His words made no sense to Grace, who could only stare at him blank confusion, her brain numbed by the constant

emotional battering she had taken from the moment she had
woken.

'I—don't…' she began hesitantly, making him sigh impatiently.

'Obviously I mean *lust*, *agape mou*,' he elucidated with
insulting care, as if explaining something to a not very
bright child. 'Hunger, desire, passion, sex…whatever label
you want to put on it. It all comes down to the same thing
in the end—the sort of craving that deprives you of reason,
leaves you incapable of thought.'

'No…' It was a low moan of despair, one she was unable
to inject any force into.

'*Yes,*' Constantine amended sharply. 'You were completely in its grip. You couldn't shake it off, could no more
deny it, say no to me, than you could have stopped yourself
from breathing.'

'No…'

Grace longed to close her eyes so that she didn't have
to see his dark, cruel face. She wanted to press her hands
over her ears to blot out the stream of terrible, distressing
words. But she knew that to do so would be tantamount to
telling Constantine he was right. Even the weak denial she
couldn't hold back had had the opposite effect she wanted,
confirming rather than contradicting his claims.

'You can't expect me to believe that, Grace!' he scorned,
leaning forward in his chair to emphasise the point, dark
eyes burning as they fixed on her pale face. 'Because I was
right there with you. I know exactly how it felt, because I
felt it too. I'd have gone out of what little was left of my
mind if I hadn't had you the night of the party, or last night,
or for many more nights to come.'

'But how many more nights?'

Once more an indifferent shoulder lifted, shrugging off
her shaken question.

'A hundred? A thousand? Who knows how long this fever will take to burn itself out?'

'So now I'm back to being an unpleasant infection once again!'

'You can call yourself what you like,' Constantine responded imperturbably. 'Just so long as you don't call the way you respond to me trust, or anything like it. Trust has nothing to do with it.'

'That's a very cynical interpretation of the facts.'

'Not at all. Look, I can smile and shake hands with business colleagues, or men I want to negotiate a deal with; I can work with them all day, laugh, share a meal—but I'll never, ever *trust* them. I know they're just waiting for me to slip up, show the slightest hesitation, the tiniest hint of insecurity and they'll stick the knife straight in, right in my back.'

'This isn't a business deal!'

'Isn't it?'

Constantine leaned back in his chair, steepling his long fingers together and pressing them against his lips for a moment.

'It strikes me that that's exactly what it is. A civilised trade-off.'

'Civilised!' Grace scoffed. 'You don't know the meaning of the word.'

'I believe I'm offering you a very fair exchange,' Constantine pointed out with a fiendish smile that sent shivers down her spine. 'I'll give you my time, my attention, my company. Materially, you will have anything and everything you want—you only have to ask. Your slightest whim will be answered.'

Materially. But what about emotionally? She knew she didn't have the nerve to frame the question. Deep down she already knew the answer was one that would break her heart.

So instead she forced herself to ask, 'And what would I have to give in return?'

She knew the answer to that too, and Constantine didn't let her down.

'You share my bed and my life. If I have to attend a reception, a dinner, party, you'll be there at my side. You'll come with me to the theatre, the opera, act as hostess in my home. In public you will be everything a man could want—a fantasy come true. You will be glamorous, elegant, beautiful…'

It was a long drawn-out sigh of sensual appreciation.

'So beautiful. I will dress you in the finest silks and velvet, deck you in the most precious jewels. You will want for nothing.'

Grace wished desperately that she could stop him. She didn't want to listen to this. Couldn't bear to hear the details of exactly what he wanted from her itemised in this way. But she couldn't find the strength to speak. She could only sit silently, wide-eyed and entranced, as that deep, husky, softly accented voice wove its spell over her.

'But wherever you are every man present will know that you are there with me. They will know that when the evening is over you will be going home with me. That you will be in my bed that night and every night. That I will be the man whose arms are round you and whose lips take yours. I will be the only one who makes love to you. The one who knows your body so intimately it will be like a brand on your skin. I, and I alone, will be the one who possesses your beauty.'

'Until you tire of me.'

Constantine's smile was bleak, cynical, totally without warmth.

'But if you are clever, as I believe you are, *agape mou*, then you can make sure that it will be a long, long time before your attractions begin to pall on me. So tell me, my sweet Grace, what is your answer?'

Could she do it? Could she be nothing more than Constantine's mistress? Wouldn't it be like selling her soul for a short time of pleasure? Everything inside her rebelled at the thought, nausea rising in her throat so that she had to swallow it down before she could speak.

'Grace?' Constantine prompted when she still couldn't find any words with which to answer him.

Twice she opened her mouth to say…to say what? No thought had formed in her mind, so that each time her voice failed her. She could only stare at him in blank silence, her grey eyes clouded and opaque.

'Perhaps you would like some time to think it over.'

Getting to his feet in an easy, lithe movement, Constantine checked the gold watch on his wrist, frowning as he did so.

'I really must be going. But I have booked a table at Reid's tomorrow night—for eight-thirty. I'll see you there…'

'No, you won't!' Anger pushed her upright too, standing up in a rush to face him defiantly.

His easy confidence, the total conviction that she would fall in with his plans without a murmur, was the last straw. He really believed that he could toss out a cold-blooded proposition like the one he had just detailed, one that was nothing more than a few crumbs flung casually in the direction of someone who was starving, and she would grasp it gratefully. He actually thought that when she had hoped for, dreamed of so much, she could be content with so little.

And the dreadful thing was that she was tempted. She had actually found herself considering his heartless scheme and the emotional death that went with it.

But not any more.

'I won't be coming.'

A swift on-and-off smile, brief as the flash of a neon light, mocked at her sincerity, incensing her further.

'I will wait at the restaurant for half an hour, no more...'

'You can wait till hell freezes over! I'm not coming! What you're offering isn't a relationship, it's slavery! You buy and I'm sold!'

'Grace, you do exaggerate! It's a sophisticated arrangement, one that suits many modern couples.'

'Well, it doesn't suit me! Forgive me if I'm not *modern* or *sophisticated* enough for you, but I'm not prepared to put up with it.'

'Don't give me your decision immediately.' Constantine cut across her tirade, reducing her to spluttering incoherence. 'Tomorrow night will be soon enough.'

He was heading for the door as he spoke, but just as he opened it he paused and looked back, subjecting her to a cool, narrow-eyed scrutiny.

'I shall leave the restaurant at nine exactly. If you know what's good for you, you'll be there.'

CHAPTER SEVEN

SHE *wasn't* going!

For the thousandth time since Constantine had walked out of the door, Grace repeated the command to herself over and over again.

She wasn't even going to *think* about going to the restaurant to meet him. She could be in no doubt at all that what Constantine really wanted was some sort of revenge on her for her lack of trust in him and his love for her, so was she going to help him carry out that revenge right to the bitter end?

No way! She had no intention of agreeing to his proposal, so he could sit there alone, wait his allotted half an hour alone, go home *alone*! He wasn't going to see her tomorrow night—or ever again!

And that was where her careful resolution faltered, weakening dreadfully.

How would she feel if she never saw Constantine again? After the pain, the aching loss, the sheer pointlessness of waking up day after day that she had endured the last time he had walked out of her life, could she possibly go through that again?

Could she turn her back on this one chance to keep him in her life, no matter what the conditions? And, even worse, knowing that she was the one who had put herself in this situation? That Constantine was prepared to continue a relationship with her but she had turned her back on him.

But what he was offering wasn't a relationship! Not the sort of relationship she wanted, anyway.

But she couldn't have what she wanted. The second-best

Constantine had offered her was all that was available. It was that or nothing. And she had been through nothing and knew it was like living in hell.

When she had phoned him to tell him the good news about Paula's confession he had been cold and distant. But what had worried her more was that he had refused to let her come to his apartment to explain, and had flatly rejected any suggestion that he might join her at her father's house.

In the end, the only compromise he had offered was that he would meet her at work, in the agency's main foyer. It was hardly the place for a tender, romantic reunion, but it had been the best Grace had been able to get out of him.

From the moment that he had come stalking into the room, it had been obvious that he was spoiling for a fight. His eyes had sparked with electricity, his face had been set into dangerous lines, his stance had been like that of an ill-tempered predator, bristling with aggression.

'Well?' He tossed the question at her as if he was a medieval knight, throwing down his gauntlet in challenge.

'Well, what?'

She wasn't ready for this. At the sight of him, so tall and dark and devastatingly sleek in the iron-grey suit and softer toned shirt, her thoughts had scattered here there and everywhere, and she couldn't even try and collect them together again.

'What do you want to say?'

'Isn't it obvious?' Anxiety made her edgy, her tone far too sharp.

'Not to me.'

'Constantine, please!'

This wasn't going at all the way she had expected. When she had anticipated gentleness and reassurance, his aggressive attitude rocked her sense of balance. Just what was going on here?

'Paula *lied*!' she said desperately. 'She made everything

up—she admitted it. There was no truth in anything she said.'

'And so?'

To her consternation he turned away from her, moving to the area of the foyer where comfortable chairs were provided for anyone needing to wait for their appointment. A pot of coffee was always kept warm on a hotplate, and Constantine lifted this now, gesturing in her direction.

'Drink?' he asked casually.

'No, I don't want a drink! Constantine, why are you behaving like this?'

'And how did you expect me to behave?' Constantine parried sardonically, glittering black eyes watching her closely.

'Oh, stop playing mind games!' She actually stamped her foot to emphasise her words, revealing how much on edge she was. 'I asked you here to tell you about Paula. I thought you'd be glad.'

She was subjected to a cold-eyed, cruelly assessing scrutiny that swept over her from the top of her smooth blonde head to her feet.

'Glad?' he said, his voice low and quiet but none the less bitingly emphatic. 'Glad to know that the little witch has finally told the truth? Glad to know that my name has been cleared? Why? It's of no importance.'

'No importance?' Grace couldn't believe what she was hearing. 'It's vitally important to you and me and our marriage.'

An arrogant flick of his hand dismissed her protest as totally insignificant.

'It's not even relevant,' he stated implacably.

Oh, dear God! It was as if all the whirling, conflicting emotions boiling up inside her had suddenly tangled themselves into a tight knot in her throat, making it difficult to breathe properly.

It was the quietness of his voice that did it. He hadn't even raised his tone above conversational level and yet what he'd said commanded complete attention.

'Not relevant?' she managed. 'But how…why?'

'Because there isn't going to be a marriage.'

'What? Of course there is! This was a terrible shock, but it's behind us now. It's in the past, and the future's what's ahead of us. A wonderful, bright, happy future together!'

'No way.'

At first Grace couldn't take in just what Constantine had said. The two stark, brutal syllables seemed to make no sense at all, repeating themselves over and over in her mind in a nonsensical litany that she couldn't comprehend. But then their true significance hit home like a blow to her heart.

'But, Constantine,' she cried, grabbing hold of his arm and holding on tight, 'you don't—you can't mean it!'

'I've never been more sure of anything in my life,' he returned intractably, shaking off her clinging hands with an abrupt movement. 'We are not going to be married. Not now, not ever.'

'But why…? What…?'

'Isn't it obvious?'

'Not to me!' she wailed. 'Constantine, don't do this to me. I love you!'

'No, you don't,' he shocked her rigid by declaring. 'You may have thought you did, but really you were just in love with the idea of being in love. Either that or you are even more shallow than I suspected and you were really only in love with my wealth.'

If he had taken her heart in his hands and squeezed it cruelly, she doubted if it would have hurt any more than this.

'That's a disgusting thought! I never… I couldn't…!'

Constantine shrugged off her protests with callous indifference.

'I'll give you credit for not being ruled by greed,' he conceded coldly. 'But love—no. You don't even know what the word means.'

'Of course I do!' Desperately Grace tried to will him to believe her. 'It means caring, and sharing, honesty, faithfulness, and…and…'

'And *trust*,' Constantine inserted savagely when she floundered, too terrified of the black, baleful glare he turned on her to be able to continue. 'The sort of trust that believes without question, without doubt, without thought! If you cannot trust your husband or wife-to-be, then who can you trust? And if you don't trust them, no matter what, then you have no right to be thinking of marrying them. Without trust, *pethi mou*, there is no love, and without love there will never be a marriage.'

'But I love you!' It was the only thing she could think of to say.

'You love me now—when your sister has confessed to her lies. But when I told you they were lies you wouldn't even listen. Then you were so sure you were right, so ready to believe someone else—anyone else—before me.'

'I—I didn't know.'

'You didn't need to *know*!' he flung at her. 'You only had to believe. You were incapable of that belief and so we have no future together.'

No future. The words exploded inside Grace's head, blasting her back to the present with a shock. No future.

So do you need any further evidence why you would be have to be crazy to get tangled up with a man like Constantine once again? Grace asked herself now, as the end of the day approached and she was twelve hours closer to the moment when she would have to make her decision. Did she really want to be involved with a man who could be so callous, so unfeeling, so totally unresponsive to the distress he had caused her?

'Oh, go to bed!' she remonstrated with herself, realising that it was well after midnight and she still hadn't come to any sort of a conclusion. 'Go to bed and sleep on it and things will look so much better in the morning.'

Or, rather, they might have done, if she had managed any decent sort of sleep at all. But the truth was that she had spent what remained of the night tossing and turning, unable to settle, the scene with Constantine that morning playing over and over inside her head like a film projected on to the screen of her mind.

And when she had drifted off it was to be plagued by heated, erotic dreams in which Constantine's long, hot body was tangled with her own, his hands on her skin, his mouth caressing the aching points of her breasts. So that when she woke she was wrung out and exhausted, feeling as if she had had no rest at all.

She couldn't go through it all again, she admitted. Couldn't endure the loss and the loneliness all over again. She had lived through that hell once; it would destroy her to have to endure it once again.

She hadn't been able to sway him then, and it seemed that his heart was still as implacably set against her now as it had been then. Knowing Constantine, she really shouldn't have expected otherwise.

But this time he had offered her the lifeline of a way to share his life, not as his wife, but as his mistress. It might not be the outcome she had dreamed of, but could she really turn her back on the chance to be something to him, however second-rate it might be?

It had taken just one night of deprivation, one night of doing without Constantine's touch, his kisses, his caresses, to make her admit to herself that she was addicted to him, and to his lovemaking. She couldn't live without him. It would destroy her even to try.

And he had said that it could take a long time before he tired of her. A hundred—a thousand nights.

A hundred nights were nothing. Three months and a little more. They could fly past in the blink of an eye. But a *thousand* nights…!

A thousand nights made up almost three years. That was longer than the time she had lived through since Constantine had broken off their engagement, and *that* had seemed like an eternity.

Surely in three years something could change. If she could only…

But she wouldn't let herself think about that. She couldn't allow herself to dream, because that was to risk the agony of having those dreams destroyed and losing everything she had yearned for.

She would take the little Constantine offered, for as long as he would let her. She had to. She could do nothing else. She would die if he walked out of her life now.

That moment would come, of course. One day. But right now that day was a long way ahead. Hopefully, in the intervening space of time she would grow a second skin, become strong enough to handle the inevitable when she no longer had any choice. But that was the future. What she had to deal with was the present.

And so she made her preparations for the evening ahead of her. She showered and washed her hair, blow-drying the silken strands until they gleamed like polished gold. She sprayed her body with her favourite perfume then applied a subtle make-up, emphasising her silvery grey eyes, the soft fullness of her mouth. After slipping on her newest and sexiest dress, a sleeveless Lycra tube the colour of rich clotted cream, she turned to contemplate her reflection in the mirror.

The dress clung in all the right places, emphasising and flattering the feminine curves of her body. Sheer silky stockings and delicate strappy sandals in the finest Italian leather made her legs look endless, touched with a subtle sheen. And above her wide cheekbones her eyes looked enormous, wide and brilliant, luminous with a mixture of excitement and apprehension.

Finally, as the last, finishing touch, she took the delicate bangle Constantine had given her from its padded box and slid it over her hand, letting it hang loosely around her fine-boned wrist.

There! She was as ready as she would ever be. She looked calm, elegant, supremely in control. So what if it was all an illusion? At least the tension that was tying her nerves into knots, the feeling like the fluttering of a thousand trapped butterflies beating their wings frantically in the pit of her stomach didn't show on the surface. She knew her appearance would deceive most people. Her only worry was, would it convince the person who mattered most?

Constantine was already at his table by the time she arrived. He had a drink before him, but no food. He obviously did not intend to dine alone.

As she paused in the doorway to study him for a moment she saw him push back his shirt-cuff to check the time on his watch. The small gesture made her smile secretly to herself. She had planned her arrival carefully for just this effect. She had barely five minutes left of the half an hour he had allotted her. It would do him good to be forced to wonder if in fact she was coming at all. Schooling herself to move slowly, nonchalantly, she strolled forward.

'Constantine…'

His dark head snapped up quickly, narrowed black eyes fixing on her face. So he hadn't been quite as sure of himself as he had seemed. This time her smile actually touched her lips.

'So you came.'

Impeccably polite as always, he was already on his feet, pulling out a chair for her opposite his own.

'Did you really think I wouldn't?'

She was proud of her voice. It sounded cool, light, unconcerned, which was just the way she wanted it.

'It may be cold outside,' Constantine drawled dryly. 'But I don't think it's quite bad enough to make hell freeze over just yet.'

Using the actions of shaking out her napkin and placing it on her lap to avoid having to look him directly in the face, Grace inclined her head in acknowledgement of his reference to her defiant declaration of the day before.

'It's a woman's privilege to change her mind. Surely you knew that.'

'And have you changed your opinion of the arrangement I offered? Or do you still see it as a form of captivity and humiliation?'

Grace reached for her water glass and took a careful sip in order to ease her suddenly parched throat.

'I prefer to see it as a business deal. One in which you pay handsomely for the sort of services I provide. And I intend to take full advantage of your generosity.'

'I wouldn't expect anything else.' Constantine's tone was darkly sardonic. 'That way at least we both know where we stand. So, do we shake hands to confirm our agreement?'

It was what she had come here to do, Grace told herself furiously. What she had told herself she wanted. So why should she find herself hesitating now, when the matter was all but decided?

'Second thoughts, Grace?' Constantine questioned when she sat still in her chair, unable to move.

With a struggle Grace forced a smile on to her lips, and made herself meet that searching ebony gaze head-on.

'Not at all,' she returned smoothly. 'You see, I really think that in this matter I've got the better half of the bargain.'

'In that case...'

He held out his hand and this time she was able to put her own into his, not even flinching at the inevitable sense of electrical shock as skin touched skin, palm against palm.

It was as his firm grasp closed over her fingers that she realised that the hand she held out was the one on which she wore the gold bangle Constantine had given her. And it was only now that she remembered that this particular piece of jewellery was usually described as a slave bracelet.

CHAPTER EIGHT

'GRACIE, darling, you look decidedly peaky these days! What's the problem? Is that Greek of yours not looking after you properly?'

'Not at all.' Grace switched on a smile in response to Ivan's teasing question. 'On the contrary, he's looking after me only too well.'

'Oh, I *see*.'

The exaggerated way Ivan rolled his eyes made it plain just what sort of 'looking after' he had in mind.

'No, Ivan, I do not mean sex!' This time her smile was more genuine, less forced. 'Well, not just sex! He's always giving me presents as well.'

Presents. If the truth were told, she was drowning in the things. From the very first, almost from the moment she and Constantine had come to their agreement, he had proceeded to put his half of the bargain into action—with a vengeance.

That first day he had arrived with another gift-wrapped box, much larger than the one the bangle had come in.

'I promised you something much more flattering,' he had told her. 'This is to replace the one that I ripped.'

'You don't sound exactly apologetic about it,' Grace responded, unfastening the silver and white ribbon fastened around the box.

'Apologetic?'

Arrogant black brows rose in disdain merely at the word.

'I do not apologise for destroying something less than third-rate and replacing it with something much more ap-

113

propriate. Something more suited to the beautiful woman who is to wear it.'

That *beautiful* became a two-edged sword, the huskily spoken compliment taking on another, less welcome significance, when Grace finally opened the box and carefully took out its contents.

I shall buy you a better one, he had declared, scorning the homely comfort of her towelling robe. And the simple nightdress she'd worn underneath had been ripped in two at the height of their shared passion. Now Constantine had fulfilled his promise.

But the robe and nightgown she unfolded carried a very different message from the clothing they were to replace. Made of the finest heavy silk-satin, they were blatantly, undeniably sexy. The rich, deep scarlet colour was something she would never have chosen for herself, and the simple, severe lines of the nightdress couldn't hide the fact that the neckline was slashed as low as it could go, and there was very little back at all.

It was perfectly obvious just what had been going through Constantine's mind when he'd bought them. They were the sort of clothes that a man would give to his lover. They were not meant to be worn for any length of time but simply slipped on in order to seduce and tantalise, to arouse passion mainly at the thought of taking them off again. They didn't so much scream sex as murmur it seductively, but Grace felt that if they had borne the label 'Lingerie for Your Mistress', then she wouldn't have been surprised.

'They're—lovely.' It was impossible to hide the catch in her voice, so she could only pray he would take it for excitement.

'Not as beautiful as the woman they were chosen for, Grace, *pethi mou…*' Constantine's voice deepened noticeably on the last words, his accent thickening markedly. 'Put them on. Model them for me.'

'I don't…' Grace demurred, ducking her head to avoid the burning intensity of his gaze. 'I'm not sure…'

It was one thing to agree to Constantine's terms in a rush of determined resolve at the end of two days of wavering backwards and forwards, quite another to play out the part of the mistress in cold blood, so to speak.

'Don't be shy, my Grace,' that soft, husky voice cajoled. 'You know how I feel about that glorious body of yours. And besides, there isn't a single inch of you that I haven't seen or touched or kissed…'

But that had been in the heat of passion, when she had been head over heels in love and had believed she was loved in return. It was quite, quite different from modelling this slinky sliver of silk, parading up and down before Constantine's coolly appraising eyes, knowing that all he felt for her was desire, the lust he had described to her so eloquently before.

'Constantine…I can't…'

But he took her in his arms and kissed her softly, persuasively. With calculated skill he gently woke her senses, roused the hunger that lay only just beneath the surface and brought it swiftly to clamouring, urgent life.

In the end, the nightdress and robe weren't needed. The aching need that swept over them like a tidal wave drove away any thought of hesitation or titillation. Neither was prepared to wait, to allow time for the sort of love games Constantine had originally had in mind. But later, with their need for each other temporarily appeased, Grace was persuaded to slip them on, which, of course, started the whole thing all over again…

That night had set the pattern for all the rest. By day they were both busy with their jobs, but it seemed to Grace that she was only functioning on automatic pilot, barely fully awake or aware of her world. She only truly came alive in the evenings, when Constantine sometimes took her out for a meal or to the theatre, as he had promised, but more often than not they simply stayed in her flat, in her bed.

It didn't seem to matter how many times they made love, it was never enough. Each shattering orgasm only eased the craving just long enough for them to recover, for their breathing to slow, the frantic pounding of their hearts to ease.

But even as they lay spent, their sweat-slicked bodies splayed in total abandonment on the bed, the insidious hunger was creeping through every cell, every nerve, wakening them, tormenting them until they could do nothing but reach for each other once more. In the end, only the total exhaustion that drove them into the oblivion of sleep granted them any reprieve from the incessant demands of their bodies.

'...in September. Will that be okay?'

'What?'

Blushing fierily, Grace realised that while she had been lost in her erotic memories Ivan had been speaking to her and she hadn't heard a thing.

'I'm sorry—my mind was elsewhere.'

'Obviously!' Ivan's tone was arch. 'And I can guess just where it was. Gracie, darling, you really have got it bad. And what about the gorgeous Constantine? Is he as deeply involved as you are? Does this mean we can soon expect to hear the sound of wedding bells?'

Grace shuffled a pile of papers quite unnecessarily, moving them from one side of her desk to another in order to hide the pain that question brought her. She was sure it must show in her eyes, betraying her innermost feelings to someone who knew her as well as Ivan did.

'It's a little early for that yet,' she hedged awkwardly.

'Grace, you've been back together for nearly four months

now. The first time round you'd announced your engagement by this point.'

'Yes, well, we did rather rush into it then. We want to take things more steadily this time—be sure of what we feel.'

The bitter irony of that remark stabbed sharply even as she spoke. If anything, both she and Constantine were much surer of their feelings this time round than they had been last time. It was the conflict between those two very different emotions that kept them apart.

'So what was it you were telling me?' With a determined effort she managed to push the misery that thought brought her to the back of her mind. 'Something about September?'

Ivan nodded.

'The annual meet-and-greet, drinks and networking do,' he said, referring to the yearly reception the advertising agency held for their major clients. 'Bob Cartwright suggested the last Friday in September. Will that be okay for you?'

'Let me check… Yes, that'll be fine. I suppose that means I shall have to spend another evening being nice to Les Harvey.' A faint grimace twisted her soft mouth at the thought of the unwanted attentions the owner of a furniture chain constantly subjected her to whenever they met. 'That'll be fun.'

'Maybe by then you'll have a brand-new engagement ring to show you're off-limits.' Ivan's laughter turned to a frown as he saw the way colour leached from her cheeks at his comment. 'Are you sure you're okay? Grace—you're not…?'

'Of course I'm not!'

With what she hoped was an airy gesture, Grace waved away the idea that she might be pregnant.

There was no chance of that. From the first, Constantine had made his position only too clear.

'We'll have to lay down a few ground rules,' he told her bluntly, even before their meal had been served on the night she'd had dinner with him at Reid's. 'For one thing, we've been playing with fire, sexually, and that has to stop. I'll make arrangements for you to see my doctor tomorrow.'

'I have my own doctor!' Grace declared, bristling with indignation. 'If you're talking about contraception, then—'

'Of course that's what I'm talking about! Believe me, I am not usually as irresponsible and careless as I have been the past couple of days. But I never quite anticipated that things would go this far this fast. I don't need any unwanted complications.'

'That makes two of us,' Grace muttered. Of course, the woman who was not considered suitable to be his wife was in no way fit to be the mother of the next generation of the Kiriazis family. 'But how do you know it hasn't happened already?'

'You assured me it was safe.' The words were accusatory, sparking her volatile temper.

'I said I thought it was! I'm not infallible!'

In spite of the fact that her nerves quailed inside at the problems that would ensue if she did turn out to be pregnant, she couldn't help imagining it just for a moment. Just the thought of a baby, girl or boy, with Constantine's dark hair and eyes was enough to twist a knife deep into an already vulnerable heart, making hot tears sting her eyes so that she had to blink furiously to fight them back.

'All the more reason to consult Dr Carr.'

Constantine might simply have been discussing the meal they were eating, rather than the possibility that she might have conceived his son or daughter. The casual indifference of his tone had Grace gritting her teeth against the sort of outburst that would have created a very ugly scene indeed in the elegant restaurant.

'I said I have my own—'

'And I said you'll see mine!'

He hadn't raised his voice, but the forceful emphasis of his words was enough to silence Grace far more effectively than any shout.

'I promised you the best of everything while we are together, and I intend to keep that promise. As long as you are mine, you will have the finest medical attention money can buy...'

He made her sound like a prized brood mare, Grace thought bitterly. With one vital difference, though. He would want a horse to become pregnant, while he had made it plain that it would not please him if she did.

'And if there should be any repercussions from the nights we spent together—well, we'll cross that bridge when we come to it.'

Much as she wanted to, Grace didn't have the nerve to ask just what crossing that bridge might involve. When they had been engaged before, Constantine had made it plain that he wanted children very much. *That* Constantine would have welcomed the idea of a baby, whether its conception had been planned or not.

But the man who sat before her now, dark eyes hooded, his stunning features shuttered, his thoughts closed against her, was a very different prospect from the man she had so wanted to marry. *This* Constantine was an unknown quantity, and she had no idea which way he might jump if he was forced into a situation that was not to his liking.

Which still didn't stop her from being weak enough to pray that she *was* pregnant, no matter what problems that might bring. And on the morning when she woke with the familiar ache low in her body that told her her prayers had not been answered she was so desolated that she had to hurry to the bathroom to hide her misery.

Turning the shower on at full power, she stood under it for a long time, letting the rush of the water hide the tears that streamed down her cheeks until she had wept her fill and was calm enough to face Constantine again.

'I think perhaps I'd better have words with Constantine.' Ivan's voice broke into Grace's reverie, making her wonder just how long she had been wrapped up in it, oblivious to the fact that he was still standing there. 'You really are not your usual lovely self. What you need is a holiday, somewhere hot…'

'What do you feel about a holiday—somewhere hot and sunny?' Constantine said that night, making her start with surprise. 'Now what have I said?' he asked, frowning as she stared at him in bemusement.

'Oh—sorry—it's just that that's exactly what Ivan said he thought I needed. He—he said he thought I looked a bit tired… Did you have anywhere particular in mind?' she hurried on, fearful that Constantine might question her further. She could just imagine his reaction if she told him of Ivan's speculations as to exactly why she might be tired.

'I thought we could spend some time on Skyros.'

'Skyros,' Grace echoed, struggling to keep her voice even.

She had only once visited the beautiful Greek island where Constantine had been born and where his parents still had their family home. That trip had changed her life because it had been there, on a beautiful early spring evening, that Constantine had asked her to be his wife.

Just for a second, a wild, crazy thought flared in her mind, but she clamped down on it hard before it even had time to form properly, let alone take root. She couldn't allow herself to dream of another special evening, another proposal. Constantine had made it painfully clear that nothing like that lay in the future and she would only be deluding herself if she even considered it.

'Do your parents still live there?' she asked carefully,

stacking the plates they had used for their meal, ready to take them into the kitchen.

'Of course.'

Something about his casually dismissive tone rubbed the wrong way over nerves already very close to the surface of her skin.

'There isn't any "of course" about it!' she snapped sharply. 'We've been together now for almost four months, but we might have just met for all that I know about you. You keep me strictly on the edges of your life, giving me time only when you can spare it from the demands of your work. We only ever meet here, or in some neutral place like a theatre or a restaurant! I'm never allowed to set foot in your home...'

'I thought you wouldn't want to,' Constantine inserted harshly, stunning her into silence.

'I—I don't understand,' she managed when at last she could speak again. 'Why wouldn't I...?'

'One word,' he returned laconically. 'Paula.'

'Paula?' she echoed dazedly. 'But why?'

'Grace, I still have the same apartment that I lived in before. I assumed that you wouldn't want to set foot in the place because being there would remind you of the fight we had over... Here, let me take those!'

Moving forward swiftly, he took the plates from Grace's suddenly insecure hold, grasping them just in time before she let them drop in shock.

It was the last thing she had expected. It had never even crossed her mind that Constantine had kept her away from his apartment in order to protect her from the unhappy memories she might have of the place. If anything, she had thought that he believed that as his mistress it was her place to stay at home and wait until her lord and master could spare the time to visit her, that he didn't want his flat sullied by her presence.

'Constantine…' she said shakily. 'Tell me about Paula.'

He had taken the plates into the kitchen and she heard him deposit them on the draining board with a distinct crash. But if her question had thrown him at all, then he showed no sign of it when he appeared in the doorway again, once more completely back in control, the assured, composed man she knew only too well.

'What about Paula?'

'The truth.'

'The truth?' he muttered cynically. 'Now would that be her truth or the one you thought…?'

'Constantine! We both know she lied. But what went before that? Because there was something—I know there was.'

'You mean the way she came on to me? From the first moment we met she was all over me. I couldn't turn up at your home without meeting her on the stairs half dressed, or in some skirt that barely covered her behind. I thought I'd made it plain that I wasn't interested, but you know what they say about a woman scorned.'

'Why didn't you tell me?'

The look he turned on her was one of pure contempt.

'And you'd have believed every word?'

'If you'd told me, I would! I *would*!' she protested at Constantine's snort of disbelieving laughter.

'You didn't believe a word I said when I said I'd never seduced her.'

How she wished she could deny it, but it was only now that she realised the wrong she had done him. She should have trusted him. Should have refuted Paula's accusation at once.

'I should have believed you…' she said shakily, looking up into his darkly watchful eyes.

But even as she spoke she saw some change in his expression, the tiniest flicker of something behind the controlled mask that was all he ever showed her. In the space of a heartbeat she was transported back to that day over two years before, hearing her own angry, accusatory voice—and seeing a similar betraying reaction in Constantine's face.

It hadn't been all her own fault. It hadn't been just her lack of trust that had torn them apart. There had been something more...

'But you were feeling guilty about something that day!' she flung at him, wincing as his grip tightened on her arms.

'*Theos!* You never stop, do you?'

A stream of darkly eloquent and obviously obscene Greek left her in no doubt as to the violence of his feeling.

'Even now, even knowing your sister's part in it, you still cannot bring yourself to—'

'I *do* trust you!'

'Of course you do!' he derided, releasing her so abruptly that she was badly off balance and had to reach out hastily to steady herself against a chair. 'You can say the word so easily, *pethi mou*, but it is only a word! There is no real feeling behind it.'

'Because you won't let me *show* the feeling!' Grace protested vehemently. 'You had me tried, convicted and condemned before I even had a chance to speak! I'm only fit to be your mistress, nothing more! So what makes you the moral judge in all this, Mr Oh-So-Perfect Kiriazis? Why don't you acknowledge that you still have something on your conscience that you're not admitting to?'

Oh, *why* had she had to go and say that? Why couldn't she keep her big mouth shut and let the storm pass over her head for once? She could see Constantine's withdrawal in his face, stretching the skin tight over the sculpted cheekbones before he actually moved away from her. How she wished the foolish, unthinking words back, all the while knowing it was completely impossible.

'I think we'll forget about dinner tonight.' Each word was cold and clipped, completely without emotion. 'Perhaps we have spent too much time cooped up together. I, for one, could do with a break.'

'Constantine, no...' Grace began, but he ignored her, his face closed against her, hard and uncompromising, as if carved from granite.

'I have to go to New York on Sunday, so I'll be away for a week or so. I'll call you when I get back.'

Looking round for his jacket, he snatched it up and began pulling it on.

'Think about the holiday. When I get back would suit me—oh, here...'

Sliding one hand into his jacket pocket, he pulled out a gold-coloured box and tossed it carelessly on to the nearest chair.

'I thought you might like that.'

'Oh, Constantine, not another present!' Grace protested. 'I don't need any more jewellery.'

But she was talking to empty air. Constantine had already gone, marching from the room without so much as a kiss goodbye. The sound of the door slamming to behind him had an ominously final emphasis to it.

But at least he had said he would call. And he had told her to think about the holiday. That had to mean that he was planning on coming back. He had to come back. She couldn't have driven him away again!

Drearily she surveyed the box that lay on the cushions, her heart feeling as if it was being slowly torn in two.

Another present. Earlier that day she had felt as if she was drowning in the gifts that Constantine had brought her. Now she felt as if she was very definitely going down for the third time. Couldn't he see that there was only one thing she wanted from him?

But of course the one thing she needed from Constantine

was the one thing he was unable to give her. He didn't love her; he had made that quite plain.

Materially, you will have anything and everything you want. Inside her head she could hear Constantine's voice as clearly as if he was actually standing behind her.

Well, he'd kept his promise and been as generous as he'd said, in every way but emotionally. And it was that lack of emotional response that was slowly killing her.

'Oh, Constantine!'

Miserably she sank down on the chair and picked up the small golden box, plucking listlessly at the ribbon around it. It must have been fastened rather more loosely than she had realised because it came adrift at once, the lid falling off and its contents spilling out on to her lap. And what she saw made her catch her breath in sharp distress.

'Oh, no!'

The necklace was pure gold, obviously of the finest workmanship. It was made up of twelve separate links, and each link was in the shape of a leaf, a delicate piece of work with all the lines and veins perfectly traced out in the fine metal.

One for every month of the year.

It had been almost in the first week they had met that she had told Constantine of the superstition that if you caught a falling autumn leaf before it hit the ground, then it guaranteed a happy month for the following year. He had listened in silence, a wry smile curving his lips at the eccentricities of the crazy English people, but a few days later he had brought her a small carved wooden box that had made a strange rustling sound when she shook it.

'Constantine? What on earth...?' she had asked in confusion.

'Open it,' he had urged. 'Open it and see, *agape mou.*'

Her hands had trembled so that she had had trouble lifting the lid, but when she had she'd found herself staring at a small collection of tiny leaves, each one crisp and bright in the tawny colours of autumn. When she'd counted them, she had found that there were twelve exactly.

'One for every month of the year,' Constantine had told her. 'To guarantee that every month will be the happiest you have spent, because we will spend it together. And when that year is up I will bring you twelve more, and again at the end of the following year, for the rest of our lives. So that the time we are together will always be the happiest part of your life.'

But of course that promise had never been fulfilled. Before that first year was over Paula had spread her malicious lies, Grace and Constantine had fought, and the marriage had been called off.

'Oh, Constantine! Constantine!' Grace sobbed, holding the necklace tight against her, the tears streaming unchecked down her colourless cheeks.

She was weeping for the innocent, gentle days, when the gifts Constantine had given her had been so special, so simple, not the unwanted expensive luxuries he now showered her with. The days when she had known that she loved him and had believed that she was loved so deeply in return.

But most of all she was weeping in despair at the thought that those days had been destroyed so completely, and there seemed no hope at all of them ever being brought back to life ever again.

CHAPTER NINE

GRACE stepped into the cool of the shady hallway and sighed faintly, flexing her shoulders to ease their stiffness.

'Tired?' Constantine's keen hearing had caught her re-action and he slanted narrowed black eyes in her direction.

Wearily she nodded, wishing it was really that simple.

'It was a long journey—and it's hot!'

She plucked uncomfortably at the smart grey trouser suit she was wearing. It had been quite appropriate for London's much cooler August, but here, in the baking temperatures of the Sporades group of islands set in the Aegean Sea, it was definitely too heavy.

'You should be thankful for the helicopter,' Constantine returned dryly. 'It would have been a much longer journey if we'd come by ferry or hydrofoil. Even under ideal conditions the ferry can take up to seven hours to get here from Athens. Skyros is the most remote island in this group—that's what gives it its character.'

'It certainly has that!' Grace commented, thinking of the old men in their baggy blue trousers, black caps and flat leather sandals with many straps, the women wearing long headscarves they had passed on the way to the villa. 'Driving here was like going back in time.'

'The islanders certainly cling on to the old customs.'

'But your family didn't. You wouldn't be where you are now if that had been the case.'

'True.' Constantine nodded his dark head. 'My grand-father grabbed at the twentieth century as hard as he could. He wanted more than just this small, rugged island... Ah, Florina...'

He greeted the small, stocky woman dressed all in black who had appeared at the far end of the corridor.

'You remember Miss Vernon?'

Florina's only response was a swift duck of her head in Grace's general direction. It was only too obvious that she remembered very well, but that that memory included the way the younger woman had behaved towards Constantine, the adored only son of the Kiriazis family. Mute hostility and criticism were stamped on the blunt features.

Grace's smile faded rapidly, her small white teeth worrying at the softness of her bottom lip. She shouldn't have come. Deep down, she had known that from the start. It was impossible not to contrast her arrival today with the time she had first visited Skyros, two and a half years before.

Then she had felt as if she'd been floating six inches or more above the ground. Already head over heels in love with Constantine, she had been idyllically happy, so full of joy that nothing could have brought her down. She had adored this large, century-old stone house with its red slate roof set on the hilly coastline of a remote bay in the north of the island, and it had seemed that everyone, from Constantine's parents to the servants who tended his home, had loved her too.

But now Florina's grudging welcome had brought her hard up against how very different the reality was this time around.

'Florina!' Constantine's tone was sharp and he added something, obviously a rebuke, in stern Greek. 'Florina will take you to your room,' he added, turning to Grace. 'I'm sure you will need to rest and freshen up after travelling for so long, and I have some phone calls to make.'

That was different too, Grace reflected miserably as she followed Florina's stiffly hostile back up the polished wood staircase and across the landing, turning to the right. The last time she'd been here, Constantine had taken her to her room himself.

They had arrived while his parents were out, and he had shown her all round the house himself, almost boyish in his enthusiasm, his determination that she should see his childhood home. And when he had finally led her into the small, cool room at the back of the house, he had gathered her into his arms and kissed her thoroughly.

Clearly he had no intention of doing any such thing now. And, equally clearly, the unwelcoming Florina knew all about her change in status. The bedroom the maid led her to was not the comfortable single one, decorated in soft pastels, that she had slept in before, but a much larger one, its crisp navy and white décor uncompromisingly masculine. A room that seemed dominated by the king-size bed with a beautifully carved wooden headboard that stood in the centre.

'Your bags will be brought up here. Would you like anything to eat, *despinis*?' Florina asked stiltedly.

'Nothing, thank you—but I would like something to drink—some tea, perhaps.'

What she really wanted was to be left alone, to have a little time to think. With another silent nod the woman turned and left the room and Grace sank down thankfully on the bed. Had she made a terrible mistake in coming to Skyros?

Constantine had been distant, both physically and mentally, for the past fortnight or so. Ever since the night that she had accused him of still hiding something from her, the night when he had given her the gold leaf necklace, he had been difficult and unapproachable. So much so that she had begun to wonder.

Was it possible that the accusation she had flung at him that night had some grounding in fact? Had she touched on some nerve, ripped away some carefully protective mask that Constantine had been concealing the truth behind, and come closer to the truth than she dared admit?

But what? Paula had admitted that her story was lies, so what else could Constantine have to feel guilty about?

Unless…

Wearily, Grace kicked off her sandals and curled up on the wide, comfortable bed. Resting her head back against the soft, downy pillows, she stared up at the white-painted ceiling, lost in thought.

Was it possible that something Constantine had done, something he'd said, had given her sister the idea in the first place? Or could there have been someone else? Someone other than her sister, someone she had never suspected? Or, even worse, had her then fiancé got to her sister and forced her to say that her story had been completely made up?

No!

No sooner had the thought insinuated its nasty way into her mind than she pushed it away again. She couldn't let it take root or it would destroy her.

But Constantine had been hiding something…

The fatigue of the journey was overwhelming, sleep claiming her before she could even begin to work it out.

The sound of movement brought her slowly awake, blinking dreamily, her unfocused eyes gradually becoming aware of the long, masculine figure, casual in white polo shirt and black jeans, seated in the chair opposite the bed.

'You sleep like a child,' a soft, accented voice murmured on a note of amusement. 'Lying absolutely still, with your cheek pillowed on your hand.'

'Constantine!'

Shock had her sitting upright in a rush, confusion filling her at the thought of being observed while she had been so completely unaware.

'When did you come in?'

'I brought you the drink you asked for.'

'I would have thought that Florina…'

Constantine's beautiful mouth twisted in sardonic humour.

'I would have thought that Florina had done enough damage to your self-esteem already,' he commented with an underlying dark thread of disapproval that made Grace shiver in sympathy for the unfortunate Florina at the thought of that censure being turned on the other woman.

'She's only being loyal,' she demurred quietly, still rubbing sleep from her eyes. 'You told me yourself the Greeks are a proud race. If I offended one then I offended all.'

'Loyal and discourteous,' Constantine declared sharply. 'Whatever, I thought you would prefer it if I brought you your tea.'

A wave of one strong hand indicated the tray on the bedside table.

'Oh—I'm sorry—I must have dozed off. I'll drink—' She broke off abruptly as he shook his dark head. 'No?'

'It will be completely cold and undrinkable by now.'

'Why? How long have you been there?'

Only now did she become aware of the change in the light in the room, the shadows that spoke of the end of the day, revealing that she had slept for far longer than she had realised.

'An hour. Perhaps more.' A movement of his broad shoulder shrugged off the question.

'An *hour*!'

Grace smoothed a distracted hand over her disordered hair, struggling to collect her thoughts. She found it intensely disturbing to think of Constantine sitting there, silently watching her while she had been so unaware of his presence, so vulnerable, so exposed.

It was crazy to think that way, she knew, when all those other days and nights in her bed he had seen her wearing far less, or every bit as deeply asleep. But somehow now, with the worrying thoughts that had been preying on her mind still lingering inside her head, she found it so much more difficult to cope with the idea. What if she had talked in her sleep, murmuring something she had tried so hard to keep from him in her waking life?

'You must have been bored stiff!'

Nervously she swung her feet to the floor, hunting for her shoes.

'You should have woken me.'

'Quite the opposite,' Constantine contradicted. 'I was quite content. It was a rare opportunity to see the real Grace, the woman you—'

'I don't know what you mean.'

Uneasiness made her tone sharp. *Had* she said something? Or had some other thing, some betraying movement or gesture, given her away? Had Constantine somehow been able to read in her sleeping face the love she tried so hard to conceal from him in the daytime?

'This is the real me.'

A wild gesture swept her hands from the top of her head and down over her body, drawing his obsidian eyes with it.

'You make it sound as if I'm someone else with you— as if I'm playing a part. This *is* the real me!' she added more emphatically when the swift narrowing of his eyes seemed to question the vehemence of her response. 'What you see is what you get. If you don't like it, you can lump it.'

'Oh, I like it…' Constantine assured her smoothly. 'I like it very much. In fact…'

With a slow, indolent movement, he levered himself up out of his chair and leaned towards her. Instinctively Grace lifted her face for the kiss that she knew was coming, all her stiffness, the prickling indignation, melting away from her at the first touch of his lips.

His mouth was soft on hers, gently cajoling, the sensual slide of his tongue easing her lips apart. Strong hands tangled in her hair, holding her so close that she could smell the scent of his skin, the sun-warmed fragrance that was essentially his and his alone.

'I'd like to see so much more of you...'

Gently insistent pressure was pushing her back on to the bed and at first Grace went with it, her body limp and pliable in his hands. But then a sudden unwelcome recollection, the memory of the worries that she had been struggling with before she'd fallen asleep, had her stiffening again.

'No...' The word escaped her lips before she had time even to think about it.

It obviously surprised Constantine almost as much as it did herself to hear it.

'No?' he questioned sharply, stilling abruptly.

The swift frown that drew his dark brows together made plain his displeasure—and no wonder! Never before had she had the nerve to say no. 'No' was not supposed to come into their relationship. It was one of the unwritten, unspoken rules of their arrangement. Constantine showered her with luxuries and she provided sex on demand. And so far both of them had kept scrupulously to their share of the bargain.

'Constantine, please!' Grace said edgily, hunting for a reason that would convince him without revealing any of the concerns that were in her mind. 'I—I feel dreadful.'

Those brilliant black eyes moved over her appraisingly once again, raising stinging trails of awareness on her skin, as if they had actually touched her.

'You look fine...'

'I've been sleeping in my clothes! I feel hot and sticky

and...' She wrinkled her nose in genuine distress as she looked down at her crumpled clothes. 'And disgusting. I need a shower to freshen up.'

The silence that greeted her words stretched her already taut nerves almost to breaking point. If he said no, if he so much as kissed her again, turned on the seductive charm that she knew so well was lethal to her self-control, she would be lost. She couldn't resist him again.

But she needed time to think. Time to collect her thoughts and try to put them into some sort of order. If he made love to her now, Constantine would know something was wrong. She wouldn't be able to hide it from him. He would know, and then, if he even began to suspect that her trust in him was being questioned once again... She shuddered inside simply at the thought of his possible reaction.

'A shower...'

For a moment she was sure he was going to suggest sharing the water with her, something they had done so many times in her flat since they had become lovers. But even as she tensed, hunting for something to say that would put him off without offending him, he seemed to change his mind, pushing himself up and away from the bed.

'Fine.' The single syllable was crisp and curt to the point of coldness, speaking of a mood a million miles away from the easy composure it was meant to imply. 'You shower and change. I'll wait for you on the terrace. I'll make you a fresh drink. You must be really thirsty, having missed your tea.'

'I am.'

The look of gratitude she flashed him was heartfelt, but even as she directed it at him she felt her own change of mood. Perversely, now that he had moved away, she felt the loss of the warmth of his body, the touch of his lips, like an ache deep inside. Her skin hungered for his caress, her mouth for his kiss.

She didn't care what he had felt guilty about—if in fact he had felt any such thing! She only knew that without the solid strength of his body close to hers she felt lost, totally bereft, alone in a very disturbing way.

'Constantine...' she managed, her voice just a thin thread of sound.

But he didn't appear to have heard her whispered entreaty, or if he had he chose to ignore it.

'I'll see you in—what? Half an hour?' He was moving towards the door as he spoke.

'Th-that should do fine.'

Call him back, an insidious little voice inside her head whispered provocatively. Call him back! Tell him you've changed your mind!

She wanted to. She even opened her mouth to say the words, then closed it again, ignoring the hungry protests of her yearning senses as she watched Constantine stride from the room, handsome dark head held arrogantly high, not sparing her a backward glance.

Grace stripped off the crumpled trouser suit and hurried into the shower. Turning the water on to full power, she stood under its pounding force, willing it to drive away her fears and anxieties in the same time that it washed off the dirt and stickiness of the day.

But it did no good. Ten minutes later, although her body was clean and refreshed, her mind was still clogged by disquiet and uneasiness. A feeling like the fluttering of trapped butterfly wings started up inside her stomach as she pulled on a sleeveless dress in a pale pink soft cotton, brushed a single coat of mascara on her long lashes and a slick of lipgloss over her mouth.

It was too hot for any proper make-up, she told herself, surveying her reflection in the mirror. But the wide, apprehensive, shadowy grey eyes that stared back at her told a very different story.

'If you're honest,' she told herself severely. 'You'll admit that all this pretence is tying you in knots!'

The truth was that she felt so nervous about the prospect of facing Constantine again that she couldn't trust her hands not to shake. She felt sure that she would smudge any make-up she tried to apply, or put it on so heavily that she would look like a clown at a children's party.

The butterflies in her stomach seemed to have fluttered up into her throat, almost choking her, by the time she made her way out to the terrace at the back of the house. Constantine was there waiting for her, leaning against the stone parapet at the edge of the flagged floor. His strong back was towards her, his dark head averted as he stared out towards the horizon where the sun was slowly beginning to sink downwards towards the night.

'Con...'

Grace found her voice was weak and unsteady, croaking embarrassingly so that she had to swallow hard before she could complete his name.

'Constantine,' she managed, still unevenly, but at least it was audible this time.

She didn't know what she'd expected to see in his face, in the jet-black pools of those deep-set eyes when he turned to face her. She only knew that it wasn't the easy calm, the smiling sociability that he seemed to be able to turn on at the flick of a switch. Suspicion, hostility, anger even, these she had been prepared for, but not this relaxed, casual man who strolled towards her without a hint of hesitation.

'Feel better now?' he enquired.

'Much!' The butterflies in her throat made her breathless. 'I hate sleeping in my clothes. You feel so dreadful afterwards.'

'The journey must have taken more out of you than you realised.'

If his reaction to her arrival had been disconcerting, then

the brief, almost indifferent kiss that he brushed over her freshly washed hair was even more bewildering. They might have been strangers who had met only a short time before, mere acquaintances, not the passionate, unrestrained lovers who had shared a bed and. been intimate with every secret part of each other's bodies over the past four months.

But of course she had forgotten about that fierce, burning pride of his. A pride that, once she had seemed to reject him in the slightest way, would not allow him to make any further advances again. And now that pride had made him determined to act as if nothing had happened, so he had switched on his best social manner, the smooth public veneer that hid any private feelings from the world.

'I thought you would like something cool to drink now.' A wave of his hand indicated the bottles of wine and mineral water that stood on a table nearby. 'But if you still prefer tea, I can ring for Florina.'

'No, there's no need for that. Some sparkling water would be wonderful, thank you.'

If she had sounded stilted before, it was much worse now. Even her footsteps seemed stiff and unnatural as she made her way to the edge of the terrace. Leaning on the wall where he had been when she had arrived, she looked out at the gardens that sloped away from the house, leading down to the beach and the Aegean Sea. In the daytime it was a clear turquoise-blue, but now its softly lapping waves were gilded by the light of the evening sun.

Behind her she could hear the faint hiss of a bottle being opened, the clink of ice on glass, and the gurgling sound of the water pouring into the glass. But she couldn't turn because a cold hand seemed to have reached out and gripped her heart, twisting it mercilessly.

It had been in just this place that Constantine had proposed to her. He hadn't gone down on one knee, of course, that Kiriazis pride was too strong for that, but he had produced the most beautiful diamond ring and, with his voice husky with emotion, had said...

'Grace...'

For the space of a couple of heartbeats she didn't know if the voice she heard was in the past or the present. It was only when Constantine repeated her name again that she realised he had come up behind her. Whirling round nervously, she almost knocked the fine crystal glass from his hand.

'Oh, I'm sorry! I was miles away!'

'Obviously.' His tone was dry. 'You always were fascinated by the sea,'

Did he truly believe that it was only the sight of the *sea* that had held her so absorbed? Did he not remember that special night, the feelings they had shared? Obviously not.

But then, of course, he must have visited this house many times in the past two and a half years. It was more than likely that familiarity had bred contempt, any residual pain that the emotive location brought back being worn away by the passage of time.

If, of course, he had felt any such thing. Hastily Grace sipped at her drink to cover her disturbed reaction, finding it difficult to force the cool liquid past the tight knot in her throat. Wasn't it more likely that her own foolish actions, her weak lack of trust, had destroyed the love he had felt for her so completely that he would be totally indifferent to this place that had once been so magical to her?

'If—if you lived in London all the year round, then you'd love to see the sea as well,' she managed unevenly, grateful for the excuse to turn back to stare at the waves and so hide the bitter tears that burned in her eyes. 'I can't wait until tomorrow when I can go down to the shore and actually get into the water.'

'Why wait?' Constantine surprised her by saying. 'There's plenty of time before dinner is served. Oh, not for a proper swim, perhaps, but you can always dip your toes in the surf.'

'I'd love that!'

Impulsively she held out her hand to him, and to her delight he took it, removing the glass from her grasp and placing it on the wide stone balustrade before leading her to the steps that led down from one side of the terrace.

Dusk was just beginning to gather as they made their way down the slope, thickly planted with fruit trees and pines. The flowers that had bordered the path on her previous visit in the spring were gone now, shrivelled by the burning sun, the ground beneath their feet baked brown. Their footsteps were silent, the only sound the gentle lapping of the waves against the shore.

Reaching the tiny cove, Grace immediately slipped off her sandals and dashed across the pebbly beach towards the water. With a sigh of delight she let the small waves wash over her feet, the foamy spume breaking softly over her skin.

'You look like a child!' She couldn't tell if the note in Constantine's voice was one of amusement or remonstrance, but she didn't care.

'Perhaps the Turn Back the Clock party worked after all,' she laughed, and knew her words to be a mistake as soon as she saw his face change, all the warmth leaching from it, leaving it hard and distant.

Did he think that she was angling for the chance to truly go back in time? That she was hinting at a possible return to the time when they had last been on Skyros together, when they had been so secure in the knowledge of each other's love that he had proposed, begging—no, *insisting*— Constantine Kiriazis never begged—that she should be his bride as soon as was humanly possible?

Oh, if only they could! If only it was possible to return to those happier, innocent days! But of course it could never be. A strong dose of reality had been injected into her life, destroying all the dreams of happiness she had had then.

'I feel like a child!' she improvised hastily. 'And this feels wonderful! So cool and refreshing! You should try it… Come on, Constantine!' she urged when he held back, looking reluctant. 'Let your hair down for once!'

Still he looked reluctant. Inspired by some wicked little imp of mischief, Grace bent down and scooped up a couple of handfuls of the salty water. As soon as Constantine came within range, she flung them in his direction, spattering the immaculate white polo shirt with wet drops.

'Hey! What the…?'

She had barely a second's grace. Kicking off the canvas shoes that he wore with no socks, he paused only to remove the gold watch from his wrist and stuff it into a protective pocket before he came after her, splashing water in her direction as he ran.

Shrieking in delight, Grace turned and fled, dashing through the waves, heedless of the way that the hem of her dress was getting soaked as she ran. At first she went as fast as she could, making it seem as if she wanted to put as much space as possible between herself and Constantine, but then, slowly, she let him gain on her. A few minutes more and he was right behind her, one strong arm reaching out and grabbing hold of her, bringing her swinging round to face him.

'You little witch!'

Giggling and struggling, she was swung off her feet and carried away from the sea, up on to the powdery sand. Once they were away from the water, Constantine tumbled her down on to the ground and came down after her, the heavy weight of his body covering hers as his hard lips captured her still laughing mouth, driving her giggles back down her throat.

'You are a temptress!' he muttered when at last he drew in a much needed breath. 'What man could resist you? You are beautiful and cool as the moon, yet wild as the sea.'

She felt wild at this moment. Wild and uninhibited, as elemental as the waves breaking against the shore, the sand against her back.

Constantine's mouth ravaged hers again, his hands hot and urgent as they moved over her body. The pink dress was rucked up around her waist and it didn't take him long to discover that a delicate pair of white lace briefs was all she wore underneath it. Moments later that fragile barrier too had been ripped away and tossed carelessly aside.

Grace didn't care. All the inhibitions, the worries of earlier in the day had been swept aside, washed from her as if she had actually been submerged in the sea that lapped just inches away from them. She wanted this, wanted it with a hunger that was hot as the sun, a hunger that had her lifting her hips eagerly, encouraging the hard, powerful thrust of his body into hers.

This was who she was, what she had been born for. She loved Constantine, she had always loved him, and she could do nothing at all to release herself from the golden fetters that bound her to him. But as she clung to Constantine, her nails digging into the tightly clenched muscles of his back, as the passion flared and spiralled out of control her last rational thought was that she never, ever wanted to be free from this glorious, sensual slavery.

CHAPTER TEN

'ANY particular plans for today?' Grace enquired lazily, stretching luxuriously in the warmth of the morning sun beating down on the terrace.

The day had begun in the same way as every one since they had come to Skyros, with a late awakening followed by an even later breakfast. The latter was the result of Constantine's insistence on never letting her out of bed until he had made love to her with a thoroughness that left her limp and satiated, unwilling to move ever again.

So now, lingering over a light meal of crusty bread, creamy Greek yoghurt, peaches, melons and honey, she felt as idle as a cat lying in the sun.

'Well, I had considered a swim, a little sunbathing, perhaps a light snack. After which I will definitely need a siesta.'

The glint in his eyes as he slanted a wicked, sidelong glance in her direction told her exactly how he planned to spend that siesta, and that he had no intention of wasting any of the precious time on *sleep*.

'Then dinner tonight…some wine…'

'A packed schedule, then,' Grace commented dryly.

She was finding it difficult to adjust to the man Constantine had become in the days they had spent on Skyros. He seemed to have shrugged off his role as the archetypal workaholic and become someone else, growing more relaxed and indulgent as each day passed, his mood improving as steadily as his native sun gradually darkened the natural tan of his skin to a deep, burnished bronze.

Looking at him now as he lounged back in his seat, the

sun making his dark hair gleam and gilding the skin exposed by the vee neck and short sleeves of his black tee shirt, she thought that if she was a contented cat then he was a sleek, sun-warmed panther, indolent and sensual.

'Well, what else is there to do here?' Constantine drawled easily. 'This is such a tiny island, and we've visited the major tourist attractions—the beaches, the tavernas, Rupert Brooke's grave...'

Grace nodded, recalling the trip to Tris Boukes, at the southernmost point of the small island, where the famous poet lay buried in what was officially now six feet of British soil. There, she had been enchanted by the sight of the Pikermies, the herd of tiny wild ponies, native to Skyros, who roamed freely across the barren countryside.

'You're forgetting Skyros town itself,' she pointed out.

She had enjoyed exploring the island's main town, where the white houses were stacked almost on top of each other along the steep, narrow, pedestrian-only lanes and steps.

'The woodwork was just amazing.' Her eyes lit up with enthusiasm for the beautifully hand-carved furniture on sale in the folk-art shops. 'I could have spent a fortune there.'

'My paternal grandfather started out as a woodworker,' Constantine astounded her by saying. 'He made much of the furniture in this house.'

'I didn't know that!

If the truth was told, Constantine had never been exactly loquacious on the subject of his family. She knew that his grandfather had been born on Skyros, as had his father and Constantine himself, and that although he had come from humble beginnings he had been the founder of the now multi-million Kiriazis Corporation. But never before had Constantine opened up about him.

'So how did he...?'

'Make his fortune?'

Constantine pushed both hands through the black silk of his hair, stretching luxuriously.

'He worked harder and longer than anyone else. Invested what he earned first in educating himself, and then in buying first a small guesthouse and then later his first hotel. It was close to the port at Linaria, perfect for travellers arriving on the ferry, so it turned into a little goldmine. With the profits from that he bought another...and the rest is history.'

'Is he still alive?'

Constantine shook his head, regret clouding the brilliance of his eyes.

'He was already sixty when I was born. He died four years ago.'

'But he meant a lot to you?' It was obvious that he had cared deeply for the old man. His feelings were etched into his face, the set of that finely carved mouth.

'He was a character—strong, wise, generous...'

Long, tanned fingers touched the gold watch on his wrist, his faint smile gently reminiscent.

'He gave me this. It was my twenty-first birthday present—but I had to earn it.'

'Working as a waiter in one of the hotels?' Grace guessed, her perspicacity acknowledged by the slight inclination of his head. Now she understood why he never let the watch out of his sight, why he always took such great care of it. 'I wish I'd been able to meet him.'

That brought those ebony eyes swinging up to her face, the momentary softness fading rapidly, leaving them suddenly disturbingly cold and distant.

Of course, she thought uncomfortably. If Florina, who was only the family's maid, treated her as a pariah because of the way she had behaved towards Constantine, then naturally his grandfather, the patriarch and founder of the Kiriazis dynasty, would hardly welcome her into his home.

But then another thought struck her, one that had her mouth opening on a soft gasp of shock.

'Your grandfather was a woodcarver. Then that box…the one with…'

'He made it,' Constantine finished for her, not needing her to explain that she meant the decorated box which had contained the twelve autumn leaves he had once given her.

'I never knew…'

She had never realised that he had given her something so very special. Something that meant so very much to him personally.

'W-would you like it back?'

The blazing look that seared over her was savage in its rejection of any such idea. Constantine didn't need to use words to emphasise just how even to think of doing any such thing made him feel.

'It was a gift,' he stated harshly. 'I do not ask for my presents back.'

She'd caught that ferocious pride on the raw once again, destroying the peaceful atmosphere of earlier in the morning. The lazily contented panther was no more. Instead, he was bristling with hostility, reining in his black temper only with difficulty.

Desperately she cast about, looking for some other topic of conversation to distract him.

'You never told me—how did your parents take the news of the cancellation of our wedding?'

Oh, Lord, no. That was even worse! Why couldn't she engage her brain before putting her mouth into gear? The golden fire of anger was still there in his eyes, only now the flames were freezingly cold, shards of pure ice in the inky depths.

'They were shocked, naturally, and angry,' he stated, glacially distant, the bleak cynicism of his tone having the bite

of concentrated acid, making her wince painfully deep inside.

'At me?'

A swift frown drew together the dark brows,
Constantine's glance in her direction expressing incredulity
that she should even ask the question.

'At *me*,' he corrected tightly.

Grace knew she was staring, shock and disbelief showing
in her eyes.

'At you? But why? I mean, I was the one who...'

'You were the one who postponed the wedding—but I
was the one whose actions seemed to be responsible for
that. If I had been unfaithful to my bride even before we
were married, then such behaviour would cast a terrible slur
on my family's honour.'

'But surely they didn't believe...' She saw the yawning
trap gaping wide at her feet just too late to stop herself
from blundering right into it.

'My fiancée believed accusations that had been made...'
The savagery of the statement tore at her heart for all that
it had been expressed in a flat, emotionless tone. 'So naturally they were afraid that there was more evidence of
those accusations than at first appeared. But when I assured
them—'

'You assured them!'

Wonderful, gloriously liberating anger boiled up inside
Grace's mind, freeing her from the shock and concerned
guilt that had had her in their grip only moments before.

'You *assured* them!' she repeated, lacing each word with
corrosive sarcasm. 'Oh, that's just great! You explained
things to your parents, assured them there was no truth
behind Paula's stories, but you left me floundering.'

'If you remember rightly, I did try,' Constantine inserted
coldly. 'I shouldn't even have needed to do that when you
claimed to love me.'

'Your mother loves you!'

'My mother loves me, but she is also realistic. She knows that since I became a man, my private life has been exactly that—private. I do not discuss my sex life with her any more than she would discuss hers with me.'

Grace winced away from the blunt brutality of the *sex life* that reduced their relationship to the purely physical, with nothing of the emotional in it at all.

'She needed me to tell her—'

'*I* needed you to tell me! Yes, I know I was angry, but you must have seen how upset—and how afraid I was. You could have tried harder to convince me of the truth.'

'And *you* should have laughed in your sister's face. You shouldn't have believed for one second that her stories had any credence!'

Pushing back his chair with an ugly scraping sound on the stone-flagged floor, Constantine got to his feet and moved to the edge of the terrace, bracing his arms on the stone parapet as he looked out at the sea.

Behind him, Grace could only stare miserably at the long, straight back, narrow hips and long legs in well-cut chinos, every inch of them taut with aggression and rejection. Even angry and distant from her, as he was now, he still had a forcefully sensual impact that was like a mule's kick in her stomach.

She longed to go to him, slide her arms around that narrow waist, press herself close up against the hard length of his body and just hold him until slowly, unwillingly perhaps, he softened, turned, took her in his arms…

No! What was she thinking of?

Oh, she could bring him out of his present vicious mood easily enough. She could entice him out of it using the wild sexual pull that their bodies had for each other, like the most powerful, irresistible magnets. She could seduce him into making love to her and so forgetting this disturbing confrontation, satiate his body so that his mind was incapable of thought. But it would be no answer. When they woke later today, or tomorrow, the problems would still be there.

'So it was a test.'

As she spoke she realised that she still held the piece of bread she had picked up long minutes ago, just before she had asked him about his parents. Now it was crushed and ruined by her convulsive grip, crumbling into nothing as she slowly released it.

'A test that it seems I failed.'

Slowly Constantine turned back to face her, resting his lithe hips against the stone wall, his tanned arms folded across his broad chest just as they had been more than two years before, when he had confronted her over Paula's accusations.

'I think we were both testing each other, Grace,' he stated flatly. 'And perhaps in our own ways we both failed.'

And then, while she was still digesting that, trying to work out exactly how he had meant it, he seemed to shrug off the black mood that had enclosed him. The coldly withdrawn look vanished from his face as if wiped away with a cloth as he stood upright again, straightening his shoulders.

'Well, if we are to go down to the cove you will need to change into something more casual. And don't forget the sun cream. I wouldn't want that beautiful skin to burn. We'll meet back here in—say half an hour?'

He didn't wait for an answer, obviously taking her acquiescence for granted as he strode back inside the house.

Left alone, Grace could only stand and stare. Was that it? Could he really just shrug it off like that—water under the bridge? Well, one thing was for sure: she couldn't!

But now was not the time to go after him, try to have it out with him. She'd seen Constantine in this sort of mood often enough to know that to push him would only make him dig his heels in even harder. She might as well batter her bare hands against a brick wall as try to talk to him in this intractable frame of mind.

So she would follow his lead—for now. She would continue with their holiday, go swimming, sunbathe. She would let him think that he could have everything his own way, until it suited her to do otherwise.

And then, at some point when he least expected it, she would tackle him about the enigmatic statement he had made. And this time she would want some answers.

After such an inauspicious start, the day went surprisingly well. It followed exactly the pattern Constantine had mapped out: the refreshing swim in the sun-warmed sea, sunbathing in the privacy of the cove. And then, in order to escape the blazing heat of the middle of the day, they retired to the bedroom, cool and air-conditioned behind closed shutters.

And in the bedroom it was as it always had been. Constantine had only to take her in his arms, kiss her with the special magic that only he possessed, and all thought of the morning's confrontation melted from her mind like a mist before the sun. She could only abandon herself to the sensual mastery of his touch, the skilful enchantment that awoke all her senses one by one until she was just a molten, mindless creature moaning her need in his arms.

But there was something new this time. Something that made their lovemaking more urgent, more hungrily passionate than ever before. With her thoughts too hazed by drugging need, her body on fire, the spiralling yearning completely out of control, Grace had no way of knowing just what it was that was different. It was only when the long, carnally hedonistic afternoon was over, when exhaustion rather than repletion forced them into sleep, that she managed to wonder if the things he had said that morning had anything to do with it.

Perhaps in our own ways we both failed.

The cryptic comment was the last thing in her thoughts when sleep claimed her, the first when she woke again.

The day had slipped away unnoticed; already the earliest signs of dusk were beginning to gather. At her side Constantine still slept, his stunning features relaxed, long thick lashes lying in jet-black arcs above the wide cheekbones.

Her thoughts preoccupied, Grace slipped from the bed and went through the usual routine of showering and washing her hair. She put on a simple soft green dress, preparing for the evening meal they would share. But all the time her mind was buzzing, thinking back, considering, wondering.

We both failed. Had the arrogant, implacable Constantine Kiriazis actually admitted to being in the wrong? Never! But it had sounded as if he was at least making a concession.

She was out on the small balcony letting her blonde hair dry in the weakening sun when she finally heard Constantine stir and head for the shower himself.

He had loved her so much before, she reflected, recalling the moment when he had given her the box of autumn leaves. But what did Constantine truly feel for her now? It was said that the opposite of love was hate, but she didn't think that quite fitted. She wouldn't be here, on his beloved Skyros, in the family home, if that were the case.

But perhaps the real truth was that the opposite to love was *nothing.* That all Constantine really felt was the blazing physical attraction that he had declared so openly, and nothing more. And yet he had loved her once. Was she only fooling herself to dream that perhaps one day that love could be revived?

A light touch on the back of her neck made her jump

like a startled cat. A moment later she felt the warm pressure of Constantine's lips on her skin, just above the fastening of the gold leaf necklace.

'A penny for them,' he murmured, coming to her side, dark and devastating in a crisp black shirt and black trousers.

'Seeing as we're in Greece, shouldn't that be a drachma for them?' Grace hedged nervously, trying to collect her scattered thoughts into something she could tell him so that she didn't blurt out the truth. 'But if you must know I was wondering how you ever manage to leave this island. It's going to be such a wrench when I have to go.'

Which she would have to inevitably—and soon. The holiday was drawing to a close. A couple of days more and they would be heading back to England.

'It isn't easy,' Constantine admitted. 'But there's always the thought of coming back.'

The thought of him coming back, or both of them? Grace found that the question meant too much to her to be able to find the courage even to ask it.

'We'll talk about it over dinner. That and other things.'

'What other things?'

But Constantine simply shook his head and, taking hold of her hand, led her out of the room.

'Later,' was all he said. 'We'll eat first. I, for one, am ravenous.' The look he slanted in her direction had a wicked, teasing glint in it. 'Anyone would think I had been doing something active this afternoon, instead of just lolling in bed.'

When he looked at her like that she could almost convince herself that he felt more for her than he admitted. With those piercing dark eyes softened by a trace of warmth, a slight smile curving his lips, he was so much closer to the Constantine she had known at first. The man who had brought her here to his island home to ask her to marry him.

Grace's heart lurched so violently that she almost missed her footing on the stairs. Could it happen? Could those 'other things' he wanted to talk to her about include the possibility that he was planning to repeat their private history and propose all over again?

It was not a thought that made for a relaxed state of mind, as a result of which her appetite totally deserted her. She could only pick at her food, pushing the tasty dish of stuffed aubergines around on her plate. Constantine too seemed absorbed in his own reflections, only coming out of them briefly when a phone rang inside the house.

'Shouldn't you answer that?' Grace asked when he didn't move.

'Florina will get it. If it's important, she'll come and fetch me.'

It was the longest speech he had made for some time, after remaining taciturn and withdrawn, his answers to the few questions she had formed monosyllabic and vague.

In the end, Grace could stand it no more.

'Constantine…'

But she got no further. Even as she spoke the door swung open and Florina stomped in, blatantly ignoring Grace as she directed a flow of incomprehensible Greek at Constantine. Seeing his swift frown, the way he snapped out a couple of sharp and obviously probing questions, she felt anxiety twist in her stomach. And when she caught a couple of words she actually understood her concern grew.

'What is it? Constantine, what's happening?'

She was ignored as he issued a string of instructions to the maid, and only when Florina had left the room did he direct his attention back to her.

'Is something wrong? I heard the words *mitera* and *pateras*—your mother and father—what's happened to them?'

'Nothing has happened. It is simply that my parents have telephoned to say that they are coming here tomorrow. I was not expecting them so soon. They had been staying with my sister in Athens, but for some reason they have cut short their visit.'

The sense of release from tension was like a rush of adrenaline, making her smile her relief straight into his dark eyes.

'But that's wonderful! I'd love to see them both again!'

But something was wrong. No answering smile softened Constantine's face. Instead he seemed even further away from her than before, every muscle in his face tight, black eyes hooded, his mouth clamped into a hard, unyielding line.

'I am afraid that will not be possible.'

'Not possible! But why?'

'We are leaving Skyros tonight.'

Grace's head went back slightly, her grey eyes widening in shock.

'And just when was this decided? We have nearly three days...'

'The holiday is over.' It was brutally autocratic: a decree issued by a tyrannical ruler to his lowly subject. 'The helicopter will take us to Athens airport. My plane will be waiting for us there.'

'But I don't want to go! I won't—'

'You have no choice!' Constantine snapped. 'It is already decided.'

'Yes, by you! But what about me? I demand some sort of an explanation. I don't want to be rushed off like this. I would like to see your parents again.'

'But they would not want to see you.'

Fired by indignation, Grace had been pushing herself to her feet, but now she subsided back into her seat, feeling as if a cruel blow had just driven all the breath from her body. The wash of angry colour leached from her face, leaving it ashen pale.

'W-what?'

'My parents would not wish to see you,' Constantine repeated implacably. 'And I would not want you to see them. I have never made it my habit to introduce my parents to any of my mistresses. That is an honour I reserve solely for the woman I intend to make my wife.'

Which left her completely without a leg to stand on. Feeling as if she was coming to pieces inside, Grace knew that the only option left to her was to get out of this with as much dignity as she could manage.

Blinking back the tears that burned at her eyes, determined that Constantine should not see them, she forced herself to keep her expression as cool and indifferent as his as she rose to her feet.

'I'll go and pack, then.'

She was proud of her voice. It sounded perfectly controlled, revealing no trace of the explosive mixture of violent emotions roiling savagely in the pit of her stomach.

'Florina is already doing that. I told her to have your cases ready as soon as possible.'

With an imperious gesture he indicated the meal on the table, her barely touched plate.

'You still have time to finish your dinner.'

But that was just too much. Drawing herself up to her full height, Grace looked him straight in the eye, her chin lifting defiantly.

'There is nothing to finish,' she told him. 'If I ate another mouthful it would choke me. I have had more than enough of it—and of you.'

CHAPTER ELEVEN

'Do YOU ever intend to speak to me again?'

The journey from Skyros to London, and its final stage back to her own home, had been completed before Grace could bring herself to speak to Constantine at any length.

Since the moment she had walked away from him and the remnants of their meal, every action she had taken had been performed in almost total silence. She hadn't even been able to bring herself to look at him, but had sat first in the helicopter, then the plane and finally in the luxurious chauffeur-driven car that had met them at the airport with her face carefully averted, staring stonily out of the window, seeing nothing.

She hadn't even felt very much. Shock seemed to have numbed her brain so that no emotion could take root. This must be how it felt to lose a limb in an accident, when the trauma was so great that for a long time the mind simply refused to accept that it had happened and so felt no pain.

'What is there to talk about?' she asked drearily as Constantine dropped her bags to the floor of her sitting room in evident annoyance. 'I think you've already said everything there is to be said. You've certainly made your opinion only too plain.'

'You knew what the arrangement was when you went into it,' he stated callously.

Yes, she had, and then she had thought she could handle it. But not any more. She had told herself that being with him was worth any price, but now she was paying far too much for the pleasure of simply having him near. It hurt too much knowing that he would never love her—and if she had had any doubts on that score, then his behaviour before they had left Skyros had driven home the truth with a sledgehammer.

But how would she live without him? It seemed to her that she risked leaping out of a very hot and torturous frying pan into an even hotter and very much more dangerous fire. She couldn't live with either situation but she had to choose one, even if it tore her heart and her mind apart to do so.

'I knew what you wanted from the relationship! The rules you were at such pains to lay down that I should follow!'

She knew from his swift dark frown that her tone and her words were a mistake, but she couldn't find it in her desolated heart to care. Suddenly the dam that had been holding back her feelings ever since the island had burst, and the words flooded out with a vengeance.

'You told me how I should live my life, what I should wear, how I should behave. You ruled my days with your occasional calls, your late, late visits, and your insistence that I should be available when you wanted—and exclusively to you! You ruled my nights with your—your sexual demands, the satisfying of which was all that you thought I was fit for! You practically told me what to eat, when to sleep—how to breathe! You took over my existence and now I want it back!'

'You don't mean that!'

'Oh, so now you've taken over my mind as well, have you? Well, let me tell you that this time your telepathic powers have let you down.'

In a gesture that mirrored her inner turmoil, she pulled off the white linen jacket she was wearing and tossed it angrily on to a nearby chair, wishing she could jettison her emotional distress at the same time.

'Because I do mean it, Constantine! I mean every word. I want you out of my life, right now, and—'

'You don't... *Theos!*' Violently he corrected himself, shaking his dark head in frustrated fury as he did so. 'Grace you *can't* mean this!'

From her defensive position on the far side of the room, Grace could only stand and stare, blinking in sudden confusion. She almost expected to see that Constantine had vanished in a puff of smoke and someone else had appeared to take his place.

Because something had happened in the last few seconds: something she couldn't yet be quite sure of and something she couldn't begin to interpret.

For one thing, part-way through that last declaration Constantine's voice had changed dramatically. It had ceased to be the arrogant, inflexible set of commands that was typically Constantine, and had become instead something that sounded unnervingly like a—a...

When Grace hunted for words to describe it, the only one she could come up with was an entreaty.

And in the same moment something had come over Constantine's face. Something desolate and bleak that dulled the brilliance of his eyes, filling them instead with turbulent shadows like the clouds that gather on the horizon in advance warning of a violent storm.

'What did you say?' Suspicion and uncertainty blended together on the question.

Sighing deeply, Constantine raked both hands through his hair, his bruised-looking gaze fixed on her face.

'I said you can't mean this. You can't end it now.'

'I can do whatever I want.'

'But, Grace, *agape mou...*'

'Don't call me that!'

Throwing aside her jacket had been a definite mistake. She was still wearing the green dress she had put on for dinner at the villa, a dress that had been suitable for the much warmer conditions of Greece. Here, on a typically rainy late summer English night, the temperatures had dropped considerably, so that her exposed skin felt chilled and clammy. She had to struggle against the need to rub her hands up and down her arms to ward off the shivers.

Constantine, on the contrary, looked supremely comfortable. The lightweight jacket he wore over his black shirt and trousers was much more protection against the cold. It was one more thing to hold against him, and she tried to inject all the resentment and anger she could into her feelings. At this moment hate was so much safer than love.

'If you call me that again, I swear I'll kill you! *Agape mou!*' she echoed cynically. 'My love—my *love*! You don't even know what the word means!'

'I know what it means to me,' Constantine snarled. 'It means that I cannot let you go. That without you I can't sleep, I can't work, I can't *live*! Without you my life is empty, unendurable! I have had more than two long years of that and I will not take any more!'

There was a roaring, booming sound inside Grace's head. Her heart was pounding so hard that her blood was thundering through her veins, making her feel dizzy and faint so that she had to reach out to a nearby chair for support. Drawing a deep breath, she forced herself to speak.

'I don't know if you realise what you said then, Constantine.' It was a struggle to keep the words calm and even and not gabble them out in a desperate rush to ease the tension inside her head. 'But it sounded remarkably like a declaration of love.'

Her words fell into a stunned silence that dragged on and on, stretching her already over-sensitised nerves almost to breaking point. She felt as if all that had gone before had flayed off a protective layer of skin, so that she was even more vulnerable to what was to come, too scared even to hope.

'Constantine…' she prompted fearfully when he didn't speak.

The man before her stirred slowly, as if waking from a long, drugged sleep. Briefly he closed his eyes, and when he opened them again it seemed to Grace that they were focused on something else, something far, far away.

'Love,' he echoed cautiously, as if testing the word, his mouth twisting on the sound. 'Love—well, yes, what the hell, why not admit it?'

It was impossible to believe what she was hearing.

'You love…'

Suddenly it was as if someone had flicked a switch inside Constantine, driving away this bewildering, confusing stranger and bringing back to life the strong, dynamic man she knew. His head went back proudly, the shadows clearing from his eyes so that they were cold and cutting, cruel as any knife.

'I love you, Grace. I always have, and I fear I always will. But that doesn't mean I'm going to act on it. I have never made decisions based on emotions and I certainly don't intend to start now!'

'That doesn't sound like any sort of love I've ever known!'

Love didn't talk of fear or refusing to act. Love just was; that was all.

'I don't believe you know what you're talking about.'

'*Christos*, Grace!' Constantine blazed, covering the ground between them with swift, angry strides. 'It is you who doesn't know what you are talking about!'

Reaching her side, he caught hold of her chin, lifting her face to his, studying it so intently that it seemed he wanted to commit every feature to memory in case he never saw it again.

'Loving you is not a choice I made. It's who I am. I could no sooner stop myself from loving you than I could will my heart to stop beating, my body to stop breathing. I think I fell in love with you in the first moment I saw you. In that moment I was lost and I knew I would never be the same again.'

Hearing that rawly voiced declaration of feeling, Grace felt as if her heart, every vital organ, even her breathing, had suddenly closed down, leaving her in a state of suspended animation. Her blood had frozen in her veins, holding her immobile. She couldn't think, could barely see his white drawn face, so close to her own. She could only focus on the fathomless pits that were his eyes, drawing her in deeper and deeper until she felt she was drowning in them.

Abruptly Constantine released his grip on her, his hand falling away to his side.

'But I do not intend to act on that emotion.'

At another time, in another existence, it seemed, she would have welcomed such an avowal of love, letting it fill her mind with an explosion of sheer delight. It should have made her heart soar, singing for joy, but the true effect it had was exactly the opposite.

What Constantine had given with one hand he had immediately snatched away with the other. No sooner had the words of love been spoken than he had revoked them, making them worse than worthless. And the pain was all the worse because just once she had heard him say what she'd most longed to hear. The words she had only ever heard him speak in her dreams over the past two and a half years.

'I don't believe you can do that!' It was a cry of anguish, all the bitter pain welling up inside and spilling out at last.

'Believe it!' he ordered coldly. 'I can do anything I want. That is where I do have a choice. I can decide what I'm going to do about the way I feel—whether I let it influence me.'

'Influence...?'

Grace lifted shaking hands to her head, pressing her fingers hard against her temples to ease the pain that throbbed there. It was as if someone had placed a steel band around her head and was tightening it slowly and inexorably, piling physical agony on top of the mental pain she felt.

'I—I don't understand.'

The breath hissed in through Constantine's clenched teeth in a sound of pure exasperation and he swung away from her, striding over to the bay window. He stared out into the dark, deserted street, much as he had done on the second morning after the party, the time when he had told her she would never be his wife. And just as it had done then, so now every taut line of his body screamed hostility and total rejection of her presence.

'I choose not to let myself feel this love,' he said at last, still keeping his face averted. 'I will not let it into my mind or my heart, or whatever other organ the purple-penned writers of poems or stories would have us believe harbours such an emotion.'

'How can you can do that?'

It was a sound of horror, of sheer incredulity, her wide, stunned eyes fixed on the tight muscles that hunched that normally long straight back.

Hearing it, Constantine moved suddenly, flexing his broad shoulders as if he felt the imprint of her gaze. Slowly he turned to face her, his features set into such a remote, expressionless mask that she didn't need an answer to her question. She could see it stamped into the white lines his ruthless control had etched around his nose and mouth.

'The way I feel is as much a fact of my life as that I am Greek, or that I have black hair, black eyes, and olive skin. It *is*. I can do nothing about it. But I have to get on with my life, so I refuse to let it even register on my thoughts. It is much the same as the fact that I am afraid of lifts, but I never give in to it.'

'You're...'

Momentarily diverted from her misery by this totally unexpected development, Grace could only stare at him in stunned bemusement. Had Constantine actually admitted to a failing, a weakness? She couldn't believe that he could ever be afraid of anything!

'You're afraid of...'

'Of lifts,' Constantine confirmed curtly with a swift, brusque movement of his head, as if challenging her to make something of it.

'But all the time I've known you—I'd never have guessed.'

'Precisely. I feel it, but I do not let it affect me.'

'And that's what you believe you can do with your feelings for me?'

'I do not feel—I know.'

'Oh, you know, do you?'

Just as it had on Skyros so much earlier that evening, once more anger proved her salvation. Feeling it run through her veins, warming, revitalising, driving away the fear and confusion that had held her frozen, she welcomed it gladly. Not giving herself time to think, she acted on its impetus, moving forward in a rush, heading straight for Constantine.

He watched her approach warily, his expression guarded, black eyes narrowed. But he didn't make any move, either towards her or away from her, and before she was quite ready she found herself close up against him; almost cannoning into the hard wall of his body before she actually managed to come to a halt.

'So you know that if I do this...'

Deliberately she lifted her hand and let it rest briefly on his shoulder before sliding it slowly and with deliberate sensuality down the length of his arm and on to his hand, gently smoothing over the warm skin, the strong muscles, the long bones. She felt his fingers move, just once, under her touch, then become still.

'Or this…'

Both hands moved to his face, caressing the lean planes of his cheeks, the tense jaw. Moving round to the nape of his neck, she wove her fingers into the dark silk of his hair, feeling its softness slide under her touch.

Silently Constantine watched her, ebony eyes hooded and withdrawn.

'Or even this…'

With her arms looped around his neck, she moved closer, pressing the softness of her body against the broad strength of his. Her breasts were crushed against his chest, her hips against his pelvis, and she could feel the heat and hardness of the immediate physical response he couldn't hide from her. It was there in the ragged nature of his breathing too, and the feverish slash of colour along the wide cheekbones.

'And, oh, Constantine…' she murmured in his ear. 'If I do this, then will you be able to control how you react?'

Her lips drifted from the corner of his jaw, over his cheekbone and down towards his mouth. But when she finally pressed the kiss she had been aiming for on to his lips, his response made her recoil in shocked dismay.

Or rather his lack of response. Because when she had been expecting the usual instantaneous response, the flaring passion, the searing demand, to feel his rock-hard stillness, the silent rejection of her caress, was like a blow in her face. She felt bruised and sullied, as if she had had her head slammed hard up against a granite cliff-face.

She couldn't move away quickly enough. She just couldn't bear to stay close to him, to touch him, feel the total rejection in every muscle, see it burning in those brilliant eyes.

'Point taken!' she flung at him, her voice raw with pain

as she put much needed distance between them. 'You certainly know how to get your message across.'

'Don't you English have a saying about being cruel to be kind?' Constantine returned with shocking imperturbability.

'Kind!' Grace spat the word out. 'There was nothing at all *kind* about what you just did.'

'I didn't want you to be under any illusions.'

'Oh, you needn't worry about that! I lost every trace of any illusions I had about you a long, long time ago.'

If only it was the truth. If only she really had had every foolish delusion stripped from her at the start. And she should have done. After all, Constantine had been totally straight with her. Brutally so, if she was honest with herself. It was only her foolish dream that things might be different that had got in the way.

'And that's why I think it would be better if we called a halt to this right here and now.'

It was obvious that he hadn't expected anything like that. His dark head went back sharply, black eyes narrowing in stunned disbelief.

'That isn't what I want.'

'Well, it's what I want, damn you!'

Stubborn pride refused to let her show how much it hurt, giving her the courage to hold her head up high and look him straight in the face.

'Be honest, Constantine. It isn't working.'

'It seems to be working fine to me. This is exactly what our arrangement was supposed to be...'

'But it isn't *enough*!'

She even stamped her foot to emphasise the words. What did she have to do to get this through to him? If he continued to fight her, she didn't know how long she could hold out.

'What do you want? More money? Clothes? A better flat?'

Grace couldn't believe what she was hearing. Her head swam in horror so that she felt nauseous and weak. Did he really think that was all she needed?

'I don't want more *things*! I don't want jewels or clothes or to be set up in a luxury apartment like some long-ago courtesan kept by her lover!'

'Then what *do* you want? You only have to say.'

'I want...'

Tears blurred her vision, making it impossible to focus on his face, but she wouldn't let them fall, even though it meant she couldn't actually see his expression.

'I want what you can't give me,' she said despondently. 'I want a love that includes commitment and—and trust, and a hope of a future together. And we don't have that.'

'Grace...'

Constantine's swift strides took him across the room to her side. One hand closed around a slender wrist, the other clamping itself to her waist, holding her prisoner when she would have twisted away.

'Oh, Grace, what we do have is too good to lose.'

He was coming close. Too close. His warm lips were on her forehead, pressing heartbreakingly gentle kisses on her skin.

'Can you really bear to live without it?'

God help her, he had only to touch her and already she was melting. The dark enchantment that he wove so easily curled around every one of her senses, filling them with the sight, the sound, the scent of him.

Weakly she swayed into his arms, let him pull her close. The touch of his hands was like fire on her skin, burning through the fine material of her dress as his fingers circled her breast, teasing the already sensitive nipple into demanding life.

'You know how it can be. How it has been. How it can be again.'

'And marriage?' It was just a whisper, a thin thread of sound that he had to bend his proud head to hear.

'Marriage…'

He didn't need to answer. She could read his thoughts in his face, in the sudden closing up of those handsome features, the way heavy lids swiftly hooded his eyes.

'Grace, *agape mou*…'

The muttered endearment was the last straw. It slashed through the fog inside Grace's head, driving away the heated haze that had held her prisoner.

'No!'

With an effort that tore at her heart she wrenched herself out of his arms, driving herself halfway across the room as she did so. Unshed tears made her eyes brilliant as diamonds as she forced herself to face him, forced the words to her lips.

'No. It won't work! I can't do it! I can't live like that! I won't live like that! So it has to be over. I want it to be over. That way you can find someone you consider fit to be your wife and I—I…'

She couldn't finish the sentence. Couldn't claim that she too would find someone else. Because if she couldn't have Constantine, then there would be no one else she could ever love in the same way.

'Grace…'

Oh, why wouldn't he give in? Why wouldn't he go and leave her to break her heart in peace?

'No, Constantine,' she managed flatly, lifelessly, the words dragged up from the very bottom of her desolated soul. 'Don't say any more. There is nothing you can say. I've made up my mind and there's no way I'm going to change it. I want you to go.'

CHAPTER TWELVE

GRACE surveyed the scene before her with a faint grimace of distaste. The Henderson and Cartwright reception was in full swing, but she was really not in any mood for socialising. If she could have come up with a viable excuse for not attending, she would have seized on it gladly, but she knew that to miss what her employers considered the social event of the year was very definitely regarded as dereliction of duty. Like it or not, she was expected to turn up.

But her mood was very far from sociable. All she ever wanted to do these days was to get through her work as well as she could and then hurry home, lock the door, and leave the world behind.

Not that she could leave all of it behind. It didn't matter where she was or what she did, but the memory of Constantine and the way he had looked on the last day she had seen him came back to haunt her again and again. Even in her sleep he was there, tormenting her with a terrible sense of loss. Or, worse, she would dream of his lovemaking, enduring heated, erotic images that drove her nearly insane with pleasure and from which she would wake, shaking and sweating, in a tangle of bedclothes that were a mute testimony to the disturbed nature of her sleep.

But tonight she had done her duty, she told herself. It would be more honest to say that she had had enough. If she had to smile at one more client or pretend to listen to one more pompous managing director trying to tell her what was wrong with the country she would scream.

No one would see her go. They were all at the stage of the evening where the generous amounts of wine provided and a lavish buffet meant that no one was too clear about who was there and who wasn't. She could slip away quietly without being seen.

The air in the hotel garden was cool and fresh after the overheated smoky atmosphere inside. Grace drew in deep, appreciative breaths of it as she let the door swing to behind her, cutting off the sound of music and chatter in the ballroom she had just left. She would just take a couple of minutes' peace and quiet and then she would make her way to Reception and ask them to ring for a taxi to take her home.

'So this is where you've been hiding yourself!'

Oh, no, Grace groaned inwardly. Not again! Not now!

Les Harvey had been trying to flirt with her all evening. From the moment she'd arrived he had made a beeline for her, and had continued to dance attendance on her ever since. But, feeling as she did, she just wasn't in the right mood to handle him properly. And as one of the most important clients the agency had, Les Harvey had to be handled with kid gloves.

'I missed you in there. Looked round and you'd gone—like Cinderella, but no glass slipper.'

'I needed some fresh air.'

This was even worse than she'd imagined. Les had obviously been taking advantage of the free drinks provided, and he was decidedly more drunk than he had been when she had last seen him. His round face was flushed, his pale blue eyes glittered unnaturally, and the lank fair hair was plastered to his scalp by his own sweat.

'Oh, come now.' Les wagged a reproving finger so close to her face that she had to flinch back hastily in order to avoid it going into her eye. 'You've been teasing me all night, playing hard to get. I know a come-on when I see one.'

'A—a come-on! Mr Harvey,' Grace managed, praying

that the formality would put some necessary distance between them. Already he was invading her personal space with a vengeance, breathing heavily as he swayed on his feet, and peering down at the scooped neck of her black silk dress in a way that was an offence in itself. 'I was just going home.'

'Great idea.' Leaning forward suddenly, he planted a wet, slobbering kiss on her mouth. 'Your place or mine?'

Shocked and appalled, Grace took a hasty step backwards, out of reach.

'I think you've made a mistake...'

'No mistake.' One heavy hand clamped over her shoulder, the other capturing her chin and twisting it round so that she was forced to face him again. 'I know what you're after. I heard about you and Kiriashiz.'

'Constantine?' Even the sound of his name so mangled by this drunk was enough to weaken her, driving a wedge into the normally secure armour of composure she wore at work. 'What about—'

'Everyone knows you were his bit of stuff—that you sold yourself out to the highest bidder...' The hand on her shoulder began to move, pawing clumsily so that Grace shuddered in horror. 'But now he's dropped you—so naturally you're looking for someone else to be your sugar daddy.'

'No...'

Her protest went unheard. The hand that held her chin squeezed it hard, the thumb rubbing over and over her mouth, while the other hand slid down her back, exploring her hips, her buttocks. With an effort, Grace wrenched herself free.

'I said no!' she declared, all thought of trying to be polite driven from her mind. 'And I meant no. Take your hands off me, you filthy louse! I can't stand you touching me!'

She recognised her mistake, saw the danger it had put her in as soon as she saw his face change.

'What's this?' he snarled. 'Am I not good enough for you? Not rich enough, I should say. Well, let me tell you, darling, I may not have the Greek's millions, but I'm every bit the man he is, and I'll prove it…'

She saw what was coming but didn't dodge quite quickly enough. Moving with surprising speed, Les grabbed hold of her, pulling her roughly towards him.

Acting purely on instinct, Grace kicked out hard, a sense of triumph filling her as she heard his muffled grunt of pain. It was enough to distract him just long enough for her to wrench herself away. But she didn't get off scot-free. The large signet ring Les wore scraped uncomfortably over her skin, and a loud ripping sound told her that her freedom had been bought at the expense of the destruction of the top of her dress.

But she didn't care. All she could think about was getting away, putting as much distance between herself and Les Harvey as possible. Already he had recovered and she could hear his heavy footsteps behind her, his furious voice calling her every name under the sun. He was between her and the door back to the hotel, blocking her way there. Panic putting wings on her heels, she fled.

She had no idea how long she had been running for or how far she had come. She only knew that when the panic eventually subsided and her pace gradually slowed it was obvious that she had managed to leave her tormentor far behind. There was no sign of him along the whole length of the street, and now she was thinking again she vaguely remembered him tripping over something and falling face down on the ground.

But where was she? Where had her blind flight taken her? Had she escaped one peril only to plunge straight into another, even worse?

Looking round, she was stunned to find that she knew exactly where she was. She had been here many times in the past. The building ahead of her had once been where she had thought she would live at the start of her married life. It was the one where Constantine had his apartment.

Constantine. Just his name was an invocation, a charm, a form of protection against danger. She hadn't come here by accident. Like a small hunted animal, fleeing straight for its home, instinct had brought her here, to the only place where she could feel truly safe.

She didn't care any more about marriage or commitment. She only knew that she needed Constantine, that only he could fill the emptiness inside her. It was his arms that she needed round her, his strength that she wanted to lean against. If that was all he could give her, then she would welcome it and be happy with it. Because the truth was that she was dying without him.

'Oh, please let him be in!' she prayed as she pressed the bell that she knew would ring the security telephone in Constantine's apartment. 'Dear God, please, please let him be in!'

'Yes?' Curt, and clearly angry at being disturbed, Constantine's voice through the speaker was still the most wonderful, the most welcome sound she had ever heard.

'Constantine—it's Grace.'

Even from this distance she could sense the invisible Constantine's immediate withdrawal, his impulse to put the phone down on her.

'Please!' she said hurriedly. 'Please let me in! I—I need you.'

The silence that greeted her entreaty stretched out through perhaps a hundred fearful uneven heartbeats. Then, just as she was convinced that he would turn her away, reject her completely, she heard his sigh, a perfect blend of exasperation and resignation.

'Come up,' was all he said as he pressed the button to release the door-lock.

The journey up to the penthouse seemed endless, in spite of the speed of the fast, efficient lift. As she was carried upwards Grace suddenly remembered the last time she had seen Constantine, the way he had unwillingly admitted to his fear of being in this enclosed space.

So what on earth had possessed a man who hated lifts to buy an apartment at the very top of a high building? Had he done it simply to prove to himself that he could defy that fear, that, as he had declared so emphatically, he could refuse even to let it register on his mind while he got on with his life?

She still hadn't solved the problem when the lift came to a halt and she stumbled out into the brightly lit hallway of Constantine's apartment.

He was there, waiting for her, his clothes an un-Constantine-like white tee shirt and denim jeans, his face dark as a thundercloud.

'What the—?' he began ominously but then he took in her appearance fully and his expression changed abruptly.

'Grace!' This time his tone was very different. 'What the hell happened to you?'

His concern was the last straw. Suddenly all the tears she had managed to hold back until now were there. They coursed down her cheeks, unstoppable, blinding her so that all she could do was hold out her hands, groping for him desperately.

'Grace!'

Her hands were taken in a strong, warm grasp, and the next moment she was gathered into the comfort and safety of his arms. It was like a dream come true. *All* her dreams come true. And she couldn't tell if the convulsive sobs that broke from her were of remembered fear or pure joy at the sense of coming home at last.

She was scarcely aware of Constantine manoeuvring her into his flat, of him settling her on the settee and coming down beside her. She only knew of his silent sympathy, his support as he held her, gently stroking her hair, patiently waiting for the storm of weeping to burn itself out.

When at last the racking sobs had subsided to intermittent gasps and hiccups, and Grace found herself reduced to sniffing inelegantly, he reached across for a box of tissues and pulled out a handful, pushing some into her limp hand and using another to wipe the tear stains from her cheeks.

'Do you feel ready to talk?' he asked softly. 'Can you tell me what happened?'

His gentleness was almost more than she could bear. It stole her tongue so that she could only shake her head in despair, unable to say a word.

'*Christos*, Grace! You have to say something! You turn up here—in this appalling state. You're shaking like a leaf—and you won't say why! Oh God…!'

He caught himself up sharply, shaking his head in despair at his own foolishness.

'I'm sorry—that's the last thing you need. Forgive me, sweetheart…'

But surprisingly his outburst had had the opposite effect of the one he'd feared. Hearing the raw edge to his words, something close to desperation in his tone, had jolted her out of the frozen state of fear into which she had fallen.

When her tear-swollen eyes flickered open they looked straight into his blazing black gaze, surprising there a look of such uncertainty, such distress, that she was swamped with an overwhelming need to help him rather than have him help her. She felt she would do anything at all if only to smooth that disquiet from his mind.

'It's—it's all right,' she managed shakily. 'Obviously you need to…to…'

She had started out bravely enough, but now her voice failed her again. With a muttered curse Constantine got to his feet and moved to the far side of the room. Grace heard the chink of a bottle against glass, and when he came back to her again it was to push a crystal brandy balloon into the limp fingers of her right hand.

'Drink that!' he commanded sharply.

'I don't like brandy!' It was a wail of protest.

'You don't have to like it, just drink the damn stuff!'

That was so much more like the Constantine she knew that it brought a weak smile to her quivering lips. This was her Constantine, the one she knew and loved.

'What did you say?'

To her consternation, Constantine's sharp ears had caught her foolish muttering of the words aloud.

'Nothing…'

She didn't feel strong enough to tell him yet. He might be anxious and concerned, but that was a natural enough reaction from anyone confronted by someone in the state she had been in when she'd arrived. She couldn't just blurt out the way she was feeling baldly and without any preparation.

So she forced herself to sip at the brandy, grimacing as the fiery liquid burned its way down her throat. It did make her feel better, she had to admit, feeling the warmth creep along her veins and drive away some of the bone-freezing cold she had been experiencing, for all that the night was so mild.

Constantine sat silently beside her, his long body held tensely so that she couldn't be unaware of the struggle he was having not to demand an explanation for her dramatic appearance at his home. But neither by word or gesture did he give any sign of impatience or attempt to push her into something she was not ready for, simply waiting until she turned to him again.

'I—I owe you an explanation—' she began, but broke off in shock as she saw him shake his head emphatically.

'You owe me nothing,' he said huskily. 'I was all sorts

of a fool even to ask. You came here obviously in distress, too shocked to speak, and I come on like the counsel for the prosecution, only making matters worse. Forgive me— I was out of my mind with worry and I wasn't thinking straight.'

'But I would like to tell you.' Her voice went up and down in the most peculiar way in reaction to that *out of my mind with worry*. 'I want you to know what happened.'

It didn't take very long. Strengthened by a few more fortifying sips of brandy, she found that the whole sorry tale tumbled out in a rush, with only a few stumbles here and there over a particularly difficult bit.

She didn't even have to finish it. Because as soon as she mentioned Les Harvey a dark, dangerous scowl descended on to Constantine's beautifully carved features, and when she touched on the assault on her he was there before her, letting out a litany of rasping profanities, white-hot fury blazing in his eyes.

'The bastard!' he roared, getting to his feet in a rush, his anger too great to let him stay still. One clenched fist slammed into the palm of the other hand with a violent sound that made Grace wince inwardly.

'Constantine…' she began, but he simply ignored her.

'I will kill him,' he declared, his tone suddenly very different. The anger was still there, but now it was expressed with a cold, deadly purpose that was somehow much more frightening than the rage of seconds earlier. 'I will push his filthy words down his throat and I'll—'

'Constantine, no! You mustn't! That isn't what I want!'

At first she thought that he hadn't heard her again, but then, slowly, he turned to her, obviously reining in his fierce temper only with considerable effort.

'The police, then.' It was a statement, not a question.

'No. Not that either. I—I don't want you to do anything.'

'Not do anything! But, Grace, look at yourself! How can I let a man do that to you and not want to punish him?'

His wild gesture towards her with his hand made Grace look down at herself for the first time since reaching the sanctuary of Constantine's apartment. Her breath stilled, her eyes widening as she saw just what Constantine meant.

The neck of the black dress was torn wide open, a large flap of material hanging loose so that the lace of her bra was exposed. And where the signet ring had caught her, the white flesh was raised in an ugly red weal.

'It looks worse than it is—it does!' she insisted when he looked frankly sceptical, his expression refuting the truth of her declaration. 'I was frightened, shocked, but he didn't really hurt me. Please, Constantine, leave it! I just want to forget that tonight ever happened.'

He was strongly tempted to ignore her appeal. Rejection flared in his eyes, fought a fierce battle with reason, and finally, she was thankful to see, conceded defeat.

'If that is what you want,' he said reluctantly. 'But if anyone other than you had asked me...'

The way his right hand closed again into a tight, clenched fist revealed the violence of his feelings more eloquently than any words, and Grace couldn't suppress a shiver of reaction at the thought of that icy fury turned on anyone—even Les Harvey.

'It's what I want, Constantine,' she confirmed shakily. 'Really, it is. If you love me—'

Oh, no! How had that slipped out? Panic flared in her mind as she wished the foolish words back, but it was too late.

'If I love you!' Constantine echoed on an odd note, one she couldn't begin to interpret. 'Grace, I have told you how I feel.'

Love, but no commitment. The sort of love he would bend ruthlessly to his will, as he had his fear of lifts. Well, she'd already told herself tonight that she would accept that. It was that or nothing. And she couldn't live with nothing.

'I...' she began, but suddenly he was shaking his head.

'I cannot give you any more than I have already.'

'I understand,' Grace whispered, struggling to make her voice audible.

'I wonder if you do,' he responded enigmatically.

Suddenly he moved, coming to sit beside her again, taking both of her hands in his and closing his fingers over them.

'Grace, will you answer one question?'

'If I can. What do you want to know?'

'Just this—why are you here tonight?'

'Why?' Grace frowned her confusion. 'You know why! Because Les—'

'But why did you come *here*? Why not go to your friends or to Ivan?'

'I couldn't go anywhere else,' she said simply and honestly. 'As soon as I started thinking again, I knew I wanted to be with you and only you. And I knew you'd be there for me. Constantine—what is it?'

He had dropped his face into his hands, bronzed fingers hiding his eyes from her.

'*Theos!*' he groaned in harsh self-reproach. 'I have been so blind!'

'Blind? Constantine, please, I don't understand!'

Slowly he straightened his head, and when he took his hands away there was something new in his eyes. Or, rather, not new, but the expression she had once seen there every day, in the days leading up to their wedding. The days before Paula.

Then she would have called it love; now she did not dare to put so emotive a name on it.

'Trust,' was all he said, his accent strangely thick, his voice cracking on the single word.

'Trust?' Grace echoed shakily, her mind whirling, but Constantine pressed a gentle hand over her mouth to silence her when she would have said more.

'Please, just listen,' he begged. 'I have so much to tell you. So much you need to know. Please listen and then answer me one question.'

Even when he took his hand away again Grace couldn't find the words to answer him, but simply nodded silently, tension making her heart beat high up in her throat. She couldn't be in any doubt that what he was about to say was terribly important. It was written all over Constantine's taut face, etched into it by the strain that pulled his beautiful skin tight over those amazing cheekbones.

'I think perhaps I'd better start with my grandfather.'

'Your grandfather?' She'd resolved to stay silent, but this was such a surprise that she couldn't stop herself from re-acting. 'What has he got to do with this?'

'More than you could imagine. You remember I told you how he was such an influence on me when I was growing up? Well, one of the things that he instilled into me was the fact that I should never sit back and rest on my lau-rels—or, rather, his laurels. That just because the Kiriazis family was now so wealthy, we should never take our for-tune for granted. We had been poor once; we could be so again. He always quoted the old saying: rags to riches and back again in three generations.'

'He needn't have worried about that with you.' Grace's voice was shaky. She didn't quite see where this was lead-ing. 'After all, if your grandfather made a fortune, you've made a second one all of your own.'

'Yes, but that was only half of what he taught me.'

Constantine pushed a hand through his hair, ebony eyes

slightly unfocused, as if they were looking back into the past.

'The other thing he wanted for me was a marriage like his. He met my grandmother when he was nineteen, and they were together for over sixty years. She married him when he was just a woodcarver, but she died the wife of a very rich man…'

Long fingers fretted at the strap of the gold watch on his wrist, betraying a lack of composure that was otherwise hidden by his rigid self-control.

'When he gave me this watch, he made me swear to him that I would never marry unless I was absolutely sure. That only when I met someone who I believed had as much faith in me as my grandmother had had in him would I make her my wife. I gave him my word.'

'Oh!'

It was a long sigh of comprehension and distress. Now she saw exactly what had motivated Constantine. How he had felt bound by the promise he had made to his grandfather, and how her own actions had led him to believe that she was not the sort of woman the old man had wanted for him.

'I understand,' she said softly. 'I see now why you can't offer me marriage, but it no longer matters—'

'Of course it matters!' Constantine broke in on her harshly. 'It matters like hell! Because I have been so wrong, so stupid, so out of my head blind not to see what was right before my eyes. I wanted to kill that rat Harvey, but the truth is that I have behaved every bit as badly as he has. When you told me about tonight, it was like looking in a mirror, and, believe me, I didn't like what I saw. There are some pretty ugly similarities between my behaviour and the pig who—'

'No!' Grace couldn't let him continue, and this time it was she who laid a finger on his lips. 'Constantine, no!'

'Yes!'

With an angry gesture he twisted away from her restraining hand, grabbing at it and holding it and its partner tightly in his lap.

'All I offered you was money and sex. I claimed to love you, but I let my pride blind me to the truth. Right from the start, I believed that if you loved me you would never doubt me, not even for a second, and yet I doubted you, but I was too damn proud to admit it. That day you came to confront me, after Paula spewed out all her filthy lies, I didn't try hard enough to convince you. Instead, I saw the whole thing as a test of your love. A test I had no right at all to set.'

'But I failed…'

'No.' Constantine shook his dark head violently. 'No, I failed you. Because deep down I was afraid. I was terrified that you might not love me as much as I believed. That you might actually believe I was capable of being so faithless, so heartless…'

'If that was fear then you hid it very well.'

Just as he had always hidden the way he felt about being in a lift, refusing to let it show, believing that if he refused to acknowledge its existence it wouldn't affect his life.

'You just looked cold, and so very distant.'

'That was just a mask,' Constantine assured her. 'And behind it was the fear—total, gut-wrenching panic—that and a terrible sense of guilt.'

'Guilt?' Grace echoed, looking back, seeing him again on that dreadful day, seeing that momentary flash of something in his eyes, the look that she had believed betrayed his lack of innocence at the time.

'I felt guilty at treating you that way. Somewhere deep inside I was ashamed of the way I was behaving, and the fact that I was hurting you so much, but I would rather have died than admit it. I let my pride get in the way of everything and so I lost you.'

Black eyes locked with grey, holding her mesmerised with the intensity of feeling that burned there. She couldn't speak, could hardly breathe. Even her heart seemed to have stopped beating, so fiercely was she concentrating on what he was saying.

'I went away, told myself I could forget you. But I couldn't get you out of my mind. After two years I just couldn't take it any longer. Any one of a dozen people could have sorted out the problems in the London office, but I snatched at the chance to come back to England, and Ivan's invitation to the party gave me the perfect opening I was looking for. But I would have found you anyway. I couldn't live without you.'

Releasing one of her hands, he reached out to touch her cheek, his caress infinitely gentle.

'And still my damn stupid pride got in the way. That was why I forced you into that appalling arrangement. I would have done anything I could to keep you with me for as long as possible.'

His thumb smoothed over her skin, erasing the last traces of the storm of tears, his expression watchful and concerned,

'I told myself I wanted proof that you truly loved and trusted me, when all the time it was right there before my eyes in the fact that you took me back, the way you behaved, the way you let me treat you. But I couldn't see it. I couldn't even see my own feelings clearly. But I knew my mother would. That was why I rushed you away from Skyros. I knew that if she took one look at my face she would see that I was still crazy about you—and there was no way she'd keep quiet about it. And then tonight...'

The words deserted him as he shook his head in despair at his own behaviour. But Grace didn't need an explanation.

Now she saw just what that single word 'trust' meant. Her instinctive, unthinking flight into Constantine's protection had provided the proof of the faith in him he had needed so much.

'Grace, my love, forgive me. Forgive my blind stupidity, my arrogant pride, my ignorance, my—'

She couldn't let him continue with the litany of self-reproach, but stopped his mouth with her own, making it clear that no words were necessary, that he hadn't needed to ask.

'And you must forgive me my doubts,' she whispered against his lips. 'I should have known that the man I love could never have done those appalling things. And I do love you, Constantine. I love you so much it hurts even to think about it.'

They were the last words she said for some time. Because even before she had spoken the last one Constantine had taken her mouth again in a hot, yearning kiss. A kiss that led to a thousand other kisses, each of them more passionate than the first. And those kisses led to caresses, the caresses to openly urgent demand.

Without quite knowing how it had happened, Grace found herself on Constantine's bed, her clothes discarded somewhere she neither knew nor cared. All she felt was that this was where she truly belonged, that this was her heart's one real home, the place she had been born to find, the destiny that had always awaited her.

And as she welcomed the fierce, primitive thrust of Constantine's body into hers she could not hold back a cry of sheer delight and wonder at the thought that this was the first time they had truly made love together. That for the first time their minds and hearts were united as well as their physical selves.

'One thing puzzles me,' she murmured a long time later

when, their hunger sated, they were lying, heavy-limbed with exhaustion, in each other's arms.

'And what is that, *agape mou*?' Constantine's voice was thick with satisfaction, lazy as his strong body, lying tangled up with her own.

'You said you had a question you wanted me to answer. What was that?'

'Couldn't you guess?' he teased softly. 'Isn't there only one possible question it could be? I wanted to know if you would marry me. If you would do me the very real honour of becoming my wife.'

'Your wife!' The shock brought her upright in the bed to look down into his dark face in stunned confusion. 'But you said that you couldn't give me that...'

'I said I couldn't give you any more than I have already,' Constantine corrected gently. 'Because it would be impossible. How can I give you any more when you already have it all? When my heart, my mind, my body, even my very soul are totally enslaved by you? I would give you the world if I could...'

'I told you, I don't need *things*,' Grace reminded him, her heart singing in unbounded joy. 'If you want to give me anything, a wedding ring will be more than enough. That, and perhaps the twelve autumn leaves you promised me for every year of our married life. No?' she asked in confusion as Constantine shook his head against the pillow, his mouth curving into a warm smile.

'Don't you know you have them already as well? The necklace I gave you—the leaves are real. I collected them for you before we broke up and had them preserved in gold so that they would last for ever. They were to have been my present to you on the day we married.'

'I'll wear them on my wedding day,' Grace promised, bending her head to kiss him again.

They would have no need of such superstitions in the future, she knew. Once she was Constantine's wife, every day of every year to come was guaranteed to be happy ever after.

Don't miss *Book Ten* of this BRAND-NEW 12 book collection 'Bachelor Auction'.

Who says money can't buy love?

On sale 6th June

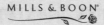

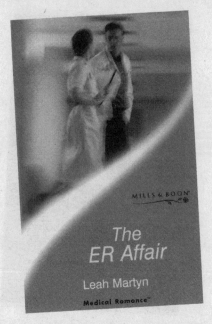